A FAMILY REUNION

A FAMILY REUNION

BRENDA JACKSON

St. Martin's Griffin   New York

www.stmartins.com

ISBN 978-0-312-31508-5

First published in the United States by St. Martin's Paperbacks

P1

ACKNOWLEDGMENTS

To three important men in my life: my husband, Gerald Jackson, Sr., and my sons, Gerald Junior and Brandon. I love you guys.

To my very own family, whose love from my childhood has helped to make me the person that I am: the Streater family, the Randolph family, and the Hawk family.

In loving memory of my grandmother, Josiephine Randolph Streater Threatt, who was a very strong influence in my life and whose earthly presence I will forever miss.

To my friends who shared fond memories with me about their family reunions, this book is especially for you.

In loving memory of my childhood friend, Willie James Hodge (Bill)—October 12, 1952 to May 20, 2000. You are deeply missed.

To Brenda Arnette Simmons for her helpful feedback on the finished product.

To my cousins, Barbara S. Love, Gwendolyn Streater, Jessie S. Wilson, Bettye D. Wendt, Maretha C. Hines, and Jackie Johnson. Remember our early teen days sitting on Gramma Josie's porch, talking and sharing secrets.

And to my Heavenly Father, who makes all things possible and who gave me the gift of writing.

An old man's grandchildren are his crowning glory.
A child's glory is his father.
—PROVERBS 17:6, THE LIVING BIBLE

A FAMILY REUNION

PROLOGUE

His eye is on the sparrow and I know he watches me . . .

Ethan Allen Bennett had lived a very long life, and today he felt every bit of his eighty-nine years. Each time he closed his eyes seeking a peaceful moment, he heard the sweet sound of his late wife, Idella, softly singing the lyrics of her favorite church song.

Since he was blessed not to have Alzheimer's, it must be his imagination, he concluded ruefully, closing his eyes once more to enjoy the spiritual melody. He was sitting in his favorite chair in a room that was kept warm by the huge old-fashioned heater. It was a heater that had been in his home pretty close to sixty years. After Idella's death ten years ago his six children, worried about his solitary state, had wanted to come in and modernize the place. For starters, they had wanted to remove his heater and replace it with central heat and air.

"That heater's no longer any good. It's dangerous," his eldest son, Ethan Junior, had declared louder than a Baptist preacher on a first Sunday morning. And as usual the other five siblings had agreed.

"*That* heater warmed all of your backsides at one time or another," Ethan Senior had forcefully reminded them. "It stays and so does everything else. Everything stays just like your mama left it."

And that had settled that.

They had not understood that when a man had been married to a woman for over sixty years, like he had been married to his Idella, and the other half departed to meet their Maker, the one left behind needed something of her to remember, to hold on to, and to cherish, even if it was the one picture on the wall that absolutely rattled his grands and great-grands during their visits. It was the huge picture of the blond-haired, blue-eyed Jesus that had been hanging in that very spot on the wall for over forty-five years.

Jesus, as Idella had visualized him to be, was flanked by a portrait of Martin Luther King, Jr., on one side and one of John F. Kennedy, Sr., on the other. A picture of Robert Kennedy—not as large as the others but just as visible—had been added years later and hung underneath Jesus. Until the end Jesus had been Idella's Savior, the Almighty, the calm in the wake of a storm, the Prince of Peace. Martin, John, and Bobby had been her boys, her heroes who could do no wrong. She would defend their honor to her dying days. In fact, she had.

Ethan heard the singing once again.

It was at times like these, when he was all alone, that he missed his Idella more than at other times. It would probably be somewhat different if he was still allowed to drive; then he could spend more time at the Masonic Lodge every day. Right now he had to depend on his children to take him wherever he wanted to go. Although he knew they didn't mind, he didn't like being a burden to anyone.

He hated that he'd let them talk him into giving up his driver's license but had understood their reasoning. He would be the first to admit that his eyesight wasn't as good as it used to be. Besides, it was either giving up his license or agreeing to their suggestion of installing one of those devices to have some emergency service monitor his house every evening, since he lived alone. He definitely hadn't wanted that. Nor had he wanted to follow their other suggestion of letting his oldest great-grand, sixteen-year-old Jerrell, live with him. He loved his first great-grand to death, but the boy played his music too loud to suit him. Although Ethan's eyesight wasn't what it used to be, so far he didn't have any problem with his hearing and wanted to keep it that way. Living with Jerrell would damage his eardrums for sure.

He heard the singing once more.

I sang because I'm happy. I sang because I'm free. His eye is on the sparrow and I know he watches me.

He wondered just how happy Idella would be in knowing the sorrowful state of the family she had left behind. How would she feel to know that her baby boy, Victor Senior, was now on his third wife and had so many outside children it had become a joke to everyone.

But not to Ethan.

Outside or inside, they were still his grandchildren, grandchildren he would claim although he didn't even know half of them.

And what about his grands that he did know about? Last count there were fifteen. Two by way of Ethan Junior, three from Joe, three by way of Emery, one from Prentice, one by way of Colleen—his deceased daughter—and the rest from his youngest son, Victor Senior. Ethan Senior had seen his fifteen grandchildren off and on over the years but never together and never at the same time. At least not since the last family reunion, fifteen years ago. Everyone had enjoyed themselves and had had a good time, not knowing that in less than five years the matriarch of the Bennett family, his Idella, would pass away peacefully in her sleep. Since then there hadn't been any more reunions. There were seldom any visits. Everyone was busy doing their own thing. Last he'd heard, his grandson Victor Junior was busy making babies, outside babies, just like his father had done. Lord knows the boy got it honest.

Then there was his granddaughter Rae'jean, the one the family had boasted as being the "pretty" one, with her high yella coloring and white folks' hair. He was proud of her, the only doctor in the family. He'd heard through the family grapevine, the all-knowing, all-gossiping Cuzin Sophie, that Rae'jean was dating a white boy, another doctor.

He couldn't think of Rae'jean without thinking of Taye and Alexia. Growing up while Idella was alive, those three granddaughters of theirs were always into something. As little ones, their weekend visits had been the highlight of his and Idella's lives. Taye had been the smart one. She could add, subtract, multiply, and divide numbers in her head in mere seconds. She had been the one the family just knew would go far. He remembered the day her ma, Otha Mae, had taken her to college, some prestigious school up north. She had left Taye on the dormitory steps with strict orders to keep her books open and her legs closed. Lo and behold, no sooner had

Otha Mae rounded the corner to return back home to Georgia than the girl had gotten buck wild and had opened her legs as wide as they could go. By the end of the first semester she had returned home pregnant. Taye had finished school a year early and had been too young to go off somewhere to college. But her parents hadn't listened to him and Idella. In the end they wished they had.

Alexia, bless her heart, had been another matter altogether, he thought, smiling proudly. To him and Idella, Alexia had been the most beautiful child anyone had ever seen. But he'd known a few of the Bennetts had thought otherwise, with her dark skin, unruly hair, weight problem, and crooked teeth. So Alexia was never showered with the same type of praise and compliments that had been bestowed upon Rae'jean and Taye. The only thing some family members thought Alexia had going for her was her voice. It was the beautiful voice of a songbird. It was a voice that she had inherited from her Gramma Idella, since everyone knew neither of Alexia's parents could hold a decent note, although Prentice and Alma still insisted upon singing in the church choir every second Sunday morning.

That's why now, with Alexia being a successful singer who was a part of that popular singing group, and whose picture, just last month, was in an issue of *People* magazine claiming her as one of the fifty most beautiful people in the world, those who'd thought she hadn't had anything going for her were walking around holding their heads down in shame.

Just as well.

Last but not least, his thoughts shifted to Michael, who was the grandson of his first cousin, Henry Bennett. Michael had gone through some tough times a few years back after learning he'd been adopted. It was something he hadn't found out until he had left for the air force right after the last family reunion.

The last family reunion.

Since that time the family had begun dwindling away and so had the values Ethan and Idella had tried to instill. He wondered how he could make his children, his grands and great-grands, understand what a real family meant. It meant more than getting together occasionally for the holidays. It meant being there for one another, through thick and thin, the good times and the bad. It also meant that when friends deserted you, you could always depend on your family to be there.

Ethan slowly stood and crossed the room to the phone. He would call his cousin Agnes. Even at the age of seventy she was still a mover and a shaker and was the one person he knew who could be counted on to get things done, especially the one thing he wanted. The one thing the family needed.

The Bennetts needed to come together for another family reunion. The first one in fifteen years.

CHAPTER 1

TAYE

Taye, are you going to the Firemen's Ball or not?"
Sharon Langley's question unsettled Octavia Bennett to no end. She fought to suppress her aggravation so she could give a calm answer. But first she needed to finish getting all of the relaxer out of Mrs. Walker's hair.

"Taye, I asked you a question."

Nerves on edge, Taye glanced up from the washbowl and gave her best friend a leveled glare. It didn't matter that Sharon owned the most exclusive beauty salon in Atlanta, where Taye worked as a stylist in the day while juggling the chore of raising two daughters and going to school at night. Nor did it matter that they had known each other since second grade. Taye would say her piece to Sharon . . . in private. "We'll talk later, OK?"

Sharon couldn't do anything but nod, caught off guard by the curtness of Taye's tone. Taye was known for her subtle wit and soft-spoken manner. You would have to push really hard to get a rise out of her. Sharon couldn't help wondering what wrong button she had pushed.

Once Taye had gotten Mrs. Walker's hair rinsed and conditioned and had placed her under the dryer, she motioned for Sharon to meet her in the supply room.

"OK, Taye, what's wrong with you? All I asked was whether or not you're attending the Firemen's Ball. The look you gave me sent chills up my spine."

The look Taye now slanted Sharon was partly amused and partly apologetic. Taye had reacted rather badly but felt she had done so with good reason, although Sharon didn't know that. She owed her an explanation. "Monica's father is a fireman."

Sharon's hand flew up to her mouth and her large bulging eyes told Taye she had literally shocked her speechless, which wasn't easy to do, since Sharon could be counted on to always have something to say. The identity of Monica's father was something Taye had never discussed with anyone, not even with Sharon. It had been bad enough that she had gotten pregnant in her first semester of college and had to return home and listen to her mother's constant spiel of how she'd disappointed the family. Then as if that hadn't been bad enough, she had screwed up again three years later by getting pregnant for a second time, this time from a man who conveniently forgot to tell her he was married. A second child out of wedlock had been a final blow to the already-strained relationship she'd had with her parents.

"Monica's father was a fireman?"

Taye nodded. "He still is." Since Sharon had been away at college at the time, she had never met the man Taye had dated for nearly three months. There was no reason to tell her that not only was he a fireman, but now he was a captain in the Atlanta Fire Department. Back then, ten years ago when they'd dated, he'd been a rookie who'd just made the squad. She had been a lonely young woman of twenty, a single mother with a two-year-old who had fallen under his spell and had believed his story that he was a single man sharing an apartment with a buddy. Even now she cringed every time she thought about all the lies he'd told and how she had foolishly fallen for them.

Sharon's footsteps furiously clicking on the tiled floor reeled Taye's thoughts out of the past and back to the present. Sharon was no longer speechless. She was angry and was pacing the room getting madder by the minute. Taye regretted that she had told Sharon anything. The main reason she'd never done so before was because Sharon was like a dog with a bone. Once she got ahold of something, she wouldn't let go. Besides, when it came to Taye, Sharon was fiercely loyal and protective.

"Octavia Louise Bennett! Here you've been working your butt off for ten years trying to make ends meet raising Sebrina and Monica, and Monica's father has a good job, but you refuse to make the scumbag pay child support!"

Taye sighed. She'd had this conversation about Monica's father not paying child support with Sharon many times. "You know why I haven't done that. In order to file for child support I'd have to reveal his identity, and I refuse to do that."

Sharon's heated face told Taye just what she thought of that. "Girl, why are you still protecting him? Even after ten years you won't tell anyone who he is, not even me, and I'm your best friend."

"You know why I won't tell you, Sharon. You'd take actions into your own hands and do something stupid."

Sharon drew in a deep, ragged breath, fighting for control. "It's not stupid to make a man take care of his child! Why are you protecting him?"

"I'm *not* protecting him. Don't you think I've thought about confronting him and demanding that he do what's right by his child? But what would that do other than hurt his wife, who doesn't know he's a low-life? They even have a daughter who was born a day or so before Monica."

"Jeez! You mean he was sleeping with both you and his wife at the same time?"

"Yes, but if anyone should have been sleeping with him it was her. She had all the rights to do so; I had none."

Sharon rolled her eyes. "But you didn't know."

"Still, I was a fool to be taken in by him. You'll never know how awful I felt when I found out I'd been sleeping with a married man. But it was my mistake and not his wife's and I refuse to ruin his marriage."

"What kind of marriage is it if he screws around on her?"

"That was ten years ago."

"And you think his penis has dropped off since then? Get real, Taye. Men like that don't know how to keep their pants zipped. I bet Monica isn't the only outside child he has. He's probably no better than your uncle Victor or your cousin Victor Junior. I bet he has—"

"I don't care, Sharon. Monica is all I care about. She's doing OK. She's never even asked me about him."

"But she's asked me!"

Taye suddenly felt dizzy. She placed a steadying hand on one of the shelves for support. Had she heard Sharon right? "Monica has asked you about her father?"

"Yes, more than once. She didn't feel comfortable coming to you and asking you about him, and since I'm her godmother she asked me."

A lump formed in Taye's throat. "What did you tell her?"

"Not what I wanted to, believe me. I told her that I honestly didn't know a thing about him. The only thing I did know was that he must have been good-looking for her to be such a beautiful child."

Sharon paused for a moment as she considered Taye. "But don't you see, Taye, she's getting older. She wants the same thing Sebrina has. She sees Gary coming here every summer to get Sebrina and wonders why she doesn't have a father coming for her."

Taye thought about the guy she'd gotten pregnant from while in her first semester at college, the one who had taken away her virginity, Gary Stevens. He was a senior who knew what he was doing when he targeted her. At seventeen, still wet behind the ears, she had played right into his hands and, in no time at all, his bed. "I can't force a man to want his child."

"But you can force him to take care of her financially. It's been ten years. Do you want to know what I think?"

Taye raised her eyes to the ceiling. "No, not really."

Sharon ignored her and told her anyway. "I think you still feel something for this guy and that's why you're protecting him. Don't hand me that cock-and-bull story about your protecting his wife. If he cared anything for his wife he wouldn't have been unfaithful."

"But that's no reason to destroy their marriage."

"What marriage? If I were a married woman I'd want to know, even ten years later, that my husband had screwed around on me. And you can't convince me he still isn't out there screwing around."

"Maybe."

"Maybe my behind. You can't convince me he's not."

Taye would never admit to Sharon that she knew for a fact that he was. Over the years she had run into him a number of times with different women, none of whom was his wife. She ran her fingers through her short hair. "Look, Sharon, I need to check on Mrs. Walker. This conversation is over and you're wrong. I feel nothing for Monica's father. At one time I wanted to hate him, but now I actually thank him for her. I just wish the circumstances surrounding her conception were different."

"If you still don't want to tell me who he is, then that's fine. But I think it's time that you sit down and talk to Monica about her father, Taye."

Taye nodded. "I will."

Without saying anything else, she turned and walked out of the room.

Two hours later Taye was hanging up her cape for the day when Sharon entered the back room with a deep frown on her face.

"You may as well put that cape back on, girlfriend. The Wicked Witch of the South just blew in on her broomstick."

Silently Taye cursed. "Please tell me you're lying."

"I wish I could, but I can't. She's here with her nice-nasty self."

"But she doesn't have an appointment."

"Does she ever? All she needs is some news to rub in your face about her precious Brandy, and she feels she can prance her butt in here at any time to deliver it."

Taye sighed, knowing Sharon was right. The woman they were discussing was none other than Valerie Constantine. Thirty years ago at the age of sixteen, Valerie had gotten pregnant from Taye's uncle Victor. Victor had refused to do the honorable thing and marry Valerie, and she had placed the blame for his decision on the Bennett family. She accused them of poisoning Victor's mind against her by making him doubt the child was actually his. Even if that had been true, any such notion had gotten dispelled once Brandy had been born looking just like Uncle Victor. But Valerie had never forgiven Victor's family and she enjoyed rubbing any available Bennett's nose in the fact that Brandy, who was the same age as Taye and was a professor with a Ph.D. at Howard University, was doing extremely well. Valerie figured that if she made it a point to tell Taye, then she would pass the word on to all the other Bennetts and make them pea-green with envy. Little did Valerie know that due to her busy schedule, Taye rarely saw her family, who mostly lived in Macon, which was an hour's drive from Atlanta.

Ignoring Sharon's "tell the witch off for once" expression, Taye walked out of the room into the front of the salon.

Sharon's beauty salon, Total Elegance, was just that. Cashing in all of her savings she'd earned while working five years in the corporate world, Sharon had gone from employee to entrepreneur, coming up with an idea for what would be every woman's dream—a one-stop beauty salon. The decor was one of total sophistication and style. There was a special room for manicures and pedicures, one for facials and body massages, and another for stylists specializing in all types of hair care services and makeup applications. The shop also contained a library with books on spiritual and personal growth. Future expansion plans included a spa as well as a lingerie shop. Total Elegance was specifically designed for the sistah on the go who believed in making every minute count and wanted to face the world feeling her best as well as looking it. Absolutely no one was seen without an appointment, so it rattled Taye to know each time Valerie Constantine visited she was breaking the rules by being a walk-in. It was time she was reminded of that fact.

Words failed Taye when she walked into the room and saw Valerie standing in front of a makeup display. Evidently she had a lot to boast about today, Taye thought, studying the woman's anxious air without letting her presence be known. Valerie was wearing a long black fur coat that was superbly tailored to fit her tall form. The coat screamed money, and no doubt Valerie was here to flaunt that fact. Taye shook her head. Of all the women she'd known her uncle Victor to either mess around with or marry, Valerie was one she could give credit to for keeping herself looking good. At the age of forty-six she was still a nice-looking woman.

Taye took a deep breath before she spoke. "Valerie, I'm surprised to see you here today. I checked the books and you don't have an appointment."

Valerie's beautifully carved mouth twisted in an expression of haughtiness that was heightened by the flare of ire in the inky darkness of her eyes. Taye knew Valerie hadn't liked being reminded of the fact that at Total Elegance she was no better than anyone else. That was a point she seemed to overlook at times.

"Really, Octavia, I'm sure you can squeeze me in today," Valerie returned silkily. "All I want is a wash and set . . . and if you can, I'd like you to give special attention to the gray hair at my temples. I want you to do something with it."

Taye lifted a brow, wondering just what Valerie thought she could do with her gray hair other than color it? She wasn't a miracle worker.

"Besides," Valerie was saying, "I have some absolutely wonderful news to share with you about Brandy."

Like there's any other reason for your visit, Taye thought. "Unfortunately, I won't be able to accommodate you today, Valerie. I promised the girls I'd take them for pizza and a movie this evening. I was just about to leave."

"Really? I thought you'd jump at the chance to earn an additional dollar or two. I heard you've finally moved out of those apartments and purchased a home. I'd imagine it's not easy being a single mother."

"You of all people would know." Taye smiled. It was time she took the bull by the horns and put Valerie in her place as Sharon had suggested many times.

Valerie's dark eyes turned on her. "Actually, Octavia, that was years ago and I really don't remember. As you know, Brandy has been doing extremely well for herself. In fact . . . how do you like my coat?" Valerie asked, giving an arrogant sweep of her hand down the full length of the fur coat.

Before Taye could respond, Valerie said, "It was a gift from Brandy's fiancé."

Taye nodded. So that was Valerie's news. She decided to play along for good measure, hoping it would get Valerie out of the salon a lot quicker. "Brandy's getting married? Why, that's wonderful. When you speak to her again, tell her I said congratulations."

"I'll be sure to pass that on to her," Valerie responded in an amused tone. "Of course her wedding will be a very elaborate affair. She may decide to include you, Rae'jean, and Alexia as bridesmaids. After all, the four of you were born the same year and are first cousins."

Taye rolled her eyes. She doubted very seriously that Brandy would include her, Rae'jean, or Alexia in on anything. Brandy, the spoiled, bad-mannered brat, had grown up to become the witch's daughter, a title she wore well.

"And you can tell your Uncle Victor not to worry," Valerie was saying. "I won't be hitting him up for any money to pay for his daughter's wedding. Brandy's fiancé is loaded, and I mean loaded, and he has offered to pay for everything. He even wants to have the wedding in Jamaica. Isn't that just wonderful?"

"Yes, off the chain," Taye said in a dry tone.

Valerie's face brightened. "Cheer up, Octavia; maybe your day will come eventually. I'm sure there's some man out there willing to take on a wife with a ready-made family."

"Really?" Taye said with a wry twist to her mouth. "In that case, I guess I'd remain a single woman. It seems to have worked for you all these years." She couldn't help but smile. She'd made another hit. The darkening of Valerie's eyes indicated that she had.

Valerie tightened her coat around her. "Well, I must be going. You will tell your family the good news whenever you see them again, won't you?"

"If I happen to remember," Taye said on a note of satisfaction. She had put up with Valerie's rudeness enough over the years and refused to tolerate it anymore. "I tend to forget trivial things, since my mind is cluttered with far more serious matters."

It was of great comfort when she watched an angry Valerie, with all her snooty airs, turn to walk out of the shop. Her comfort was short-lived when Valerie turned back around and said, "It must be a huge burden of guilt for you to carry around the fact that you're such a big disappointment to your family. I'm sure you know they used to put you on a pedestal, always bragging about how smart you were with your gift for numbers and how far you would go. Idella and Ethan would even brag about your growing up and becoming the first black woman Secretary of the Treasury. Imagine that. Now just look at you and what you're doing. What a shame."

With a haughty smile on her face, Valerie walked out of the shop.

Taye's nerves were still on edge when she left Total Elegance and headed for home. Her confrontation with Valerie had not helped matters, because Valerie had hit a sore spot with her, a very sore spot. She *had* let her family down, but who'd given them the right to put her on a pedestal anyway? After all, she was human and was allowed to make mistakes.

Even what they considered as two of them.

When she came to a traffic light, Taye momentarily took her eyes off the road and glared at her reflection in the rearview mirror. She hadn't particularly liked herself lately, and thanks to Valerie she'd been reminded why. Everything the woman said was true. Taye was carrying a burden of guilt around and had done so for thirteen years. Her family had bragged from the day she'd entered preschool that one day she would be somebody. Why couldn't they see that she *had* become somebody? Maybe she wasn't who they had wanted her to be, but still, being a single mother raising two girls did make her somebody.

No one, other than Sharon and the people Taye had grown close to at church, ever complimented her on how well mannered her daughters were or how, compared to other kids their age, they were extremely considerate, mindful, and obedient. She was proud that Sebrina and Monica were her daughters and no one else's. And no matter what mistakes she had made in bringing them into the world, she was trying to not make any mistakes in raising them.

Taye shifted her thoughts from Sebrina and Monica to her cousins Rae'jean and Alexia. She couldn't help but wonder if they had any burdens they were bearing that the family had shouldered on them. *Probably not,* she thought. Rae'jean had always been considered the "pretty one," and she was still absolutely beautiful. The last time Taye had seen her was at Rae'jean's mama's funeral. Because of the number of people who had attended, it had been nearly impossible for the two of them to spend a lot of time together. At the time Rae'jean had been in her third year of medical school, fulfilling her lifelong dream of becoming a heart specialist. Now she worked as a cardiologist at a huge hospital in Boston.

Then there was Alexia. Taye doubted Alexia was carrying around any burdens, since some family members hadn't ever showered her with any glowing expectations. She'd had a beautiful voice and everyone in the family had known that, but none of them ever suspected her voice would carry her as far as it had. At least no one had known other than their grandparents, Mama Idella and Poppa Ethan, and Taye and Rae'jean. Now Alexia had made it big as part of that singing group Body and Soul and was living on easy street. She never failed to remember the girls' birthdays and always sent them advance copies of Body and Soul's new releases.

Taye thought about all those weekends as teenagers they had spent with Mama Idella and Poppa Ethan. Those had been special times for her, Rae'jean, and Alexia. At least they were special times until Valerie forced Brandy's company on them. Brandy had always been a pain in the butt . . . just like her mother.

Taye then thought about another cousin named Michael, who often had spent those weekends with them. Three years older than they were, he was the grandson of Poppa Ethan's first cousin, Henry. She smiled remembering the crush she'd had on Michael from the time she'd turned thirteen, a secret she'd only shared with Sharon, Rae'jean, and Alexia. News that you thought yourself in love with your cousin wasn't something you wanted to get out. But still, as a teenager, she'd gone to sleep several times with thoughts of him on her mind. Her feelings for Michael had lasted until he left for the air force just a mere two months before her sixteenth birthday. She shook her head, thinking it was hard to believe that as close as she, Rae'jean, Alexia, and Michael had been, now they rarely communicated with one another because of everyone's busy schedule and lifestyles.

Alexia was busy out in LA making hit records, and Michael, the last Taye had heard, was living somewhere in Minnesota working as a pilot for a major airline. His wife had gotten killed in a car accident around six years ago, and he was a single father raising his daughter.

As Taye pulled off the main road onto the lane leading into her subdivision, her brows drew together when for no reason she began to feel uneasy. It was only after she had turned the corner to her street that she understood the reason behind her uneasiness.

Her parents' car was parked in her driveway.

Deliberately Taye straightened, lifted her chin, and inserted her key in the door. She didn't want to remember the scene that had ensued the last time her parents had visited. Her father, as usual, had tried being the peacemaker, which wasn't an easy task when you were married to Otha Mae Robbins Bennett. She had had the nerve to question how Taye could afford such a home in a nice area of Atlanta. She'd all but accused her of being a kept woman.

What her parents didn't know and what she had refused to tell them was that Sharon had loaned her the money for the down payment and she was in the process of paying Sharon back. If things stayed on track, the loan would be paid off by the end of the year.

Her mother, Taye accepted, would forever blame her for the embarrassment she'd caused the family by having not one but two babies out of wedlock. Although she knew her parents loved her and their granddaughters dearly, the fact still remained that she had messed up her mother's well-laid-out plans for her future.

And to this day Taye's mother never let her forget it. That was the main reason Taye rarely traveled to Macon, where the majority of the Bennetts still lived. She would love to take the girls and just spend a peaceful and relaxing day with Poppa Ethan. But if word got out that she'd visited Poppa Ethan without visiting her own parents, it would create an even bigger division between them.

Taye nervously opened the door, wondering why her parents were here. Had something happened to Poppa Ethan or one of her brothers? Bryan, her oldest brother, was almost forty, and Darryl was thirty-six. Both were married and had two kids and lived in Dallas.

Taye entered her living room and looked around. There was no sign of Sebrina or Monica, or her parents for that matter. In fact, the house was unusually quiet.

"Sebrina. Monica. I'm home!" she called out.

When she didn't get a response she walked through the house, only to turn up nothing and no one. When she got to the kitchen she noted the back door was slightly ajar. Walking over to it, she then noticed her father and her daughters in the backyard on their knees. They appeared to be burying something.

Taye went to the window for a closer look. They weren't burying anything but were on their knees planting something. Tears formed in her eyes when she realized what her father and the girls were planting. It was a peach tree.

Her father, who enjoyed the outdoors, had helped her plant her very first peach tree when she was Monica's age. Together they had planted it and together they had watched it grow. From her father's love of nature she had grown up appreciating the environment, and she had taught her daughters to do the same.

As she blinked back her tears, she saw that Monica had looked up, noticed her standing at the window, and waved. Whatever her younger daughter said to her grandfather made him and Sebrina turn their heads and look up, too. Taye was then reminded of the information Sharon had shared with her about Monica's curiosity regarding her father's identity. Taye knew it would be a good idea for her to have a discussion with Monica this weekend about her father, since Sebrina would be spending the weekend over at a friend's house. Just what she would say to Monica she wasn't quite sure, but one thing was for certain: she wouldn't divulge his identity just yet.

As Taye brought her focus back on the three people outside the window, she noticed they were now heading back toward the house. She walked over to the door to meet them.

Automatically, unashamedly, her daughters embraced her and told her how glad they were to see her. She had always encouraged their open display of affection. She told them daily that she loved them, and they did likewise with her. They didn't know how much she needed to hear that. Everyone needed to know they were loved.

"Grampa helped us plant a peach tree in the backyard," Monica said excitedly. "Isn't that great?"

"Yes, sweetheart, that's wonderful." Sebrina, Taye noticed, was hanging back with an all-knowing and an ever-observant eye. Three years older than Monica and three years wiser, her older daughter had long ago picked up on the strained relationship between Taye and her parents.

Taye let her gaze leave Sebrina to come to rest on her father, the mighty Joe Bennett. For some reason today he appeared taller and his shoulders wider. Since his retirement from the railroad four years ago, he still dressed in the work clothes he'd worn for years, denim overalls over a blue shirt and a billed cap that covered his graying head. She thought he looked in pretty good shape for a man who would be fifty-seven later this year.

"Dad, it's good seeing you. What brings you here for a visit?"

"I had you and the girls on my mind and thought I'd drop by and see you. On the way in I stopped by Victor's nursery and got that peach tree for the girls."

Taye smiled. Victor Senior, her father's youngest brother, and his son, Victor Junior, owned Bennett's Nursery. Since Macon was a good hour away, there was no way her father could have just dropped by. It had to have been a planned trip.

"Besides," he was saying, "I promised Cousin Agnes I'd get this to you." He pulled a folded letter out of his pocket.

"What is it?" she asked, taking the letter from him.

"Something about the family reunion."

Taye's head snapped up. "The Bennetts are having a family reunion?" At her father's nod, she asked, "When?"

"Sometime this summer. Agnes is running things, so I expect the gathering will take place come hell or high water. You know what a meticulous planner she is, never leaving anything out."

Taye nodded as she read the letter. The Bennetts were having a family reunion. It would be the first one in fifteen years. The first one since Mama Idella had died. "What gave Cousin Agnes this idea?"

"Pop did."

"Poppa Ethan? Why?"

"Probably because he knows he's getting older and wants to spend as much time with his family while he can. The Bennetts are so spread out now, I don't know the last time we were all in the same place at the same time."

Taye nodded in agreement.

"Well, I'd better go wash my hands and head back toward Macon."

Taye wasn't ready for him to leave yet. He may have spent some time with the girls before she arrived, but he hadn't spent any time with her. "Dad, the girls and I are going out for pizza. Would you like to come with us before heading back?"

"Yeah, Grampa, come with us. Pleeze," Sebrina and Monica pleaded with enthusiasm while jumping up and down and grabbing hold of his hand.

Taye watched as he smiled warmly at her and his granddaughters. "I think I will. Thanks for asking."

It was Monday and the salon was closed; however, it was a study day at Morris Brown University for Taye. She and Sharon made it a point to take time out of their busy Monday schedules to have lunch together at the Pizza Hut that was located not far from campus. Sharon was a pizza junkie and had been for as long as Taye had known her.

"Guess what?" Taye said, wiping her mouth with a napkin.

Sharon's brows lifted. "What?"

"The Bennetts are having a family reunion. It will be the first since Mama Idella died."

Sharon nodded. "You're going, aren't you?"

Taye took another bite of her pizza before answering, "I haven't decided yet."

"What's there to decide? You're a Bennett. Why wouldn't you go?"

Taye shrugged. "I don't know."

Sharon looked up in time to catch the brief flicker of pain that crossed Taye's features. She'd been her best friend long enough to know how she was thinking. "You should go, Taye. I bet when you get there, you'll find that you aren't the only Bennett who's a single mom. Mrs. Otha Mae has brainwashed you into believing you're an isolated case."

"There may be a few others, but I'm probably the only one the family had high hopes of making it to the top."

"And you still can and you will. It's not easy holding down a job, taking care of two kids, while pursuing a college degree. You should be proud of your achievements, and I bet once your family hears about all of them, they will be, too."

A smile touched Taye's lips. Sharon always took the liberty to toot Taye's horn and knew just the right words to get her out of the slump at times.

"Besides," Sharon continued. "If for no other reason, I think you should go just to see if your cousin Michael looks as good as he used to."

Taye met her best friend's gaze. She had thought that very same thing a few times herself since her father had handed her the letter. "You remember Michael?"

"Remember him? Who can forget him? Even back then he was a good-looking brother. The only reason I never went after him myself was because I knew you were interested."

"He was my cousin."

"So? That didn't stop you from having the hots for him, and I know for a fact you did because you told me so. Besides, it's not like he's your first cousin or even a second. What is he, a fourth or fifth? And him being your actual cousin is a moot point now anyway, since we found out a few years ago that he'd been adopted. So the two of you aren't even related."

Taye shook her head, smiling. "It may be a moot point but as far as the family is concerned Michael is still very much a Bennett. From what I understand, he's the one who had problems dealing with the fact that he'd been adopted, not the family."

Sharon looked at her pointedly. "I really think you should go, Taye. It will be good for the girls, especially for Monica. Sebrina already has another large family, thanks to Gary and his folks. Monica needs to know she has a large family as well."

Taye took a sip of her soda. "I'll think about it."

Two days later and Taye was still thinking about it. During the little spare time she'd had, she'd gone through numerous photo albums looking at pictures she'd taken as a teenager after getting a Polaroid camera one Christmas. Most of the photos had been of Michael. Sharon was right. Michael had always been a good-looking brother. Tall, dark, handsome, and well built was the only way Taye knew to describe him.

She shook her head. Although biologically he wasn't her cousin, technically he was. She could understand and accept having thoughts and dreams about him as a wide-eyed fifteen-year-old, but now as a thirty-year-old woman having those same thoughts about him just couldn't be normal. Could it?

As she closed the photo album, she couldn't help but wonder how he looked now. Sharon was right. It just might be worth it to go to the reunion to find out.

CHAPTER 2

RAE'JEAN

Feeling warm and freshly showered, Rae'jean Bennett walked out of her kitchen with a cup of hot chocolate in her hand and curled her body in an armchair. For what had to be the hundredth time that morning, she mentally asked herself whether or not she had made the right decision by agreeing last night to marry Grady Fitzgerald.

She tightened her hand on her cup. Yes, she had made the right decision. They had done all the normal things couples did that led up to this point. They had dated exclusively for almost a year and had become best friends before they had become lovers. All through college and medical school she had avoided any type of serious relationships. After she met Grady things had changed.

He had joined the staff of Boston University Medical Center the same time she had, and instantly they had become good friends. That friendship deepened, mainly from the mutual respect and admiration they had for each other. She'd been moved by the care and concern he showed while taking care of his patients as well as his dedication to the medical field. At first they'd end up leaving the hospital around the same time each night and join each other at the hospital staff's favorite watering hole for beer and chips before heading home. After they had been doing that routine for almost a year it became apparent to the both of them that they felt something for each other that was stronger than friendship and wanted an exclusive relationship. The issue of his being white and her being black had not once been taken into consideration, nor had it entered into their decision.

Rae'jean took a sip of hot chocolate. There was no reason not to have said yes to his proposal last night. None whatsoever.

Then why was she plagued with a fit of nervous tension about it?

She tried convincing herself that it had nothing to do with everyone's reaction at the hospital last year when word had first gotten out they were dating, not that they'd tried to hide it. But until that time she had never known so many people had a problem with interracial couples.

"It really shouldn't matter," one nurse had whispered in confidence to her during lunch one day. "It's not like you're really black anyway."

Rae'jean's jaw had literally dropped at the insinuation that she wasn't a sistah. So what if she was light-skinned with straight hair? Being born a Bennett meant she had just as many roots in Africa as Alex Haley. Together she and Grady had somehow weathered the storm, and now most of the hospital staff saw them for what they were—another couple in love.

Then what's the problem?

Rae'jean slumped down deeper into her chair and gazed at the huge diamond engagement ring on her finger. One of the problems, she inwardly admitted, was the fact that they hadn't had to deal with their families yet. In other words, after a year of dating neither had taken the other home for dinner. For Grady it was excusable, since both his parents were deceased and the closest relatives he had were an older sister and brother-in-law who spent more time out of the country than they did in. But for Rae'jean the situation was an altogether different matter. There were more Bennetts living in Macon, Georgia, and the surrounding counties than you could count. The letter she had received in the mail yesterday from her grandfather's cousin Agnes announcing the family reunion planned for that summer only served as a reminder of that fact.

Would the family see her choice of Grady for a future husband as some sort of radical statement on her part? It was evident that she was mixed with something, and just what that something was had always been a closely guarded secret in the Bennett family, a secret her mother had taken to the grave with her. It irked Rae'jean to no end that to this day she still didn't know a thing about the man who had fathered her and for the past thirty years no one in the family had given her even a hint or a clue. Even Cuzin Sophie, who was the known gossip in the family, for once had miraculously zipped her lips.

Letting her head fall against the back of the chair, Rae'jean couldn't help but wonder just what was the big deal. All she had to do was take a look at herself in the mirror and take note of her coloring and hair texture to know that her father must have been white. But just who that white man was she had no idea. What she intended to do was attend the reunion and get one of her closemouthed relatives who knew something to finally talk. She would get some answers even if she had to go straight to Poppa Ethan for them. It was time she knew the truth about her parentage once and for all.

A knock at the door shattered her thoughts. She slowly got up and crossed the room to the door. "Yes?"

"It's me: Grady."

Rae'jean immediately placed a smile on her face. She didn't want Grady to know she was nervous about agreeing to be his wife or that she needed to see him to reaffirm she had made the right decision. She opened the door and he stood before her with a huge bouquet of flowers in his hand.

"These are for the woman who has agreed to be my wife," he said in a voice that was sweet as warm honey.

Suddenly and inexplicably, Rae'jean felt every nervous tension she'd experienced before he'd arrived dissolve. There was no way she could not marry this man, this wonderful, giving man who was also her best friend. Tears began forming in her eyes.

"What's wrong, sweetheart?"

"Oh, I'm acting ridiculous," she said, swiping at her tears.

He smiled as he entered her apartment and handed the flowers to her. "No, you're not. You're acting just like a blushing bride-to-be. Speaking of which, don't you think we should move ahead and set a date?"

Rae'jean's heart lurched sharply in response to his question, and she was grateful that her head was bent over the flowers, inhaling their fragrance.

That way he could not see the look of sheer panic in her eyes. She willed the look away before lifting her gaze and meeting his. "Do we have to do it right away?"

"Not as long as you know what the wait is doing to me," he said, grinning.

Rae'jean returned his grin, knowing he didn't need to elaborate. His eyes told her everything. Although they had already slept together a number of times over the past year, last night after saying yes to his proposal, she had requested that they hold out and not sleep together again until their wedding night to make the physical consummation of becoming husband and wife that much more anticipated and special. Grady had reluctantly agreed to do so but had unashamedly warned her that he wasn't averse to applying a little pressure if he thought it would break her resolve and make her regret making the request. The look he now slanted her from his gleaming blue eyes let her know this would be one of those times.

"Can I at least get a kiss out of you?"

Placing the bouquet of flowers on the table, she turned and willingly walked into his arms and held her face up to his. His lips were cold from the icy weather outside, but even that thought was erased from her mind as his mouth crushed hers in an urgent demand for her lips to part under his.

"Umm, you taste good," Grady murmured against her hair when their kiss ended. "And you feel good, too. Are you sure you don't want to—"

"Grady, you promised," Rae'jean said, smiling up at him.

"And you plan to hold me to it?"

"Most definitely."

He pulled back and smiled down at her. "In that case, I suggest we set a date for our wedding over something to eat." He placed another kiss on her lips. "Go on and get dressed. I'm taking you to Riley's for breakfast."

"OK. Have you heard from your sister?"

Grady smiled. "Yes, I spoke with her last night. Candace and Ron are back in the States for a while. I told them about our engagement. They're dying to meet you and have invited us to drive up to Maine to visit with them for the weekend. What about it? Can you get the time off at the hospital?"

Rae'jean's smile widened. From what Grady had told her, there was a five-year difference between him and his sister. Since he was thirty-two, that meant his sister was thirty-seven. "Yes, that shouldn't be a problem. I'll ask Lori to cover for me."

"Good. I'll let them know we're coming."

"All right."

They never made it to breakfast. Grady's beeper went off moments before they were ready to leave. Rae'jean braved the cold to walk to the sandwich shop on the corner for bagels and coffee. No longer filled with nervous tension or doubts about her decision to marry Grady, she decided to make full use of her day off from the hospital by staying busy.

After writing out bills and putting a few things in order around the apartment, she glanced out the window and saw a large moving van out front. Evidently another tenant was moving in, she thought as she watched the movers unload furniture. Her upscale apartment complex was in a ritzy area of Boston, and most of the tenants were professionals. With her busy schedule she was only acquainted with the couple who lived in the apartment directly across from hers.

She was about to turn from the window when a movement next to the moving van caught her eye. A man stood talking to the driver of the truck, apparently giving him instructions. Rae'jean could only assume he was the new tenant. As she continued to watch him from her second-floor window, she couldn't help but notice how well his body fitted into a pair of jeans. He was by far one of the most well built men she had ever seen, except for the men on that calendar her cousin Alexia had sent her for Christmas. But still, seeing a well-built man on a calendar was one thing and seeing him in the flesh was another.

She took a long, deep sigh and reminded herself that she was now an engaged woman. However, she concluded, some things deserved to be appreciated, and this fine specimen of a man was one of them. Besides, she was engaged, but she wasn't blind, and the brother standing below in the parking lot was pretty good on the eyes. So she continued to stare, unable to help herself . . . until she noticed he had turned and had seen her at the window and had begun staring back.

Deep. His stare, Rae'jean thought, was deep. It was deeper than any stare had a right to be. His gaze seemed to swallow her whole, and the heat of it was definitely doing unimaginable things to her body parts. He was staring at her like a wild animal surveying his prey, and the thought of that made shivers race up and down her body and started a heated flutter in the pit of her stomach. Amazing. She had never gotten this sort of intense reaction when Grady stared at her.

Grady!

Rae'jean drew up short, appalled at the fact that for the past two to three minutes she had been standing at the window openly ogling a man. A very good-looking man who had seen her and who was still looking at her with intense dark eyes. She hoped she had not sent the wrong message to him, that she was available or anything like that, because she wasn't. She was engaged to be married. Reacting quickly to put an end to her foolishness, she pulled the curtains closed and placed a hand over her fluttering heart.

She released a deep sigh and then on impulse sneaked a peek through the curtain to see if he had gone. Her heart did a somersault when she saw he was still below, standing in the same place, looking up at her with a heart-stopping smile on his lips. She dropped the curtain back in place and took a step back. She had played with fire more than she needed to today.

"I must admit that you're quite different from any woman Grady has brought here for us to meet before."

That simple statement coming from Grady's sister's lips should have offended Rae'jean. After all, it went along with everything else that had been said to make her feel unwelcome since entering the Stanhopes' home. To say she had totally surprised the couple would be an understatement.

"Then it's good to know I'm in a class by myself," Rae'jean responded, smiling, although she was steaming inside. She was determined not to lose her cool and had forced herself to "chill" a number of times. She was reminded of what Gramma Idella had told her once: "Even people with money can have bad manners."

Rae'jean had felt the couple's coldness as soon as they opened the door to greet her and Grady. At first she had decided to give them the benefit of the doubt and be patient; after all, it was evident she was a surprise to them, which indicated Grady had not mentioned anything beforehand about their being an interracial couple. Then later, when their attitudes hadn't thawed, she'd resigned herself to the fact that there was no way Candace and Ron Stanhope would give them their blessings.

She glanced around the patio, wondering what was taking Grady and Ron so long. She had been left alone with Candace on the patio sipping martinis while the two men had gone upstairs to check out Ron's new state-of-the-art music system he'd had installed.

"I know you're of mixed heritage," Candace was now saying, reclaiming Rae'jean's attention. "What is it? Mexican? Italian?"

"African," Rae'jean said quickly with just enough of a sweet smile on her lips to let the other woman realize she had known that simple word would set her on edge.

After Candace recovered, the smile she gave Rae'jean did not quite reach her eyes. It was coy and as phony as a four-dollar bill. "How does your family feel about you and Grady getting married?"

Rae'jean crossed her legs to get comfortable. "We haven't told them yet. Although they know I'm dating Grady, they haven't actually met him. Once they do I'm sure they'll be happy for us."

"You think so?"

"Yes."

"And if they're not?"

"Then they'll have to deal with it, because Grady and I plan on being happy anyway. We're marrying each other and not our families."

"So their opinions don't matter?"

"Only up to a point. Grady and I will be getting married, Candace, with or without our families' blessings," Rae'jean said pointedly.

Silence ensued for a moment and Rae'jean took that time to study her surroundings. Everything around her indicated money, and plenty of it. The grounds were immaculate and included a swimming pool, a tennis court, and a garden with beautiful blooming plants.

Candace saw her studying everything and said, "The Fitzgeralds and the Stanhopes are both very old and distinguished families. Our history can be traced back to England, before they sailed to America aboard the *Mayflower.*"

Rae'jean smiled. "Is that a fact? Well, the Bennett family is one that's rich in history, too. We traced our roots and discovered there were a number of African kings and queens in our family." She leaned forward on the chaise and added, "Of course that was before they sailed to America aboard the *Amistad.*"

Candace settled back on the rattan love seat and reached for her drink and took a sip from it. Then another sip. "You're not the first, you know."

Rae'jean lifted a dark brow. "The first what?"

"Fiancée. Grady's been engaged before, while he was in medical school."

Rae'jean nodded. Evidently Candace thought she was telling her something she didn't already know. "Yes, I know about her. Lynn, wasn't it?"

Candace sat up. "Grady told you about her?"

"Yes."

Candace's eyes narrowed. "Did he also tell you that he loved Lynn very much?"

"He didn't have to. I assumed if he asked her to marry him he felt some deep affection for her. But he did tell me why they broke up. She chose the opportunity to teach school in England over marrying him."

Candace placed her glass back on the table, evidently ready to set the record straight. "It wasn't just any school in England. It was the school inside Buckingham Palace, and her students were part of the royal family."

Rae'jean glanced down at her watch, wondering for the umpteenth time what was taking Ron and Grady so long. She was getting weary of her conversation with Candace. "Should I be impressed?"

"Most people would be."

Rae'jean took a sip of her drink. "But then we've already established the fact that I'm in a class by myself."

"Ah, that's right. We did, didn't we?" Candace didn't say anything else for a moment longer. Then, "Lynn's back in the States. In fact, she moved to Boston a few weeks ago. Isn't that a coincidence?"

Rae'jean shrugged. "Not really. I think it's a good place to live. Boston is a beautiful city."

"Yes, that's what I told her. I also told her that she should look Grady up when she got there. I was sure he'd be glad to see her. Evidently he was. When I talked to her last week Lynn told me she had looked him up and that he'd taken her out to dinner." She smiled.

So did Rae'jean. Although she wanted nothing better than to throw the rest of her drink in the woman's face. "I wouldn't expect Grady to treat an old friend any other way."

They both looked up when Grady and Ron made their way back to the patio. From the hard set of Grady's jaw and the frown on his face Rae'jean could only assume Ron had taken the liberty to give Grady his thoughts on their engagement like his wife had done to her.

Grady came straight to where she sat and pulled her to her feet. "Missed me?" he asked, replacing his frown with a smile and planting a kiss on her lips.

"You'll never know how much," she whispered.

His chuckle gave her the distinct impression that he did.

Two days later, during the drive back to Boston, Rae'jean's thoughts kept dwelling on what Grady's sister had told her. His old girlfriend had moved to Boston and he'd not only seen her but taken her out to dinner as well. Why hadn't he mentioned it to her?

"Grady?"

"Yes, baby, what is it?" he asked, not taking his eyes off the road.

"Why didn't you mention that Lynn had moved to Boston and you had taken her out to dinner?"

He casually shrugged his shoulders. "It wasn't a big deal. I thought it was the decent thing to do. You aren't concerned about it, are you?"

"Should I be?"

He pulled the car to the side of the road, turned off the ignition, and twisted his body around to face her. "No, and I resent Candace telling you about it to put any type of doubt into your mind about us. I would have told you myself had I thought it was a big deal."

Rae'jean nodded. "She and Ron think we're making a mistake getting married."

Anger crossed Grady's face. "They can think whatever they like." He studied her. "Candace didn't get to you, did she? You're not beginning to think that we shouldn't—"

"No," she quickly assured him. "What about you? Ron didn't get to you, did he?"

Grady's face broke into a relieved smile. "No, but it wasn't from lack of trying on his part. He claims he's concerned about all these babies we haven't had yet. He thinks they'll grow up confused."

"About what?"

"What race they'll belong to."

Rae'jean rolled her eyes. "What race did you tell him?"

"The human race."

Rae'jean's shoulders shook in laughter. "Good answer. Good answer." When she finally got her laughter under control Grady pulled her into his arms and captured her mouth in a kiss.

When he finally released her, she slid a manicured finger along his cheek. "Promise me if for some reason you change your mind and begin having doubts about us I'll be the first to know."

Her words spoken softly in a whisper penetrated the tender and loving moment they'd just shared. "I won't change my mind, Rae'jean, and I won't have any doubts."

"But promise me that if you do, I'll be the first to know."

He looked at her intently. "I promise. And what about you? Will I be the first to know if for some reason you change your mind or begin having doubts?"

"Of course, but that won't happen."

Grady chuckled. "You haven't taken me home to meet your family yet."

"You're marrying me, Grady Fitzgerald, and not my family. Speaking of which, I know the perfect time for you to meet the entire Bennett clan."

"When?"

"In a few months. They're having a family reunion in Macon in July. Will you go with me?"

Grady smiled. "Sweetheart, I wouldn't miss it."

Monday morning Rae'jean left her apartment on her way to work and walked across the hall to the elevator. Her mind was on one of her patients, and she didn't see the man until she'd bumped into him.

"Oh, excuse me; I'm sorry; I wasn't looking—" She suddenly stopped talking. The man she had just bumped into was the same one she had watched from her window moving into the apartment complex almost a week ago. "—where I was going," she said, finishing her apology. Up close, he was even more handsome than he'd appeared through the window. She glanced down at him, dressed in Wrangler jeans and a denim shirt, and thought, on top of that, he was even more well built.

"No problem," he said, dropping his hand from her elbow, where he'd automatically reached out to keep the both of them from tripping over each other.

Hearing him speak made Rae'jean's pulse rate increase. He had a voice as deep and melodic as Barry White's. He'd removed his hand from her arm too late, she thought. Already the heat of his touch had swept a wave of desire over her so thick, it had her mind reeling in confusion. Nothing like this had ever happened to her before, and certainly not with a stranger. She loved Grady. Why was the mere touch from this man having such an effect on her?

She didn't know and she didn't want to know.

She took a step back, inhaled, then let out her breath slowly. "Thanks for not letting me fall."

His intense dark eyes held hers. They were brown eyes, the color of early-morning coffee with a touch of cream. "Don't mention it."

Rae'jean nervously moistened her dry lips before saying, "I'd better go so I won't be late for work. I'll pay better attention to where I'm going." Without waiting for a response, she rushed off toward the elevator door when it opened. Turning around, she saw he was still standing there watching her with an intense look. Then suddenly, without warning, his lips smoothed into a warm smile.

When the elevator door closed on him she thought his smile had charmed her. By the time the elevator had reached the ground floor her mind was a mass of confusion.

How could you love one man and lust after another?

When the elevator let her off on her floor later that evening as she returned home from work, Rae'jean glanced around. Evidently the stranger lived on her floor, since it was here they had bumped into each other that morning. Not wanting to run the risk of bumping into him again, she walked quickly to her apartment, unlocked the door, and went inside.

With all the activity that had gone on at the hospital that day, she had managed to keep thoughts of the stranger at bay. But now, the fact that they lived in the same apartment building and shared the same floor was something she couldn't help but think about.

She had placed her medical bag on the table when the phone rang. She immediately crossed the room to pick it up. "Hello?"

"Dr. Bennett, please."

Rae'jean's brow raised inquiringly as she tried to recognize the feminine voice. Had a family member of one of her patients somehow obtained her phone number and called her at home? It wouldn't be the first time. "Yes, this is Dr. Bennett."

"I swear, girl, you're one hard person to get ahold of."

Rae'jean shook her head, smiling, finally recognizing the voice. "Taye! Girl, it's been years. I never see you when I come home to visit. What's going on with you?"

"Not a thing. What's going on with you, *pretty girl?*"

Rae'jean laughed. "OK, Octavia Louise, don't start that mess with me," she said as she plopped down in the armchair. "But to answer your question, I'm doing fine, just keeping busy. How's the girls?"

"They're fine, just getting bigger each day. Sebrina turned thirteen two months ago."

"Get outta here! Boy, I feel old. And Monica is ten now, right?"

"Yeah, can you believe that?"

"I don't want to believe it. I was there when you gave birth to her, remember?"

"How could I forget? You were a medical student, yet you fainted watching me give birth."

Rae'jean snorted. "I didn't faint. That was the lie Alexia told."

"Then why were you on the floor?"

Rae'jean chuckled. "A contact popped out of my eye and I was down there looking for it."

"Flat on your back?"

"Again, that's Alexia's version and it's a lie."

Taye couldn't stop laughing. "Rae'jean, I hate to tell you this, honey, but there was another eyewitness. Have you forgotten Sharon was there that night, too?"

"So? She was so busy bawling she didn't see a thing."

Taye continued laughing. "That's right; she was crying all over the place. The doctor threatened to put her out."

"He threatened to put us all out. He almost did, too."

Taye wiped tears of laughter from out of her eyes. Her grandmother Idella had died a month before she'd discovered she was pregnant with Monica and hadn't been there for her. Her mother, Otha Mae, had barely spoken to her the entire time during her second pregnancy. Taye had felt alone and unloved except for Sharon, who had promised to come home from college during the time she was due and had attended Lamaze classes with her. But then, so had Rae'jean and Alexia. Both of them had come home from college just to be with her during that time, to give her support and to prove that they still loved her no matter how many mistakes she made. "Those was the best of times, weren't they, Rae?"

"Yeah, Taye, you want to do it again?"

"Hell, no!"

"Go ahead; get pregnant. It's time Aunt Otha Mae had another cow."

"She'll have more than a cow. She'll have a heart attack."

"No problem. We got a doctor in the family. Heart attacks are my specialty."

"Well, you can forget about me having another baby. I'm safe."

"Girl, you didn't get a tubal, did you?"

"No, I just don't do the thang anymore."

Rae'jean raised a brow. From the last photo Christmas card Taye had sent of her and the girls, Rae'jean knew that Taye was still a very attractive woman. She couldn't imagine her not having a lover. "You're kiddin'. You mean to tell me that you're celibate?"

"Yep. I haven't been serious about anyone since Monica's father. I guess you can say he cured me for life."

"Dang, girl. Are you trying to tell me that you haven't had any in ten years?"

"That's exactly what I'm telling you."

Rae'jean shook her head. If she continued to hold Grady to that promise it might be a good six to seven months before she got any again herself ... but ten years? That was a bit much. "How do you manage to keep sane?"

"I don't think about it. Besides, with working at the salon, going to school, and taking care of the girls, I don't have the time or the energy."

Rae'jean chuckled. "I think for that I'd always make the time, and as far as energy goes, all you gotta do is lay there and enjoy it. That's why it's called a good lay. A man is supposed to do all the work anyway."

"Is that a fact?"

"Yes."

"Speaking of a man, rumor has it that you've finally got one. Only problem is that he's white."

Rae'jean smiled. "Oh, that's supposed to be a problem?"

"For some members of the family, but not for those who could care less what color he is as long as he has all the necessary body parts in working order and treats you right."

Rae'jean shook her head. "Trust me, he has all the necessary body parts in working order and he treats me right."

"Is it serious?"

"Definitely. He asked me to marry him last week and I accepted."

"Rae'jean, that's wonderful! Congratulations, girl. When will I get to meet him?"

"At the family reunion. You going?"

"Yeah, I think so. I wasn't at first, but then I decided to go."

"So have I. Besides introducing Grady to the family, there's something else I want to accomplish while I'm there."

"What?"

"Somebody is going to give me information about my daddy."

"Good luck. That's been the best-kept family secret for years."

"Well, I got news for you: when I get to Macon somebody's gonna talk."

"I don't know about that. On some things those Bennetts stick together like glue."

Rae'jean frowned. "Then I'll find one that's no longer so sticky."

"Like I said, good luck. When was the last time you heard from Alexia? Do you think she's coming?"

"Lex's still on tour in Europe with her singing group. She probably hasn't heard about the reunion yet. She won't be back in the States for another two weeks."

"What about Michael?"

"Gosh, I haven't heard from Michael in years. Last I heard he was still a pilot for a major airline and still living in Minnesota. He sort of lost touch with the family after finding out he'd been adopted. He was really torn up about it. Lex and I went to his wife's funeral six years ago and tried keeping in contact with him, but he stopped returning our calls. Last time I was home I asked Cousin Henry about him and he said Michael rarely calls him, too."

"So you don't think he'll come?" Taye asked, hoping Rae'jean didn't pick up on the disappointment in her voice.

"I don't know, but I hope he does. I think he needs to know that no matter what, we're family and we'll always be there for each other. Right?"

Taye couldn't help but smile. "Right."

CHAPTER 3

MICHAEL

Michael Bennett took in his hotel room at a glance. Tonight it was his home-away-from-home due to a flight layover. After studying the weather reports, as the captain of the 737, he had decided it was too risky to fly to Chicago due to the snowstorm there.

He dropped his gear on the bed and went immediately to the phone to place a call home. His live-in housekeeper and baby-sitter picked up the phone on the second ring. Mrs. Duncan had been with him for a year now, ever since his last housekeeper, Mrs. Boswell, had moved away from Minnesota. The one thing he liked about Mrs. Duncan was the way she handled his thirteen-year-old daughter. Kennedy was known to be a handful at times. The tricks she used to get away with things while in Mrs. Boswell's care didn't seem to work with Helen Duncan. Having been a single mother who had raised six kids and three grandkids, she'd heard and seen it all.

"Hello, this is the Bennetts' residence."

"Mrs. Duncan, this is Mr. Bennett. How are things going?"

"Fine, sir. Kennedy did her homework and went to bed early."

Michael raised a brow at that. Usually his daughter was a late-nighter. "Is she all right?"

"Yes, sir. She said she's fine but just tired. Today was cheerleading try-outs."

"How did she do?"

"We won't know until Friday. Will you be back home by then?"

"I hope so. I canceled the flight out of Texas that was going to Chicago due to weather conditions there. I'm staying here tonight. Hopefully the weather will improve in Chicago overnight and I'll be able to fly the plane there in the morning. This is the phone number at the hotel where you can reach me tonight if you need me."

"All right, sir."

He smiled. Mrs. Duncan was old enough to be his mother, but she insisted on calling him sir. After giving her the number, he said, "Good night, Mrs. Duncan. Will you let Kennedy know in the morning that I called?"

"Yes, sir."

Michael chuckled as he hung up the phone. He checked his watch for the time before heading to the bathroom to take a shower. When he walked out of the bathroom twenty minutes later fully refreshed, he smiled when he heard the knock on his door. Perfect timing.

The moment he opened the door lust flared through his entire body. Stephanie Myers on occasion served as a flight attendant under him. At other times, when the two of them could arrange it, she served as a lover . . . under him . . . as well.

Tonight would be one of those times. He couldn't wait for her to get under him in the bed.

"I take it you found your accommodations adequate," he said as he stepped aside to let her into his hotel room and closed the door behind her.

"Very," she said as she immediately began removing her clothes. "This is a good night for making love, don't you think, Captain?"

His body hardened as he watched her undress, piece by piece. "Any night is a good night with you, Steph," he said, meaning every word. He couldn't help but remember the first time he'd slept with her. It had been their second flight together, two years after his wife had died. He'd been celibate since Lynda's death, and Stephanie had known just what he wanted, just what he needed. During the four years since then, she was the only woman he'd made love to. He was a widower and she a divorcée with no plans to ever marry again. What they shared was mutual satisfaction and friendship. No love, no forever-after, just plain sex. Good, mind-blowing sex that had to last him until he saw her again. When that would be neither of them knew. For the past year they'd been lucky and had gotten assigned to at least three flights together.

"Flattery will get you everywhere," she said, turning to him, now completely naked. She smiled broadly as she glanced down his body and saw that he was ready, aroused. "I take it you've missed me since the last time."

"Very much so." His nostrils flared as they inhaled the tantalizing scent of her heated flesh. She was just as hot and ready as he was. "Did you miss me?"

"More than you'll ever know." She came to him and reached out and opened his robe, groaning sensuously as she rubbed her naked body against his. "This feels good," she purred in his ear before pulling his head down for a kiss. When he reached down and cupped her bottom and lifted her against his hardness, a passionate groan escaped both their lips. He gripped her upper arms as burning desire pulsed through him, swiping any control he had. It had been four months since he'd had her last, and he wanted her with a vengeance now.

"I want you," he told her seriously as he picked her up and headed toward the bed. His lips sought hers the moment the bedcovers touched her back. He guided her legs around his waist, fitting his body to hers as he slid into her. It was a welcome reunion of flesh, mind, and spirit. She tried to hold him within her to savor the moment, but he refused to be still. He began moving, his thrusts powerful and urgent, and then she began matching him stroke for stroke, her movements just as powerful and just as urgent as his.

The end, when it finally came, swept them both away in a gigantic burst of pleasure . . . to last them until the next time.

Michael turned his body toward the sound of the phone and discovered he could not move. Something or someone had him pinned in place. He slowly opened his eyes and discovered Stephanie's weight curled atop him as she slept. It was a very soft, a very feminine weight. However, at the moment it was hindering him from answering the phone.

He inhaled deeply when he remembered why she was on top of him. After he had made love to her several times while she'd been under him, she had wanted to take the dominant role and had pushed him on his back to give him the ride of his life. The experience had left him deeply satisfied, although at the moment he felt weak as water.

Mustering up all the strength he could manage, he gently lifted her off him and placed her beside him in the bed. Without waking up, she turned her face toward his shoulder and cuddled closer to him.

He reached out and grabbed the ringing phone. "Yes?"

"Oh, Mr. Bennett, I was just about to hang up. I'm so glad I was able to reach you."

He recognized Mrs. Duncan's voice immediately. He also heard the distress in it. Reacting to it, he moved to sit up on the side of the bed. His abrupt movement brought Stephanie awake. "What is it, Mrs. Duncan? What has happened?"

"It's Kennedy, sir."

Michael was on his feet now. "What's wrong with Kennedy?"

"I told you earlier when you called that she had gone to bed."

"Yes."

"Well, I went in there right after our conversation to check on her. I opened the door and peeked my head in her room to make sure she was fine, since she usually doesn't go to bed so early."

"And?"

"From a glance she appeared all right. But then a few minutes ago I got up to get some water and decided to check on her again and noticed something strange."

Michael drew in a deep breath, hoping Mrs. Duncan would get to the point she was trying to make and not be such a stickler for detail. "What was strange, Mrs. Duncan?"

"Her body was in the same place. No one can sleep for two hours without moving their body to another position. Then I knew I'd been had."

Michael was pacing the room as Stephanie sat in the middle of his bed naked, looking at him with a sleepy but concerned look on her face. "How had you been had, Mrs. Duncan?"

"Kennedy wasn't there. She'd put a pile of clothes under the bedcovers to pretend she was there. Oh, Mr. Bennett, I don't know where she is or how long she's been gone."

Now Michael was just as frantic as Mrs. Duncan. "Have you called the police?"

"Yes, sir, they're on their way."

"What about her friends, those twins, Faith and Grace?"

"Yes, sir. I just finished talking to Mrs. Larson. The twins are missing, too."

Several earthy expletives flowed from Michael's mouth. "Call Morgan, Mrs. Duncan. He lives in the next county, but at least he'll be able to get there before I do." Morgan Viscount was a fellow pilot and a good friend.

"All right, sir. Will you be coming home?"

"Yes, just as soon as I can get a flight out of this place tonight."

"And what do you want me to tell Kennedy when they find her?"

Michael stopped pacing. "Tell her I said no more chances," he said before hanging up the phone.

"So, are you really going to put your foot down this time, Michael?"

Michael glanced over at the bed. Not only had Stephanie been his lover for the last four years; she'd also become his very good friend and confidante. In addition to making love to her each and every time he saw her, he'd also given her updates on the problems he'd begun having with Kennedy. Since becoming a teenager his daughter had turned into a hellion. They'd had several arguments about his refusal to let her get a tattoo and his objections to her wanting to get her nose pierced. He'd heard countless times from Kennedy over the past year just how uncool he was. If being a concerned and caring parent made him *uncool,* then so be it. He would stay uncool.

"I put my foot down all the other times, Steph."

"But maybe not enough, Michael. Don't you see what she's doing? She fighting for attention."

Michael ran a frustrated hand across his head. "I give her as much attention as I can. I'm a pilot, for heaven's sake! I have to be gone away from home at least three or four nights each week."

"Then make sure she understands that."

"Don't you think I've tried, Steph? It's like Kennedy has turned into another person, a total stranger. Where is that little girl I used to read a story to each night when I returned home from a flight? Where is the little girl who would come sit in my lap and tell me over and over how much she loved me? Where is she?"

Stephanie got out of the bed and walked over to him and placed a hand on his arm. "She's still there, Michael; you just have to do whatever you can to bring her back out. But you may not be able to do it alone. I know you have a large family who you can call on if you'll only reach out to them."

Michael shook his head. "The majority of my family live in Georgia, and other than my grandfather, Kennedy doesn't know any of them. Besides, she's my responsibility, not theirs."

"But I'm sure they wouldn't mind helping—"

"No, damn it, she's my responsibility! I don't need their help!"

Stephanie knew when to back off. She and Michael had had discussions about his family many times. He'd been very close to them as a child growing up, but for some reason once he'd found out that he had been adopted, he had taken that discovery hard. "All right. Then what are you going to do?"

Already Michael was moving around the room packing. He paused and met her gaze. "The first thing I'm going to do when I get home is give Kennedy the behind whipping she deserves."

As soon as the airline was able to secure another captain to take over his flight, Michael caught a plane in the middle of the night to go home to Minnesota. A call from Mrs. Duncan before he'd left the hotel indicated the police had found Kennedy and the Larson twins. The three of them had gone joyriding with a sixteen-year-old girl from their school. There had been an accident, a minor fender bender. After the police officer had given the girls a good tongue-lashing he had taken them home.

By the time Michael drove up into his driveway at three in the morning, he was furious as well as shaken up over the entire ordeal. The house was completely dark, which meant Mrs. Duncan and Kennedy were asleep. With as much rage and anger as he was feeling he knew the best thing to do was wait until morning and confront his daughter. But still he had to see for himself that she was safe and sound asleep in her room.

Taking the stairs two at a time, he entered his daughter's bedroom. Walking over to the bed, he stared down at her sleeping form. From the streetlights shining through the window he saw her features, so much like Lynda's, as she clutched her teddy bear while she slept. How could such a tiny and petite person be such a hellion while she was awake and appear to be such an angel while asleep? He glanced past his child to the framed picture of his wife that sat on Kennedy's nightstand.

Suddenly at that moment the weight of all he'd endured for the past six years came crushing down on him. He thought his world had come to an end when he lost Lynda in an auto accident six years ago. How on earth would he have survived if he'd lost his daughter tonight the very same way? For heaven's sake! She'd been out joyriding with friends when she should have been home in bed, safe and protected.

After pulling the covers over Kennedy, he left her room and walked across the hall to his own. Going over to his dresser, he picked up Lynda's picture, a duplicate of the one in his daughter's room. As he stared at it, he felt tears he hadn't wept in six years wet his face. He had promised his wife that day at the hospital, just moments before she'd taken her last breath, that he would take care of their daughter and always keep her safe. He wondered if Lynda thought the way he now felt, that he was doing a damn poor job of it.

No. Lynda would understand like she always had that due to his profession he had to be gone from home a lot. She would believe in her heart that he would make things work for him and their daughter, always putting Kennedy first.

"Where is she, Lynda?" he whispered to the portrait he held in his hand, the likeness of the wife he'd loved so much. "Where is our little girl? The one you left for me to take care of? I want her back. I don't know if I'm equipped emotionally to deal with the person she's become. I need help. I need help, sweetheart. I don't know if I can handle it alone any longer. I wish so much that you were here with me. You would know exactly what to do."

Inhaling a deep breath, he placed the picture back on his dresser. Before he went to bed he would thank God for not taking his daughter away from him tonight, and he would do something that he had not done in a long time.

Tonight he would pray and he would pray hard.

. . .

"We're moving to Atlanta."

At first after he'd said those words Kennedy just stared at him like he had suddenly grown two heads. Then she quietly shrugged, met his gaze, and said, "I'm not moving anywhere."

"You don't have a choice, young lady."

When she saw that he was dead serious the crying and screaming began, putting the tantrum in full swing. "How can you think about forcing me to leave? My friends are here. What about Faith and Grace? What about my school? What about—"

"What about putting a lid on it, Kennedy? Being dramatic won't do you any good. We're moving. As far as I'm concerned, none of those things you named makes a bit of difference to me, especially Faith and Grace. What type of friends would encourage you to pull a stunt like you did last night? All of you could have gotten killed."

"We didn't," she countered.

"But you could have and that's all that matters to me."

"Well, that's not all that matters to me. My friends matter to me. You're never here. I need someone I can relate to."

Michael took a deep breath. "And that's why we're moving. I'm taking this job that was offered to me a month ago. I'll still be flying, but for a private corporation with flights only in the Southeast. That way I'll be home more." The decision had come to him last night after much soul-searching and prayer. He would take only a small cut from his current salary, but in a few years he'd be right back on top of his range again. But at the moment that didn't matter. What he cared about most was his daughter and trying to coast her through these turbulent teenage years with as much ease as possible and without him losing his sanity in the process.

He had known he made the right decision when he went through his mail at breakfast and came across the letter from Cousin Agnes. There would be a Bennett family reunion in July. It was time for him to stop carrying that chip on his shoulder about being adopted. Donnel and Zoe Lee Bennett had given him a loving home for the first twelve years of his life. After their deaths his grandfather, Grampa Henry, had raised him and the rest of the Bennett family had given him a strong sense of values to live by. The close relationships he'd shared with all of his cousins, especially Taye, Rae'jean, and Alexia, had always given him a feeling of belonging.

He wanted Kennedy to have that same feeling of belonging as well.

It takes a village. That very thought had suddenly struck him last night, and he realized the importance of a strong, loving family system. Lynda was gone, but he still had a loving family he knew was there for him. All he had to do was reach out. Stephanie had tried to make him see that many times, but he had refused. If anything happened to him Kennedy would be completely alone, and he didn't want that. Lynda's parents had died years ago, and she'd been the only child. The only relative she'd known about was an elderly aunt who'd died the year before she had. Therefore, his family would be the only one Kennedy had, and except for his grandfather, she didn't know any of them. Living in Atlanta would put them within an hour's drive of Macon, where most of the Bennetts lived.

"I won't go. I'll run away first."

Kennedy's threat interrupted his thoughts. "Yeah, sweetheart, you do that. Think of all the money you'll be saving me on food, clothes, hair, and nails."

The tears and the screaming started again. "I hate you!"

He tried to let her words, spoken in anger, roll off him. But they hurt nonetheless and his heart skipped a painful beat. "That may be the case, Kennedy, but I do love you."

He then turned and walked out of the room.

Three weeks later and his plans had been finalized. He and Kennedy would be moving to Atlanta at the end of her school term. Kennedy was still pouting and was beginning to be a sheer test of his patience and control, but he was determined to ignore her antics. Her negative mood and attitude would not change a thing. In fact, they only reinforced his belief that he was doing the best thing for the both of them.

With the help of a realtor Michael had located a very nice home for him and Kennedy close to the school she would be attending. If everything worked out as planned, he would be settled in his home a few weeks before the family reunion, which was something he was beginning to look forward to. He had been gone away from home too long. After high school he had immediately joined the air force to fulfill his lifelong dream of becoming a pilot. His travels had taken him just about everywhere, but it was when he was sent to Japan that he met Lynda. She'd been a nurse working at the base where he'd been assigned.

"Hi, Captain."

Michael looked up and smiled. Stephanie was leaning her shoulder against the wall just inside the door of the employees' lounge. "Steph, I didn't know you'd be flying today. I thought you were off this week."

She returned his smile. "I am. I came by especially to see you. Is there a place we can go and talk?"

He lifted a brow, noticing the serious look behind her smile. "Sure. My flight doesn't leave until three, and I was about to go grab lunch at Larry's. Would you like to join me or do you prefer that we go somewhere more private?"

"Larry's will be fine."

Due to the lunch crowd, Larry's Seafood Grill was loud when Michael and Stephanie stepped through the doors. As he led Stephanie to an empty table he couldn't help notice a number of familiar faces in the place. Because it was located in the airport, a number of other pilots and flight attendants ate there on a regular basis in between flights.

When the waiter left after taking their order Stephanie asked him, "How's Kennedy?"

Michael released a frustrated sigh. "As well as can be expected for someone who claims her world is going to fall apart with the move to Atlanta." He had called Stephanie the day after returning home like he'd promised her he would do. She had been concerned about Kennedy and wanted to make sure she was all right when he got there. It was then that he had told Stephanie about his decision to quit his job with the airline and go work as a pilot for a private company. She had understood his decision. She'd also understood that his decision had virtually meant the end to their four-year relationship, unless either of them wanted for it to continue.

"But I'm sure you didn't want to have lunch with me just to talk about Kennedy. What is it, Steph?"

Stephanie glanced up at him. "I've met someone. I know we've pretty much decided to end things between us anyway, because of your move, but still I wanted you to know."

Michael leaned back in his chair and tipped his head back and studied Stephanie. She had come to mean a lot to him over the past four years. She had been everything he had needed to help get over losing Lynda. Stephanie was a woman with a giving heart who had never made any demands on him. She had been a special lover, and even more important, she had been a good friend. "This sounds serious, Steph. Is it?"

She met his gaze. "It could be. I met him two weeks ago on one of my flights. He's a rancher from Montana. We've been communicating a lot by phone, and a few days ago he invited me to spend a week at his ranch. I just wanted to make sure things were completely over between us before I accepted his invitation."

Michael nodded. When he and Stephanie had decided just to date exclusively four years ago, they had done just that, dated exclusively. But they'd also agreed that if either one or the other met someone, then it would be just a matter of letting the other know.

He had enjoyed her companionship. He was definitely going to miss her, but she deserved more than what he would ever be able to offer her. "Are you having second thoughts about your decision to never marry again?"

"Yes."

He paused from drinking his water. A small smile touched his lips. "I'm glad. I think you have a lot to offer someone. You're a special woman, Steph."

"And you're a special man, Michael. You helped me get over some rough times in my life."

The rough times she was referring to were the years she'd been married to an abusive husband. After three years of enduring constant beatings and ridicule she had ended the marriage. She had been divorced less than a year when she and Michael had met. "My involvement with you helped rebuild my self-confidence, Michael. It also showed me that a physical relationship with a man didn't always end up brutal. I'll always appreciate you for doing that."

"You helped me as well, Steph."

She smiled up at him. "That's something else I want to talk to you about. I care for you a lot, Michael; you know that. You are a warm, caring person. You're a person any woman could easily fall in love with. I know how much you loved Lynda and the idea of another woman ever taking her place in your life right now is unthinkable to you. But I believe there is a special woman out there for you. And although she won't ever take Lynda's place, I think she'll be able to carve her own special place in your heart if you let her. Promise me that when you do meet her you'll give her a chance and that you won't let anything come between you. You will need her and Kennedy will, too."

Michael considered her words for a moment. He doubted another woman would ever be able to carve a place in his heart. If Stephanie hadn't been able to do it in the four years they had been together, he doubted any other woman would even venture close.

"Promise me, Michael, that you won't give up on love and that one day you'll give it a second chance . . . just like I plan on doing."

She had breathed out the words in a low whisper. It was a heartfelt plea, and Michael knew she would continue to go at it until he said what she wanted to hear. Although in his heart he doubted there would ever be another woman for him, he owed it to Stephanie to let her believe there was hope not only for her but for him as well. She deserved believing that, as much as he believed in his heart that she was also deserving of some man's complete love and devotion.

He met her intense gaze and reached across the table and captured her hand in his. "I promise."

CHAPTER 4

ALEXIA

Men. Who could understand them? And what woman wanted to waste her time trying?

Alexia Bennett shook her head and returned to what she was doing, trying to dismiss from her thoughts the empty doorway and the man who had angrily walked out of it. She gritted her teeth. Franklin Devine had really rubbed her the wrong way. What was his problem? Why couldn't he understand that when the affair was over, then it was over? Finished. Final.

She shook her head, sending the long mass of hair that cascaded down her back flying wildly. She stood, walked to the window, and watched as Franklin got into his BMW and drove away. Unfortunately, he hadn't taken her news very well.

Why did some men make ending a relationship so damned difficult? Why couldn't they understand that there were some women who actually wanted nothing more than a "wham, bam, thank you, ma'am"? Men had been resisting serious relationships for years. Why did they get pissed when a woman did it?

Why couldn't Franklin accept and understand what she'd explained to him up front at the beginning of their relationship? She wanted intensity and not intimacy. At least not the level of intimacy some men wanted. To her, intensity did include an element of mind-blowing sex that resulted after a hot look, a sudden connection, a series of dates, and maybe even a little infatuation thrown in for good measure.

But to men like Franklin that wasn't enough. They always wanted more. They wanted the depth of intimacy that involved a willingness to let someone else know who you really were, what you were made of, and what made you tick. It was the level of intimacy that revealed yourself and everything about you. The kind that exposed your flaws as well as any hidden secrets.

That level of intimacy also meant letting your guard down, which was something she had done with her first husband and would never do again.

It was the kind that could lead to being trapped in a relationship and afraid of the pain if things didn't work out. It was the kind that also led to the fear of rejection. That's why her motto was *Reject them before they can reject you.*

Taking a deep breath, Alexia dragged her thoughts away from the scene she'd had with Franklin and forced them on the party she was attending that night. It was a party for D'Angelo and would be held at some extravagant club in the heart of LA. Everyone who was somebody in the music industry was expected to be there. She had a lot to do to get ready. The first thing she would do was call her hairstylist, Naomi. She needed something done to her hair. She had so much weaved hair on her head that she was beginning to feel like Diana Ross's kid sister. She smiled. That wouldn't be so bad, since Diana was her idol, her number-one diva, and had been since Alexia was a teenager living in Macon, Georgia. The highlight of her day had been pulling out her mother's old Supremes albums and singing along with Diana, Mary, and Flo to her heart's content.

As she crossed the room to her bedroom she concluded that she and Diana were a lot alike in a number of ways. One day Diana had made the decision to cut loose from the Supremes and go out on her own. Few people knew that Alexia had that same goal. She had been with Body and Soul for ten years, but now she wanted more. It was time to move on to bigger and better things—alone. She wanted to go solo, and she had big plans to do just that.

There was only one way to handle her agent, Alexia decided as she stepped off the elevator two days later. And that was by using scare tactics. Abbott Bodie needed to know that she would find a replacement for him and find one fast if he didn't work on cutting a deal with her and Dunning Records. If she had to endure another rehearsal like she had today, she would go bonkers. Raisa and Chloe had been in rare form, snapping at each other like two mad dogs, and when she had tried to intervene to bring about a semblance of peace, they had both turned on her. How the three of them, opposites in every way you could name, had remained together as Body and Soul and in the process had become one of the biggest-selling female groups of all time was beyond her.

She and Chloe were the two original members. Raisa Forbes had joined the group three years ago after founding member Mia Combs got married and decided the group's grueling cross-country tours weren't worth the time spent away from her new husband. When Mia had been a part of the group everyone had mainly gotten along, since the three of them had a history. They'd been friends attending Tuskegee University in Alabama when the same man who had discovered the Commodores at their college years before had offered them a chance of a lifetime. Since they'd all been seniors at the time, they were able to finish school before the group cut their first record. When they had emerged onto the scene they had done so in a big way. With Alexia singing lead, their first single, "Some Like It Hot," went platinum and their debut album, *Test of Time,* had held the number-one spot for more than six months. Mia had been the peacemaker in the group. Whenever tempers flared she knew how to soothe them by reminding everyone that the main focus was the success of the group and not individual egos.

Raisa's take on things was altogether different. She enjoyed being a hell-raiser and kept mess going all the time among the three of them. Her philosophy was to give the newspapers something to print, whether it was good or bad, and for some reason she preferred bad. She didn't care that any negativity about her was a bad reflection on the group as well. And Raisa couldn't be trusted. Chloe had discovered that the hard way when she found out a couple of days ago that Raisa had hit on her boyfriend one night at a party Chloe had not attended. There were some who even claimed Raisa left the party with him. Chloe had broken things off with Myron and had come within two feet of giving Raisa a good behind whipping today at the recording studio.

Alexia took a deep breath. She was too old for this. Most of the new all-girl groups hitting the scene were in their early twenties. She and Chloe would turn thirty-one later this year, and Raisa, the youngest member of the group, was twenty-seven, which probably accounted for her lack of maturity. It may account for it, but it didn't excuse it. As far as Alexia was concerned, there was no excuse for one sistah betraying another by coming on to her man. How low could you go?

She shook her head in disgust and walked over to the secretary's desk and spoke to the young woman sitting behind it. "I believe Mr. Bodie is expecting me."

The girl smiled up at her. "Yes, he is, Ms. Bennett; however, he's with someone. As soon as he's free I'll let him know you've arrived."

Alexia had not yet taken a seat when the door to Abbott Bodie's office opened and he walked out with a very good-looking man at his side. She immediately began checking the brother out, breaking her long-standing rule of not showing interest in another man any sooner than three months after ending a relationship with one.

The man was well over six feet tall, with broad, muscle-layered shoulders that were covered in an expertly tailored suit. Another thing she noticed about him was his features. In one scope she'd taken in the richness of his medium brown skin, his straight nose, and his firm, sensual lips. He had close-cropped black hair and a dimple displayed in his chin when he smiled, like he was doing now while talking to Abbott.

He happened to glance up and their eyes met. Alexia suddenly felt goose bumps rise on the skin of her arms and legs. Then, on the flip side of that, she felt heat pool in the bottom of her stomach. Actually, it was a little lower than her stomach, she thought, as the heat intensified and settled between her thighs. She shifted her weight from her left foot to her right, then back again. Nothing worked. The heat was still there and was getting hotter by the second.

She couldn't help it. The man was drop-dead gorgeous.

"Alexia, you're early," Abbott Bodie said the instant he saw her. He walked over to her with Mr. Drop-Dead-Gorgeous by his side.

"Abbott." She may have greeted her agent, but her full attention was on the man with him.

"Alexia, may I introduce Quinn Masters. Quinn is my new attorney."

Then to Quinn he said, "This is Alexia Bennett, both the body and the soul behind the singing group Body and Soul."

Alexia smiled as she held her hand out to Quinn. "Mr. Masters."

He took her hand in his in a firm handshake. "Ms. Bennett."

With the feel of his hand on hers, Alexia almost forgot to breathe. And when she noticed his eyes inspecting her from beneath dark brows, every feminine hormone in her body went on alert. She even thought she heard the sound of music in her ears.

Impossible.

But when she looked into his eyes and saw the intensity there, she thought that maybe she did hear a symphony after all.

"Alexia?"

Seemingly from a distance she heard Abbott Bodie call her name, and that immediately grabbed her attention. She swallowed several times to get rid of the sudden dryness in her throat before answering. "Yes?"

"I'm ready to meet with you in my office now."

"Oh. Yes, of course." She then looked down at her hand. Quinn Masters was still holding it. He released it and she felt an acute sense of loss.

"Be sure to get back with me, Quinn, on that issue we were discussing," Abbott was saying.

Quinn smiled as he nodded his head. "Sure thing." He then turned his attention back to Alexia. And when he did, a sudden, undeniable wave of acute passion swept over her. Her mind reeled in confusion and she knew she had to put as much distance between her and Quinn Masters as possible.

"It was nice meeting you, Mr. Masters."

His smile widened. "The pleasure, Ms. Bennett, was all mine."

"Hmm, and he looked that good?" Ivana Perkins asked as she sat at the desk with a pair of eyeglasses perched on her nose.

"He looked even better," was Alexia's reply. Ivana, who was old enough to be Alexia's mother and didn't have a problem with reminding Alexia of that fact, served as her secretary, handling all the numerous correspondence she received as well as organizing her social calendar. She had just finished telling Ivana about Mr. Drop-Dead-Gorgeous. To say the man had been a tempting sight would be an understatement. Although Alexia was definitely one who believed that there was more to a person than just great looks, she had to hand it to the brother for being able to send a tremor of excitement down her spine. She'd been attracted to other men before but never this sudden and this intense. And definitely never to the point where they dominated her thoughts like Quinn Masters was now doing. Besides that, the man had somehow set off a deep dormant longing within her. She had never encountered the promise of such raw passion the way she had during the few brief minutes of their introduction. The center between her legs still throbbed just at the thought of it. The dark intensity of his eyes had held invitations to things she didn't know if she was quite ready for.

Get a grip, Alexia, she said to herself. *Of course you aren't ready for it, nor will you ever be. The last thing you need is to get involved with a man who seems to have an overabundant supply of take-charge genes.* There was also something about the way he had looked at her, alerting her to the fact that with any relationship he was involved in, he would be the one calling the shots and in total control. Those were the types of men she tried avoiding at all costs.

"Here's a letter you might want to answer yourself," Ivana said, interrupting her thoughts. "It's from one of your family members."

Alexia's lips tilted in a smile as she moved across the room to get the letter from Ivana. She looked the envelope over. "It's from my cousin Agnes. I wonder why she's writing me."

Moments later, after Alexia opened the envelope and read the letter, the smile on her face widened. "The Bennetts are planning a family reunion the second weekend in July."

"I hope you're not contemplating going."

Alexia raised her brow as she looked at the other woman. "I wouldn't miss it."

Ivana took off her glasses and looked at her intently. "You may have to. That's the same weekend you're scheduled to do that concert in D.C."

A frown marred Alexia's features. That concert had been Raisa's idea, and she hadn't discussed things with her and Chloe before she'd committed them to it. "The details of that concert haven't been finalized yet. I'll just let Chloe and Raisa know I won't be able to make it. This is far more important. My family hasn't had a family reunion in fifteen years, and this is one I don't plan to miss. I want all those fuddy-duddy Bennetts, the ones who thought I'd never amount to anything, to eat their hearts out."

. . .

Alexia took a sip of wine as she enjoyed a luxurious soak in her Jacuzzi. Leaning back, she couldn't help but feel giddy at the thought of seeing the majority of her family again. Because of her hectic tour schedule she hadn't been home in almost a year, and then the visit had been so quick, she hadn't a chance to see anyone other than her parents and Poppa Ethan.

Poppa Ethan.

She smiled as she remembered her grandfather and the impact he and her grandmother had had on her life. When others thought she couldn't or wouldn't make it, her grandparents had always known that she would. "You're a special child, Alexia Idella Bennett. And don't let anyone tell you differently," her grandmother Idella used to tell her all the time.

Alexia then curved her mouth into an even bigger smile when she thought about her cousins, especially three in particular, Taye, Rae'jean, and Michael. Bless Michael's heart, when she, Rae'jean, and Taye had gotten to be teenagers who could get into even more trouble than they could manage as youngsters, their grandparents had assigned Michael to be their watchdog and protector. Wherever they went, he would have to go to keep them out of trouble, which wasn't an easy thing to do.

She, Taye, and Rae'jean had called themselves the three musketeers. All for one and one for all. She grinned softly to herself when she remembered some of their escapades, like the time Michael had caught the three of them smoking a pack of Uncle Victor's cigarettes under the house and how they'd sworn him to secrecy.

After a while indulging in more of her childhood memories, which she found herself laughing at out loud, Alexia rose from the tub and dried off her body. She would be retiring for bed early so that she could be on time for the practice session at the studio at the crack of dawn.

"Just where the hell is Raisa? She knew we were supposed to be here at five this morning to get started."

Alexia shook her head as she watched Chloe angrily pace the confines of the room they used for practice sessions. "Chill, Chloe; she's probably just running late."

"Or she's somewhere in bed with Myron. I still can't believe she would do something like that."

Alexia decided not to say anything. It was obvious that Chloe was all keyed up and just itching for a fight. Alexia didn't want to be around when Raisa did show up. To be quite honest, it would be in Raisa's best interests if she didn't show.

"There's something I need to talk to you about before Raisa gets here anyway," Alexia found herself saying to Chloe moments later.

"What?"

"There's going to be a conflict with me and that D.C. concert. Is there any way we can get out of it before the plans are finalized? My family is having a family reunion that same weekend."

Chloe nodded her head. "I don't see why we couldn't get out of it, since it's still a 'maybe.' I don't have a problem with it, but I'm sure Raisa will since the whole thing was her idea in the first place. She graduated from Howard and likes going back there to show off."

They both nodded their heads as they remembered their last concert in D.C. and the mess Raisa had made of things. She had tried letting half of the student body at Howard into the concert for free, which didn't sit well with the promoters.

"Besides," Chloe was saying, "I'll probably be out of the picture by then."

A sudden lump formed in Alexia's throat. "Out of the picture? What do you mean?"

Chloe met her gaze with sad eyes. "I may as well let you know that I found out yesterday that I'm pregnant."

"Pregnant? From Myron?"

"Yes, who else other than that jerk?" Chloe said through clenched teeth. "Isn't it a flip that I'm pregnant and the father of my child is now having an affair with Raisa?"

Alexia couldn't help but nod. It was more than a flip. In her opinion, it was downright disgraceful. "What do you plan to do?"

"Leave the group, since I have no intentions of leaving my baby to anyone to take care of while I travel across the country doing concert tours. My child deserves more than that. And due to wise investments I've made, I have enough money saved to hold me over for a while."

Alexia felt now was not the time to tell Chloe that by this time next year there may not be a Body and Soul because she had all intentions of trying to launch her career as a solo artist. "If you need anything you'll let me know, won't you, Chloe?"

Chloe smiled. "Yes. Just don't say anything to anyone about this yet. I'm still trying to work out some minor details before I officially announce that I'm leaving."

Alexia nodded. "Does Myron know about the baby?"

"No, and he's the last person I want to tell right now."

The soft chime of the elevator let them know that someone was arriving on their floor. When it stopped, Raisa stepped out with a huge grin on her face. "Sorry I'm late, but I had some things I needed to do."

"Like you're the only one with things to do!" Chloe snapped.

Alexia looked up toward heaven. It was going to be one of those days again.

By the end of the day Alexia didn't feel in the mood for anything but going home and taking something for her headache. Chloe and Raisa had bickered back and forth continuously for the balance of the day. Now with Chloe pregnant and contemplating leaving the group, this would be a good time to cut out herself. If Raisa wanted to continue Body and Soul, then it would be up to her to come up with two replacements. That would serve her right for being the cause of so many of their problems.

The phone rang just about the time Alexia was about to go into the kitchen to fix a sandwich. "Yes?"

"Alexia, this is Abbott. Are you sitting down?"

She raised a brow. "No, why?"

"I think for this you should. I just got a call from Chad Dunning. He wants to sign you on—solo."

Hearing Abbott's news made her shoulders shake with laughter of joy and happiness. "Oh, Abbott, that's wonderful!"

"Yeah, I think so, too. And the deal they offered isn't half-bad. In fact, I think you'll be pleased. How soon can you get to my office in the morning to meet with him?"

"How soon do you want me there?"

Minutes later, after hanging up the phone with Abbott, Alexia knew at least one of her dreams had come true. Now it was time to seriously think about doing something about the other one.

Her dream to have a baby.

Her marriage to Richmond Fulton never had a chance. He had been controlling and manipulative from the start, which was one of the reasons she would never let herself get involved in a serious relationship again, especially with a man who liked calling the shots. He'd gone so far as to tell her how she should look and act in public. He'd even wanted to send her to a speech therapist to try to get rid of her southern accent. The pain of the breakup wasn't worth it. She did want a child, always had from day one, but Richmond had staunchly refused to let her do anything that would ruin her figure or require time away from her tours.

Now that she'd turned thirty she could hear her biological clock ticking. More than anything she wanted to have a baby by the time she turned thirty-two, and since she had no intentions of ever marrying again, that meant, like her singing career, she planned to go solo. She had no qualms about being a single mother.

She had ruled out artificial insemination since the process was so clinical, so technical, undependable, and, therefore, totally unacceptable to her. She wanted to experience a man making love to her, planting his seed inside her body, and then watch for nine months as that seed blossomed into a life, a life she would bring into the world.

Lately she'd tried not to think about her burning desire to have a child, but now, after learning about Chloe's pregnancy and with the news of a solo career, she believed it was there within her reach and the time was right to act on it.

The only thing missing was the man who would go along with getting her pregnant and who would agree to relinquish all ties to the child afterward. She had all these grandiose ideas of finding the ideal man to get her pregnant. There were certain criteria he would have to meet. She wouldn't let just any man place a baby within her body. He would have to be someone she considered the perfect specimen of a man to father her child.

She knew finding such a man wouldn't be easy, but she was determined to do so.

BENNETT FAMILY REUNION

JULY 12–JULY 15
MARRIOTT HOTEL, MACON, GEORGIA

Agenda

*For there is hope for a tree—if it's cut down it sprouts again;
and grows tender, new branches.*
JOB 14:7

THURSDAY JULY 12	7:00 P.M.	Welcome Reception
FRIDAY JULY 13	2:00 P.M.	Memorial Service (Mount Olive Cemetery)
	4:00 P.M.	Activities at Poolside
SATURDAY JULY 14	3:00 P.M.	Family Fellowship Hour
	7:00 P.M.	Reunion Banquet (semi-formal affair)
SUNDAY JULY 15	8:00 A.M.	Family Breakfast
	11:00 A.M.	Church Service (Mount Calvary Baptist)

---

*Supper will be served immediately after morning service on the
grounds of the home of Ethan Allen Bennett, Senior.*

CHAPTER 5

Taye stood in the middle of her room at the hotel where the Bennett family had decided to stay for their family reunion weekend. She appreciated the fact that her brother Bryan had graciously offered to pay for her and the girls' hotel stay. She stared at the king-size bed they would be using for the next four nights. Monica was a wild sleeper who didn't know the meaning of staying on her side of the bed. She had a tendency of wanting to sleep all up under you.

Taye's mind wandered when she remembered that Monica's father had pretty much slept the same way, barely giving her breathing room. Even now she wondered what excuse Lynell Joyner had given his wife those two or three times he had spent the night over at her place. Chances were Mrs. Joyner probably thought he was out of town on a business trip for the fire department or something.

Taye balled her hands into fists at her sides. Lies, lies, lies. Everything Lynell had told her and everything he'd been about ten years ago had been lies. Even now the thought of it still hurt. He had been a man living a double life, one that included a wife and the other that included a girlfriend who actually thought he hung the moon. But like she'd tried explaining to Sharon, she had not been the only injured party. His wife, whom he'd neglected to tell her about, unknowingly had been injured just as much. In a way, even more so, because she was possibly still in the dark regarding her husband's past and current backstreet activities.

"Boy, what a big bed!"

Taye turned around at the sound of Monica's voice. She and Sebrina had just come inside the hotel room from out in the hallway where they'd been chatting with their cousin Victoria. Victoria was the daughter of Taye's first cousin, Victor Junior. Taye couldn't help but see the sparkle of mischief in Monica's eyes. "Don't get any ideas, young lady," she said, smiling at her younger daughter. "I don't care how inviting that bed looks; it is not a trampoline."

She couldn't help but recall a time when at the age of nine she, Rae'jean, and Alexia had accompanied Gramma Idella on a train ride up north to see her brother Aaron. Halfway there they had spent the night in some hotel that had a bed just as big as this one, although not as fancy. As soon as Gramma Idella had left them alone to go into the bathroom to take a bath, Taye, Rae'jean, and Alexia had attacked the bed for the fun they knew they would have jumping all over it. What they hadn't counted on was Alexia falling off the bed and hitting her head on the metal frame. Blood had begun gushing everywhere and Taye and Rae'jean began screaming, thinking their cousin was surely dying.

Gramma Idella had come rushing out of the bathroom and had immediately taken in the scene before her. Without panicking she'd quickly walked around the hotel room, looking up in every nook and cranny until she found what she'd been looking for—spiderwebs. They watched in absolute horror as Gramma Idella gathered as much spiderweb as she could get, then proceeded to place the webs over the wound on Alexia's head. Miraculously, the bleeding stopped.

Taye shook her head, smiling. That was just one recollection of the miracles of life her grandmother had seemingly been able to perform. While growing up she couldn't ever recall going to the doctor for any of her childhood scrapes. Gramma Idella seemed to know what to do in every situation, even the time Taye had gotten a huge splinter in her backside from sliding across their wooden porch one summer. Instead of taking her to the hospital so a doctor could get it out, Gramma Idella had taped a piece of thick bacon over the area, and by the next morning the splinter had worked its way out of Taye's butt.

"Mom, can we go and sit by the pool with Victoria later today?"

Taye glanced around at her two daughters. Already signs of excitement shone in their eyes. She wanted their first family reunion to be a fun one for them while they spent time with relatives they knew as well as getting to know those they had never seen or met before. "Yeah, maybe later, but first we need to unpack and then go find Cousin Agnes to see if she needs help putting those family reunion souvenir bags together."

She watched how her girls went about working together to get the luggage unpacked. Although Sebrina and Monica were separated in age by three years, they'd always had a close relationship and gotten along well together. Monica thought the world of her older sister, and Taye knew she had missed Sebrina last month when she went to visit her father and grandparents like she did at the beginning of every summer. Taye was grateful that her brother Darryl had invited Monica to come spend some time with him and his family in Texas before school started in August.

"Mom, do you actually think your cousin Alexia is coming?"

Raising her head from putting away some of their things in the dresser drawer, Taye couldn't help but smile at Sebrina's question. When she had told Sebrina about the family reunion that was her first question. Alexia was Sebrina's idol. Taye's teenage daughter got a thrill knowing she was related to the world-famous singer.

"I haven't talked to Alexia directly myself, but according to her mother, Alexia is coming. Like everyone else, she should be arriving sometime tomorrow. The reason we checked into the hotel a day early is to help Cousin Agnes get things together."

"I'm so excited about the family reunion, Mom. I can't wait to see and meet all the people I don't know who are some kin to me," Sebrina said in an energized voice. "Monica, Victoria and I are hoping there are more cousins around our ages. Wouldn't that be just cool?"

Taye couldn't help but smile. "Yes, sweetheart, that would be just cool."

The afternoon and evening passed in a furor of activities. Poppa Ethan had selected the right person to head the family reunion committee, Taye thought as she watched her seventy-year-old cousin Agnes move around the hospitality room making sure everything was in order. They had stuffed close to two hundred souvenir bags that each attendee would receive as well as a T-shirt that proudly and boldly boasted the BENNETT FAMILY RE-UNION on the front and a family tree listing the names of the key persons who began the Bennett dynasty on the back.

"Do you think this many people are actually coming?" Fayrene Bennett whispered the question to Taye as they went back through the bags to make sure nothing was missing.

Taye smiled at Fayrene. "Evidently Cousin Agnes thinks so, and you know her; she has to plan accordingly."

Taye couldn't get over how good Fayrene looked. It seemed the older she got, the better she looked, which goes to show that some men would be dogs no matter how good a tasty bone they had at home. Fayrene, Victoria's mother, was only two years older than Taye and had dated Victor Junior all through high school and college and had been his first wife. As far as the family was concerned, she was his only wife, since no one could stand his second wife, Evelyn. Evelyn enjoyed keeping mess going on in the family.

Besides being a pretty person on the outside, Fayrene was such a warm, loving, and caring person on the inside as well. The family simply adored her and had decided long ago that she was way too good for Victor Junior, who, like his father, just couldn't keep his hands off other women, which was the reason Fayrene had divorced him a few years ago.

"I'm excited about everyone who's coming; aren't you? It will be so good seeing Rae'jean and Alexia again," Fayrene said as her gaze swept over Taye. "You know Michael is coming, don't you?"

Taye met her gaze. "No, I wasn't sure if he would, although I was hoping so. It will be good seeing him again."

"I'm sure it will be for you. I can remember how close the two of you were."

Taye's forced smile attempted to hide her increased pulse rate upon hearing that Michael had planned to come. "Actually, he was close to all three of us, me, Rae'jean, and Alexia." Taye felt the need to clarify.

"Probably so. But I always thought you and he had a special bond for some reason, more so than the others."

Taye couldn't help but wonder if that was true, and if that had been the case, they evidently had lost it over the last fifteen years, since it had been nearly just that long since she had last seen or spoken to him. She went about the task of stuffing some items into a souvenir bag that she'd discovered was missing a few things. "Will he be bringing someone with him?" she asked, keeping her tone light.

"Other than his daughter I don't think so. In fact, I heard Cousin Henry tell Agnes that Michael has moved closer to home. I believe he said that he recently moved to Atlanta."

Taye's head jerked up from bending over the souvenir bag. She sat up straight, not sure she'd heard Fayrene right. "Atlanta?" At Fayrene's nod she asked to be certain, "Are you sure?"

"That's what I heard his grandfather telling Agnes." Fayrene studied Taye's features. "Imagine the two of you actually living in the same city."

After a long silence Taye finally said, "Yeah, imagine that."

CHAPTER 6

Slowly, silently, Rae'jean shook her head. Being a doctor herself, she clearly understood what Grady was telling her, but still she didn't like it. Because he had to perform open heart surgery first thing in the morning, he could not fly out with her that day for Macon, Georgia. Instead, barring any unforeseen complications with his patient, it would be sometime late Friday afternoon or early Saturday morning before he could get a flight out to join her at her family reunion.

He seemed to sense her disappointment and reached across the table in the hospital's cafeteria and took her hand in his. "You do understand, don't you, Rae'jean?"

She met his gaze. The last thing he needed to be concerned with was how she was handling the disappointing news. Grady needed to have his mind completely clear. The complexities of open heart surgery required total and complete usage of a surgeon's mind both before and after the operation.

She forced a smile up at him. "Yeah, I understand. I'm a doctor, too, remember. Some things just can't be avoided. How about if I just wait and fly out the same time you do and—"

"No, Rae'jean. I know how much you've looked forward to seeing your family again and spending time with them. I don't want you to change

your plans because of me. I'll join you late Friday night or early Saturday morning, just as soon as I can get a flight out."

She nodded. She did look forward to seeing her family again and spending time with them. She had spoken to Alexia earlier that morning. The two of them would be arriving at the hotel around the same time. Already she, Alexia, and Taye had made plans to get together in Alexia's suite later that night. "I'm going to miss you."

Grady smiled at her admission. His hold on her hand tightened. "Not half as much as I'm going to miss you. I hope you know that Christmas won't get here fast enough for me."

Rae'jean nodded, smiling. "I'm waiting for it with bated breath myself," she whispered softly, and watched as his eyes darkened with more than a hint of longing and desire. They had decided on a small wedding on Christmas Day. That meant they would be husband and wife when the New Year rolled in. Although the date for their wedding was five months from now, they were looking forward to the night they would become sexually intimate again. Keeping their hands off each other was a sheer test of their wills. But like she'd told Grady, the abstention would make their wedding night the best ever.

He leaned forward toward her across the table. "Are you absolutely sure I can't get you to reconsider your request for us to hold out?"

Rae'jean sadly shook her head no and smiled at the pout that appeared on Grady's face.

"Well, how about if we moved our wedding date up sooner? The wait is about to kill me."

Rae'jean threw her head back and laughed with sheer delight. He was determined not to give up on making her change her mind. The thought that she could put that deep, dark, sensuous glaze in Dr. Grady Fitzgerald's eyes was some pretty heady stuff. She had opened her mouth to respond when a feminine voice interrupted her.

"Grady?"

She and Grady turned to take stock of the woman who stood next to their table. For some reason Rae'jean knew immediately who she was. The way the very attractive blond-haired, blue-eyed woman was looking at

Grady with such familiarity said it all. This could only be the renowned former fiancée, Lynn.

A few seconds later Grady confirmed Rae'jean's suspicion when he stood and said, "Lynn. Hi. What are you doing here?"

"I had an appointment here and thought I'd look you up."

"An appointment? You're OK?"

Lynn smiled. "Yes, I'm fine. My third-grade class at school drew pictures about the dangers of smoking, and the hospital agreed to display them on the wall in the main lobby starting next week."

Rae'jean sat there wondering if Grady had completely forgotten her presence. She was about to clear her throat to remind him of her existence when he looked down at her and smiled. It was a reassuring smile.

"Lynn, I'd like you to meet my fiancée, Rae'jean Bennett," he said to the woman. To Rae'jean he said, "Rae'jean, this is Lynn Whitworth, an old friend."

Rae'jean nodded, not bothering to stand. She reached her hand out to the woman. "Hi. Nice meeting you, Lynn."

The woman took her hand in a friendly exchange, but Rae'jean was fully aware that she was being checked out from A to Z. "The same here, Rae'jean." Lynn returned her gaze back to Grady. "How have you been?"

"Fine," Grady answered her. "What about you?"

"I've been doing OK."

After a few moments of silence, Lynn said, "Well, I'd better be going. It was good seeing you again, Grady."

"Yeah, same here."

Lynn then turned her eyes to Rae'jean. "I'm glad to have met you, Rae'jean."

Rae'jean blinked. What she saw in Lynn's blue gaze was something only another woman would notice. Especially one whose profession could easily recognize signs of pain, despair, and regret. The woman standing before her had once loved Grady very much. Chances were she still did.

Rae'jean took a quick glance up at Grady. He seemed not to have noticed the look in Lynn's eyes. In fact, he wasn't looking at her at all. Instead, he was checking his watch. It was time for him to leave and go make his rounds. It was time for Rae'jean to leave as well. She glanced

back at Lynn and stood up from her chair. "I'm glad I got the chance to meet you, too, Lynn."

"I hate to run, ladies, but I have to go make rounds," Grady said, smiling first at Rae'jean and then at Lynn. "I'll be sure to check out that display from your class when it goes up next week, Lynn," he said as he quickly began walking away. He stopped, turned, and gave Rae'jean a warm, seductive smile. "I'll see you again later, before you leave for the airport."

Rae'jean returned his smile. "With your busy schedule will you be able to get away?"

"I'm going to make it a point that I do."

Rae'jean's smile widened as she watched Grady turn back around and continue walking. She noted that Lynn kept her eyes on him until he disappeared around a corner. Then the woman nervously turned and met her gaze and said, "Well, I'll be going now. Again, it was nice meeting you."

I just bet it was. Rae'jean was never one to hold her tongue when she felt she had something to say. She quickly decided now was one of those times and came right out and asked, "Lynn, why are you really here?"

At first the woman frowned in puzzlement. "I don't understand what you mean."

"I think you do," Rae'jean responded in a clipped tone. "Did Grady's sister Candace suggest that you come here to see him just like she suggested that you look him up when you got to Boston?"

Lynn stared at her. "Candace is concerned and suggested I talk to him."

Rae'jean smiled briefly. "In my opinion Candace is a lot of things. And at the moment none of them are nice."

Lynn met Rae'jean's gaze. "Candace loves her brother and wants what's best for him."

And no doubt Candace believes you're what's best for him, Rae'jean thought to herself. "At least that's something Candace and I agree on. I want what's best for Grady, too."

Lynn nodded her head slowly. "Candace isn't the reason I came here today. I had to see for myself."

Rae'jean lifted a brow. "See what?"

"I had to see if he was truly as happy as he pretended to be at dinner that night."

"Oh, and what's your verdict?"

"He wasn't pretending. He is truly happy," Lynn said, her voice flat and defeated. She then turned and walked away.

CHAPTER 7

I don't want to go!"

Michael gritted his teeth against his daughter's words as well as the tone of voice she was using with him. As a child if he had spoken that way to either one of his parents or his grandfather, he would be picking his teeth up off the floor this very minute. At times he was starkly amazed at how much the world had changed over the past twenty years. But then he knew it was the people in the world who had actually done the changing. They were more tolerant and their kids were less respectful.

"And you can't make me go, either!"

Michael placed his arms across his chest and gave Kennedy a look that clearly said he could make her do anything he wanted and that he was at the end of his patience with her. She had the good sense to read the silent message in his glare and take a step back. "Do you want an instant replay of what you got the week before we moved here, Kennedy?"

He watched as she slowly shook her head no. He didn't think that she did, but he thought he would ask anyway just to make sure. The week before they had moved to Atlanta, he had whipped her behind in good fashion, getting her for "the old and the new," as his parents would have said. The next day after she'd gone to school he had waited for the school officials to call him and accuse him of child abuse. He'd been almost certain she would take the opportunity to claim as much to the school administra-

tors. But no one called, and if they had called, he'd have a thing or two to tell them or any judge or court of law that would question him about giving Kennedy the whipping she'd rightly deserved. Under no circumstances would he be made to feel like a criminal for giving his daughter the type of discipline she needed to make her straighten up and fly right. As a loving parent he appreciated anyone, teacher, school administrator, or child welfare official, who was concerned with a child who routinely came to school with bruises or broken limbs. But as far as Michael was concerned, when it came to a good tanning to the backside of a disobedient or disrespectful child, especially someone with a lot of mouth like Kennedy, that was the only way to get through to him or her.

As a parent Michael didn't want to ever hurt Kennedy by having to spank her, but then as a parent he felt it was something he had to do. What she needed to take her through life was a good attitude and respect for herself as well as for others.

Michael ran a hand over his stubbled chin. He was grateful that he and Kennedy understood each other—for now. "OK then," he said, glancing at the kitchen clock. "I'm going into my room to finish packing and to shave. I want you to go to your room and finish packing as well. I plan to leave around four o'clock. It will take us an hour to get to Macon, which will put us at the hotel around five, plenty of time to make the welcome reception at seven. Understood?"

He watched as Kennedy glared at him before stomping out of the kitchen without bothering to say whether she understood one way or the other. Later as he stared at himself in the bathroom mirror while he shaved, Michael couldn't help but think of Stephanie and the promise he'd made to her about letting another woman come into his life and heart. What woman in her right mind would want him if Kennedy was a part of the package? His daughter would give any woman he showed an interest in pure hell. But then he knew that he would never get involved with any woman who would not accept his child. She was his and he wouldn't neglect or ignore her for anyone. That was the main reason he avoided his neighbor across the street, Marcella Boykins, at all costs. Although she was around ten years older than he was, it was quite obvious that she was interested in him, as she didn't bother hiding it. The first time they had met was the day he and Kennedy had moved into their new home. Marcella Boykins had boldly strutted across the street to officially wel-

come him to the neighborhood. She had flirted shamelessly with him in front of Kennedy, who had watched the entire thing with curious eyes. The woman had dressed to garner attention and interest by wearing skin-tight jeans and an all-too-revealing top. She had licked her lips the entire time she'd been talking to him, undressing him with her eyes, and had told him her life's history in a little over thirty minutes.

Although Marcella was a very good-looking woman with a put-together body, he'd found her lacking in a number of ways. Her age didn't bother him, but the way she dealt with Kennedy whenever his daughter was around did. Marcella liked bragging about how quickly she had given her kids to her husband to raise when they got unruly and began cramping her style.

"I just didn't have the time or patience to deal with them anymore," she had told him as she batted her long lashes and licked her lips while looking at him like he was a bowl of cream and she was a hungry cat. "Kids can be such a bother," she'd added. "If I had known they would be such a pain, I would never have consented to getting pregnant," Marcella had concluded.

He and Kennedy had been in the grocery store at the time Marcella made that comment. She had run into them there and had invited herself to follow them from aisle to aisle offering idle, meaningless conversation while he and Kennedy did their grocery shopping. After hearing Marcella's words, Kennedy had looked at him with questioning eyes at the same time she had reached for a jar of mayonnaise, as if wondering if perhaps he felt the same way about her that Marcella felt about her kids.

To rid his daughter of any such thoughts, he had quickly said to the woman, "You're right, Marcella; kids are an awesome responsibility and only the strongest of parents will survive. But I wouldn't have it any other way. I can't imagine Kennedy not being a part of my life each and every day. There's no way I would ever slack off on my responsibilities as a parent, because she means the world to me. I love my daughter very much."

His words had brought a huge smile to his daughter's lips, and he knew Kennedy had needed to hear his affirmation that she still meant everything to him and that he loved her. It seemed from that day forward things had gotten better between them.

Until today, when she found out she had no choice but to go to the family reunion.

"I may as well warn you that she's on her way over here," Kennedy said, entering the bathroom.

Michael looked up and met his daughter's gaze in the mirror as he continued shaving. "Who are you talking about, Kennedy?"

"The man-hungry Mrs. Boykins."

He frowned as he continued to shave. "That's not a nice thing to say, young lady."

"It's true, Daddy, and you know it. All she wants is for you to unzip your pants and get into her panties."

The heavy lashes shadowing Michael's cheeks flew up and the razor fell from his hand into the sink. He whirled around and stared at his daughter, tongue-tied. Kennedy merely looked at him with a smug smile on her face. Nothing, not even the sound of the doorbell ringing, broke his stare. He was too stunned. Finally he was able to find his voice after taking a deep breath of utter astonishment. "What do you know about someone unzipping their pants and getting into someone's panties?"

She had the nerve, he thought, to actually laugh. "Oh, Daddy, I'm not a child," she said. She sobered up quickly when she noticed that he wasn't cracking a smile. "I'm thirteen, remember," she rushed in and said. "There are a lot of things I know. Since moving here, with nothing else to do, I've been reading a lot of books and watching a lot of television."

He leaned against the vanity cabinet, thinking he'd better start paying closer attention to what books she was reading and what shows she was watching on television. "We'll definitely talk about this later, Kennedy. Go and get the door."

"She doesn't want to see me. You know as well as I do that Mrs. Boykins only came over here to see you."

He glared at her. "Do what I said and get the door, Kennedy," he said in a stern voice.

He watched as she turned and left the room. He couldn't help but shake his head. Just last month after Kennedy had gotten her first monthly period and he'd survived that, he had hoped that surely with her official emergence into womanhood and their move to Atlanta, the worst part of dealing with a teenage daughter was past him. It seemed his hope was in vain and he was wrong.

Dead wrong.

CHAPTER 8

Following the instructions of the FASTEN YOUR SEAT BELT sign, Alexia buckled up as she settled comfortably in the seat of the large jet bound for Atlanta. Once there she would get a rental car, preferring to drive into Macon instead of transferring flights to a smaller plane. She was about to close her eyes to relax when she happened to notice the last passenger boarding the plane. She blinked.

Quinn "Drop-Dead-Gorgeous" Masters!

Alexia watched as he glanced down at his ticket, then looked over in her direction. She knew the exact moment he saw her. He blinked, surprised. Then he stood starkly still as their gazes connected. His eyes tilted higher in a silent acknowledgment, and his lips parted in a smile that showed perfect white teeth. He began moving down the aisle, and she couldn't help but wonder if perhaps the empty seat next to her in the first-class section belonged to him.

It did.

"Ms. Bennett." His low-pitched voice was smooth as silk, and the velvety soft sound of it made a strange warm feeling wash over her.

"Mr. Masters," she responded with a smile that was appropriate, knowing she had to be careful, really careful, with this particular man. She thought about holding her hand out to him in a form of greeting, since this was the first time she'd seen him since they'd met three months ago.

But then she remembered that day and the length of time it had taken him to release her hand and the feelings his touch had evoked, and thought better of it.

"Excuse me, sir, but you need to take your seat for takeoff," a flight attendant came by and said.

"Certainly," was his response, and Alexia watched as he placed his carry-on in the compartment overhead before settling in the seat next to her. He snapped his seat belt in place. His smile, the one Alexia thought had enough sensual power to make a nun question her vow of celibacy, was turned on her again. It caused a hot sensation to move through every lower part of her body before coming to rest dead center between her legs.

"So, where are you headed, Ms. Bennett?"

Straight toward an orgasm if you continue to look at me like that, Alexia thought as she shifted in her seat and tightened her thighs together. She cleared her throat. "Please call me Alexia," she said softly, noticing his mouth. He had very nice lips. "I'm on my way to Macon, Georgia, for a family reunion. I'm picking up a rental car in Atlanta and driving the rest of the way. And you?"

"Home to Savannah for my sister's wedding."

"You're from Georgia?" she asked, looking at him with surprise. There wasn't a hint of a southern accent in his voice. She'd assumed when she met him that he was from the West Coast.

"Yes. I was born and raised in Savannah. I still have a lot of family there, although I haven't lived there since leaving home for college over eighteen years ago. I was seventeen at the time and had gotten a scholarship to attend UCLA. Once I got to California I quickly decided I liked the Pacific Ocean better than the Atlantic and made California my permanent home."

Alexia did quick calculations in her head. If he left home at seventeen and that was eighteen years ago, it meant he was now thirty-five. "Any regrets on leaving?"

"None whatsoever. There were seven of us and we're scattered all across the United States. It gives my mother a reason to travel when she comes to visit each of us."

Alexia nodded. Then, careful in her approach, she asked casually, "And your father?"

Quinn Masters continued to smile as he met her gaze. "I never knew my father. He died a month before my twin sister and I were born."

Alexia raised a brow. "You're a twin?"

"Yes. My sister, the one getting married, is my twin. I'm the oldest by six minutes. She and I are the youngest of the Masters siblings."

"Excuse me," a flight attendant interrupted them. "Would either of you like something to drink?"

He looked up and flashed a smile to the attendant before ordering a beer. He then turned to Alexia. "What would you like?" he asked, leaning slightly closer to her.

Hmm . . . that's a loaded question, Alexia thought, meeting his gaze. Up close, in addition to his nice lips, she noticed that he had a nice set of eyes. They were slightly slanted, something she hadn't really zeroed in on before. "I'll take a Diet Pepsi. Since I'll be driving for an hour after this plane lands, I want to stay away from alcoholic beverages."

Quinn nodded and then gave the flight attendant Alexia's order. When they were alone once again he settled back in his seat and began studying her.

"What?" she asked moments later when he'd said nothing but had continued to watch her.

His expression was that of a rueful grin. "I was just remembering an article I read in People magazine a few months back about you. The article named you as one of the fifty most beautiful people in the world, and I happen to think the magazine was right on target. You are beautiful, Alexia."

The reaction of her body to his words was immediate, automatic. She felt the unwinding in her abdomen heat up and move down to settle in her lower extremities once again. This man was doing crazy things to her body parts. "I'm flattered that you would think so, Mr. Masters," she said softly. She couldn't remember the last time a man's opinion of her, other than her father's and grandfather's, had meant anything to her.

"If I'm to call you Alexia, then you'll have to call me Quinn. Agreed?"

She smiled. "Agreed, Quinn."

The delivery of their drinks saved either of them from having to make any further comments for a while. It definitely gave Alexia a few minutes to think. She couldn't help wondering just what there was about Quinn

Masters that somehow pushed all of her buttons. In her brief conversation with him she was able to pick up on his confidence as a black man, his humor, and his intelligence. She had picked up on his sexiness the first day she'd seen him. He was definitely cover model stuff, but then at the same time she sensed that he could be a very strong, domineering type male.

She sighed. And that was the problem. She didn't need a strong, domineering type male in her life. So why was she attracted to Quinn Masters?

"So are you from Macon, Alexia?"

After taking a sip of her Pepsi, she tilted her head back and looked at him. "Yes. I left there twelve years ago at eighteen to attend Tuskegee University in Alabama. Body and Soul was actually formed on campus when the three of us, me, Chloe, and Mia, were in our junior year of college. We had worked different gigs on weekends to earn extra money. It wasn't until the beginning of our senior year that we signed a contract for our first single."

"And the rest is history."

"Yes, I suppose. I'm bracing myself for when the announcement is made that I'll be leaving the group. So far things have been hush-hush." Alexia watched as he nodded. She was certain that as Abbott Bodie's attorney he had been aware that she would be going solo. "You don't think Raisa Forbes will try to cause problems when she finds out, do you?" she asked.

"Don't worry about that. Let me and Abbott handle any problems Raisa Forbes may want to make."

Alexia took another sip of her soda. "I'll be glad to do that. The word is out in LA that you're a pretty damn good attorney."

Quinn's initial response was a rueful chuckle. "There's nothing like having a beautiful, sexy woman stroke a man's ego," he whispered in a voice filled with vibrant undercurrents.

She looked at his broad shoulders and thought that her head would fit perfectly in the hollow between his shoulder and neck. Probably just as perfectly as her body would fit between his firm, warm, pulsing thighs. She felt the peaks of her breasts grow to pebble hardness with those thoughts.

"Do you know what I think, Alexia Bennett?" he asked in that same voice she found to be extraordinarily sexy.

Hopefully not the same thing I was just thinking. "No. What do you think,

Quinn Masters?" she asked, pulling her thighs together even tighter when she felt a deep throb return there.

"I think this five-hour trip to Atlanta with you as my flight companion will be the best I've had in a long time."

Alexia's mind began reeling with all kinds of delicious illicit thoughts. She knew he would be the best of anything she'd ever had in a long time. She was intrigued as well as cautious.

"May I ask you something, Quinn?"

"You have my permission to ask me anything."

"OK then." She leaned closer. "What's a nice brother like you doing still single?"

Grinning, he took a sip of his beer. "Waiting for a nice sistah like you to show interest."

Alexia couldn't help but throw her head back and laugh. The last thing this man had to wait on was some sistah showing interest. A woman would have to be half-dead not to notice him and want a piece of him.

She shook her head. She was doing it again . . . falling under Quinn's spell when she knew the best thing was to keep her distance. But for some reason she enjoyed flirting with him.

"Will you be in a rush to get to Macon when we get to Atlanta, Alexia?" he asked with a voice that was simmering in sensuality and was doing all sorts of things to her mind and her good sense.

She met his gaze over her cup of Pepsi. "Why?"

"I'm going to have a three-hour layover before my plane leaves for Savannah. I thought you could join me for dinner somewhere."

Say no, girl. Don't let this man start messing with your mind or your good sense. He is not your type. But then another part of her mind said, *Girl, go for it. He may be one strong brother, but you're an even stronger sistah. You can handle him. You can handle any man who comes your way, because you've learned your lesson the hard way.*

Smiling, she said, "Sure, Quinn. I'd love that."

CHAPTER 9

"Gee, Mom, you look beautiful."

Taye turned away from the mirror and met her older daughter's gaze and smiled. "Thanks, sweetie." She looked down at the dress she was wearing to the family reunion welcome reception. It was an outfit she had purchased a few weeks ago while out shopping with Sharon. "You don't think it's too short?"

Sebrina cocked her head to look at her mother's outfit. "Nope, it's not too short. I think it looks absolutely cool on you. You have nice-looking legs, Mom; you need to show them off more."

Taye chuckled as she raised a brow at her daughter's comment. "Now why would I want to do something like that?"

A distinct twinkle shone in Sebrina's eyes when she said, "To show what a beautiful woman you are." She hesitated for a second before saying, "I think you need a boyfriend, Mom."

Taye lifted an amused brow. "Why on earth do you think I need a boyfriend?"

Sebrina came farther into the room and sat on the bed. "Because you need to get with it, Mom. You never have fun. You don't go anywhere and you don't do anything. All you do is spend your time taking care of Monica and me. I don't think you've been out on a date since Monica was born."

The *kid* had that right. Taye leaned back against the dresser in the hotel room. Her daughter had just painted a very clear picture of her life. "Sebrina, I do go places. I go to work and school. My free time is limited since I usually have a lot of studying to do. And as far as my taking care of you and Monica goes, that's what I'm supposed to do." She walked over to where her daughter was sitting and sat next to her on the bed. "Why the concern all of a sudden?"

Sebrina shrugged before she began speaking. "Because the last time I talked to Daddy he told me he's decided to get married."

Taye took a deep, steadying breath and hoped the shock she felt didn't quite reach her face. Gary had always sworn he would never marry. No woman, he'd said, would ever get him to the altar. He claimed he wasn't the marrying kind. "Your father is getting married?"

"Yes, he's getting married to Maureen."

Taye looked down into her daughter's downcast eyes. Gary had been seeing Maureen for at least two years, and whenever Sebrina returned home after spending time with her father she'd had nothing but nice things to say about the woman. "But you like Maureen, don't you?"

"Yes, but that's not the point, Mom."

Taye nodded slowly. "All right then, how about if you tell me what *is* the point?"

Sebrina raised her head and met her mother's gaze. "You are so much prettier than Maureen, Mom. And with your new haircut you can pass for Nia Long's twin sister, and most men think she's da bomb. I just don't get it. I don't understand why Dad can't see how pretty you are and get interested in you again. He evidently liked you a lot before, since the two of you made me."

Taye took a deep breath. How could she explain to her thirteen-year-old daughter that people who slept together didn't always love each other? That wasn't the way it should be, but that was the way it sometimes happened. For her it had been love; at least at the age of seventeen that's what she'd thought at the time. For Gary, who'd been twenty-one and in his last year at college, getting her into his bed had been a game, an ego trip, and a chance to add another notch to his bedpost. What he hadn't counted on was the condom he used being defective.

"Sebrina, whatever your father and I felt for each other back then ended a long time ago, sweetheart. The only thing we have in common now is you. We both love you very much. I'm happy that he's finally found someone to share his life."

"But you don't have someone to share yours, Mom. It's not fair that you center your life around Monica and me. What will you do when we leave home for college?"

Taye smiled. "By then I should have my college degree and will be pursuing a promising career." She pulled her daughter to her in an affectionate embrace. "Don't worry about me, hon; I'm fine."

Taye sat for a long, quiet moment, hugging her daughter and convincing herself that everything she'd just told Sebrina was true and that she was fine.

Taye arrived downstairs where the festivities were to be held. She was thirty minutes early, since she had promised Cousin Agnes that she would help make sure everything was in order. Sometime later she glanced up from what she was doing and heard the sounds of people arriving, her parents among them.

"That dress is kind of short, don't you think, Octavia? And it's way too airish in here for those thin straps," her mother said, frowning.

And I'm glad to see you, too, Mom, Taye thought to herself. Her mother hadn't bothered to say hello and already she was digging into her about what she was wearing. She always called her Octavia when she was not pleased with her about something. "This is the latest style, Mom."

"Maybe for someone younger but not for you. You'll be thirty-one in November."

"Leave her alone, Otha Mae; Taye knows when her birthday is. Besides, I think she looks good in the dress."

"Thanks, Dad." Taye gave her father a smile of thanks for interceding in her behalf. Ever since he had joined her and the girls that night for pizza, he'd made an extra effort to speak up for her more and tried to keep her mother from riding her back about every little thing. "Where are Bryan and Darryl?" she asked.

"They're around here somewhere," her father answered. He glanced around the room. "Cousin Agnes has gone all-out, like she's expecting a huge crowd. I hope she's not disappointed."

Taye followed his gaze. "Yeah, I hope she isn't disappointed, too. She's put a lot of time into all of this."

"Where are the girls?" Otha Mae asked.

Taye met her mother's inquiring glance. Although she hadn't been happy about Sebrina and Monica being born out of wedlock, it was evident to all those who knew Otha Mae that she simply adored all six of her grandchildren. "They're upstairs and will be coming down with Fayrene later. You know how it is when they get with Victoria, Lauren, and Cody. They want to stick together, since they rarely see each other." Lauren was Darryl's ten-year-old daughter and Cody was Bryan's fourteen-year-old daughter.

Otha Mae nodded. "That's how it was with you, Rae'jean, and Alexia. Everyone is wondering if Alexia is going to show up or if she thinks she's gotten too famous to spend time with her family."

Taye couldn't help but smile. "Alexia is coming. I doubt wild horses will keep her away."

Alexia stepped out of the shower and began drying herself off with one of the thick velour towels. She figured it would take her at least an hour to get completely dressed.

Her original plan had been to arrive at the hotel before five o'clock, but because she had accepted Quinn Masters's invitation to dinner she'd been thrown almost two hours behind. The welcome reception had officially started downstairs, and here she was just getting out of the shower. But knowing the Bennetts, she wouldn't be the only person who would not be on time.

Luckily, when she had arrived at the hotel there had not been any familiar faces about. She had been able to register and catch the elevator up to her suite without being seen. Even after the hour's drive to Macon from Atlanta, she'd still been too wrapped up in memories of her dinner date with Quinn to have small talk with anyone.

Walking out of the bathroom, she sat on the bed and momentarily closed her eyes as she relived the scene that still had parts of her body simmering. In a cab from the airport Quinn had taken her to a very nice restaurant in Atlanta. They had sat at a table where the lighting from the chandelier that hung overhead somehow made Quinn's features that much more striking.

Over dinner, they had spent an hour and a half talking about various things. She could not remember the last time she had enjoyed holding a conversation with a man. Quinn shared with her stories about his childhood in Savannah and his other siblings, and she had provided him with entertaining tidbits about the Bennett family. However, even while they had been conversing she had felt his penetrating gaze on her face, especially each time his gaze had lingered on her lips. Whenever his gaze had met hers she'd been forced to remember that Quinn wasn't her type, no matter how much she enjoyed his company and no matter how attractive she found him to be.

But still, that did not stop her from wondering how it would be to get seduced by him or, better yet, how it would be if she were to seduce him. The thought of either of those things happening had hastened her into thinking of their naked bodies, tossing about on silken bed sheets. No amount of common-sense logic could counteract the powerful physical attraction she felt for him. His warm, seductive smile had continuously thrown her senses into overload. His gaze had caressed her like an intimate touch, and her body had betrayed her time and time again by responding to it.

After dinner they had caught another cab back to the airport. He had remained with her until she had gotten the rental car, and then before she had gotten inside he had lowered his head and brushed a kiss across her cheek and said, "I hope you enjoy being with your family this weekend."

"And I hope you enjoy being with your family as well," she had responded in a breathless whisper. He had given her one last dazzling smile before walking back inside the airport terminal to catch his connecting flight.

Alexia reopened her eyes. There was no doubt about it: Quinn Masters was one smooth and suave brother. He was as polished as the family's best-kept silver. "Well," she said to herself when she stood up to begin getting dressed. "He definitely was the highlight of my day."

As she walked to the closet to get the outfit she had planned to wear tonight, she couldn't help but wonder if he would ever be the highlight of one of her nights as well.

She hadn't been home in almost two years, Rae'jean thought as she stared at the door that led to the banquet room where the reception was being held. Sucking in a deep breath, she squared her shoulders. It would have been a lot easier if Grady could have been here with her tonight. *Then maybe not,* she thought. She definitely had to prepare the family for him, although she was sure that by now most of them had heard she was marrying a man outside of her race.

She continued to stare at the door that was less than ten feet away. Just beyond were probably more Bennetts than she'd been in the company of for years.

Rae'jean also knew that beyond that door were answers to questions she was determined to get regarding the man who had fathered her. Someone, she had decided, was going to loosen his or her lips and talk. She would not return to Boston without knowing the truth.

"Rae'jean?"

A deep masculine voice called her name just to the right of her. She half-turned and saw a very good-looking man standing beside a pretty teenage girl. Rae'jean blinked when recognition hit. "Michael!"

She crossed the room in quick strides and was engulfed in a huge bear hug, feeling the welcoming warmth of her cousin's embrace.

Coming home, she thought, wasn't so bad after all.

CHAPTER 10

R ae'jean Bennett," Michael said, smiling down at her. "You look the same."

Rae'jean gave him a huge smile. "Give or take a few pounds."

"No," he said, taking her hand in his and twirling her around. "You look great. I always thought you were too skinny back then anyway. Now you have some meat on your bones."

Rae'jean chuckled and then looked at the very pretty girl standing next to Michael, amazed. "Oh, Michael, please don't tell me this is Kennedy. She was seven years old when I saw her last. She's simply beautiful."

Michael looked at his daughter and beamed proudly. "Yes, this is Kennedy." To Kennedy he said, "This is my cousin Rae'jean. We grew up together. Her grandfather and my grandfather are first cousins."

Kennedy, Rae'jean noticed, was more interested in her ring than she was in their family history. "Is that an engagement ring?" she asked excitedly.

Rae'jean smiled. "Yes. I'm getting married on Christmas Day. My fiancé, Grady, is also a doctor and has surgery first thing in the morning and won't be arriving until late tomorrow night or Saturday morning."

Kennedy's mouth dropped. "You're a doctor?" At Rae'jean's nod she said, "But you look so young."

Rae'jean grinned. "That's the nicest thing I've heard all day. I'm only three years younger than your father."

"You're thirty?"

"Yes, but I'll be thirty-one in two months."

"You sure don't look it. You look around twenty-two or twenty-three!" Kennedy exclaimed.

Rae'jean smiled up at Michael. "Hey, Michael, I really like this kid. She's good for my ego."

"I want to be a doctor."

Kennedy's announcement surprised her father. This was the first he'd heard of her wanting a career in medicine. "What kind of doctor do you want to be, Kennedy?" he asked.

She looked up at him. "I want to be one of those doctors who work in an emergency room," she responded quickly. "Just like the ones you told me about who tried to save Momma after her car accident."

Startled at her response, Michael stared at her. This was the first time she had mentioned her mother's car accident in a very long time. He thought she had forgotten the extraneous details of what he had told her that day when he'd had to break the news to her that her mother was never coming back home.

"Do you work at a hospital or do you have an office?" Kennedy asked Rae'jean, not aware of the tailspin she had placed her father in.

"I work in a hospital for now, but my fiancé and I have talked about going into private practice in a few years. We're both heart specialists."

"Cardiologists? Boy, that's cool!"

For a moment Rae'jean couldn't ever remember thinking her job was "cool." Mentally she went about each day fulfilling her lifelong dream of taking care of others without actually thinking about it. Being a doctor had its rewards, but then it had its letdowns—especially whenever she lost a patient. But as Grady had often told her, they had been trained to heal. The final outcome of whether a person lived or died was not their decision. It belonged to a higher being.

"If you're thinking about being a doctor, Kennedy, you need to start preparing yourself now," Rae'jean said to the teenager. "How are your grades?"

Kennedy's smile faded somewhat. "They're fair."

"They need to be better than fair. When school starts back up in the fall you'll have to concentrate on improving them. And you'll need to get a firm grip on biology and any health classes your school may offer."

"I will," Kennedy promised, energized at the thought of a future in medicine.

Rae'jean met Michael's gaze. Looking directly into his eyes, she saw his gratitude. Evidently he and Kennedy had had many discussions about improving her grades. "I see that we're going to have to catch up on a lot of things, Michael. It's been too long," she said, wrapping her arms around him again.

Wrapping his arms around her as well, Michael felt the wall he'd erected against the Bennetts when he discovered that he had been adopted break up in tiny pieces.

"Yeah, you're right. It has been too long."

Taye glanced around the room, thinking Poppa Ethan and Cousin Agnes had to be pleased with the turnout. There were more Bennetts here than she'd imagined coming. Reaching across the table that was laden with food, she helped herself to a cracker with a piece of cheese on it.

"That's gonna make you fat."

Inwardly Taye grinned, but when she turned to face the man who had made the comment she tried to appear annoyed. "Victor Junior, don't you have anything better to do than keep an eye on what I eat?"

"Hey, Cuz, gimme a break. I'm just trying to look out for you."

"Why? You never wanted to look out for me before."

"You're crazy, Taye," Victor Junior said, shaking his head, smiling. "And I would have been even crazier back then if I'd done what Gramma Idella and Poppa Ethan had wanted, which was to be your, Rae'jean, and Alexia's watchdog." He reached across the table to get his own snack. "You three were trouble."

Taye lifted a dark brow. "Are you saying you couldn't handle us back then?"

"No. I'm admitting I didn't want to handle the three of you back then.

I had other, more important things to do with my time," he said, smiling even more.

Taye frowned at him. "Yeah, I know all about those other things. I also understand that you haven't slowed down."

He shrugged. "Slow down? What for?"

"Last time I heard, Victor Junior, you were still married to Evelyn. Besides, I thought you would have straightened up after losing Fayrene over that kind of mess. She was the best thing that ever happened to you."

"Taye . . . ," he warned through his teeth. "Don't start in on me about Fayrene. There you go sounding like Momma and acting like Aunt Otha Mae, all in the Kool-Aid and don't even know the flava." For a moment Victor tore his gaze away from Taye and glanced across the room to the woman who was the topic of their conversation. Boy, did Fayrene look good. Always did. He didn't need Taye or anyone else to tell him he had literally screwed up with Fayrene. She *had* been the best thing to ever happen to him.

He then turned and glanced to the other side of the room at his current wife, Evelyn, and wondered what on earth had ever possessed him to screw around on Fayrene with her. He had married Evelyn a year ago, after their second child had been born and after her father and brothers had threatened to do him bodily harm if he didn't. Already Evelyn weighed more than his momma and wasn't even trying to lose weight. The plate she held in her hand was testimony to that, since it was filled to capacity.

"Evelyn gets upset every time we have a family function and Fayrene is invited," he said to Taye, hoping it would make her feel bad.

It didn't. "Fayrene was in the family long before Evelyn, so if she doesn't like it she can stay home."

Victor Junior frowned at Taye. "Or the family can stop inviting Fayrene to every blasted thing they have. Why should Evelyn stay home? I'm married to *her* now, not Fayrene. That's not right and you know it."

"When did you start caring how Evelyn felt, Victor Junior? If you cared so much you wouldn't be screwing around. And as far as what's right, it wasn't right for Evelyn to sleep with you when you were a married man— and you know that."

Taye dismissed the thought that she had slept with a married man herself and like Evelyn had gotten pregnant. There was a big difference between her and Evelyn. At the time, Taye hadn't known Lynell was married. Evelyn had known Victor Junior was a married man. In fact, she had relished the thought of being the other woman and had gone out of her way to cause Fayrene nothing but heartache and pain by openly flaunting the affair. If Victor Junior expected pity from her on Evelyn's behalf he was looking for it from the wrong person. Besides, she would never forget about that lie Evelyn had put out while in high school about her, Rae'jean, and Alexia being bulldaggers.

Victor gave a low whistle. "Well, I'll be damned. Rae'jean's here and she's still the family's pretty girl. Look at her. She looks good."

Taye only gave Rae'jean a cursory glance. Her gaze was immediately drawn to the tall, handsome man who had walked in with her.

Michael Alvin Bennett.

As she looked at him, Taye couldn't help but recall the boy he had once been and appreciate the good-looking man he had become.

"Hey, ain't that Michael with Rae'jean?" Victor Junior asked.

Taye nodded. "Yeah, that's him."

"Well, put that plate down and let's go over there."

Taye couldn't do anything but put her plate down and follow in Victor Junior's wake.

CHAPTER 11

Rae'jean, you look good, Cuz," Victor Junior was saying as he gave her a hug. "And Michael, man, it's good to see you," he said, releasing Rae'jean and giving Michael a brotha handshake.

Taye then hugged Rae'jean. "It's so good to see you, Rae." As soon as she hugged her she knew it had been too long and couldn't help but appreciate Poppa Ethan for wanting his family together once again at this reunion.

"Girl, you look good," Rae'jean was saying to Taye. "I can't believe you chopped off all your hair. I bet Aunt Otha Mae went bonkers. But short hair looks good on you. You had more than you ever needed anyway."

Taye grinned. "Look who's talking." She then turned her attention to Michael. Dang it, but up close he looked even better. "Hi, Michael," she said, giving him a hug. "It's been a while."

Michael's arms tightened around her. "Too damn long, don't you think, Taye?"

Taye finally caught her breath when he released her, but it didn't help matters for him to be looking at her so intently. "And I agree with Rae'jean. Short hair looks great on you."

"Thanks."

"It's hard to believe that Aunt Otha Mae's baby girl is now all grown up."

"Yes, it is, isn't it?" Taye replied as an easy smile played at the corners of her lips. She forced her eyes from him to the beautiful teenager at his side. "And who do we have here?"

"This is my daughter, Kennedy."

Taye smiled at Kennedy. "I like your name and you're a very pretty girl."

"Thanks, and you look like Nia Long. Has anyone ever told you that?" Kennedy asked.

Taye chuckled. "Yeah. My teenage daughter did just today in fact."

Kennedy's eyes brightened. "You have a teenage daughter?" she asked, looking around, unable to mask the excitement at the prospect of other teenagers being present tonight.

"Yes, I have two daughters. Sebrina is thirteen and Monica is ten. They're still upstairs but should be on their way down."

"I'm thirteen, too," Kennedy interjected.

Michael grinned. "Kennedy thought she would be the only young person here tonight," he said, meeting Taye's eyes again.

Taye smiled as she turned to Kennedy. "Tonight you'll get to meet a lot of cousins your age. Besides my daughter Sebrina, Victor Junior's daughter Victoria is thirteen and my brother Bryan's daughter, Cody, just turned fourteen last week."

"Cool!"

Taye glanced up at the entrance door. "Speaking of the little devilettes, the three of them just walked in. My other daughter Monica must be on her way down with her cousin Lauren. Come on and I'll introduce you."

Taye introduced Kennedy to her cousins Sebrina, Victoria, and Cody.

After that greeting there was a long silence as the three young Bennetts tried to politely size up their new cousin. Finally, Sebrina broke the silence when she asked Kennedy, "Where're you from?"

"I was living in Minnesota, but my dad and I moved to Atlanta three weeks ago."

"Do you know what school you'll be attending?" Victoria asked.

"Yes, Collinshills High."

"Wow! That's great," Victoria said, smiling excitedly, looking every bit like Victoria Junior and Fayrene's child. She was a pretty girl who had her father's dark eyes and her mother's flawless complexion of nut brown.

"That's the school me and Sebrina go to. Just think, there will be three Bennetts there now!"

Kennedy smiled. She'd never attended a school where she had relatives who also attended. "What school do you attend, Cody?"

The somewhat shy but cute girl smiled. "I live in Texas and attend school there. But I get to spend every summer here with my grandparents. Hopefully, we can have a lot of fun together this summer while I'm here."

Kennedy gave all three girls a genuine smile, feeling accepted by the group. "I'd really like that."

Leaving the four girls alone, Taye sought out Michael. He was standing across the room talking to Poppa Ethan, his grandfather Cousin Henry, and other male members of the Bennett clan. No doubt they were reading Michael the riot act for being separated from the family for so long.

"I guess I need to make my rounds and say hello to everyone," Rae'jean said, coming up to Taye from the buffet table where she'd been.

"Yes, I guess you'd better or you'll get talked about. I can hear some of them now: 'Yeah, chile, Miss Ann brought her half-white behind to the reunion and tried to act uppity, like she was all that and didn't know anybody.' "

Rae'jean shook her head, laughing. "You sound just like Cuzin Sophie. By the way, where is the old bat?" she asked, glancing around the room to spot the woman who claimed to have dated Otis Redding when the two of them attended high school together in Macon.

"She's around somewhere. Do you remember when she used to put that bulky handkerchief stuffed with money in her bosom?"

Rae'jean laughed. "Is she still doing that?"

"Who knows? But I do know she still hauls her purse around wherever she goes like it's a permanent fixture on her body," Taye said, joining Rae'jean laughing. "Another thing I know for certain is that she's still sticking her nose in other people's business. That hasn't changed."

"Then she'll have a lot to talk about Saturday when Grady gets here."

Taye nodded, knowing that would be true and it wouldn't be just Cuzin Sophie doing the talking. She glanced around the room that was getting more crowded with people by the minute. She saw their Grand-uncle Ray standing across the room. Even at the age of seventy, he still walked around with his bottle of Gordon's gin. In her lifetime she had seen him drunk more often than sober. She shook her head. She guessed there was an Uncle Ray in every family. "Do you know if Alexia got here yet?" she asked Rae'jean.

"Yeah, I called her room before coming down. Some good-looking man detained her in Atlanta. She's going to tell us about him later tonight. You *are* coming up to her suite after this gig is over, aren't you?"

"Yes."

"Good. And don't forget to wear your PJs. It's going to be a pajama party with just you, Lex, and me. Just like old times. You've made arrangements for someone to watch the girls, haven't you?"

"Yeah, they're sleeping over in Fayrene's room tonight. They're having their own pajama party."

"Do you think they'll invite Kennedy to join them?"

"Oh, yeah. They're excited about having another cousin to hang out with."

Rae'jean nodded. She then glanced over to where Michael was standing. "He looks good, doesn't he?"

"Who?"

"Michael."

"Yeah, he looks good. He's definitely a fine brother. I'm surprised he didn't remarry," Taye said.

"He was crazy about Lynda and probably isn't over her death, although it's been six years. I hate you never met her. I think you would have liked her."

"Maybe I would have and maybe I wouldn't have." Taye felt Rae'jean's gaze on her but refused to satisfy her cousin's curiosity.

"I just remembered, Taye, that you used to have a major crush on Michael when we were teenagers."

"So?" A quick glance at Rae'jean couldn't help but make Taye grin. For some reason, she'd never been able to hide anything from Rae'jean and Alexia. "Cut it out, Rae. That was fifteen years ago. I'm no longer a teenager anymore. Besides, have you forgotten that Michael is our cousin?"

"A distant cousin who just happens to have been adopted."

Taye shook her head. "Jeez, that would really give the family something to talk about."

Rae'jean laughed. "Yeah, and it will take the heat off me and Grady for a while. Just look at Michael. I think he's sexy as hell."

"If you think so, then why don't you go after him?"

"Because I wasn't the one he was looking at kind of funny a few minutes ago, and although you may deny it, you were checking him out kind of close, too."

"I was not."

"You were, too. Liar, liar, pants on fire," Rae'jean chanted one of their favorite sayings from long ago. "Besides, I'm an engaged woman who's in enough trouble lusting after the good-looking brother who lives in my apartment complex."

Taye lifted a brow, but before she could ask Rae'jean for details Fayrene walked up and joined them. The look Taye gave Rae'jean indicated that she expected her to tell all later tonight.

Michael looked into the face of the man who had been like a second grandfather to him, Ethan Allen Bennett, and realized that he had not heard the sound of his deep, authoritative voice for some fifteen years, at least not since the day he'd left Macon for the air force. But the sound of Poppa Ethan's voice was just as powerful and no-nonsense as he'd always remembered. Hearing it was enough to make his mind recall so many fond memories.

Both of his parents had died in a house fire one day while he'd been at school. He'd been twelve at the time. After that he had gone to live with his grandfather. Grampa Henry, like most of the older black men who'd lived in Macon, had worked for the railroad and had depended a lot on his first cousin and his wife, Poppa Ethan and Mama Idella, to help in raising Michael. That's why he had spent so much time around Taye, Rae'jean, and Alexia. And since he had been three years older than the three girls, he'd gotten charged with the task of keeping an eye out for them during their teen years. The last time the four of them had spent time together had been at the last family reunion, in '86, a week before he was to leave for the air force. He had thought he would be doing his basic training close to home at Warner Robins but soon found out the air force had plans to send him to another base out west. By then he'd discovered he had been adopted and hadn't cared where they sent him. He'd just wanted to get as far away from Macon as possible. And although he'd kept pretty close contact with his grandfather by phone or by sending for him to come visit him on occasion, he'd never returned to Macon until now.

"So now that you're back with the family, son, I hope you won't be forgettin' us again no time soon."

Poppa Ethan's words pulled Michael's attention back to the conversation. "I never forgot anyone, Poppa Ethan. I just had a lot of things I had to deal with."

Poppa Ethan nodded his head in understanding. "Well, no matter what, you're family. You're a Bennett and don't ever forget it. No one cares that your real mama was Zoe's baby sister. That means nothin' a-tall. If you ever feel the need to come by my place and visit, I'd love for you to just drop by and sit a spell on the porch and talk. It will be just like old times."

Michael smiled remembering those times. Although the Bennetts had all lived within the same rural Macon community, their dwellings had been miles apart, which made lengthy visits common. Church meetings, court days, and funerals became occasions to socialize, to hear news, to gossip, or to discuss major concerns. But the favorite place he remembered where everyone liked to gather was Poppa Ethan and Mama Idella's huge front porch. Shaded by tall trees and graced with a couple of wooden rocking chairs, it had been the ideal place to sit, relax, and watch passersby—the ice-cream man, the insurance man who went door-to-door every week, and Reverend Overstreet, who used to come visit every once in a while to discuss or debate religion with Poppa Ethan and Grampa Henry. He remembered Mama Idella's finger-lickin' fried chicken and iced lemonade on Sundays and her mouth-watering sweet potato pie that would put a smile on your face just thinking about eating a slice. Then he couldn't help but remember the games he, Rae'jean, Taye, and Alexia used to play as kids out in the big backyard—kickball, red light–green light, dodgeball, and so many others. And nothing was quite like sitting on the porch chewing Bubble Yum bubble gum, sucking on Jolly Ranchers, or chewing Bonkers or Now and Laters.

Michael's concentration shifted again when Poppa Ethan and Grampa Henry began discussing the church's plans to expand their kitchen facilities. He glanced across the room at Rae'jean and Taye. They were standing next to the buffet table talking.

Just like old times.

Other than being older and more mature, neither of them had really changed in looks. He shook his head. That wasn't exactly true. They both had changed and become even more beautiful. Kennedy would be stunned speechless when she discovered later tonight that Alexia Bennett of the popular singing group Body and Soul was actually his cousin, which was something he'd never told her, although he knew she had every record the group had recorded. He inwardly berated himself for not telling her about that, as well as for not keeping in touch with everyone over the years.

He had abandoned his family, but they had never abandoned him. Even after a fifteen-year absence the family had welcomed him back with open arms. His thoughts then went to Taye as he studied her. She had mentioned that she had two daughters but hadn't said anything about a husband. He knew from a letter he'd received from Grampa Henry some years back that she had gotten pregnant her first year at college. But he'd heard nothing about her having a second child. Was she involved with anyone, and if so, was the man nice to her? More than likely if she didn't have a husband she had a boyfriend. No woman looked the way she did and was unattached. He couldn't help but wonder what type of man had captured her heart. Was he worthy of her affections?

Michael shook his head upon realizing he still had that protective instinct toward her as he'd always had. It was hard for old habits to die, and when it came to Taye, for some reason he had been more protective of her than the others. Maybe the reason had been that, of the three, she'd been the youngest and the shyest. But still, even as a teen she'd been the most arresting and the most intriguing. Somehow he had known she would grow up to be a woman who would draw a man's interest. Pretty much like she was doing now.

His interest.

Cousin or no cousin, he had to admit that Octavia Bennett was a good-looking woman. The kind any man would look at twice. She still had that elegance about her that was somehow uniquely hers, and for some reason tonight he felt oddly drawn to it.

"Michael?"

Upon hearing Grampa Henry call his name, he cleared his throat and turned his attention away from Taye and looked at the older man. "Sir?"

"You're planning to stay for the entire weekend, aren't you, son?"

"Yes, sir."

"Good. I would love to visit with that great-granddaughter of mine. Especially since I'm the one who named her."

Michael shook his head, grinning. His grandfather had been tickled pink when he and Lynda had agreed to let him name their daughter after a prominent Democratic family whose name in a lot of elderly black folks' minds was synonymous with fairness and justice for all, especially those blacks from the South who'd struggled through the civil rights movement. "I'm sure Kennedy would like that, Grampa."

Half an hour later Alexia entered the banquet room where the reception was being held. It was evident from all the whooping, hollering, and screaming from the younger Bennetts that she had a fan club among the teenage group.

Rae'jean, Michael, and Taye stood off to the side and watched as the teenagers crowded around Alexia. Michael shrugged his massive shoulders and grinned sheepishly when Kennedy shot him a look that clearly said, *I can't believe you never told me she's a relative of ours!*

"Should we go over there and rescue Lex?" Taye asked a few minutes later.

"No, not yet," Rae'jean said. "I want tonight to be her night. I want all those snooty Bennetts who never thought she would amount to anything to see just how far she's gone. I want Gramma Idella's beautiful black pearl to shine tonight."

Taye nodded in agreement.

A few moments later Rae'jean said to the other two, "Now it's time for us to go and rescue her. All the love and admiration from the kids in the family has touched her deeply. She's beginning to cry."

And the three of them knew it took a lot to make Alexia cry.

Being the oldest, Michael led the group, making his way through the cluster of teens and coming to a stop in front of Alexia. Without saying anything he drew her into his arms.

"I'll be fine in a minute," she whispered to him, quietly drawing off his strength, the same strength she'd drawn from him in her childhood when he'd been her protector.

"Take your time," he whispered back. "Tonight among your family, you're in the spotlight. You are the shining star, and it's about time, don't you think?"

Turning, Alexia twisted her position in his arms to stare up at him through her wet lashes. "It never really mattered."

He drew her back to him and whispered softly, "Yes, it did, Alexia. But me, Rae'jean, and Taye were the only ones who knew just how much it did matter."

Rae'jean and Taye, who had been hanging back, walked up to Alexia and Michael. One by one the four cousins who'd once been thick as molasses embraced one another before finally holding on to one another and forming a circle of love that they intended never to break again.

CHAPTER 12

Alexia glanced around her hotel room. A bottle of white wine was chilling in the ice bucket waiting for her two guests to arrive. Plans had been made for Rae'jean and Taye to come up to her suite for a pajama party. The three of them wanted to spend as much time together as possible during the reunion, because when it was over they would each go their separate ways again. But this time, unlike before, they had vowed to stay in touch better.

She ran one hand through the mass of hair covering her head and took the other hand and smoothed the material of her silk pajamas. They were a deep purple, a color she would never have dared wearing as a teenager because of her dark complexion. But now she found herself not shying away from any particular colors. She wore them all.

She took a quick glance at the clock. It was almost midnight. Taye had said she would be up after she had gotten the girls situated, and Rae'jean had wanted to call and talk to Grady before coming. As Alexia walked across the room toward the bar to make sure it was well stocked, a smile touched her lips. Tonight had been special. The younger generation of Bennetts had welcomed her with open arms and had truly been proud of her accomplishments. They had made her cry, and she hadn't cried since Richmond had walked out of her life four years ago.

Alexia forced her thoughts off her ex-husband and back to the fun she'd had earlier. As the night had drawn on, what should have been a family social gathering had turned into a full-scale party when several of the Bennetts decided to get loose. Uncle Bubba and Aunt Priscilla, both in their sixties, had gotten on the floor to prove to the younger folks that the "mashed potato" wasn't just something to eat.

Not to be outdone, Cuzin Mavis, who was staring fifty in the face, wanted to show off her skill at doing something called the funky chicken. In the end Alexia, Rae'jean, Taye, and Victor Junior had shown everyone their ability to still do the Neutron Dance and the Moonwalk, which wasn't easy with the outfits they had on. Michael had stood off to the side laughing at the four of them the entire time. There was no doubt in Alexia's mind that a number of Bennetts would be too sore to move in the morning.

A moment later Alexia walked toward the door when she heard a knock. Peeking through the peephole, she saw it was Taye. After freeing the chain on the door, she tugged it wide open.

Taye looked at Alexia in her pajamas and snorted in disgust. "You would have to look good in your Persian silk when I'm dressed in my Wal-Mart cotton flannel."

Laughing, Alexia grabbed Taye's arm and pulled her inside the suite and closed the door behind her. "Tell me those are Sebrina's pajamas you're wearing and not yours, Taye."

"I can't do that because they *are* mine."

"Hell, Taye, women don't wear cotton flannel anymore. How do you manage to hold a man wearing something like that to bed?"

Taye was about to tell her she didn't have that to worry about when there was another knock at the door. "That must be Rae'jean."

It was. Rae'jean breezed into the room wearing a pair of silk PJs that were almost identical to the ones Alexia was wearing except hers were a powder blue. Rae'jean and Alexia stood in the center of the suite checking out each other's sleepwear and trying desperately to keep from laughing. Finally, turning to Taye, Rae'jean spoke. "So we both like shopping at Victoria's Secret. Big deal."

Taye chuckled. "No sweat. As you can see, I happen to like Kathie Lee's design."

"But they're cotton flannel," Alexia implored, not even trying to keep the laughter out of her voice.

"Get over it, Alexia, because I refuse to get in a discussion with you regarding the material of my pajamas."

Alexia smiled. "You don't have to discuss it with me. Discussing it with Rae'jean will do just fine." Turning to Rae'jean, Alexia asked, "What's with Taye and the cotton PJs? I can't believe her man would let her come to bed wearing something like that."

Rae'jean returned Alexia's smile. "What man? Didn't Taye tell you she's celibate and hasn't had a man in ten years?"

"You're lying."

"No, I'm not."

Alexia turned to Taye. "Tell me she's lying."

Instead of responding to Alexia, Taye walked over to the chair and sat down. She lifted her chin at the two women. "I don't like the two of you talking about me like I'm not here," she said with friction in her voice.

Alexia looked thoughtfully at Taye before going over to the bed and pulling off both pillows. She tossed one to Rae'jean and kept the other one for herself. "I'd appreciate it if you would explain why you've been celibate for ten years, Taye," she said, placing the pillow on the floor, then sitting on it.

Taye opened her mouth and closed it again. She had already given Rae'jean her reason, but she doubted Alexia would understand. Nonetheless, she decided to tell her anyway. "I don't need a man, Alexia."

"I don't, either," Alexia replied rather quickly. "But the real issue here is not the man but the sex."

Rae'jean grinned as she tossed her pillow on the floor and sat down next to Alexia. "Pleeze, give us a break. Not everyone can separate the two, Lex," she said.

Shrugging at Rae'jean's statement, Alexia turned her attention back to Taye. "Does your lack of interest in a man have anything to do with Monica's father?"

Taye inhaled deeply. Although Rae'jean and Alexia didn't know the identity of Monica's father, they did know he'd been a married man. "Yes. Even after ten years I still feel stupid for letting him sucker me in that way. Twice I've made bad choices in the men I fell in love with, and I refuse to do it again. I'm tired of the games most men play. I want to play for keeps, but they want to play the field. They don't care that when they score there's a chance some woman is left on the sidelines with a broken heart. It happened to me twice; I care about myself too much to go for a third time. I've decided it's safer to take myself out of the game and leave men alone."

"It doesn't have to be that way, Taye. There are some men who want to play for keeps, too," Rae'jean said softly.

"Maybe there are those who do, but I don't plan on wasting my time digging through those who don't." Taye positioned her body to sprawl in the chair before saying, "There's nothing wrong with being celibate."

"But for ten years?" Alexia exclaimed.

"Even if it's for twenty, it's my choice. It's my heart that I'm protecting."

"But how do you get around those sexual urges?" Alexia asked curiously.

"I don't think about them."

"What do you think about when you see a good-looking man? Doesn't jumping his bones ever cross your mind?" Alexia asked, grinning and staring at Taye.

"No." She wasn't ready to admit that she had felt a strong sexual pull toward Michael tonight. Heat had ignited in the pit of her stomach from the moment she had seen him. Deciding to turn the conversation off her, Taye looked at Rae'jean and said, "Now it's time to get into your business, Rae. You said something earlier that didn't make sense. Do you or don't you love Grady?"

"Of course I love him."

"Then what's the problem?" Taye asked, eyeing her cousin curiously.

Rae'jean sighed. Finally, after three months, she would be able to voice her concerns aloud with the two people she trusted the most. "I love Grady, but . . ."

Taye lifted a brow. "But what?"

Rae'jean met her gaze. "I'm attracted to someone else."

"Oh, is that all?" Alexia responded lightly as she rose to her feet to pour each of them a glass of wine. Cheerfully she added, "No matter who I'm involved with at the time, I still have the hots for Morris Chestnut. No big deal."

"It's not the same, Lex. I love Grady. You don't love any of the men you're involved with; at least that's what you tell me. Besides, nothing will ever come of the attraction you have for Morris Chestnut, so you don't really feel threatened in any way. The guy I'm attracted to happens to live in the same apartment building that I do."

"Another white man?" Taye asked, throwing Rae'jean a curious glance.

"No, he's a brother."

Alexia walked over and handed Rae'jean her glass of wine. "That's deep, Rae."

Rae'jean nodded. "Yes, I know." She hadn't seen her sexy neighbor too often, but whenever their paths did cross they would gaze at each other and the heat that passed between them was almost unbearable.

Taye sipped the wine Alexia had handed her and regarded Rae'jean intently. "Are you sure you love Grady, Rae'jean?"

"Of course I'm sure. Grady is the kindest and most decent man I know. He's an excellent doctor who takes care of his patients with more dedication than—"

"Forget about how well he performs in his profession, Rae'jean," Alexia interjected, drawing both women's attention to her when she sat back down on her pillow. "How do you feel about *your* relationship with him? Are you not attracted to him as well?"

Rae'jean took a sip of her wine before answering, "Yes, as well but not as deep."

"You actually want to jump this other guy's bones?" Alexia asked, grinning.

"Yeah, and in a big way," Rae'jean answered truthfully. She took a long, deep breath. "I keep telling myself that it has to be my hormones acting up and that sooner or later I'll get my head back on straight and that when December gets here I'll be fine."

"What if you aren't? What happens if you find yourself even more attracted to this man come December? Just what do you know about him?"

"That's just it. I don't know anything about him. We pass occasionally in the hall. The only time we've spoken to each other is when I accidentally bumped into him one day. And even then we barely exchanged two words." *But whenever he looks at me, I can actually feel his touch,* she thought further to herself.

Taye stared at Rae'jean, frowning slightly. "I think it's just a phase you're going through. I once read an article that said a lot of men and women, fearful of losing their freedom, are driven to have that one final fling before taking the plunge. According to the article it's normal to feel that way and the author even suggests that a person go ahead and indulge themself to get it out of their system."

"Well, I don't want to have a fling before tying the knot with Grady. I couldn't do anything like that to him anyway. Our relationship is based on mutual trust and respect. I couldn't betray him that way."

Everyone was silent for a moment; then Alexia said, "After listening to you two, my problem isn't so big after all."

"And just what's your problem?" Taye asked, putting her wineglass aside.

Alexia met her gaze. "I want a baby but not a husband."

Taye sat back in her chair, gaping at her. "What! You really want to give the family something to talk about, don't you?"

"They'll get over it."

"Wanna bet?"

"OK, so they won't get over it. I've thought it through and have made my decision. I'm going to tell my parents about it this weekend now that I've decided to move ahead with it."

Rae'jean looked at her. "And you think our problems are bigger than yours? Think again, cousin dearest. Why on earth would you want a child without a husband?"

"Because I don't need a man to jump-start my life. Times have changed. Women are acquiring things without the benefit of a husband, and like many others, I've decided I want a child without being in a serious relationship with anyone."

"You want to adopt?"

Alexia pushed her hair away from her face. "No, I want to have a child born from my body, and I don't intend on waiting to find a husband before that happens. I've been married before and it wasn't ideal. I don't ever want to remarry."

Taye nodded. "How do you think a child will fit into your profession, Lex? You're in a group that travels all the time and—"

"I'm leaving the group."

If Taye and Rae'jean were surprised to hear that news, they disguised it well. "Does that mean you won't be singing anymore?" Rae'jean asked quietly.

"No, it means I won't be singing with the group anymore. I'm going solo."

They couldn't disguise their surprise a second time. Taye sat up straight in her chair. "Starting when?"

"In another month or so. I'll be making an official announcement to the media when I return to California."

"Won't that mean that then you'll have even less time on your hands? I'd think you would have to work that much harder to get a solo career off the ground," Rae'jean said, eyeing her cousin intently. "How will a baby fit in?"

"I think rather nicely, since I intend to handle both. A lot of women balance careers and families. You're doing it, Taye."

"But it's not easy, Lex," Taye told her.

"I didn't say it would be easy, but I can and I will do it. I will make it work."

"Don't do anything hasty, Alexia," Rae'jean said, concern evident in her voice.

"I won't. Trust me. I've thought about it for a long time and now I'm going to act."

"So, if you're not going to adopt and you're not in a serious relationship with anyone, who, may I ask, will be this child's father?"

Hesitating for only a moment, Alexia said in a quiet voice, "A man I met a few months back. He's an attorney."

Rae'jean raised her brow. "Is this the same guy you mentioned who traveled with you from LA and who took you to dinner earlier today when you got to Atlanta?"

"Yes."

"And just what does he think of being used for stud service?"

Alexia tried sipping her wine gracefully but ended up swallowing a few hefty gulps. She cleared her throat and met Rae'jean's and Taye's curious gazes before answering, "He doesn't know anything about it. I made the decision that it would be him today while we were having dinner. There's a lot about him that I like, so I've decided that he's going to be the one. He's going to be my baby's daddy."

CHAPTER 13

I t was Friday morning and all the Bennetts, at least those thirty-something and older, decided to sleep in late. The others, those younger and who possessed an endless amount of energy, had gotten up early to take advantage of the delicious breakfast buffet the hotel had served.

No activities had been planned for the family until noon. After lunch they were to get in their cars and motorcade the five miles to Mount Olive, the cemetery where most of their deceased relatives had been laid to rest. In consideration of the heat, a very short memorial service, which included placing fresh flowers on the graves, was planned.

A shudder passed through Taye. She had an aversion to cemeteries. "What are my chances of getting out of going?" she asked Rae'jean and Alexia over lunch near the pool.

"Don't even think it," was Rae'jean's quick reply as she cocked a dark brow at Taye. "Poppa Ethan expects everyone to come, and that means everyone, even the teens who've been trying to talk their way out of going all morning."

"Did any of you see how Uncle Victor was checking out that lady who works at this hotel, the one who served us the food last night?" Alexia asked, changing the subject. "I bet he's hit on her already."

Rae'jean frowned. "You think so?"

"I'll be willing to put some money on it."

Taye pasted a smile on her face, trying to follow the conversation between Alexia and Rae'jean and force her gaze from Michael, who was
sitting on the other side of the pool at a table with Victor Junior. "I'm not
so sure Uncle Victor will be too quick to mess around on this third wife
he has," she decided to put her two cents in and add to the conversation.

"Why?" Alexia wanted to know. "Having a wife never stopped him
before."

"Yeah, but he's never had a wife like this one before, either. Rose is
the jealous type, and rumor has it she's threatened to cut Uncle Victor's
you know what off if she ever caught him being unfaithful," Taye informed
the others about their uncle's third wife.

Rae'jean couldn't help but laugh. "Are you serious?"

"Yeah, I'm serious," Taye said, chuckling. "So I expect him to be on
his best behavior at this reunion."

"I don't know about that," Rae'jean said as her gaze shifted around and
lighted on her Uncle Victor, the youngest of the Bennett siblings. He was
standing across the patio talking to Taye's father, Uncle Joe. Victor Bennett,
Sr., had always been an extremely good-looking man, and even now he
still looked pretty good for fifty. Rae'jean doubted if he would ever slow
down his womanizing ways. It was rumored he had fathered close to twenty
kids, including one belonging to his second wife's sister.

After checking her watch, Taye reminded everyone it was time to go
pay their respects to the deceased Bennetts.

As far as cemeteries went, Mount Olive was a really nice place, with lush
green grass, sloping hills, and huge oak trees. Currently the grounds were
being maintained by a number of black churches in the area that still buried
their members there.

Back in the 1930s, the Bennetts had purchased enough land in the cemetery to bury their kin for generations to come. This particular section of
the cemetery had been named Bennetts Row.

The day was hot. The cars had been left at the entrance of the cemetery,
and everyone had taken the walk to the family plots. Nearly everyone had
dressed comfortably for the walk and the heat, except for Cuzin Sophie
and Aunt Virginia. They had decided to dress up for the occasion by wear-

ing their Sunday-best dresses, fashionable hats, and high-heeled shoes.

When Cuzin Sophie stopped to rest her sore aching feet and leaned against a huge oak tree in Bennetts Row, she remarked to everyone, "This is a good spot with plenty of shade."

Taye whispered to Rae'jean and Alexia, "I guess now isn't a good time to tell the nosy old bat that we're glad she liked that spot since it's hers anyway. That very plot has her name on it."

It was hard for the three women to keep straight faces and not break up into stitches.

Later that day back at the hotel, Rae'jean, Michael, Taye, Alexia, and Victor Junior were sitting at a table near the pool playing bid whist. After glancing at her watch, Rae'jean pushed her chair back. "Don't deal me in this time around. I need to run up to my room and make a phone call."

Victor Junior, who was already sore about losing the last couple of games, glanced up at Rae'jean and sneered. "Whatcha gonna do? Call your white man?"

Rae'jean heard the scorn in his voice and frowned. He had snarled the words loud enough to get everyone's attention, including those relatives who were sitting at another table playing their own game of cards. Conversation at the table faltered, then stopped altogether. Apparently everyone was interested in how she would respond to Victor Junior's question. She met his narrowed gaze with one of her own. "Yeah, I'm going to call *my* white man. You have a problem with it?"

"Yeah, I do, and so do others in this family. I can't believe that you don't. You know the black folks' history. You know what the white man did to our black women long ago. How he treated them."

The look Rae'jean gave Victor Junior sent chills down everyone's spine. "Oh, you mean the same way *you* and some brothers are treating them today, Victor Junior, by screwing their brains out and getting them pregnant with more babies than you'll ever be able to claim?"

Rae'jean's words hit a nerve with Victor Junior. He stood up. "I claim any baby I make as mine."

Rae'jean stood up as well. "Really? In that case, you must never have any money for paying out child support for each and every one of them."

Embarrassed because he knew he was not doing so, Victor Junior sat back down. "I said that I claimed them, Rae'jean. You know damn well that I can't financially take care of every single one of them."

"Then you should keep that thing in your pants and not use it so often if you're not willing to be a man and take full responsibility. And I mean full responsibility. Now getting back to the issue of Grady, I would appreciate it if you never question my choice of a mate again. And don't ever throw up in my face what his ancestors did to our black women, 'cause the way I see it, you and a number of other brothers are doing a whole hell of a lot worse to them. Take my advice and get a vasectomy." Picking up her sunglasses, an angry Rae'jean placed them on her eyes and walked off.

Victor Junior looked around the table and saw the frowns Alexia, Taye, and Michael gave him. "What's the matter with her? I was just telling it to her like it is."

"Yeah, and she told it to you like it is, too," Taye said curtly. "One day, Victor Junior, you're going to learn not to rub Rae the wrong way. And if you have any thoughts of showing your butt when Grady arrives tomorrow, don't. Or you just might find yourself on the way to the emergency room. Rae'jean just might decide to personally give you that vasectomy herself."

Victor Junior squirmed in his seat at the thought of that happening. "Rae'jean ain't *that* crazy."

Alexia giggled. "That's the same thing you said right before she tied your butt up to the bedpost and shaved half your head when you really got her mad about something when we were teenagers. Remember? I would hate for you to lose your balls over some foolishness."

He tightened his legs together. He would hate to lose them over some foolishness, too.

After making her phone call to Grady, Rae'jean made her way back downstairs and stopped when she got to the lobby area. She sat down on a love seat, not ready to rejoin the group just yet. Victor Junior had pissed her off big-time.

She smiled. Talking to Grady had helped. Just listening to the excitement in his voice had renewed her spirits. His patient, the one he hadn't expected to make it through surgery, had. He wanted the two of them to celebrate when he arrived and had told her to expect him sometime tomorrow. A part of her had been tempted to tell him not to bother coming, but she changed her mind. He would have to deal with her family sooner or later, so it may as well be now. Besides, Grady could handle the likes of Victor Junior.

"You all right, girl?"

Rae'jean turned toward the deep-timbred voice and saw her grandfather standing beside where she sat. "Oh, hi, Grampa. Yes, sir, I'm fine."

Poppa Ethan eased his body in the seat beside her. "I heard you and Victor Junior had some words earlier."

"Yes, sir, we did," she mumbled.

A smile broke into her grandfather's wrinkled features. "Just like old times, uhh?"

Rae'jean couldn't help but return his smile. "Yes, sir, just like old times." She reached out and took his hand into hers. "How have you been doing?"

"Fairly well for a man who'll be ninety in a few months. What about you? I hear you're thinking about getting married."

Rae'jean lifted a brow. "Yes, sir, and what else have you heard?"

"Enough. But I'm not paying that garbage no account. I like to size a man up for myself no matter what color he is."

Her grandfather's words gave Rae'jean a measure of relief. She wished every other person in the family would be as open-minded. "Thanks, Grampa. I appreciate that."

"Will your man be here for the family supper tomorrow night?"

"Yes, sir," she responded, staring at her grandfather. "Grady is coming."

"Good. I wanna meet the man my oldest granddaughter has chosen to marry," he added.

"I think you'll really like him, Grampa."

Poppa Ethan bowed his head for a moment before lifting his gaze back to her. "Do you like him, Rae'jean?"

The tenderness in her grandfather's expression touched her. "Yes, sir."

"Then that's all that matters. You're a grown woman, aren't you?"

"Yes, sir."

"Well then."

Unable to help herself, Rae'jean reached over and hugged her grand-father. This was why she loved him and would always love him. He could make her feel so good about herself. But there was something else that was bothering her. There was something else she needed to know.

"Grampa?"

"Yeah, girl?"

"Is there anything you can tell me about my father?"

Rae'jean felt his body stiffen and heard his soul-weary sigh before he pulled away slightly and looked at her. "No, chile, I can't. I gave my word."

Rae'jean lifted a brow as confused thoughts raced through her mind. "You gave your word to whom?"

"I can't say, Rae'jean."

Rae'jean nodded, knowing that he had given her his final say on the matter. She knew that if her grandfather had given someone his word about anything then he wouldn't break it. But she was determined to leave the reunion with the information she wanted. If her grandfather wouldn't talk, she was determined to find someone who would.

"That's fine, Grampa. I understand."

After a few moments of silence her grandfather gestured to an exquisite atrium containing beautiful flowers not far from where they were sitting. "Your grandmother would have liked all those flowers, wouldn't she?"

Rae'jean smiled as she remembered her grandmother's love for flowers. "Yes, sir, she would have," she said quietly.

"I'm sure she liked the flowers we took her today, aren't you?"

Rae'jean thought about the fresh flowers they had placed on Gramma Idella's grave earlier that day. She drew in a long breath, then slowly released it. It was days like this that she missed her grandmother more than ever. "Yes, sir, I'm sure she did."

Rae'jean studied her grandfather's features. Suddenly he looked older and there appeared a faraway look on his face. He had loved her grand-mother very much, and she knew his life must be lonely without her. "Grampa, how would you like to come visit me in Boston sometime?"

His bushy brows arched at her invitation. "That place too cold, Rae'jean. Besides, you ain't gonna get me on a plane; you know that," he added as his lips twisted in a chuckle before he reached up and tweaked her nose. "If God had intended for man to fly he would have given him wings."

Rae'jean smiled as she snuggled closer to him on the seat, just like she used to do as a child. "Yeah, Grampa, I know," she said, remembering how often she'd heard him say that while she was growing up. At that moment she silently thanked God that she still had a grandfather in her life to love and who she knew loved her.

CHAPTER 14

Michael retired to the comforts of his hotel room and lay stretched atop the covers watching the evening news on television. He glanced up to see Kennedy enter the room.

"Oh, hi, Dad," she greeted him, smiling brightly. "Why aren't you downstairs by the pool having fun like the other old people?"

Michael pasted a smile on his face. *Old people?* For crying out loud, he was only thirty-three and his daughter thought he was old. "I decided to come up here and chill for a while. People as *old* as I am need frequent breaks from so much fun."

She nodded like she understood completely, which made Michael roll his eyes to the ceiling. "What have you been up to? I haven't seen you practically all day," he asked her.

Kennedy came and sat next to him on the bed. "I've been having so much fun, Daddy. I'm glad I came."

Michael looked up at her, surprised but glad. "Really? What do you like about being here other than finding out that you're related to *the* Alexia Bennett?"

A flurry of excitement immediately lit his daughter's eyes. "Oh, there's Victoria, Lauren, Monica, Sebrina, and Cody and all my other cousins. We're having so much fun together. It's been off the chain."

Michael chuckled. "That good, huh?"

"Even better. Victoria, Sebrina, and I will be attending the same school next year. Isn't that cool?"

"Yeah, I guess." While in his teens he had attended the same school as Victor Junior, but he hadn't found anything cool about that experience.

Kennedy stretched out beside him on the bed. He braced himself. This was her *let me butter Dad up to get what I want* approach.

"Daddy?"

"Yes, Kennedy?"

"You know about our trip to Disney World next month?"

"Yeah, what about it?"

"It's going to be just me and you, right?"

"That's right. Why?"

"Well, I was thinking."

That could be dangerous, Michael thought as he waited for what he knew was coming. His daughter was about to try to weasel something out of him. Before Lynda had died they had gone away every year for a family vacation. He had continued that trend after her death. Because he was a pilot, he would occasionally rent a Cessna and he and Kennedy would fly to a number of places within the boundaries of the United States. It had proven to be a great experience for Kennedy as well as a relaxing time for him.

When Kennedy hesitated in getting whatever she wanted to say off her chest, he prompted her on. "What were you thinking about, Kennedy?"

She looked at him and smiled brightly. It was a smile that reminded him so much of Lynda it suddenly made his heart ache. The older Kennedy got the more she resembled her mother. There was no doubt in his mind that his daughter would continue to blossom into a beauty, which was another thing that was beginning to worry him. How was he going to deal with her interest in boys when it became a major issue? The thought of some father's son checking out his daughter didn't sit too well with him.

"I was thinking how nice it would be if Sebrina and Victoria were to come with us. Monica won't be able to come. She's going to Texas to spend the rest of the summer with Lauren and her parents. Just think of all the fun me, Sebrina, and Victoria will have."

"Yeah, at the expense of me going bonkers. Kennedy, you by yourself are a handful. I don't relish the idea of being responsible for two others like you. We're talking about a full week vacation, sweetheart, not a couple of days." He could just see it now with him trying to keep up with three energetic thirteen-year-olds, all females. Michael tried returning his attention back to the news, but his daughter was determined not to let him.

·She rolled over on the bed and got on her knees before him, claiming his full attention. "What if we got you some help?"

Michael lifted a brow at her. She was tenacity at its best. "I doubt there's another human being a glutton for such punishment, Kennedy."

"Sebrina said her mother would do it. In fact, she said her mother needs to do it. According to Sebrina, Aunt Taye doesn't have a life."

Michael smiled at how easily Kennedy had adopted Taye, Rae'jean, and Alexia as honorary aunts, although in truth they were distant cousins. "Why does Sebrina think her mother doesn't have a life?" He hated admitting it, but curiosity had gotten the best of him.

"Because she doesn't have a boyfriend and has never had a boyfriend since Monica was born, which really doesn't make sense since Aunt Taye is so pretty and all. Sebrina thinks that since her mother doesn't have a boyfriend she doesn't have any fun. Going to Disney World would be fun. Everyone has fun at Disney World."

Michael shook his head. There was fun and then there was *fun*. He doubted the kid type fun would really interest Taye. Like him, she was probably into the grown-up stuff. But he was even more interested in Sebrina's claim that her mother didn't have a boyfriend. He agreed with Kennedy. Taye was too pretty not to have one.

"Are you sure you didn't misunderstand Sebrina, Kennedy? Could she have said that her mother didn't have a current boyfriend?"

"No, I heard her right, Daddy, because when she said it, it suddenly occurred to me that you don't have a girlfriend, either. You've been by yourself since Momma left, but you seem to be doing OK."

A part of Michael regretted that Kennedy had not known about Stephanie. "How will taking Taye to Disney World get her a boyfriend?" he asked.

"Maybe she'll meet someone there. Even if she doesn't, at least she'll have fun for a change. Sebrina says all her mother does is work, go to school, and take care of her and Monica. She thinks a week of fun will do her good. So can they come with us, Daddy? Please?"

He gazed thoughtfully at his daughter. No longer on her knees, she was now sitting in the middle of the bed, Indian-style, looking at him with such beseeching eyes. "Has anyone talked to Taye about this?" he asked, trying to ignore that look.

"No, we thought you could do that."

Michael couldn't help but smile. Oh, he just bet they did. He could recognize a well-thought-out manipulative plan when he heard one. No doubt the three girls had the week in Orlando pretty much planned already. "What if Taye doesn't want to go?"

"Oh, Daddy, she'll go if you invite her and then talk her into it. You can do it. I know you can. Don't you want her to finally have some fun in her life? Aunt Alexia said you used to look out for her, Aunt Taye, and Aunt Rae'jean while they were growing up. We think Aunt Taye still needs someone to look out for her."

"We? Who are we?"

Kennedy smiled brightly. "Me, Sebrina, and Victoria, of course."

"Yes, of course." At that moment it suddenly occurred to Michael that this was the happiest he had seen his daughter in months. Maybe even in a couple of years. She was reacting positively to being around the cousins she had met. Maybe that was what his daughter needed, cousins she could consider friends who were good kids and not like those incorrigible twins, Grace and Faith.

"Please, Daddy, will you talk to Aunt Taye about it? Please?"

Michael released a deep sigh. His daughter had him wrapped around her finger and had him wrapped tight. Besides, he was concerned with the information she had given him about Taye. She was either too busy to get involved with anyone or, like him, had managed to keep the involvement well hidden from her daughter. "All right, Kennedy, I'll talk to Taye, and if she agrees, the girls can come with us."

"Cool!" Kennedy exclaimed like she knew it was a done deal and that she and her cousins were already Orlando-bound. And then she did something that she had not done in a very long time. She reached out and hugged him and said, "Thanks, Dad, and I love you."

• • •

Michael was able to talk to Taye later that night after dinner. A group of them had gathered in Alexia's suite to play a game of How to Become a Black Millionaire. The questions asked were those pertaining to black history. Unfortunately, with the amount of wrong answers most of them were giving, it was apparent they didn't know a lot about their history. No one had made it to millionaire status yet.

While everyone took a break from playing to catch their breath, revamp their muddled minds, and take a sip of wine, Michael got Taye off to the side. "Kennedy and I are going to spend a week in Orlando next month. I've rented this huge condo and wondered if you and Sebrina would like to come with us. I'm also extending the invitation to include Victoria. I understand Monica will be in Texas with Darryl and his family during that time."

Taye shook her head, smiling. "So those little brats have been busy plotting, have they?"

Michael returned her smile. Evidently Taye knew where the idea had originated. As he studied her, he couldn't help but again notice how pretty she'd gotten over the years. There was no way she wasn't involved with anyone. "Seriously, I don't mind. It's a huge place, and I want Kennedy to continue to develop the relationships she's formed with the girls. She resented having to leave Minnesota, and I think the more time she spends with her cousins the quicker she'll get over it."

Taye nodded. She knew it was probably crazy, but the thought of spending a week with Michael made her feel giddy. For heaven sakes! The man was her cousin! A nagging voice in the back of her mind insisted she not go and that the only reason she felt an attraction to him was because she'd been without a man for too long. But deep down Taye knew that was not the case. There had always been something about Michael that had pulled her to him even when they'd been kids growing up.

"Are you sure that's what you want?" she asked him. "With me going that would make three additional females invading your space. How much rest do you think you'll be able to get?"

"As much as I would have gotten, anyway. Kennedy is a handful. At least this way we can rotate the parenting duties that week."

"Exactly what week is it?"

"The first week in August. I think it would be a good trip for them before school starts. I can rent a van and drive us all down."

"I'll split the cost of everything."

"No, Taye, it will be my treat. Besides, I want to spend some time with you and the girls." What he'd just told her was true. They had discovered from earlier conversations that he and Taye didn't live too far from each other. At one time while growing up they had been tight. As tight as two cousins could be. They used to spend a lot of time together and used to talk about everything. For some reason he wanted to recapture that closeness.

Taye knew not to make a big deal out of Michael wanting to spend time with her and the girls. After all, they were family. "We'd like to spend time with you and Kennedy as well, Michael. You were gone from the family a long time."

"Hey, you two!" Alexia called out. "The game is starting up again."

"We'll be right there!" Michael called back. He looked down at Taye. "So what about it? Do you think you'll go? Kennedy is going to bug the hell out of me until I have your answer."

Taye looked at him and smiled. It was hard to think straight when he was looking at her with those same dark, dreamy eyes that used to make her heart go pitter-pat when she was a fifteen-year-old. "I'd love to go. However, I think you and I will have to work out a plan so the girls won't think they're so smart that they can pull us into another one of their schemes."

Michael laughed. "OK, that's a bet. We'll come up with something."

CHAPTER 15

With the bellman's assistance in carrying their packages from the car, Alexia, Fayrene, Taye, and Rae'jean returned to the hotel from a Saturday morning of shopping. As they stepped onto the elevator, Rae'jean glanced down at her watch. It was almost three o'clock, and she couldn't help wondering if Grady had arrived, and said as much to the other three women.

Alexia, who was standing in front, closest to the elevator door, glanced back over her shoulder and said, grinning, "And if he has arrived does that mean we won't be seeing your face again until the banquet starts at seven tonight? I can just imagine all the things the two of you will want to catch up on."

An answering smile touched Rae'jean's lips. "Maybe." She had no intention of telling her cousins that she had made Grady promise to hold off from making love with her again until their wedding night. They didn't need to know that although Grady had a connecting room, the two of them would not be sharing a bed. There were some things a sistah kept to herself and didn't share with her kinfolks, no matter how close they were, especially if they would think she had a few screws loose if she told them.

"I'm going to my room to rest my poor aching feet," Taye said when the elevator came to a stop on her floor. Stepping out, she called over her shoulder, "See you guys later!"

"I think Taye has the right idea," Fayrene said, smiling, once the elevator closed again. "I'm going to my room and chill, since Aunt Otha Mae took the girls to a movie."

Alexia giggled. "I bet it was a Disney movie."

Fayrene couldn't help but chuckle herself. "Probably, but I told the girls to roll with the flow and not sweat the small stuff. I'll make up for it when we get back to Atlanta. They really wanted to see that new movie that just came out with Morris Chestnut."

"They got the hots for Morris, uhh?" Rae'jean asked, smiling.

"Probably no more than you had the hots for Prince when you were their age," Alexia reminded her.

Rae'jean's smile widened as she remembered those days. She'd bought every record Prince made, seen *Purple Rain* more times than she could count, and had pictures of him plastered on every wall in her bedroom. "Yeah, I did have a thing for Prince, didn't I?"

"Big-time," Alexia said, raising her eyes to the ceiling. "Your thing for Prince was just as big as Taye's thing for Michael back then."

Alexia shook her head, grinning. "I'd almost forgotten about Taye's crush on Michael. Boy, was it intense, and Michael never knew it, did he?"

Rae'jean smiled. "I doubt he noticed it."

The elevator door opened and Alexia got out after telling Rae'jean and Fayrene that she had planned to spend the rest of her afternoon in her hotel room reading, relaxing, and napping.

"You OK, Rae'jean? I heard about your conversation with Victor Junior yesterday," Fayrene said when they were alone in the elevator.

"Yeah, I'm OK. It's just that Victor Junior can aggravate the hell out of me at times. Nothing has changed there."

"I know. He can aggravate the hell out of me at times, too," Fayrene said, smiling. "Can you believe he's called me a couple of times wanting us to get back together?"

Pausing for a moment, Rae'jean considered Fayrene's words. "I hope you're not carrying a torch for Victor Junior. You know as well as I do that he's not worth it. Although it's what she rightly deserves, I hear Evelyn's catching all kind of hell being married to him."

"No, I'm not carrying a torch for Victor Junior," Fayrene said automatically. "He's permanently destroyed whatever love I had for him. Our only connection is Victoria." A smile touched the ends of Fayrene's lips. "I haven't said anything to anyone, but I started seeing someone a few months ago. He's someone I met through a friend. He's nice and I really like him. Victoria likes him, too."

"Oh, Fayrene, that's wonderful! I'm glad you're finally getting on with your life. You have too much to offer a man. You're a good person who deserves a good man."

Rae'jean was still thinking about how happy she was for Fayrene when she entered her hotel room carrying her packages. She smiled when she noticed the connecting room door was open, which meant Grady had arrived. Dropping the bags she was carrying on the bed, she slipped out of her shoes and walked to the connecting door and stood in the opening. Grady was lying across the bed, facedown and shirtless. By his even breathing Rae'jean could tell he was asleep. Deciding that he needed his rest, she pulled the door closed and went back to her room and began quietly sorting through the packages she had purchased.

"Why didn't you wake me when you got back?"

Rae'jean glanced over her shoulder. Grady stood in the open doorway between her room and his. He was still shirtless, and with the sunlight coming through the window blinds, the ray of light somehow made his brown hair appear lighter in coloring. She couldn't help but return his smile. That was something that had always been automatic between them. His smile always made her smile.

For a moment his smile took her back to that afternoon, almost a year ago, and the first time they had made love. They had gone to Texas for a medical convention, and like this time, they'd had connecting rooms, with the intent of using separate beds. Things didn't quite work out that way when she'd finished unpacking and looked up to see him standing in the doorway that separated the two rooms. He'd been staring at her with a kind of smile on his features that clearly said he wanted her. He had been the first man to catch her interest since college and the preceding years of medical school. She had been too busy studying to become involved in an in-depth relationship with anyone.

When she and Grady had made love there hadn't been an earth-shattering explosion or anything that had rocked her world. But she had preferred it that way. He had made love to her with such tenderness and such loving compassion it had brought tears to her eyes. She'd become enraptured in his special form of lovemaking, and he had fulfilled her every sexual desire. She hadn't wanted or needed anything wild and intense, and somehow Grady had known that. He had been so attuned to her mild and moderate sexual appetite. Her hectic lifestyle was filled with too much intensity as it was. She didn't want or need the same thing in the bedroom. Earth-shattering passion was something she could do without. He had made love to her the same way he did everything else, meticulously, flawlessly, and completely. At that time and every time since then, he had given her the kind of lovemaking she wanted and the type she needed. And she had found herself caring more and more for him each time.

Then why don't you love him to distraction like you're supposed to? her mind screamed at her. *Why do you often have images of that other guy and why are you craving such intense emotions now? Why every time you see that guy does your sexual hunger immediately go from mild and moderate to turbulent and extreme?* Rae'jean forced those thoughts away from her mind, knowing she had no answers to those questions.

"Aren't you glad to see me, Rae'jean?" Grady asked, resting his body against the door frame.

"Of course I am."

He quirked an eyebrow at her as he crossed his arms over his chest. "Then why are you over there and I'm over here?"

"Which is something that can easily be corrected, Mr. Fitzgerald," Rae'jean said, walking across the room to him. She placed a steadying hand on his bare chest when she reached him. "Is this better?"

"No, this is," he whispered before leaning down and kissing her.

For some reason Rae'jean couldn't get into their kiss like she wanted to. Her mind was too busy concentrating on things she felt should be happening to her but were not. For instance, although she was enjoying their kiss, she wasn't feeling weak in the knees. And then, although his breathing was getting deeper, hers was not.

Maybe if you put your heart and soul into it and not think about things that aren't important, then maybe those things will begin happening! her mind yelled at her. She decided to take her mind's advice, but it was too late. Grady lifted his mouth from hers.

"That was nice, but why do I feel I didn't have your full concentration?" he said, frowning down at her. "Something wrong?"

She swallowed thickly. At times Grady could read her so well. "Nothing's wrong. You're imagining things."

"Am I?"

"Yes."

His dark blue eyes studied her. "OK. Do you want to keep me company while I take a shower? Or better yet, do you want to take a shower with me?" he asked, bringing her closer into his arms.

Rae'jean wrapped her arms around him. "You don't know how to give up, do you?"

Grady chuckled. "No."

Rae'jean shook her head. "Go on and take your shower. I'll still be here when you finish." He slowly released her and she leaned against the door and watched as he walked back in his room and pulled his robe off a hanger in the closet. He was such a good man, with a big heart, she thought. He deserved any woman's complete love and devotion, especially the woman he had chosen to become his wife.

He turned back to her as he began walking toward the bathroom. "Oh yeah, by the way, Lynn is staying at my place while I'm gone."

Rae'jean's smile vanished. "Excuse me? What did you just say about Lynn?"

He turned back in her direction. "I said she's staying at my place while I'm away. The water pipe burst in her apartment and she had to move out for a few days."

Rae'jean instantly became livid. "Why didn't she check into a hotel?"

Grady lifted a brow at the anger he heard in Rae'jean's voice. "She was going to, but I offered to let her stay at my place."

Rae'jean walked into the room with hands on hips. "You are an engaged man, yet another woman is sleeping in your bed?"

Bewildered, Grady expelled a frustrated sigh, clearly not understanding why Rae'jean was upset. "Rae'jean, she's not sleeping in my bed. She's using the spare bedroom and will be gone when I get back."

"And what if she's not gone?"

Grady walked over to her. "Then I guess I'll have no choice but to come stay with you until she leaves," he said in a teasing fashion. "Maybe even share your bed, since you don't have a spare bedroom and your sofa won't fit me."

"This isn't funny, Grady. I know you only consider Lynn a friend, but I'm not that gullible to think that's what she wants. I know precisely what she's all about."

Grady placed his arms over his chest and frowned. "And just what do you think she's all about, Rae'jean?"

"She wants you back."

"That's crazy."

"It's not crazy. I'm a woman; I know."

"Well, you're wrong. Lynn is not that kind of person. She knows I'm engaged to be married." He frowned. "Don't you trust me?"

"This has nothing to do with trust, Grady. No black woman in her right mind would put up with another woman staying at her man's apartment, especially if that woman happens to be his ex-fiancée."

Grady's frown deepened. "I've never heard you refer to yourself that way before."

"What way?"

"A black woman."

Rae'jean automatically stiffened her spine. "I *am* a black woman, Grady."

"I'm well aware of that, Rae'jean, but you've never felt the need to remind me of that. Why are you doing so now? The issue of race has never come up with us before. Why are you making the distinction now?"

"Because this situation warrants it."

"In what way? Are you trying to tell me that you believe black women have certain standards in dealing with men that white women don't have?"

"In a way, yes. We're less tolerant of certain things and more assertive. We don't know how it feels to be privileged or protected, since we weren't ever granted that right. So we tend to take things a bit more serious. And one thing we won't tolerate is another woman, white or black, making a move on our man."

"First of all, Rae'jean, if you're aching for a fight, I'm much too tired to oblige you. Furthermore, I'm sure there're probably a number of women, including some white ones, who'd think the way you do if they felt threatened in some way by another woman, so I feel the statement you made was uncalled for and biased. Besides that, you of all people shouldn't feel threatened by any woman when it comes to me."

"But you used to love her."

"Yeah, and I'm not going to deny that I did. But that was a long time ago. If I didn't love you now I would not have asked you to marry me. Letting Lynn stay at my place while I'm gone was a favor to a friend, nothing more. I would have expected you to do the same for any of your friends, male or female. Lynn knows how I feel about you, and she knows what used to be between us is over."

Rae'jean wished she could have as much confidence in Grady's words as he seemed to have. As far as she was concerned, he was too trusting when it came to people.

"If you're concerned about competition, maybe you ought to be nicer to me," Grady said jokingly as a small taunting smile touched his lips. He reached out to pull her into his arms.

Rae'jean immediately placed her hand on his arm to stop him. "I'm not worried about competition, Grady Fitzgerald. I'm a woman who can hold her own, but I refuse to get caught up in some sort of love triangle."

"You won't."

"I'd better not."

Grady smiled. "You're kind of sassy, with a little attitude, aren't you?"

"Damn right. If you don't think you can handle it, then—"

He didn't let her finish but pulled her into his arms and captured her lips. Rae'jean tried to return his kiss with her full concentration, but deep in the recesses of her mind for some reason she felt things weren't going for her and Grady like they should be, and she knew it involved more than just her anger about Lynn.

Alexia was awakened from her nap by a knock on her door. "Yes?"

"Room service. We have a delivery for you."

Pulling her robe together, she crossed the room and opened the door. A lady stood before her with a beautiful arrangement of flowers, calla lilies.

"They're gorgeous," Alexia whispered, accepting the arrangement from the woman.

"Yes, they are. Must be from someone special."

Alexia lifted a brow at the woman's comment. She had no idea who could have sent them. To avoid the media, she had let few people know where she was this weekend. "Just a moment, please." She walked across the room and grabbed some money she had placed on the nightstand next to the bed to give the woman a tip. "Thanks for bringing them up here."

"My pleasure. I hope you enjoy them."

Alexia smiled. "I'm sure I will." As soon as she closed the door she pulled the card from the arrangement and read it:

> The article in People magazine said these are your favorite. I hope you enjoy them as much as I enjoyed having dinner with you Thursday evening.
>
> Quinn

Alexia couldn't help but smile. She was touched by Quinn's thoughtfulness. And yes, she would enjoy them and think of him while doing so.

Even though she really didn't want to.

She had thought about Quinn often since that evening they'd shared dinner. And what she had told Rae'jean and Taye was true. He was the man she wanted to father her child.

After placing the flowers on a table, Alexia slid back onto the bed. Lying on her back, she stared up at the ceiling as she forced her mind back on track. The only thing she wanted from Quinn was his child. She didn't want nor did she need a loving and serious relationship with any man, especially a man who could enslave her the way Richmond had done during the two years of their marriage. Now that she had rebuilt her heart completely, after Richmond had ripped it to shreds, she would never be that vulnerable a second time. She would always protect herself from hurt and pain.

No man was worth the agony. Not even Quinn "Drop-Dead-Gorgeous" Masters.

CHAPTER 16

"Well, there's the white man," Victor Junior said in a cold voice to the others standing around him when Rae'jean and Grady entered the banquet room. "He's about to get a taste of what it feels like to be in the minority. And I can't wait to see his reaction at church tomorrow when Aunt Sadie starts jumping a pew or two when the Holy Spirit hits her."

Alexia shot Victor Junior a deep scowl before moving her gaze across the room to Rae'jean and the man by her side. She smiled and so did Taye, liking what they saw.

"He's cute and has a nice build," Alexia said, giving Grady a thorough once-over as they watched Rae'jean take him over to Poppa Ethan to introduce him. It seemed that most everyone in the room had their eyes on the couple.

"Yeah, he is good-looking, isn't he," Taye agreed, thinking that Grady's sharp, chiseled features and dark brown hair made him look very attractive. "He sort of reminds me of movie star Alec Baldwin."

"Well, no matter what the two of you think, I just hope Rae'jean knows what she's doing crossing color lines," Victor Junior said, frowning.

"I take it you have a thing against interracial marriages," Michael said to his cousin as he watched Victor Junior's frown increase. Michael's brows beetled down and his gaze narrowed. He was bothered by his cousin's insensitivity in regard to Rae'jean's engagement.

"Yeah, I have a thing against it," Victor Junior replied brusquely. "You don't?"

Michael rolled one shoulder casually. "No. I don't have a problem with it."

Victor Junior met Michael's gaze. "Yeah, I bet you'd think differently if your daughter ever brought home a white boy."

Before Michael could respond, Alexia, who could see the anger lining Michael's features, cut in by saying, "Tonight should be interesting. Look who just walked in."

All eyes turned toward the door when Valerie and Brandy walked in. There was a nice-looking man with dreads at Brandy's side whom she was clinging to, as well as a very attractive woman who looked to be in her late twenties.

"I wonder if that's Brandy's fiancé," Taye said, giving the man a curious glance.

"Mmm, probably," Alexia said, giving him a curious glance as well. She had to admit—although she really didn't want to—that the guy was nice-looking. Even from across the room she could tell he was from the islands and was such an impressive package that she couldn't help but wonder how Brandy had gotten so lucky. "What's the scoop, Victor Junior? What's going on with Brandy?" she asked curiously.

"How in the hell would I know?" Victor Junior replied, too busy checking out the woman with Brandy to care about anything else.

"Considering she's your half sister, I'd have thought you'd know what's going on with her and just how she met this guy," Alexia said.

"Well, I don't. All I know is that Brandy is getting married over the Labor Day weekend, and according to Dad the guy's family is loaded. They are paying for the entire wedding, and it's going to be in Jamaica. All Dad has to do is be there to give her away."

Everyone stopped talking when Brandy looked over in their direction. She whispered something to the people with her; then Brandy, her fiancé, and the younger woman began making their way through the crowd over toward them. Valerie, with her head tossed in the air like that of some regal queen, headed in the direction of Aunt Otha Mae and Aunt Sadie, no doubt to boast and brag.

"Heaven help me if Brandy comes over here with those boojee ways of hers. I'm in no mood for it tonight," Alexia whispered through clenched teeth while holding her smile in place.

"Chill, girl. There's a possibility she's changed." Even as Taye said the words she knew they were a lie. Brandy still possessed her uppity-acting ways. "And if she hasn't changed, then just ignore her. She's not worth the bother."

Growing up with Brandy had always been a pain in Taye's, Rae'jean's and Alexia's rear ends. They'd tried to be nice to her, but Brandy, thanks to her mother's influence, had always acted like she had a chip on her shoulder because Uncle Victor didn't marry Valerie to make Brandy a legitimate Bennett instead of an illegitimate one.

"I wonder who's that woman with her. She's a real nice-looking piece. I hope Brandy plans to hook a brother up with her," Victor Junior said, smiling.

Alexia raised her eyes to the ceiling. "Pleeze, Victor Junior," she mumbled. "Do you need to be reminded that you have a wife?"

"I wasn't checking her out for myself. I was giving her the once-over for Michael. I'm trying to look out for my cousin here."

Taye wished there was some way she could give Victor Junior a good kick in the butt just for having that thought. As far as she was concerned, Michael didn't need Victor Junior looking out for him and certainly didn't need to be bothered with the likes of the hoochie momma walking over toward them with Brandy and her fiancé.

"Hi, everyone! I'm so glad to see all of you. It's been years!" Brandy exclaimed in a high-pitched voice and with more airs than were needed. She threw her arms around Victor Junior and gave her half brother a resounding smack on the cheek.

Taye and Alexia rolled their eyes upward and decided to play along and be just as phony as Brandy was being. They pretended to accept her hugs graciously and figured she was trying to impress her fiancé with such a warm display of family affection.

"Heaven mercy, Alexia, I swear it's been years, girl. I was just telling Mama last month while watching Body and Soul's concert on HBO that you couldn't possibly have gained as much weight as those cameras made it seem."

Taye took a deep breath as she eyed Alexia carefully, hoping she had the good sense to ignore Brandy's pointed remark. Alexia was known not to take anyone's crap. She was not one to mince words.

"And Taye," Brandy was now saying, bringing Taye's attention back to the conversation. "I hear you're still messing around with hair. Seems like you've been doing that forever."

Before Taye could respond, Brandy pulled the man next to her to the forefront. "Everyone, I want you to meet my fiancé, Lorenzo Ballentine. And this," she said, motioning to the woman, "is my best friend, Jolene Bradford. She's maid of honor in my wedding."

Lorenzo shook everyone's hand as Brandy made all the introductions. When he got to Alexia, his smile was friendly and his voice had a rich, sexy Jamaican accent as he said smoothly, "Alexia, I'm a huge fan of yours. I saw you in the same HBO special, and unlike Brandy, I didn't think you looked like you'd gained any weight. In fact, I thought you looked great, and now that I see you in person, I think you're even more beautiful," he added.

Alexia smiled, thinking it was a shame that someone this good-looking could be engaged to Brandy. "Thanks, Lorenzo; that was such a nice thing to say. You're too kind." She cast a glance at Brandy and saw the deep scowl on her cousin's face. Knowing Lorenzo's compliment had irritated Brandy made Alexia's smile widen.

"And you have a beautiful voice," Lorenzo said, recapturing Alexia's attention.

"Thanks again." Alexia looked deep into Lorenzo's gaze. There was something in the dark depths looking back at her that suddenly made her feel uneasy. That along with his lady-killer smile. Was she imagining things or was this man checking her out, giving her a thorough once-over? No, he couldn't be that brazen, not with Brandy standing right there watching the whole thing. Alexia shook her head. She had dated island men before and had found them to be—in addition to sexy and handsome—brash and possessive. They were also big flirts.

Looking past Lorenzo, Alexia released a sigh of relief when Rae'jean chose that moment to come up to join them. She went about introducing Grady to everyone.

"So, Rae'jean, when are you getting married?" Brandy asked in a tone that said it was a crying shame that she wasn't the only one in the family tying the knot.

"Grady and I are getting married on Christmas Day. It will be a very small wedding."

"Oh, well, mine will be a large one," Brandy said excitedly, thinking she had one up on Rae'jean. "Lorenzo's parents are covering all the expenses. They're so happy that he's settling down to take over the family business. They own a chain of hotels in Jamaica, the Bahamas, and Bermuda. I'm sure you've heard of the Ballentine Hotels."

Everyone nodded. Of course they had.

"We would love for all of you to come to our wedding," Lorenzo said, smiling. "If you decide to do so, my family will cover the cost of your airfare and hotel accommodations."

"Hey, we just might take you up on that, man," Victor Junior readily said, smiling at the invitation as he tried to keep his gaze off Jolene Bradford.

"I'm hoping that all of you do." Lorenzo then turned his attention back to Alexia. "I'd be honored if you were to sing at our wedding."

Alexia pasted a smile to her lips. "I'll have to check my schedule first."

"I already have a soloist for our wedding," Brandy cut in, protesting mildly.

"I'm sure you can add another song, sweetheart," Lorenzo said smoothly without missing a beat. Although he'd worded it like a suggestion, Alexia had a feeling it was understood by Brandy to be anything but.

"If that's what you want, Lorenzo," Brandy said softly.

"Yes, that's what I want."

"Fine."

Alexia inwardly frowned. She totally despised domineering men and had a feeling Lorenzo Ballentine was as domineering as they came. Her earlier opinion of him as being nice suddenly vanished. She wondered how Brandy could tolerate such a man. She shrugged. He was Brandy's problem, not hers. In fact, Lorenzo and Brandy deserved each other. She had long ago learned the truth about men and their need to manipulate and control. Maybe it was time Brandy learned the same lesson.

"After you've checked your schedule please let us know," Lorenzo said, like he was used to giving orders and having them obeyed.

Alexia was about to tell him that she had decided not to sing at their wedding when the music stopped playing and Cousin Agnes announced that everyone was to take their seats for dinner.

CHAPTER 17

Rae'jean couldn't help but hide a grin behind her napkin as she finished wiping her mouth. She glanced across the table, and the grins on Alexia's and Taye's faces matched her own. Victor Junior was getting a taste of his own medicine, which served him right.

After everyone had sat down to the table to partake in the meal, Victor Junior had deliberately started a conversation that was intended to exclude Grady. Unfortunately, Victor Junior had not known that Grady, being the type of person that he was, could hold his own in any group, even when he was in the minority.

Also, Victor Junior had not known that this was not Grady's first time being placed in such a situation. Before moving to Boston, Grady had worked two years at an inner-city hospital in Chicago. During those two years, he and three other doctors, all black, had operated a clinic in one of the worst areas of town. Therefore, none of the topics being discussed were going over Grady's head like Victor Junior had intended. Grady was just as much a part of the conversations as everyone else. In fact, he was hitting it off big-time with Michael and Taye's brothers as well as some of the other cousins. And Poppa Ethan seemed to like him. That meant a lot to her.

The only person who didn't seem to be happy about the recent turn of events was Victor Junior. He was the one on the outside of the conversation, since the topic had shifted to golf, a sport Grady, Michael, and Taye's brothers played regularly and Victor Junior didn't play at all and knew very little about.

"As soon as the food is cleared away, it's movie time," Cousin Agnes announced to everyone.

Rae'jean knew that for this portion of the evening, which would last around thirty to forty-five minutes, a video that consisted of family photos Cousin Agnes had collected over the years would be shown. She wondered at what point during the evening she would have to speak privately with her uncle Victor. She was certain he knew the facts about her father, but like the others, he would not talk. She was prepared to beg and plead with him if that's what it would take for him to tell her what she wanted to know.

Rae'jean noticed as soon as the lights were turned off for the movie Uncle Victor quietly left the room. Thinking that this would be the perfect time to talk to him, she turned to Grady. "Excuse me, Grady. I need to go talk to my uncle about something," she whispered.

Grady nodded, smiling, not taking his eyes off the video. Evidently he was enjoying watching the movie Cousin Agnes had put together.

Rae'jean stepped out into the empty lighted hallway, wondering where her uncle could have gone so quickly. After waiting outside the men's room for a little more than five minutes, she figured he must have gone someplace else.

A thorough search of the pool area indicated Uncle Victor was not there. Rae'jean was about to turn around and leave when she noticed the door from the pool area that led to the outside stairway was slightly ajar. Automatically she walked through it, and immediately she heard the moans and grunts of a man and woman entrenched in the throes of hot-blooded lust.

The stairway area was dark, so she could not see a thing, but she sure did hear a lot. She recognized her uncle's voice but didn't recognize the moans of the woman he was with and wondered if it was the woman who worked at the hotel. The sounds Uncle Victor and the woman were making went above and beyond mere sexual gratification as far as Rae'jean was concerned. She refused to believe that anyone could enjoy doing it so much that they had to make that kind of noise. They sounded like two animals who hadn't had sex in fifty years and were making up for lost time as well as stocking up for the next fifty years.

Embarrassed at the thought that the man under the stairway carrying on that way was her fifty-year-old uncle, Rae'jean couldn't help wondering if perhaps he was taking Viagra or some other type of medication to boost his sex drive. It must be in the genes, genes he had unfortunately passed on to Victor Junior, since he couldn't keep his pants zipped, either. Deciding she had heard enough, more than she'd actually wanted to, she entered the pool area and sat down on one of the recliners to wait. They had to get their fill and come out sooner or later. Rae'jean quickly decided to use her uncle's whorish activities to her benefit by blackmailing him into telling her what she wanted to know about her father.

Nearly a good twenty minutes later the woman slipped back through the door's opening and Rae'jean nearly gasped out loud. The woman who had been outside making out with her uncle was none other than the prim and proper Valerie. Talk about being shocked. It appeared that even after thirty years Uncle Victor and Valerie still had some use for each other.

Rae'jean stayed out of sight in the darkness as she continued to watch Valerie fix her hair and straighten her clothes. From the smile Valerie wore, evidently Uncle Victor's performance tonight had been well worth her time. Rae'jean wondered if anyone attending the banquet had noticed that both Valerie and Uncle Victor were missing. She wondered if Rose had noticed.

After Valerie disappeared from sight it didn't take long for Uncle Victor to make an appearance, as he hurriedly entered the pool area. Rae'jean waited until he'd finished tucking his shirt back in and zipping up his pants before making her presence known.

"Uncle Victor."

Nearly startled out of his pants again, Victor Bennett, Sr., placed a hand over his heart. "Rae'jean, what are you doing out here? Why aren't you in there watching the movie like everyone else?" he asked, catching his breath.

Rae'jean came closer to him in the light. "I could be asking you the same thing."

He had the gall to look innocent. "I decided to get a bit of fresh air."

Yeah, and that's not all you got a bit of, Rae'jean thought as she met her uncle's gaze. She checked her watch. She didn't have a lot of time to waste. "Look, Uncle Victor, I know what you and Valerie were doing out here, and I know Rose wouldn't be too happy if she found out, so I'm willing to make a deal."

Uncle Victor frowned. "What are you talking about, girl? Are you saying you'll say something about tonight to Rose?"

Rae'jean detected surprise in his voice. "Yes. I might say something unless you're willing to swap secrets with me."

Uncle Victor lifted a brow. "Swap what kind of secrets?"

"I want to know about my father."

Uncle Victor shook his head regretfully. "Can't do that, girl. All of us promised that we wouldn't."

Rae'jean frowned. "And just who did all of you make that promise to?"

Uncle Victor crossed his arms over his chest. "Can't tell you that, either."

Rae'jean rubbed both hands across her eyes. She was sick and tired of family secrets, especially one she felt she had a right to know about. "Fine, Uncle Victor, you keep your secret, but *I won't* keep mine. If you don't agree to meet with me later and tell me what I want to know, then I'll make sure Rose knows all about what happened here tonight with Valerie."

Uncle Victor looked at her, shaking his head. In his heart he knew his niece was bluffing, but he also knew how determined she was to learn the truth. "Rae'jean, honey, some things are better left alone. You didn't have a daddy all these years; why do you want to find out about one now? Didn't me and your other uncles give you everything you needed while you were growing up? Didn't we help your mama with you, girl? God rest her soul, Colleen was my sister and we all loved her dearly. Not once did any of us turn our backs on her when she got knocked up with you. She was the youngest of the girls but was the first to have a baby. She had you when she was only sixteen."

Rae'jean sighed. "Uncle Victor, I know all that, and I do appreciate everything you and my other uncles did for me but I need to know who my father is. Because of my coloring, I know he couldn't have been a black man. I need to know who he was, not just for me but for the kids I may have one day. I have a right to know about the person responsible for creating me. For once, think about how I feel. I bet all your outside children know you're their daddy." At his nod she said, "Then why can't I know who my father is? Just because he may be white doesn't change anything. I may decide not to act on the information once I get it, but I think I have a right to make that choice."

"Leave it alone, girl," he said gruffly.

"No, I can't leave it alone. If I don't get the information from the family then I'll hire a private detective and get the information that way."

Rae'jean saw her uncle swallow hard. Evidently taking that approach was something he and the family would not want her to do. "I mean it, Uncle Victor." She turned and started for the door.

"Rae'jean?"

She stopped walking and glanced back over her shoulder. "Yes?"

"About tonight. You're not going to mention anything to Rose about tonight, are you?"

Rae'jean turned and stared at her uncle for a long time before answering. It would serve him right if she did. He was a married man but was not honoring the vows he'd made. But she knew she would never do anything that could possibly cause him harm. What he said earlier had been the truth. When she was a child growing up her uncles had always taken care of her just as much as they'd taken care of their own kids.

"No, Uncle Victor, I won't mention anything to Rose."

Hunching his shoulders, he nodded his head and muttered, "Thanks. It will be best for everyone if you don't."

Rae'jean's full lips tightened as she nodded in agreement. She was certain that it would be. She turned around to leave again.

"Rae'jean?"

She turned back around to her uncle. "Yes, Uncle Victor?"

"See me after church tomorrow. We'll talk and I'll tell you everything then."

Rae'jean felt her stomach jump. "You'll tell me about my father?"

Uncle Victor nodded. "Yeah, as much as I know. And you're right, girl. You do have a right to know the truth."

"Yes," she quietly agreed. "I do." She smiled as she walked back over to him. She reached her hand out to him. "Come on, Uncle Victor; let's go back inside together. And if anyone asks why you've been gone so long,

I'll just tell them that you and I had a long uncle–niece chat just like we used to do. How does that sound?"

Uncle Victor took her hand. "That sounds good, girl. Rose will believe that."

CHAPTER 18

R ae'jean and Uncle Victor slipped into their seats just moments before the video ended and the lights in the room were turned back on.

Grady twisted around in his chair to look at Rae'jean. He reached out and smoothed her hair away from her face. "You missed seeing the video, sweetheart."

Rae'jean smiled. "Did you enjoy watching it?"

"Yes. There were a number of clips that showed you as a child. You were kind of cute, and I want a daughter who looks just like you." He leaned down and let their foreheads touch and their noses rub. Their lips came mere inches from touching before Alexia caught Rae'jean by the shoulder and tugged on her.

"Excuse us a minute, Grady," Alexia said apologetically. Nearly dragging Rae'jean out of her chair, she took her hand and headed toward an area on the other side of the room. "What are you and Grady trying to do? Give these old folks heart failure? Cuzin Sophie got some of them on the warpath already at the thought of your marrying Grady. I doubt they can handle such an open display of affection between a white man and black woman. You should have seen Uncle Bubba's eyes nearly pop out of the sockets." Alexia chuckled. "I hadn't seen his eyes get that big since that Sunday when Sister Harrison shouted so hard she passed out on the floor and showed everything under her dress—which, shamefully, wasn't much. But it was enough to keep the deacons awake the following Sundays in case there was a repeat performance."

Alexia's good humor caused Rae'jean to laugh. "Oh, I remember that." A few moments later she glanced around the room. "Where's Taye?"

"The teens are having their own little party upstairs, and she and Michael volunteered to chaperone for the first hour. They'll meet us back downstairs around eleven."

Rae'jean nodded.

"The rest of us grown-ups," Alexia continued, "those between the ages of thirty and fifty, will be partying to the sounds of the sixties, seventies, and eighties out by the pool. Grab Grady and meet us there. And remember, none of that kissy-kissy stuff from the two of you."

Rae'jean grinned. "Gotcha."

Taye and Michael caught the elevator back downstairs, leaving Taye's brother Darryl and his wife, Lisa, as chaperones for the next hour.

"I'm glad that's over," Michael was saying. "If I had to listen to another song by Ginuwine, I would have lost my mind."

Taye shook her head, grinning, understanding completely. She'd been surprised when Michael had volunteered to assist her in being a chaperone. If she didn't know better, she would think he'd done so to escape Jolene Bradford's obvious interest in him.

"So, I take it the girls are excited about this Disney trip," he said. His voice was low and deep, and Taye felt her body immediately responding to the sound of it.

"Yeah, they're excited; can't you tell? That's all they've been talking about." Taye fell silent for a moment as she remembered the last family reunion and the good time she had growing up in the eighties.

"You're quiet, Taye," Michael said after a few moments. His hand reached out and touched her arm. "What are you thinking about?"

She glanced up at him. "I was thinking about the last family reunion and those who were there then and aren't here now—Gramma Idella, Aunt Colleen, Uncle Herbert, and Aunt Bertha. And we can't forget Billy."

Michael nodded. He knew their cousin Billy was doing time somewhere in a Texas prison for armed robbery. "Does any of the family keep in contact with him?" Michael asked softly.

Taye nodded. "We all did at first, but then his letters were so negative most of us stopped writing. I think Uncle Taylor and Aunt Marcy still write to him. Even Poppa Ethan writes to him now and then, although it hurt Grampa real bad when Billy changed his name to Mohammed something or another, totally turning his back on the Bennett name and his Baptist religion."

Michael nodded. He then paused in his stride just before they reached the pool area. "Hold up, Taye; there's something I want to say to you."

Taye stopped walking. A small lump formed in her stomach as she turned to face Michael and looked up at him. She tried to keep her tone light when she asked, "What is it, Michael?"

"I watched you up there with those teens, and you can relate to them so well and on their level. Hell, you even kept up doing the latest dances. I had no idea you could dance so well. Even Kennedy was in awe of you. And your daughters are so well mannered and respectful, and your relationship with them is amazing. In my book that says a lot, and to me it means that you're a swell mom."

When she mumbled some words to try to deny that she was anything special, Michael held up a hand to silence her. "No, Taye, you've always done that, even as a kid. For some reason you refused to take compliments at face value. I'm proud of you and the woman you've become. I know being single and raising two kids, working, and going to school can't be easy, and I admire you and what you're doing. I think you're very special."

Taye chewed on her lower lip and fought back the tears that threatened to cloud her eyes. Michael had somehow seen in just three days what some of her other family members hadn't been able to see in thirteen years. Even with her mistakes from the past, she was doing a good job as a mother, an employee, and a student. "Thanks, Michael. Hearing you say that means a lot." She doubted he would ever know how much. She leaned up on tiptoe and brushed a kiss across his cheek. "And I think that you're special, too."

CHAPTER 19

Excuse me, people," Alexia said, leaning over the table and whispering to Taye, Rae'jean, and Michael. "Correct me if I'm wrong, but isn't this party supposed to be for the thirty-through-fifty crowd?"

Taye nodded her head. "Yes, that's my understanding."

Alexia snorted. "Then why is Aunt Jules's old butt hanging around? She has to be in her sixties; therefore, she should be with the others who are in the banquet room listening to the sounds of Fats Domino, the Platters, and hometown favorite Little Richard."

Rae'jean giggled. "Leave Aunt Jules alone. I can deal with her a lot better than I can deal with this forty-something crowd who's dominating the music. If I hear another song by Marvin Gaye and Tammi Terrell I'm going to scream. When are they going to play something by Prince or Janet Jackson? I'd even be happy to listen to 'We Are the World.' That was one of my all-time favorites."

Michael chuckled as he quirked an eyebrow at her. "You don't have to remind us, Rae'jean. After that song came out you were hell-bent on sending every penny you could get your hands on to Africa to feed the poor. You drove us nuts with your constant begging."

Rae'jean smiled, remembering. "Yeah, I did, didn't I? I'm glad Grady got too tired to hang and went upstairs to bed. I wouldn't want him finding out just what a softy I am. When it comes to caring and being concerned about people's welfare, he's soft enough for the both of us."

Taye nodded. "I really like Grady, Rae'jean. He's a swell guy. Besides, anyone who can hold their own with Victor Junior can't be too soft. In my opinion, that means Grady is made of some pretty heavy stuff."

Alexia glanced around. "Speaking of Victor Junior, where is he?"

Michael bit his lip to keep from grinning. "I saw Evelyn drag him upstairs a few minutes ago. I can only assume they called it a night."

Rae'jean leaned back in her chair grinning. "I'm glad Brandy and her crew called it a night as well. Jolene couldn't keep her eyes off you, Michael. The woman was downright salivating at the mouth."

Michael shrugged. "I didn't notice."

Alexia looked at him pointedly. "Now why doesn't that surprise me? For as long as I've known you, you've never noticed girls checking you out. I remember how that very thing used to make Taye cry a river of tears."

At that moment Taye wished there was some way for her to slide under the table. Michael, however, seemed a bit confused.

"Why would me not noticing girls who were checking me out bother you, Taye?" he asked, turning to her with a bemused look on his face. He then turned his attention back to Alexia when it was apparent Taye had no intention of enlightening him.

"It wasn't you not noticing other girls that bothered her," Alexia said, all too happy to explain things to him. "She cried her eyes out because you didn't notice her checking you out, either. Surely you had some idea Taye had a huge crush on you back then."

Michael's jaw dropped open. "But we're cousins."

"So?" Alexia said in a casual voice. "When you're young and in love the fact that you're related means nothing."

If looks could kill, the one Taye slanted Alexia would have made her a goner. However, Alexia chose to ignore the look and kept right on talking. "Michael, I can't believe you never figured it out," she continued. "Taye was hooked on you something awful. It lasted almost three years, from the time she turned thirteen. Poor thing cried her eyes out during the entire family reunion after you announced you had enlisted in the air force."

For the first time in her life, Taye wanted to kill her cousin. "I did not cry my eyes out, Alexia," she said in a voice filled with anger.

"Yes, you did, Taye. Don't you remember? You cried yourself to sleep that last night. How on earth can you forget something like that?"

Michael turned in his chair and looked at Taye. She refused to look at him. Instead, all of her attention was focused on the water glass in front of her. "I didn't know," he said, not taking his eyes off Taye.

Taye felt Michael's gaze on her and was compelled to lift her eyes to meet it. She forced a bright smile to her lips, shrugged, and said cheerfully, "Alexia is exaggerating, Michael. It wasn't that big of a deal. Besides, that was a long time ago." She then gave a pointed look at Alexia, aiming a command for her to keep her mouth shut for the remainder of the night.

That look was wasted.

"Actually, Taye, it was a big deal," Alexia said. "It was always 'Michael did this' or 'Michael did that.' You used to take oodles of pictures of him. I bet you probably have tons of photo albums just filled with nothing but his pictures. Then there were those love letters you used to write him that you never got the courage to give him."

"Well, what do you know? They're finally playing a song from the eighties," Rae'jean said quickly, breaking into the conversation in an obvious attempt to change the subject. "Isn't that 'Control,' by Janet Jackson?" she asked, knowing darn well that it was.

Once again Alexia did not take the hint.

"Michael, I remember one letter in particular. If you had read it, it would have really opened your eyes as to how Taye felt."

"Really?" Michael said smoothly, still watching Taye. She had resumed her interest in the water glass. He tried to force his mind back fifteen years and for the life of him couldn't remember a time when Taye could have had a crush on him. In all his recollections what he remembered about Taye was that even with the three-year difference in their ages, the two of them had been close and had hung out together a lot. She had always been his favorite girl cousin because she'd had such an easygoing disposition, and no matter when he came to visit Poppa Ethan and Gramma Idella, Taye always had a smile for him. Even now he could remember that day he'd left for the air force. She had stood on her grandparents' porch with tears in her eyes. But then everyone had been crying that day. Even he had gotten kind of weepy-eyed at the thought of leaving Macon.

"Well, Alexia," Taye's voice cut in with a sharp edge. "Since you've

wasted the last half hour discussing my business like I wasn't here, I think I'll just retire for the night."

"You're leaving?" Rae'jean asked, seeing the anger in Taye's eyes and wishing she had kicked Alexia under the table like her mind had told her to do earlier.

"Yes, I'm leaving," Taye responded, standing. "I don't appreciate being talked about to my face."

"Would you have preferred for me to talk about you behind your back?" Alexia asked good-naturedly, not put off by Taye's anger.

"No, I would have preferred you not talk about me at all," Taye responded.

"Wait. I'll ride the elevator up with you," Michael said, placing his wineglass on the table and getting to his feet.

Taye forced herself to look at him, feeling totally embarrassed that he knew how she had felt about him back then. "That's not necessary, Michael."

"It's no problem," he said, placing an arm underneath her elbow. "I was about to call it a night myself."

Taye nodded. "Good night, Rae'jean." The look she gave Alexia indicated she was not speaking to her at the moment.

"Good night, Alexia and Rae'jean," Michael said, before turning to walk off with Taye.

As soon as Michael and Taye were out of hearing range, Rae'jean turned a deep, dark frown on Alexia. She threw up her hands, completely disgusted. "What the hell was that about, Lex? Taye swore us to secrecy back then. What on earth possessed you to say those things in front of Michael? Do you know what you've done?"

A smug smile touched Alexia's lips as she watched until Taye and Michael were no longer in sight. "Yes, I know what I've done, Rae. Hopefully I've finally opened Michael's eyes."

Rae'jean frowned. "What are you talking about?"

Alexia leaned back in her chair. "I'm talking about the fact that if you had been paying attention, you would have noticed that Jolene Bradford wasn't the only one who couldn't keep her eyes off Michael. Taye was right there giving the woman plenty of competition, since she couldn't

keep her eyes off Michael, either. It's just like it was when we were teen-agers, but now I think it's even worse."

Rae'jean lifted a brow, seriously doubting that, but decided to ask any-way. "How can it be worse?"

A smile touched Alexia's lips. "Because now Taye's a woman with clearly defined urges and desires that haven't been tapped in ten years and Michael's a good-looking, hot-blooded male who probably could use some constant loving from a good woman. And unlike before, there's the fact that in truth they aren't really blood kin, which makes it perfectly acceptable if they decide to hook up." She took a sip of her Diet Pepsi before con-tinuing. "I think Michael is just who Taye needs and Taye is who Michael needs."

Rae'jean gave Alexia a look of disbelief, wondering how on earth she had figured that, but decided not to ask. She herself had thought about the idea of Taye and Michael getting together and had even mentioned it to Taye the night of the welcome reception. She had noticed Taye checking him out that night as well but had put the episode to the back of her mind. Her main focus of concentration had been on finding out her father's iden-tity. "The family will have a hissy if something develops between Michael and Taye," she finally said.

Alexia grinned. "Let them. They will have a hissy anyway when they find out I plan to have a baby without the benefit of a husband, so what's another hissy for them to endure?" She shook her head, grinning. "With your white man, Brandy's rich Jamaican, Taye and Michael getting it on, and me and my daddyless baby, this family will have enough to talk, grieve, and moan about until the next reunion."

Rae'jean couldn't do anything but nod her head in agreement. It seemed that things were about to get real interesting in the Bennett family. Real interesting.

For the first time since the reunion, Taye felt uncomfortable being alone with Michael. And here they were as alone as two people could get, since they were the only ones in the elevator. They hadn't said anything to each other since leaving Alexia and Rae'jean.

Taye decided to be the first one to speak, since she was the reason there was now an uneasiness between them. She could just imagine what Michael must think of her. And just earlier that evening he'd been singing her praises. But of course that was before Alexia had spilled her guts, telling him everything.

She cleared her throat. "Umm, Michael, about what Alexia said back there."

Michael, who had been intently studying the closed elevator door, lifted his gaze and looked at her. The gaze that met his seemed shy, almost embarrassed. "Yes? What about it?"

"I'm sorry if any of it bothered you."

He shrugged, feeling slightly awkward, but a smile tilted the corners of his mouth nonetheless. "None of it bothered me, Taye. In a way I'm sort of flattered. To be honest with you, I'm glad I was told about it. I just wish I'd known then."

Taye looked at him. "Why?"

He looked at her intently. "Because I wouldn't have felt so guilty about the time I came close to kissing you."

Taye's eyes widened. Her heart jolted and her pulse pounded. "You did? When?"

"It was that last night of the family reunion when you and I were talking under that big sycamore tree in Grampa Henry's backyard. Of all the people who I was going to miss when I left for the air force, you were the one I knew that I would miss the most, and a part of me wanted to kiss you, but not like a cousin kissing another cousin. I wanted to kiss you like a guy kisses a girl who means something to him. I felt guilty as sin for thinking that way. You were only fifteen and were my cousin. I had always protected you from older guys, and here I was with a sudden urge to come on to you myself. I felt like a pervert for even thinking about doing such a thing."

Taye wasn't prepared for this and a part of her lit up inside knowing there had been a time when he had felt something, even if it had been just that one time. Ever practical, she said, "I was closer to sixteen than fifteen, Michael."

"Yeah . . . well, that may be true, but the fact remained that you were still my cousin." He smiled. "So as you can see, Octavia Louise Bennett,

you aren't the only one who kept secrets all those years." Slowly Michael's smile wavered. "But that was some years ago, wasn't it?"

Taye nodded. "Yeah, fifteen years to be exact. People change and their feelings change."

Michael nodded, accepting and understanding what she had said. That was then and here was now. Just because she'd had a crush on him as a teenager fifteen years ago, that in no way was indicative of how she felt about him now. Before he could tell her that he understood, the elevator door opened.

"Well, this is my floor. I guess I'll see you later," Taye said. For once she was glad to part from his company.

"Are you coming down for breakfast in the morning?" he asked.

She couldn't help grinning. "Have you forgotten that I'm the one who has two daughters with healthy appetites? So yes, I'll be at breakfast in the morning. What about you?"

"Yeah, I'll be there. I'd better get a good meal. I have a feeling Reverend Overstreet will be long-winded at church tomorrow, which means it will be a long service."

"Probably," Taye said, smiling.

Michael smiled back. "Take care, Taye, and have a good night's sleep." No sooner had he said those words than he thought about the sensual image of her tossing around and getting all tangled in soft cotton sheets, and for the first time since things had ended between him and Stephanie he felt drawn to a woman. But Taye was a woman he should not be drawn to. For years he had considered her a blood relative. And although he now knew that wasn't the case, since he had been adopted into the Bennett family, a part of him felt he should still consider her kin. But he was finding it hard to do so and wasn't certain as to why.

"Good night, Michael, and I hope you have a good night's sleep, too."

He nodded. "I'll keep the elevator door open until I see that you've gotten inside your room."

Taye nodded and walked quickly toward her room door, which was in full view of the elevator. Taking out her room key, she had to force herself to enter without looking back at Michael one last time before closing the door behind her.

Later as she got ready for bed she was grateful that she had the entire

hotel room to herself, since the girls were doing a sleepover in Cody's room.

As she placed her head on her pillow, numerous thoughts tumbled through her mind—of the very cute young man of eighteen whom she'd had a crush on at the last family reunion . . . and now of the very handsome man of thirty-three he had turned out to be.

In a way nothing had changed. Even after fifteen years Michael still managed to capture her fantasies and creep into her dreams.

Rae'jean glanced around when she heard someone call her name. She inwardly groaned when she saw the "Mod Squad," the name she, Taye, and Alexia had given the three nosiest women in the Bennett family. "Yes, Cuzin Sophie, Aunt Lulu, and Aunt Lenora, what can I do for you?"

It seemed Cuzin Sophie was going to be the spokeswoman for the group. "We feel it's our duty to discourage you from marrying that white boy, Rae'jean. All it's going to do is bring you heartache later. Just think of the children the two of you are bound to have."

Rae'jean blew out an exasperated sigh and wondered if any of the three had somehow spoken to Grady's sister and brother-in-law. "Grady is a decent person and—"

"We didn't say he wasn't decent, Rae'jean," Aunt Lenora piped in. "What we said was that he was *white*. We've never had an interracial marriage in our family before and we'd prefer it didn't happen now."

"Why?"

"It just ain't right. Black folks are supposed to be with black folks and white folks are supposed to be with white folks. We tried telling your mama the same thing, but she didn't listen."

Rae'jean raised a brow. "So you know who my father is?"

There was complete silence; then Cuzin Sophie spoke. "If we do, we ain't talking."

It will be a first, Rae'jean thought, shaking her head. She felt a severe headache coming on. "I appreciate all of your concerns, but the family needs to understand that I believe love is color-blind and—"

"Has he taken you home to meet his family yet?" Cuzin Sophie asked, interrupting.

"Yes."

"And?"

Rae'jean frowned. "And what?"

"And you want to try and convince us that even with your light skin, they're overjoyed about him marrying you?"

Rae'jean's frown deepened. "It doesn't matter how anyone feels. Grady and I are getting married and that's that. Now if you ladies will excuse me, I'm rather tired. It's been a long day."

Without giving them a chance to say anything else, she walked off.

CHAPTER 20

"Good morning, Taye. I notice you're sitting alone. May I join you?"

Taye glanced up from her plate of grits, eggs, sausage, and toast and glared at Alexia. As much as she loved her cousin, she had nothing to say to her after that stunt she'd pulled the night before. When Taye refused to say anything to her Alexia sat down anyway with her own plate.

Taye ignored Alexia and looked beyond her to the beautifully landscaped yard outside the hotel. After a few minutes Alexia said, "OK, let's have it out now and get it over with. I know you're upset about last night, but I had my reasons for doing what I did."

Taye drew her attention away from the scenery and placed it on her cousin. She narrowed her eyes. "What reason could you possibly have had for deliberately humiliating me in front of Michael the way you did?"

Alexia placed her fork down. "I did not deliberately humiliate you, Taye, and I apologize if you think I did. What I did last night was something you should have been doing yourself."

Taye's eyes darkened. "And just what might that be?"

"Finally getting some guts and letting Michael know how you feel about him."

Taye looked at Alexia and actually gritted her teeth. "Alexia, my crush on Michael was fifteen years and two daughters ago. It was old news, news that I trusted you with. How I felt about him as a teenager wasn't even worth discussing."

Alexia fingered the crisp bacon in her hand before saying, "It was if you feel the same way about him now that you felt about him back then."

"I don't."

Alexia placed the bacon back down on her plate and met Taye's gaze squarely. "You, Octavia Louise Bennett, are a bald-faced liar."

Taye sat up with anger flashing in her eyes. "What did you just call me?"

"You heard me loud and clear, Taye," Alexia said without flinching, her own eyes narrowing. "Who do you think you're fooling? I know when a woman is interested in a man. I can read the signs as well as I can read a Donna Hill novel and enjoy it just as much. I see sparks of interest in your eyes whenever Michael walks into a room. I see you trying to pretend you're not looking at him when it's plain to see that you can't keep your eyes off him. And I enjoy seeing you break out in a cold sweat like you did last night when he came and sat next to you at the table." Alexia took a sip of her orange juice. "So please, girl, don't insult my intelligence by denying any of those things. If you want to lie to yourself, then go ahead and do so, but don't lie to me. I would not have done what I did last night if I didn't know for certain that you're still interested in Michael—fifteen years and two daughters later. I know what I see, Taye."

Taye stabbed her fork into her link sausage as she glared at her cousin. "You see too damn much, Alexia."

Alexia sighed. "No, Taye, I see what I want to see, and I ignore what I don't want to see. And when it comes to you and Rae'jean, I've always kept my eyes open. We promised Gramma Idella that we would always look out for each other and that's what I'm trying to do. Regardless of whether or not you think you want one, you need a man in your life, just as much as Michael needs a woman in his."

Taye's mouth dropped open and she stared at Alexia. "Good grief, do you know what you're suggesting? You're actually advocating that Michael and I have a relationship, some sort of an affair."

"Yes. I'd even go so far as to propose marriage if that'll work."

"That's insane. That's ludicrous. That—"

"Makes sense," Alexia cut in. "Think about it, Taye. Like it or not, you still have feelings for him. Feelings I can clearly see, so don't bother denying them. You owe it to yourself to be happy."

"But not with Michael. It would never work."

Alexia sliced her hand in the air to halt any further words from Taye. "Fine," she snapped. "Then stop drooling each time he comes within arm's reach of you. Stop trembling every time he innocently touches you." Leaning forward, she added, "And for Pete's sake, stop watching that doorway waiting for him to come down for breakfast."

Taye and Alexia stared at each other from across the table for a few tense moments. Then Taye bowed her head in silent acknowledgment of everything Alexia had just said. When she lifted her gaze to meet her cousin's once again, she wore a small flustered smile on her lips. "Am I *that* obvious?"

Taye's question, asked with the enraptured emotions she could no longer hide, eased the tension between them. "Only to someone who knows you so well, Taye. Although we haven't spent a lot of time together in recent years, some things don't change. One of those is your inability to hide your emotions."

"Do you think Michael has picked up on it as well?"

"No, and that's why I decided to give him a little eye-opener. I think after last night he may start noticing you more. If he does, then he'll be able to read your emotions as well as I can. But isn't that what you want, for Michael to finally notice you?"

Taye smiled at the thought of Michael noticing her. Then reality struck and a frown marred her features. "It would cause too many problems if something was to develop between us. First of all, to our family it would be taboo, forbidden, sacrilegious. They'd consider a relationship between us synonymous with incest."

"They would be wrong if they did. You and Michael are not related. He was adopted and everyone knows it, so the two of you aren't blood relatives."

"Yeah, that may be true, but to our family, we *are* family. We have the same last names. Our grandfathers are first cousins. My aunts are his aunts. My uncles are his uncles. My cousins are his cousins."

Alexia rolled her eyes. "As long as your mama ain't his mama and your daddy ain't his daddy, you don't have a thing to worry about."

Taye shook her head, still not convinced. "What about the girls? Not only would a relationship with Michael stir up bad feelings within this family, but it would totally confuse our daughters."

Alexia shook her head, disagreeing. "I think the girls would be fine with it. It's obvious that Monica and Sebrina would go along with anything that makes you happy. I know for a fact that Sebrina is excited about the two of you going to Disney World with Michael and Kennedy next month."

Taye grunted. "Yeah, she should be, since she's getting a free trip out of this and a chance to have fun and kick up her heels for a week."

"Maybe so, but from what Michael has told me, he's been having discipline problems with Kennedy lately and thinks that since she's been around your girls these last few days she's shown definite signs of improvement. I think both Sebrina and Monica are good for Kennedy."

"As cousins?"

"Even as stepsisters if it came to that. I can see you, Michael, and the girls as one big happy family."

Taye sighed deeply. "For ten years I haven't given diddly squat about a man. Now that I've seen Michael again, he has stirred up longings and desires that have been dormant for that long. I try telling myself that I shouldn't feel that way about him, but I can't help it. It's like I'm a fifteen-year-old girl all over again and he is the recipient of all my cravings. But this time they are adult cravings."

Taye decided not to tell Alexia about the dream she'd had last night. The one where Michael had played a major part. It had seemed so vivid and so real that if she missed her period and found herself pregnant next month she wouldn't be surprised. She expelled a frustrated sigh. "Oh, Lex, what am I going to do?"

Taking a deep breath, Alexia launched into Taye without showing any mercy, since she had asked for her advice. "The first thing you're going to do is stop worrying about what the family is going to think. It's your life to do whatever you damn well please as long as you aren't breaking any of the Ten Commandments." A smile tilted her lips. "I do draw the line somewhere. And speaking of the Ten Commandments, there's no place in the Bible that says you can't marry an adopted cousin. Jacob married both Rachel and Leah, and they were actual first cousins. So if it happened in the Bible it can't be wrong."

Taye smiled at Alexia's logic. "Yeah, well being wrong and being tolerated are two different things. You know as well as I that as far as the members of the Bennett family are concerned it doesn't matter if a relationship between Michael and me is right or wrong; to them it won't be tolerated. The family would probably divorce themselves from us." She sighed, deep in thought. "I'm probably getting all worked up for nothing, since my interest may be one-sided. Michael hasn't done anything to indicate he sees me as anything other than a cousin that he's fond of."

"Then you had better pay close attention, because what you see may suddenly surprise you," Alexia said, smiling, just as Michael entered the room flanked by Rae'jean and Grady. His gaze immediately sought out Taye, and he gave her a warm smile.

Alexia cleared her throat as a huge *I told you so* grin touched her lips. "See what I mean?"

"Do I detect trouble in paradise, Rae?"

Rae'jean glared across the table at Alexia. "Is there anything you *don't* notice?"

Sitting on the side of Rae'jean, Taye released a soft chuckle. "Didn't you know, Rae'jean, that Madam Alexia and her crystal ball know and see everything?"

Alexia frowned at Taye. "Shut up, Taye, before I get back into your business again."

"Heaven forbid," Taye grumbled as she picked up her glass of orange juice and took a sip.

Rae'jean glanced across the room at Michael and Grady. The two of them were in the buffet line fixing their plates. She and Grady had had their second argument in a matter of two days, and because of it she wasn't in the mood to eat anything heavy and had settled for a cup of coffee. "Grady is upset with my handling of Uncle Victor," she finally said.

"Did you explain to Grady that in the end Uncle Victor agreed to tell you what you wanted to know without being coerced?" Taye asked as she took another sip of orange juice.

"Yes, I tried to explain that to Grady, but he still thinks I went too far. He thinks I'm forcing Uncle Victor to break a promise he's made to the family. Grady believes that a promise is a promise and if you make one, then you don't break it."

Alexia snorted as she pushed her plate aside. "But in this case, it was a promise that should never have been made. For crying out loud, what's the big deal? Doesn't Grady think you have a right to know who your daddy is?"

"Yes, but he thinks I've suddenly become obsessed with knowing and he can't understand it. But then I really don't expect him to. He knew the identity of both of his parents from the day he was born. Unless you've been there and done that, you won't fully understand."

Taye nodded, wondering how she would handle it when the time came and Monica began asking more questions about her father. She knew that sometime in the future she would have to make contact with Lynell. He needed to be prepared for the fact that when Monica got older and if she asked for the name of her father, Taye would give it to her. It would be up to him to get his business in order and tell his wife about Monica before she found out another way. Seeing what Rae'jean was going through over not knowing the identity of her father, Taye refused to protect Lynell at the expense of Monica's happiness and well-being. "So what are you going to do, Rae'jean?" she asked, bringing her thoughts back to the conversation. "Have you changed your mind about getting the information from Uncle Victor?"

Rae'jean shook her head. "No. In fact, I plan to pump him for all it's worth. I think I deserve to know who got my mother pregnant and any details Uncle Victor can give me. Grady will have to accept that."

"After you find out the truth, what do you plan to do?" Alexia asked, studying Rae'jean intently.

Rae'jean shrugged. "I don't know. That will depend on what I find out. I just hope and pray that this doesn't turn into a soap opera or *Peyton Place*."

Grady and Michael returned to the table. Rae'jean watched as Michael sat down next to Taye and began sharing some of his food with her. As she studied them, she wondered if perhaps Alexia was right and Michael and Taye did, in fact, need each other. They sure as heck looked good together.

CHAPTER 21

On the steps of the Mount Calvary Baptist Church, there was nothing more pleasing to the eyes that Sunday morning than the three good-looking sistahs dressed to a tee and profiling hats, shoes, and other accessories that accented their outfits.

Rae'jean, Taye, and Alexia's attire would have made Gramma Idella proud. When the three of them had gone shopping together the day before, they had purchased outfits their grandmother would have been pleased to see them wear back to Mount Calvary, a church where the three had gotten baptized on the same Sunday morning at the age of twelve.

Alexia was dressed in a hunter green jazzy jacquard two-piece suit. She wore a hunter green asymmetrical profile hat that was decorated with a front bow of the same jacquard print as her suit. Matching hunter green shoes adorned her feet.

Taye wore a red-and-black two-piece suit that had a shapely button-front jacket. A matching red-and-black Tiffany-brimmed hat covered her head, and sleek two-tone red-and-black pumps were on her feet.

Rae'jean's suit was meant to dazzle . . . and it did. The color of rose petals, the two-piece number was made of satin and had an embroidered lace shawl-collared jacket. Her pillbox hat was of the same color, and its double-tiered veil detailed her flawless facial features. The matching satin rose petal criss-cross sling-backs on her feet provided the finishing touch.

Even Grady did a double take and smiled with male appreciation when he saw her.

The three of them were definitely Sunday showstoppers, and everyone was complimentary on their outfits, even Aunt Fannie, who was known to be stingy with her compliments to anyone.

"If I wasn't related to you ladies, I'd hit on you myself," Victor Junior said, grinning, as they entered the church. "The three of you look just that good."

Michael discovered he was hard-pressed to keep his eyes off Taye. There was just something about the way she looked in her outfit that kept drawing his gaze back to her. "You look good, Taye," he whispered to her as they were led to their seats by an usher.

Taye gazed up at him from under the wide brim of her hat and smiled. "Thanks, Michael."

When everyone had been seated, Reverend Overstreet asked that they all bow their heads in prayer for this special reuniting of the Bennett family.

"I don't like it when we're mad at each other, Rae'jean."

Rae'jean glanced up at Grady and smiled. "Me, neither." She was grateful that the loud singing of the choir was drowning out their whispers.

Grady reached over and captured her hand in his. "Love you."

Rae'jean's smile widened. The man sitting next to her was proof of God's many blessings. No matter what color he was, Grady had come into her life at a time she had needed someone, and for that he would always be special to her. He was a very special person, and she regretted that some of her relatives couldn't look beyond his skin color to see that. "Love you, too," she whispered back. "What do you think of today's service?" She knew Grady's Catholic background was a lot different from her Southern Baptist one. That was one of the reasons they had decided to get married in a private ceremony that would be performed by the brother of one of their colleagues, who was a judge.

He grinned. "Different."

. . .

Taye recognized some of the people in the congregation as being members at Mount Calvary when she was a child. The majority of the Bennetts, including her parents, still actively attended service here, but she and her girls had joined a church in Atlanta, closer to their home.

"Deacon Simon still looks the same, doesn't he?" Michael whispered to her when the older man came forward to pray over the tithes and offerings.

Taye nodded as a deep heat settled in the pit of her stomach. Because of the large congregation at church that day, the pews were full and she and Michael were squeezed close together. She inhaled deeply when she felt the hardness of his thigh pressed next to hers and the solidity of the arm he'd placed across the seat around her shoulders.

Murmured amens filled the church's auditorium when Reverend Overstreet walked back up to the pulpit. After reading the Scripture, he said, "Today, ladies and gentlemen, we are blessed with one of our very own who has returned. She started singing here at this very church as a child, and today she is a well-known singer in this country. We're proud of her. Join me in welcoming back home our very own Alexia Bennett."

The entire congregation began clapping as Alexia got out of her seat and started walking toward the front of the church. She turned to the audience when she reached the microphone. "Giving honor to God, who is the head of my life," Alexia began by saying. "To Reverend Overstreet; the mother of the church, Mother Phelps; deacons, sisters, members, and friends. I want to dedicate this song to my grandmother, Idella Bennett. This was her favorite song, and I used to sit in this very church on Sunday and listen as she sang in the choir, and I prayed that one day I'd be able to sing it just as beautifully as she did. Today, I'm going to try."

The congregation got completely quiet when Alexia closed her eyes for a few moments before any sound left her lips. Then she began singing "His Eye Is on the Sparrow."

As Alexia continued singing, the soothing, soulful, melodic sound of her voice filled the sanctuary and touched everyone present as she put her heart, soul, and mind into every note and every lyric. She sang from her heart. She sang from her soul. She sang as her mind relived memories of faithfully attending this church under the watchful and protective eyes of her grandparents, parents, uncles, aunts, and cousins.

Her family.

As she continued to sing, she couldn't help but get caught up in the spiritual significance of being at this church on this day and with her family. In her heart she knew it was time to put aside any unpleasant memories of the past. It was time to remove the animosity from her heart for those family members who had thought she wouldn't ever amount to anything. Those who had believed in her had never let her down and had given her more than enough encouragement and love to make her believe in herself.

When the song ended, she opened her eyes and saw the entire church on their feet in a standing ovation, including every member of her family. Some of them had tears in their eyes, including Grampa Ethan. Everyone was clapping and smiling, and she knew in her heart as she lifted her eyes toward the heavens that somewhere up there Gramma Idella was smiling and clapping right along with them.

CHAPTER 22

"Do you think you have enough food?" Rae'jean asked Grady, grinning. After church, dinner had been set up on the grounds of her grandfather's home, and they had found a shady spot under a huge oak tree to sit and eat.

"I hope so," Grady replied with a lovable boyish grin on his face seconds before attacking the barbecued ribs on his plate. From his expression after biting into the meat, Rae'jean could tell he thought he had died and gone to heaven the minute he licked his lips. Uncle Joe's special barbecue sauce was to die for, and it appeared Grady was practically there.

Rae'jean unfolded her hand and looked at the dollar bill she held and couldn't help but smile. For as long as she could remember, Aunt Mary had always slipped a dollar bill into her hand and folded it before whispering. "Buy something special, chile." When she got older she had understood why her grandfather's only sister had singled her out to be the benefactor of such a gift. She was the only one of Poppa Ethan's grandchildren who hadn't had a daddy accounted for. Giving her that dollar had been Aunt Mary's way of saying how much she cared. Even now, like always, Rae'jean appreciated it. And although she earned a nice income as a cardiologist, her aunt still pressed the dollar in her hand whenever she saw her and whispered the same words in her ear.

Rae'jean glanced around the grounds. Tables of food were everywhere.

There was Cuzin Sophie's delicious potato salad, Aunt Otha Mae's "git down with it" dirty rice, and Cousin Agnes's crab meat dressing. Then there was corn on the cob as well as a number of other pots of vegetables, watermelons, iced tea and lemonade, baked ham, fried chicken, all kinds of cakes and pies, as well as coleslaw and tossed salads. Everyone figured that if you were going to get together to reaffirm family ties, you may as well do it on a full stomach.

Alexia, Rae'jean noticed, was still holding Cousin Marsher's newborn baby. Even from a distance Rae'jean could see the deep longing in Alexia's eyes for a child of her own to love.

Rae'jean had decided to at least let Uncle Victor enjoy his meal before seeking him out. Like most people, she would be leaving to return home after dinner. She and Grady had already changed into more comfortable clothing and had checked out of the hotel. They would be driving to Atlanta to catch their flight back to Boston later that evening. She was just itching to know what information her uncle had for her and was satisfied in knowing she would be leaving the reunion with the information she had wanted to know for so many years.

Alexia, who had changed into a pair of shorts and top, tried to be conservative with the amount of food she placed on her plate and found that she couldn't. Everything looked too good, and she was too hungry.

" 'Bout time you put Marsher's baby down and get you something to eat," her grandfather said when he came up beside her. He glanced down at her plate. "And stop trying to eat like a bird. Put more food on that plate."

Alexia smiled at him. "You know me, Grampa; I have to watch my figure." He snorted, shaking his head. "Food was meant to be eaten and not nibbled," he said as he piled more of Aunt Julia's candied yams on his plate as well as on Alexia's. "Prentice and Ruth tells me you gonna stay in Macon one more day."

"Yes, sir. I'm not leaving until tomorrow evening." She wouldn't mention to him that the reason she was staying the additional day was so she could talk to her parents about her plans to have a baby out of wedlock. As Alexia was their only child, she and her parents always had a rather close relationship, and although she was old enough to make her own decisions, she always wanted to keep them abreast of what was going on with her. There was no doubt in her mind that they would try to talk her out of it, but her mind was set and she planned on going through with it.

"Would you like to have breakfast with me in the morning?" Grampa Ethan asked.

"I'd love to, Grampa. You name the time and I'll be here."

"It has to be early. You know I don't believe in sleeping late."

Alexia nodded, grinning, as she remembered how he would always get up at the crack of dawn each morning. "Yes, sir. I know."

Her grandfather's eyes crinkled up in a well-worn smile. "You sounded downright pretty today at church, Alexia. Your gramma would have been downright proud of you. We always knew you would be somebody someday. I want you to keep right on singing. Your voice is a gift from the Almighty, and you should use it well."

Alexia thought of her plans to go solo. "Yes, Grampa, I plan to do just that."

"The girls told me that the two of you are taking them to Disney World," Aunt Otha Mae was saying to Michael and Taye as they sat on benches eating. "I think that's wonderful. There's nothing like kinfolk spending time together whenever they can."

Taye tried to keep her face emotionless as she continued to eat her food. She wondered what her mother would think if she knew that at the moment what Taye was feeling toward Michael had nothing to do with kinship.

"You're a widower, Michael, and we know it ain't easy raising a child alone. The family will do anything we can to help out," Otha Mae continued. "Since you and Taye are living in the same city, the two of you should depend on each other. I'm always worrying about Taye and the girls living up there in Atlanta by themselves, but now I'll rest easier knowing you'll be there to look out for her, just like you've always done."

Michael smiled as he glanced over at Taye before returning his attention to Aunt Otha Mae. "Yes, ma'am. I think I did the right thing by moving closer to family. I know for a fact that Kennedy has enjoyed herself at this reunion."

Otha Mae nodded. "Yeah, that chile needed to meet her relatives. If anything were to happen to you, she'd belong to us, since your wife didn't leave any family behind."

Michael nodded. That thought had been heavy on his mind for quite some time. He had discounted the possibility of his grandfather raising Kennedy since he would be celebrating his eighty-seventh birthday later that year.

Michael glanced over at Taye, who was listening to what her mother was saying. Aunt Otha Mae had changed subjects and was now talking about Taye's brother Bryan's new job. Michael knew that if anything were to happen to him, Taye would be the one person he would want to raise Kennedy. Even as a single mother she was doing an outstanding job with her own girls, and in just three days Kennedy had taken to Taye in a way she had never taken to anyone else. But then, he thought, that was not surprising. Taye had always been down-to-earth, well liked, and approachable.

After a few minutes Aunt Otha Mae finally ran out of conversation and decided to move on, leaving Michael and Taye alone.

"I agree with Momma, Michael. I want you to know I'm available if you ever need me. I know with your job you travel a lot. Kennedy is welcome to stay at my place anytime you're out of town. Since she and Sebrina will be attending the same school it won't be any trouble to include her in our plans."

Michael smiled, appreciating Taye's offer. "Thanks; I'll keep that in mind. I hired an elderly lady to stay over on those nights I'll be away, so hopefully things will work out. Kennedy has met Mrs. Frazier and seems to be OK with the arrangement, which is similar to what I had in place in Minnesota. Hopefully with this new job I won't be away from home as much."

"Well, if you are and you need to put a backup plan in place, don't forget me," Taye said brightly.

Michael grinned and inwardly thought Taye was not a person anyone could easily forget, especially if that person was a man. He shifted in his seat, wondering why he was beginning to notice her as a woman the more time he spent around her. Once again he was transported back in time to that night of the last family reunion when he'd almost kissed her. She'd had a crush on him then and he hadn't known. He wondered if things would have been different if he had known.

Before allowing his mind to answer that question, he picked up his glass of lemonade and took a huge swallow. He didn't want to think about the answer to that question now.

"Are you still sure you want to go to Orlando with me and Kennedy?" he asked to break the silence that had suddenly cropped up between them.

Taye glanced over at him and smiled. "I couldn't get out of going now if I wanted to. The girls are looking forward to it."

He nodded and tried to keep his face a mask of indifference when he asked, "Is there any reason you wouldn't want to go, Taye?" His gaze locked on hers for a long moment, and he wondered if he was imagining things or if she could feel the sexual tension flowing between them like he did.

Taye looked at Michael a long while before answering his question. No matter how attracted she was to him, she couldn't think of just herself and her feelings. She had to think of her daughters, Michael's daughter, and, most important, the family. She could never let anything develop between her and Michael. "No, Michael, there isn't any reason I don't want to go. Are you sure you want me to go?"

"Yes, I'm sure." As he said those words, he knew that although he was sure about wanting her to come to Orlando with him and Kennedy, there were a number of things he wasn't sure about. He wasn't sure about this strong attraction he felt for her, and he wasn't sure just where it would lead.

But most important, he wasn't sure he wanted it to lead anywhere.

"You might want to sit down, Rae'jean."

Rae'jean lifted a brow at her uncle's suggestion. "I'm fine standing," she said, wondering if Uncle Victor thought the name of her father would make her fall flat on her face. They had decided to hold their private discussion in an empty room in her grandparents' home. Since everyone was still outside, it was the perfect time.

"I think I'll sit, then," Uncle Victor said as he dropped down in the cloth-covered chair. He wiped the sweat from his forehead with a well-worn handkerchief. "Somehow I just knew I'd be the one to have to tell you this."

"How you figure that?"

"Just did."

Rae'jean decided not to get her uncle off on a tangent to explain why. Time was of the essence. Michael, Taye, and Alexia could only keep Grady occupied for so long. "Who is he, Uncle Victor? Who's my father?"

A few tense, quiet moments passed. Uncle Victor cleared his throat and released a slow breath. "When Colleen turned sixteen, a young white fellow started coming around the neighborhood. I believe he was only twenty or so. He was clean-cut and well mannered. Ma and Pa really liked him. I guess Colleen liked him even better and let him come around a couple of times when Ma and Pa weren't home."

Rae'jean raised a brow. "Who are you talking about, Uncle Victor? Who was this white guy who came around the neighborhood?"

Uncle Victor looked at her like he had expected her to figure it out and was disappointed that she hadn't. "The insurance man."

Rae'jean blinked. "The insurance man?" she repeated.

"Yeah, the insurance man."

Rae'jean frowned in deep concentration. She remembered when she was a little girl an insurance man used to come around to her grandparents' house every Monday to collect insurance premiums. In fact, he made his rounds to every house on their street. Poppa Ethan and Gramma Idella used to have a ton of policies on all their grandkids nailed to the wall by the front door and paid less than a dollar a week for each one. "The insurance man: Mr. Taylor?" she asked when a name suddenly popped out in her mind. "Mr. Taylor got my mother pregnant?"

"No, Mr. Taylor became the insurance man later, after you were born, Rae'jean. Before then, there was a younger white man by the name of David Turner. He was only supposed to come around for about three months to get some experience working the neighborhood before going inside the office to work. Evidently, experience wasn't all he got after meeting Colleen. The next thing we know is that your ma got pregnant and said the insurance man did it, and he admitted to doing it."

Rae'jean shook her head. "And?"

"And it was decided the best way to handle the situation was to take what the insurance company offered to the family to keep the business out of the streets. They didn't want anything blown out of proportion, no sort of scandal to deal with about one of their men messing around with any of the Negro girls in the neighborhood. Some even said Turner was the grandson of the owner of the company, so they offered to make things right with Pa."

Rae'jean's head began spinning at what she was hearing. Her mother had gotten pregnant from a door-to-door insurance man? She wondered just how the insurance company thought they could make things right when an unborn child was involved. "What did they offer to do?"

"For our word that we would never mention the details surrounding your ma's pregnancy, they offered the entire family paid-up insurance policies and some cash on the side."

Rae'jean didn't want to believe what she'd just heard. "Paid-up insurance policies and hush money?"

"Yeah, can you believe that?" he asked smiling like what they'd been offered was something worth smiling about. "We got eight paid-up policies of ten thousand dollars each."

Rae'jean decided it was time for her to sit down, so she did. "And all of you kept quiet all these years because of those paid-up policies and the money you were given?"

"Yeah." Uncle Victor looked at her. "So now that you know the truth, what are you planning to do?"

Rae'jean shook her head. "I don't know. Nothing for now. I just want to go somewhere and absorb all this."

Uncle Victor nodded in understanding. "We looked out for you, Rae'jean. We didn't forget you. You got a paid-up policy, too. That was part of the agreement. You were the only grandchild who got one."

Rae'jean wondered if he thought that was consoling news. "You said David Turner was the grandson of the man who owned the company?"

Uncle Victor shrugged. "That's what your mama claimed, but I can't rightly say. Colleen used to exaggerate at times."

Rae'jean nodded.

"You and you mama are a lot alike when it comes to that one particular thing."

"And what particular thing is that, Uncle Victor?"

"Both of you seem to have a thing for white boys."

Rae'jean rolled her eyes heavenward. "The only thing I have for Grady is love."

"You sure of that?"

"Of course I am."

"You know what I think?"

"No, Uncle Victor, what do you think?"

He lowered his voice to an almost-whisper. "I think you can't help yourself. It's in your genes passed down from Colleen. Your mom was afflicted with it; now you got it."

"Got what?"

"That mess they call jungle fever."

Rae'jean knew better than to waste her time debating otherwise with her uncle. "Thanks for telling me everything, Uncle Victor."

"I wished I could have told you more."

In truth, Rae'jean was glad there hadn't been more to tell. There was some truth in that old saying "beware of what you ask for." She stood. "I'd better go back. Grady will began wondering where I've gone off to." She turned to leave.

"Rae'jean?"

She turned back around. "Yes, Uncle Victor?"

"Ma and Pa did what they thought was best for everyone, including you. There was no way that white man would have claimed you as his child. The insurance company did the right thing by making things right."

Rae'jean nodded and then walked out of the house.

After Rae'jean left Uncle Victor, she had immediately rounded up Taye and Alexia and herded them inside the house and into Grampa Ethan's bedroom and closed the door. Michael was still outdoors keeping Grady company.

Sighing, Taye ran her hands over the quilt work of the beautiful spread that covered her grandfather's bed. She remembered the time her grandmother had made it. "So, the identity of your father has been kept a secret all these years because of paid-up insurance policies and hush money?"

Rae'jean nodded, still feeling numb from the impact of what she'd found out. "Knowing how things were back then for blacks, I guess I can understand how Gramma and Grampa thought they were getting justice by getting those policies and money on top of it."

Alexia nodded in agreement. "I wonder how much money they got."

Rae'jean sighed. "Who knows? I was too shocked to ask. But it had to have been enough for them to be willing to keep quiet for so long. Even Cuzin Sophie has kept her lips zipped."

Taye shook her head. "So what do you plan to do now?"

Rae'jean moved one tired shoulder. "I don't know. I'd like to hire a private detective to find my father."

"What for?" Alexia asked.

"Just to meet him and to see if he had any feelings whatsoever for my mother."

"And if he didn't?" Taye asked.

"Then I'll accept it. But a part of me has to know one way or the other."

Taye and Alexia nodded.

Rae'jean looked at her watch. "It's time for me and Grady to hit the road." She looked at Taye and Alexia intently. "We're all in agreement that we'll do a better job of staying in touch?"

Taye and Alexia smiled and nodded again.

"And the three of us are going to try real hard to make it to Brandy's wedding? Right?"

Alexia frowned. "I never agreed to that, Rae'jean."

"Come on, Lex," Rae'jean was saying. "No matter what a pain in the butt Brandy can be at times, she's still family."

"Let me know when she starts acting like it; then I might reconsider," Alexia responded curtly.

"You know why she acts the way she does. She's always felt like the cast-off because Uncle Victor never married Valerie."

"No one in the family ever treated her that way," Alexia defended her kin. "She has the Bennett last name for Pete's sake! It's Valerie's fault for pumping Brandy's head with that garbage because of her own disappointment about Uncle Victor not marrying her. Brandy always wanted to take it out on us, and it wasn't fair."

"No, it wasn't fair, but at least we should try and understand why she acts the way she does."

"That's no excuse."

"I'm not giving you an excuse. I'm giving you the reason, at least how I see it." Rae'jean smiled. "Besides, Lorenzo asked you personally to sing at their wedding. Aren't you going to do it?"

"I don't know, since I'm not so sure I like him, either."

Rae'jean rolled her eyes upward. "For crying out loud, Alexia, stop being so difficult. I thought he was nice."

Only because you weren't the one he was eyeing like he would enjoy having you for breakfast, lunch, and dinner, Alexia thought. She hadn't said anything to the others, but a couple times during the banquet dinner she had caught him paying more attention to her than to Brandy. "I'm not sure I want to go to Brandy's wedding," she finally said.

"Well, think about going. It will give us a chance to be together again before Christmas. The two of you will try to come to me and Grady's wedding, won't you?"

"I'll be there with bells on," Taye said, smiling.

"Good. What about you, Lex?"

"Yeah, yeah, I'll be there." Alexia smiled. "I can't let you tie the knot without me. And I'm hoping to have some good news to share with the two of you. If things work out the way I plan, I'll be pregnant way before then."

Rae'jean nodded. She wanted to suggest to Alexia to really think through that plan, then decided if her cousin's mind was made up about it, there was nothing she could do other than be there to give her support. "All right, you guys, give me hugs for the road."

And they did.

Each of them knew that over the past four days they had done more than reaffirm their family ties. They had renewed their bond, a bond that meant they would always be there for one another, through the good times as well as through the bad.

It was an affinity, an allegiance, and a pact they planned to keep.

CHAPTER 23

"Welcome back, Rae. How was the family reunion?"

Rae'jean acknowledged Shawna Harper's question with a lift of her head and a smile on her lips. Shawna was a trauma physician in ER and someone Rae'jean considered a friend.

"It was nice going back home and seeing everyone," Rae'jean said as she closed the patient's chart in which she'd just made an entry. Her first day back at the hospital and working a shift that began at midnight and ended at eight in the morning had her feeling bonelessly tired, especially since her shift had ended hours ago and she hadn't left the hospital yet. "How were things around here while I was gone?"

"Quiet," Shawna whispered in a surprised, hard-to-believe tone as she raked her fingers through the mane of braids on her head. "Last weekend was uneventful except for a few cases of food poisoning."

Rae'jean quirked her brow. "Anyplace I should avoid dining at in the future?"

Shawna chuckled. "No, it was a private affair, a wedding. The caterers served a bad batch of potato salad."

Before Shawna could say anything else her pager went off. After checking it, she immediately reached for the phone at the nurses' station and dialed an extension that connected her to ER. The expression Shawna wore alerted Rae'jean that the call involved something serious. As soon as Shawna hung up the phone, she said, "Gotta go," and took off walking quickly toward the elevator.

Rae'jean was right on her heels. "What is it?"

"A shooting at an elementary school in one of the upscale areas of town. A third-grader brought a gun to school and decided to take aim at a couple of his classmates he didn't like. The bullets hit his teacher when she threw herself over the students to protect them. A bullet did hit one of the students, though. They're life-flighting them over. It sounds serious."

Rae'jean nodded as they stepped onto the elevator. "Can you use another pair of hands, Dr. Harper?" The last remnants of exhaustion dissolved from Rae'jean's face in the wake of the pending emergency.

Shawna forced a smile. "ER can always use another pair of hands, Dr. Bennett."

When Rae'jean and Shawna stepped off the elevator they saw ER turn into a madhouse as the paramedics rushed through the ER doors wheeling in their patients. Familiar with the routine of the trauma team, Rae'jean stepped aside as the doctors and nurses went into action. Her colleagues knew she was there, ready to give assistance if needed. She glanced across the room and studied the face of the unconscious little girl on a stretcher who was quickly hooked up to an IV and monitors. She couldn't have been more than seven or eight. Rae'jean couldn't help wondering what it would take for people to see the need for gun control. No gun should have been accessible to a third-grader.

Rae'jean's attention shifted from the little girl to the other patient also being hooked up to an IV and monitors. It was the teacher who had placed herself in harm's way to protect her students. Rae'jean's intense gaze skimmed over the woman, studying the features she could barely make out from a distance. Blood soaked the sheet covering her, and her hair lay limp around her face. But there was something about the shape of the woman's face, even with her eyes closed in unconsciousness.

A shudder raced through Rae'jean when recognition hit her. The teacher who had taken two bullets in the back and was fighting for her life was Lynn Whitworth.

• • •

Grady's muscular form was sprawled across the bed as he slept. He had performed an emergency heart operation his first night back at work. His patient had been a newborn, a little girl who had come into the world with a huge hole in her heart. It was a hole that he and a colleague had successfully closed.

He muttered to himself when the sound of the phone disturbed his sleep. Without opening an eye, he reached out and picked it up immediately, hoping complications hadn't developed with his young patient. "Dr. Fitzgerald."

"Grady?"

He lifted an eye and turned away from the sunlight that slanted through the window in his bedroom. Yawning, he turned his body over in bed. "Rae'jean?" It was unusual for her to call not long after his shift ended. She knew the importance of uninterrupted sleep whenever a doctor could get it.

When she didn't say anything he slowly pulled himself up in bed. "Rae'jean, what is it?"

"Grady, I think you need to come to the hospital right away. There's been an emergency, a shooting at a local elementary school. A teacher and a student were injured."

The doctor in Grady locked onto Rae'jean's every word. *A shooting at an elementary school?* He glanced at the clock. It was just past noon. "Is ER short-handed?"

"This isn't a professional call, Grady. For you, it's personal."

Grady's brow lifted and mere seconds later he was on his feet. "Lynn?"

Rae'jean's voice was soft when she answered, "Yes."

Somehow Grady had expected the worst when he got to the hospital, and what he found wasn't far from it. Lynn had been taken to surgery and was fighting for her life while surgeons tried removing two bullets from her body.

Rae'jean sat on a sofa in the waiting room and watched as Grady paced the floor. Lynn had been in surgery three hours already. "You need to eat something, Grady."

"I don't want anything now," he murmured as he stopped and hooked the leg of a chair with one foot and sprawled down in it. He rubbed his hand across his face. "How could something like this happen?"

Rae'jean said nothing. Grady knew the answer to his question. They'd had numerous discussions on gun control and the need for it. What he really wanted to know was how such a thing could happen to Lynn.

"Did you notify Lynn's family?" she asked him.

Grady lifted his gaze to hers. "There's no one left in Lynn's family. Her parents died when she was in college, and her grandmother died a few years ago."

Rae'jean nodded. "Did you call your sister?"

Grady nodded. "Yes. I was able to locate Candace in the Middle East. It will take her a few days to get a flight out, but she's on her way."

At that moment one of the surgeons, Dr. Jason Hudson, came into the waiting room and Grady immediately got to his feet. "How is she, Jason?"

Dr. Hudson sighed deeply before saying anything. "We were able to get both bullets out, which was no easy task, Grady. They went through her back, barely missing the spine and lodging in her chest. Her condition is still critical and the next forty-eight hours will be crucial. She lost a lot of blood and is still in a coma."

Grady nodded as a deep, intense expression covered his face. "How soon will she be placed in a room?"

"One is being prepared for her now. She did a very courageous thing by taking those bullets to protect her students. I hope to God she pulls out of this."

Grady shook his head. "So do I."

A few moments later, after the doctor had left, Rae'jean asked Grady, "Are you sure you don't want me to get you something to eat?"

He tried to place a smile on his lips. "No, but thanks for asking." He sat back down and leaned back against the chair. "I know you just got off work a couple of hours ago and must be tired. You don't have to hang around here if you don't want to."

"No, that's OK. I'll wait with you a little while longer, until they bring her out of surgery; then we can leave together."

Grady shook his head. "No, you go on. I'm going to stay. I want to be here when they get her settled into a room to see for myself that she's OK."

Rae'jean forced her mind to understand Grady's need to do that. After all, he had once loved Lynn. "All right." She stood. "Will you call me if anything develops?"

He stood and reached out and pulled her into his arms. She felt the shudder that moved through him. "Yes, sweetheart, I'll call you."

Rae'jean awoke from a long nap and noted Grady hadn't called. In a way that was good news, since it meant Lynn's condition hadn't worsened.

She arrived at work earlier than usual so she could go by Intensive Care to see how Lynn was doing. She was not surprised to find Grady still there. He wasn't in the waiting room where she had left him earlier that day but was now in Lynn's hospital room, sitting by her bed where an IV and monitors were hooked up to her. Grady was asleep in a chair next to the bed.

He immediately came awake when Rae'jean touched him lightly on the shoulder. "You OK?" she whispered to him.

He nodded, then stood slowly, stretched, and yawned. Taking Rae'jean's hand, he led her from the room so they could talk.

"How is she?" Rae'jean asked, noticing the tired lines of fatigue etched in Grady's face.

"The same. She hasn't come out of the coma."

Rae'jean nodded. She knew that under the circumstances Lynn's being in a comatose state was not at all surprising, considering the extent of her injuries and the amount of blood she had lost. Like Jason had said, the next forty-eight hours would be crucial.

She handed Grady the bag in her hand. "I brought you something to eat. You should be hungry now."

He took the bag from her hand. "Thanks, and you're right. I am."

Rae'jean glanced down at her watch. "I got an hour before duty. Do you want to go to the cafeteria and grab some coffee to go along with your sandwich?"

"No, I want to stay here just in case Lynn comes out of the coma. She needs to know someone is here."

Rae'jean nodded as she considered his words. She wondered just how long he planned on staying. "Aren't you on duty tonight?"

He shook his head. "No, I've asked for a couple days off. Hopefully by then Candace will have gotten here."

Rae'jean studied Grady. Her gaze was intense and assessing. It was on the tip of her tongue to ask if he thought a twenty-four-hour watch was necessary. "I'll check by in the morning before I leave," she said quietly.

He nodded. "All right."

She leaned forward and kissed his check. "I'm praying that Lynn pulls through this, Grady."

He nodded. "Thanks. She's going to need all the prayers she can get."

Rae'jean was able to take a lunch break a little before two in the morning and caught the elevator to the floor where Lynn's room was located. The corridors of the Intensive Care Unit were quiet. Shawna looked up when she approached the nurses' station.

"Hey, girl, busy night?" Rae'jean asked.

Shawna smiled. "No, luckily it's been pretty peaceful, for which I'm glad, considering the happenings yesterday. This place was swarming with reporters."

Rae'jean nodded. "I can imagine. How's the little girl?"

"She's improving. Luckily, the bullet was lodged in tissue and not muscle of her arm. That made removing it easier, although it was still a bit much for a seven-year-old to have to go through. Her condition will be downgraded from critical to serious in the morning."

"I'm glad."

Shawna moved closer to Rae'jean so they could have a private conversation away from a nurse who'd walked up. "What's Grady's connection to the teacher? He hasn't left her bedside since she came out of surgery."

Rae'jean wasn't surprised that others were noticing Grady's concern for Lynn. "Lynn Whitworth and Grady go way back. They're childhood friends." Rae'jean knew she could be completely honest with Shawna and added, "And they were engaged to be married three years ago."

Shawna nodded. "Oh, I see."

At that moment Shawna's pager went off and Rae'jean was grateful for the interruption. "I'm needed elsewhere," Shawna said before taking off and leaving Rae'jean to continue her walk to Lynn's room.

She quietly pushed the door open. The room was dark and the only light was from the television that was on. Grady had moved his chair closer to the bed and was asleep.

Rae'jean was about to turn to leave the room when something suddenly struck her. The reason Grady had moved his chair closer to the bed was so that he could hold Lynn's hand.

He was sound asleep with Lynn's seemingly lifeless hand securely gripped in his.

When she was calm enough to think clearly the next morning, Rae'jean couldn't help wondering if perhaps Grady cared more for Lynn than he realized and the shock of possibly losing her was what he was going through. That thought was heavy on her mind when her shift ended and she headed toward the floor where Lynn was.

She paused when she reached Lynn's hospital room door. Grady was still sitting next to the bed, but this time he was wide awake. He looked scruffier than she'd ever seen him look before. It was obvious he hadn't shaved, and his thick brown hair looked as if he'd run his fingers through it several times.

He was reading the newspaper out loud, the comics. Apparently he knew just what Lynn enjoyed from the paper the most. Medical experts claimed that in most cases comatose patients retained their sense of hearing, and encouraged talking or reading to them to bring them out of a coma. Grady was giving it his best shot.

"Good morning."

He glanced up from the newspaper and smiled. "Good morning, Rae'jean."

She walked into the room. "How are things here?"

"The same. I've been watching her closely and I haven't detected any sign of movement in her body."

Rae'jean nodded. "We still have to keep hoping."

"Believe me, I am. Jason stopped by earlier, and he says she seems to be breathing better."

"That's a good sign."

"Yes, but she's far from being out of danger. I'll feel a lot better when she comes out of the coma."

Rae'jean shook her head in understanding. "Look, I can stay here for a while if you want to go home and freshen up."

Grady placed the newspaper aside. "I can't ask you to do that. You just finished your shift."

"You're not asking me, Grady. I'm volunteering. I know how much it means to you for Lynn not to be alone. Besides," she said, smiling, "I had a pretty easy night last night and I'm not as tired as I normally am."

Grady looked at her as an abundance of gratitude filled his gaze. "Are you sure?"

"Yes, I'm sure. If it was a close friend of mine you'd do the same thing for me." And Rae'jean knew that he would. Grady was just that kind of person.

"Thanks, Rae'jean. I appreciate it."

Later that evening Rae'jean sat in her living room curled up in her favorite chair with her fingers around a cup of coffee. After Grady had returned to the hospital she had left to come home to get some sleep. Instead of sleeping at least four to five hours like she normally would have done, she had only gotten three hours of sleep at the most.

She kept her head bowed down and her fingers gripped tight around the cup as she mulled over Grady's behavior over the past day and a half. Was it only deep concern for a friend that had him acting the way he was? She doubted he even realized the way he was acting. A lump formed in Rae'jean's throat. Grady was behaving like a man on the verge of losing the woman he loved.

She took a sip of her coffee as she forced her mind to concentrate deeply on that thought. Grady loved her; she was sure of it. But was he in love with her? Some people claimed there was a difference between loving someone and being in love with that person. Did Grady understand the difference? Did she? Was that the reason she'd had those lustful thoughts about her neighbor? Were she and Grady turning their backs on the chance to have the kind of love they both deserved by unknowingly pretending to be satisfied with the simple, easy, and safe relationship they shared?

Before she could think about it anymore, the phone rang. Placing her coffee cup on the table, she reached over and grabbed the phone.

"Hello."

"Rae'jean, this is Shawna. Lynn Whitworth's condition just took a turn for the worse." She took a moment before adding, "I think Grady needs you."

Rae'jean was already on her feet with her heart pounding a thousand beats a minute. "I'm on my way."

When Rae'jean arrived at the hospital she found Dr. Hudson and a couple of nurses in Lynn's room readjusting the life-sustaining apparatus connected to her. "What happened?" She glanced at the bed where Lynn still lay in a coma.

"Her breathing slowed, almost came to a stop. We were able to bring her back around, although it was touch-and-go for a while. We've been able to stabilize her condition for now."

Rae'jean nodded. "Where's Grady?"

Dr. Hudson heaved a deep sigh. "You might want to check the chapel."

That's where Rae'jean found him, sitting in a middle pew. At first Rae'jean decided not to go to him, to let him have his quiet, personal moments alone. But then she decided that she had to go to him to make him see things not as they were but as they should be. She owed him that.

Without saying anything, she slipped into the seat beside him and took his hand in hers. "She's all right, Grady. I just left Dr. Hudson and he said they were able to stabilize her condition."

Without looking at her, Grady nodded. He continued to look ahead at the front of the chapel. "Did Jason tell you she came out of her coma, for a little while?"

Rae'jean's brow lifted. "No."

Grady took a deep breath before turning to meet her gaze. Her heart went out at the pain and torment she saw in it. "I was holding her hand and felt it move. I lifted my eyes to hers just in time to see them open and to hear the words, although they were weak and slurred."

Rae'jean nodded. "What did she say?" She watched as Grady pressed his lips together like he couldn't bear to repeat the words Lynn had spoken.

She could tell from his expression that the pain of doing so would be great. She felt his grip on her hand tighten, although his palms were moist. They were as moist as his eyes were at the moment.

"Grady, what did Lynn say?" she felt compelled to ask him again.

He lifted his moist gaze to her and their eyes met and held. Then he spoke. "She said she loved me."

Rae'jean wasn't surprised by the words Lynn had come out of her coma to say to Grady. "Did you have a chance to say anything to her before she lapsed back in a coma?"

"No. What could I say?"

"You could have told her you loved her, too."

Grady looked at her sharply. "You think I should have lied to her?" he snapped.

Rae'jean was not put off by his attitude. "It wouldn't have been a lie, Grady. You do love Lynn and I think it's time you accepted that."

He pulled his hand from hers. "What are you talking about? Of course I care for her. She's a friend. I'll always feel something for her, but I love you."

"Yes, you love me, but you're *in love* with her."

"Rae'jean, that doesn't make sense."

"Yes, it does, and I think it's time for you to accept that. *I* have. The sooner you accept it the better off me, you, and Lynn will be. You and I love each other, Grady, and we will always love each other, but it's not the same as being head-over-heels in love. We would have gotten married and lived together happily, or at least we would have tried to because we have so much respect and admiration for each other. That's what our love is based on, Grady, respect, trust, and admiration. But what you feel for Lynn, what you're trying hard to suppress, is a whole lot more. It's the all-passion, all-consuming kind of love that few people have. And it's the kind of love you and I could never have together."

Grady shook his head. Tears he couldn't hide appeared in his eyes. "You're wrong, Rae'jean."

She bit her lip to stop her own flow of tears. "No, Grady. I'm right. In a way I've known it for a while, but loving you, having you love me that way, was simple, easy, and safe. Even when some people weren't ready to accept us together as an interracial couple, to us it still felt right. I didn't want nor was I ready for intense emotions like heart-stopping passion or fiery desire. Nor did I want an all-consuming love. And I guess you didn't, either. But now you need to take another look at things and so do I. Lynn needs you, Grady. She needs you to forget about whatever drove the two of you apart, and more than anything she needs you to tell her you love her. Forget about reading her the comics. The only thing that will bring Lynn out of that coma is for her to know you love her and just how much. She needs to believe that there's someone back here worth surviving for. Without believing that, she'll give up. You don't want her to do that, do you?"

Grady didn't answer. He really didn't have to. The one lone tear that fell from his eye told Rae'jean everything. He reached out and hugged her against him. "I love you," he whispered softly.

Rae'jean shook her head. "And I love you, too. But you're not in love with me and I can accept that. So go to her, Grady. Bring the woman you're in love with back. You can do it. You're the only one who can."

Grady's arms tightened around her and she clung to him, comforted by the fact that she had done the right thing. Lynn needed him and Rae'jean wasn't going to hang on to him out of selfishness or spite.

After a few silent moments, Grady released her and kissed her forehead. "You're special; you know that?"

She smiled through the tears that wet her eyes. "And so are you, Dr. Fitzgerald. That's why you'll always be my friend. My very special, dearest friend." She took the engagement ring off her finger and placed it in the palm of his hand. Kissing his cheek, she stood and walked out of the chapel.

"I can't believe you gave up your man to another woman, Rae'jean."

"Believe it, Lex," Rae'jean responded with a breathless chuckle. She, Alexia, and Taye were having a three-way conversation on her speaker-phone. Today she felt better than she'd felt in a long time. It had been almost a week since she had broken off her engagement to Grady, and she had been down in the dumps and feeling sorry for herself. But Grady's phone call a few days ago, letting her know that Lynn had come out of her coma, had reinforced her belief that she had done the right thing.

"Well, what do you have to say about it, Taye?" Rae'jean asked.

"You did the right thing, Rae."

Alexia snorted. "You would think so, Taye. You're too soft."

"And you, Alexia, are too hard. Give it a break and admit Rae did the right thing."

"But I like Grady," Alexia grumbled. "I had gotten used to the idea of him being part of the family with his good-looking fine self. I dread everyone in the family hearing about this. I bet Victor Junior and the 'Mod Squad' take credit for running him off."

Rae'jean shook her head. "No one ran him off. The decision to end our engagement was a mutual one."

"Well, now you can check out your sexy neighbor without going on a guilt trip," Alexia said brightly.

"I don't plan to get involved with anyone anytime soon. Besides, he's moved."

"He moved? Boy, Rae, you've had nothing but rotten luck lately."

Sitting on the carpeted floor in her apartment, Rae'jean wrapped her arms around her legs. She had wondered why she hadn't seen her good-looking neighbor after she returned from the family reunion and had casually asked another neighbor about him. She found out that he moved out of the apartments the week she left town for the family reunion. *It's just as well,* she thought. She sighed deeply as she searched her mind for something to say to shift the conversation off her to someone else. "Taye, when was the last time you saw Michael?" she asked.

"I haven't seen or talked to him since the family reunion, although the girls talk almost every day. I'll see him in a few days, since Kennedy is spending the weekend with us."

"Umm, that means he'll be fancy free for two days," Alexia said thoughtfully. "Be careful with that, Taye. You don't want to free up his weekends too often. You never know who he might be spending his free time with. I hear there's a lot of man-hungry women in Atlanta."

Taye didn't say anything as she listened to Rae'jean and Alexia lapse into another conversation about a movie that had come out the weekend before. Her thoughts, unfortunately, remained on what Alexia had just said. It didn't help matters that she'd overheard a conversation Kennedy had had with Sebrina about Michael's neighbor, the man-hungry Mrs. Boykins.

"Taye, are you still there?" Alexia asked her.

"Yes, I'm still here."

"So what do you think?"

"What do I think about what?" Taye asked.

"Girl, you weren't listening," Alexia admonished. "I want to know what you think of Dominic as a boy name and Dominique for a girl?"

Taye lifted a brow. "You're pregnant already?"

"Of course not, Taye. Please keep up. I haven't seen Mr. Drop-Dead-Gorgeous since I've been back."

Taye shook her head, smiling. "You're not one to waste time on anything, so what's the holdup?"

"Some things aren't meant to be rushed, Octavia. Besides, I heard he's out of town on business and won't be back for another week."

Taye nodded. "But when he returns . . ."

Alexia giggled. "The man's a goner."

Rae'jean shook her head, still not sure her cousin was doing the right thing. "Did you have a chance to tell your parents about your plans, Alexia?"

"Yes."

"And what did they say?"

"The expected. 'Don't do it. It will be a mistake. Think things through first. Adopt.' " She smiled. "Momma even suggested I take one of Victor Junior's kids off his hands since he got so many. I told them my mind was made up about it. They still weren't happy with my decision but will support me anyway." After a slight pause, she said, "What about you, Rae'jean? Is your mind made up about your father? Will you try and find him or will you forget the idea?"

Rae'jean took a deep breath. "I've had too much on my mind lately to think about it."

"That's understandable, Rae," Taye said soothingly. "Take your time and don't make a hasty decision about anything."

"I won't." Rae'jean knew that taking the time to think things through was what she had to do.

CHAPTER 24

A fter entering the recording studio, Quinn Masters came to a stop when the evocatively beautiful voice of Alexia Bennett caught his ears. The sound was soft, soulful, and sensuous—intensely so.

He continued walking and every step he took he was getting more entranced with the passionate melody, the soothing rhythm, and the woman whose voice had him spellbound.

That morning after opening *USA Today*, he had read the headline, "Alexia Bennett Quits Body and Soul to Go Solo." The article had been a rather lengthy one, providing first the group's history, then fans' reaction to the announcement, and, last but not least, statements from the other two group members.

Chloe Parelli had taken the news in stride and wished Alexia much success, probably because she had plans to split herself once her pregnancy kept her from touring. Raisa Forbes was another matter. As expected, she had not taken the news well, and she had filled the reporter's ear with unflattering remarks about Alexia. Quinn immediately dismissed Raisa Forbes from his mind. He preferred concentrating on the melody, as well as on the woman singing.

Rounding a corner, he saw her, standing behind a glass wall. Her head was thrown back; her eyes were closed. The mass of hair covering her head fell like a silken curtain around her face. Her body appeared calm and relaxed as her voice penetrated the air while belting out lyrics of love and desire.

He wondered how such a heartrendingly beautiful sound could come from any voice. It was strikingly moving and was pulling every emotion he possessed, setting the mood, stirring deep-rooted desire within him, and compelling him to finally do what he'd avoided doing since meeting her— make his move.

The reason he had not done so before now was that, other than the strong sexual attraction he knew they shared, they had nothing in common. He was a forever kind of guy, one who wasn't afraid of marrying one day and having a family. It wasn't a secret in the entertainment business that Alexia Bennett dropped men like hot potatoes, especially when they began showing attachment tendencies. Everyone knew she did not want nor was she interested in a clinging male or a lasting relationship. It was rumored the word *commitment* wasn't in her vocabulary. And because of a failed marriage, one that had left her extremely bitter and way too wary, her motto was, *If at first you don't succeed, say the hell with it and don't think about trying again.* She saw life as neat columns and slotted men wherever she wanted to put them. Abbott Bodie's opinion of Alexia Bennett was that in addition to being an extremely gifted artist, she was a tigress with long, sharp claws who didn't mind using them if she felt her livelihood threatened by a man. Rumor had it that the last man she'd been involved with was still licking his wounds.

Quinn Masters was determined not to be a victim. Call him insane, but he had decided to tame the tigress. In due time he planned to have her not scratching but purring in his arms and his bed—for a lifetime. The bottom line was that the woman set his blood on fire. Ever since he had met her, she had constantly invaded his thoughts, taken over his dreams, and pulled at his gut. No woman had ever affected him that way. She was the first. And just like she was the first with him, he planned on being the first with her. He intended to be the man who would make her want to take a second chance on love.

If she was a tigress, then he intended to be the hunter. She was his prey. She was marked for capture, and he would do that very thing by utilizing his skill as a man. There was no doubt in his mind that Alexia, although they were opposites in a lot of ways, was his soul mate. He knew convincing her they had a connection would be a long process, but he was prepared. When it came to what he wanted, he was a very patient man.

And he wanted Alexia Bennett.

Seeing her again reinforced what he'd thought wasn't possible. He had fallen in love with her.

No sooner had that last thought left Quinn's mind than the song ended and Alexia lowered her head and slowly opened her eyes.

Then she saw him.

Alexia's breath caught in her throat. She had been thinking of Quinn Masters while singing. Thoughts of him had penetrated her mind, rumbled through her soul, and touched her music. No man had ever done that before. No man had ever been the focus of her deep longing and intense desire while she sang.

Until now.

As she watched him studying her, she could barely handle the intensity he emitted. The penetrating magnitude of his gaze was forceful, potent. The expression on his face seemed to convey a passion, stroke a promise, and display persistence. That thought made her shiver, feel panicky. She didn't want anyone that strong, that confident, that capable in her life. But then he was the embodiment of everything she wanted in the man who would father her child. He was a flawless specimen of a man. He would be absolutely perfect.

She would find a way to cope with and control her strong physical attraction to him. There were a lot of men out there, but she had only one heart. A heart that had been tested once and had barely survived. She would protect that part of her at any cost, which meant she would have to be careful and cautious with Quinn Masters. He was dangerously sexy, drop-dead gorgeous, and had eyes that generated searing heat, exuded sensuality, and promised earth-shaking passion.

Transfixed, she watched as he walked toward the room where she was, stopping when he could go no farther. Even the glass surrounding her didn't protect her from his heat. And when his lips curved upward into a sexy smile, she felt her legs weaken as the force of that heat shot through her.

She ignored the sounds around her and had dismissed everyone from her thoughts until Frank Farmer touched her arm, reclaiming her attention, forcing her to breathe again.

"What is it, Frank?" she asked breathlessly, breaking eye contact with Quinn and looking up at the man who was the studio manager.

"I said you sounded good, Alexia. I don't think I've ever heard you sing that way before. This will garner attention, that's for sure. You won't have any problems with a solo career."

She smiled, appreciating his comments. "Thanks, Frank."

When she turned back around Quinn was still standing there, outside the glass room, looking at her. For a moment she wasn't sure if she should leave the safety of her enclosed surroundings. He was out there and she was in here. But then, she couldn't hide from him forever.

Unhooking the recording equipment from her body, she opened the door and stepped out. Most everyone, including Frank, had gathered their stuff and was about to leave. It was lunchtime.

A part of her panicked. She wasn't sure she wanted to be left alone with Quinn Masters. She had never been completely alone with him before. Even while she was sharing dinner with him that evening in Atlanta, others had been around, close by. She had felt safe. Now she felt cornered, at risk, in jeopardy.

"See you after lunch!" Frank hollered to her over his shoulder as he headed out. Giving Quinn a nod, Frank walked past him, and moments later the sound of the door shutting vibrated through the room.

They were alone.

Alexia took in a deep breath of air. She had to stay in control of her mind and her senses. She wanted and needed this man for one thing and one thing only—to give her a child. For days since making her decision she had wondered how she would go about convincing him to father her child. She had immediately dismissed complete honesty as the way. No man in his right mind would willingly get a woman who was not his wife pregnant. He would think being the baby's daddy would come with strings attached. Strings he'd want to avoid. He would see twenty-one years of child support payments and a postulation on him that he didn't want. Few would believe her claim of not wanting anything more from them than a child, a child she could afford to take care of herself. They would not believe that she would want them to relinquish all rights and leave her to raise her child alone with no plans to ever come back and hit them up for anything.

Since complete honesty was not the way to go, she would just have to let nature take its course and be prepared for the consequences. She and Quinn were sexually attracted to each other, and in time the urge to do something about it would drive them to take care of their needs. And when that time came, no matter how careful Quinn Masters was in protecting her from getting pregnant, she was determined to get pregnant anyway.

"I don't think I've ever heard anyone sing a song so beautifully, Alexia."

Quinn's words, spoken in a husky voice, captured her complete attention. She swallowed the lump in her throat and found her voice. "Thanks, Quinn. It's good seeing you again. How was the wedding?"

"It was beautiful. How was the family reunion?"

His question made her smile. "It was fun, and thanks for the flowers. They were beautiful."

"I'm glad you liked them."

She watched as he slipped his hands into his pockets. The movement placed emphasis on just what a good-looking body he had, especially the lower part—well defined and firm. She cleared her throat. "What are you doing here, Quinn?"

"I came to see you," he murmured softly. "I spoke to Abbott today and he mentioned you called him last week trying to reach me when I was out of town on business." He paused. "Was there anything in particular that you wanted?"

If only you knew, Alexia thought as she gazed at him through the thickness of her lashes. "Yes, there was. I wanted to invite you to dinner as a thank-you for your kindness in Atlanta when you took me out to eat. It's my belief that one good meal deserves another."

Or a debt to be repaid, Quinn thought as he nodded. He had a feeling Alexia's dinner invitation stemmed from her not wanting to feel beholden to a man for anything, in any way, shape, form, or fashion. "That isn't necessary."

"Yes, it is. It's something I want to do."

Quinn nodded. "When do you have in mind?"

"Saturday night at my place."

He took his hands out of his pockets and crossed his chest. "Can you cook?"

His question made another smile touch her lips. One thing Idella Bennett made sure of was that her granddaughters could cook, whether they wanted to know how or not. "I can cook just as good as I can sing."

Quinn lifted a brow. "Really?"

"Yes, really."

A smile touched his lips. "I'm impressed. What else are you good at?"

A quiver of warmth spread through her with his question. She suddenly felt aroused, daring, and reckless. "That's for me to know and for you to find out, Quinn Masters."

He took her challenge and moved toward her. The attraction she'd felt upon first meeting him intensified, became even more potent, and the heat radiating from him touched her in all sorts of places.

"I plan to do just that, Alexia," he said huskily when he came to a stop in front of her. "Starting now."

His tone was lighthearted. But there was nothing light about the look in his eyes. They were dark. Turbulently dark. Smoky. Seductive. Gazing deep into her eyes, he reached out and closed his hands around her arms. Then, slowly, he drew her to him.

When their mouths met, Alexia knew that this was something that she wanted. It was what she had craved ever since meeting him, so she didn't hesitate in opening her mouth under the full pressure of his. Wild, turbulent, hot feelings tore through her when she welcomed his tongue into her mouth, getting acquainted with the taste of him. And when he changed the angle of his head to feed more off her lips and mouth, she found out what it felt like to be kissed senseless. The man knew how to invoke passion. He knew how to strip emotions, dissolve your strength, and eradicate your mind of logical thoughts.

Alexia's stomach clenched and a part of her wanted to pull away. This was too much and all they were doing was kissing. No, Quinn Masters was doing more than just kissing her. He was blatantly making love to her mouth. Slow, passionate love. The rhythm he was using as his tongue moved in and out, around and about in her mouth, touching her everywhere, would be the same rhythm he would probably use making love to her. Deep and thorough. Fire scorched through her at the thought and she somehow found the strength to hold on.

She wanted to do more than hang on. She wanted to participate. His kiss was the kind that encouraged you to be more than a willing partner. It seduced you into being an active participant. When her tongue joined his in the duel, the exploration, the quest for fulfillment, she felt his body harden even more, and she heard a groan from deep within his throat. She almost came unglued when he deepened the kiss.

Heat spread through to her every nerve as the taste of him flooded her mind, her senses, her body. His flavor was all-consuming, all-devouring, too delicious. She wanted to swallow him up whole. She felt heat pool between her legs and wondered if it was possible to have an orgasm from kissing a man, then realized she would find out soon enough if she didn't end this by pulling away. But she didn't have the mind to do so, nor the strength. Nothing had ever tasted this good, this rich, this intoxicating. If mating with his tongue generated this much heat, she didn't want to think what would happen when he got inside of her. He would send her up in flames.

When at last he pulled away, only because they needed to breathe, she looked up at him, stunned, speechless. She needed time to clear her mind. Regroup. Rethink. Regain control. Quinn Masters had her shaking in passion so profound, so shattering, she couldn't think straight. To be perfectly honest, at the moment she couldn't think at all.

"You're more than good at this, Alexia. You're perfect," he whispered softly, not loosening his hold on her.

Alexia shook her head to clear her mind. When she met his gaze again the expression on her face was troubled. "That was supposed to have been just a kiss, Quinn," she said in a voice suffused with desire.

He smiled. "It was."

The hell it was, Alexia thought. If he believed that, then she was in way too deep. There was kissing and then there was devouring. Quinn hadn't kissed her; he had devoured her. Now she wasn't sure if it was safe to have him at her place alone for dinner. She had planned on taking things slow so he wouldn't get suspicious of her motives. If their kiss was any indication, it appeared slowness would get tossed out of the window rather quickly and they would be making love a lot sooner than she'd anticipated.

She couldn't handle too many more of his kisses without wanting to tear the clothes from his body, without wanting to taste him all over, and without wanting him buried inside of her—deep.

"I can't wait for dinner Saturday night at your place," he whispered in her ear before totally releasing her and taking a step back.

Alexia nodded. She had a feeling that she would be the main course. For a reason she couldn't explain, her heart began pounding with excitement at the very thought of that. But then another thought suddenly brought her back down to earth. Quinn Masters wasn't a man she would be able to handle as easily as the others. She definitely had to rework her strategy.

CHAPTER 25

Taye stood on the other side of the door and stared at the tantalizing vision in a blue denim shirt and tight faded jeans as he escorted Kennedy up the walkway. She tried not to frown when the conversation she'd had a few days ago with Alexia and Rae'jean crossed her mind. Did Michael have plans to spend the weekend with someone? She forced herself not to think about it. After all, what he did with his free time wasn't her business.

"Hi, Aunt Taye," Kennedy said cheerfully. "Thanks for having me over."

Taye smiled and gave Kennedy a hug before saying, "You don't have to thank me, Kennedy. You'll always be welcome here, and I'm looking forward to spending time with you." She then glanced up at Michael. "Hi, Michael. Did you have a hard time finding the house?"

He smiled. "No, you gave great directions. I didn't know we lived so close by."

Taye moved aside to let them enter. "Yeah, but the homes in your subdivision are a lot more upscale and the yards are humongous."

When Michael and Kennedy stepped into Taye's living room, Michael's first impression was that he was seeing what a real home should look like. Although everything was neat and tidy, the room looked lived in. There were magazines on her coffee table and a number of throw rugs on the floor and wall shelves overflowing with books, which reminded him of how much she enjoyed reading. She had live plants in various places and several black art pieces hung on her wall. Everything he saw created a warm, cozy, and homey atmosphere for Taye and her daughters. "Where do you want me to put this?" he asked, indicating Kennedy's overnight bag.

"Just leave it there. The girls should be able to get it upstairs. I'll call them down."

As soon as Sebrina and Monica found out Kennedy had arrived they ran down the stairs, eager to see her again. Taye and Michael found themselves alone when the three girls raced up the stairs dragging Kennedy's overnight bag.

Michael stood at the bottom of the stairs and watched his daughter scamper off without telling him good-bye. "Kennedy, haven't you forgot something?" he called after her.

Kennedy turned around with a bemused look on her face. "What?"

"Your father."

It took her a minute to get what he meant. She raced back downstairs, gave him a quick hug, then raced back up the stairs again. Moments later she and Taye's daughters disappeared into a bedroom and closed the door behind them.

"I'm crushed," Michael said softly.

Taye couldn't help smiling. "Cheer up, Michael; it's not that bad. At least she's still giving out hugs, and that's good."

Leaning against the banister, he asked, "Are you sure?"

Taye nodded her head. "I'm positive. Trust me." She checked her watch. "But if you're hopeful they'll be back down anytime soon, don't hold your breath. The big news of the day is Alexia's decision to leave Body and Soul, so they have a lot to talk about. They'll stay up there until I call them down for pizza."

"Pizza? What time are you serving pizza?"

"Around six. You're welcome to stay if you'd like."

He shook his head. "Thanks for the invite, but I can't do that. Kennedy will wonder why I'm hanging around and think I'm having a hard time letting go. I've never let her spend the night away from home before."

Taye lifted her brow, surprised. "She's never had friends whose parents you trusted?"

"That wasn't it exactly. It's just that I always wanted her to sleep in her own bed at night where I always felt she'd be safe."

Taye nodded as she remembered the first time the girls had spent a night away from home. She understood how he felt. He was a loving and protective father. "Well, I'm glad you feel comfortable enough to let her stay here with me and the girls."

"I didn't think twice about it. I know you'll take good care of her."

"Thanks, Michael."

"Don't mention it." After a brief pause he said, "Well, I guess I'd better go."

Taye nodded. "Are you sure you don't want to stay for pizza?"

"Yes, I'm sure, but thanks again for asking."

"Don't mention it."

They looked at each other and grinned when they noticed their responses were repetitive.

"I'd better go," he said, once again repeating himself.

Taye nodded. "I'll walk you out."

As they walked out of Taye's house together, Michael complimented her on how well kept her yard was. He also mentioned that he spent a lot of time in his. While he was discussing their yards, Taye's mind momentarily drifted elsewhere. She couldn't help wondering if Michael had a date for the weekend. When they reached his car, he turned to her before walking around to the other side. "I plan on staying home all weekend, so if you need me for anything that's where I'll be. And tomorrow I plan to work outside in the yard all day."

Taye shook her head. He hadn't said anything about having a date. "The girls are going to take in a movie tomorrow." She smiled. "In fact, they plan on taking in three movies, back to back. I'm dropping them off at the theater, and I'll return to pick them up seven hours later." Her smile widened. "And before you ask, yes, they'll be safe. My girls do it all the time. My friend Sharon's sister Danielle manages the place, and she always keeps an eye on the girls for me. Plus, I bought Sebrina a cell phone to use in cases such as this. They have strict orders not to leave the premises until I get there, and Danielle makes sure of it."

Michael nodded. "I trust your judgment, Taye, but thanks for telling me about your plans anyway." He tapped a few times on the top of his car before asking, "What do you plan to do for seven hours while waiting on the girls?"

Taye shrugged. "I don't know. I'll probably come back here and mess around. Why?"

"Why don't you come to my house?"

"Your house?"

"Sure." His smile was slow and his eyes glittered from the reflective light that shone off his car. "I live closer to the theater than you do. You can come by my house and kill seven hours. I can use an extra hand in the yard since you've taken away my free labor for the weekend. Have pity on me and come help me out tomorrow."

Taye grinned. "I guess I could do that, since you're looking like a pathetic little puppy. Just go easy on me, all right?"

"Hey, I'll even let you ride the mower."

"A riding mower?" At his nod she said, "Wow! Since I still have the push kind, that ought to be fun."

Michael chuckled. "It will be. And bring your bathing suit. After we've worked our tails off we can take a swim in the pool."

"All right."

"I'll see you tomorrow, then," he said before walking around the car to get inside. He waved to her as he drove off.

Taye remained standing in her driveway, watching until he was no longer in sight.

"Gee, Aunt Taye, I'd think twice about helping Daddy with yard duty tomorrow if I were you. He can be a slave driver at times."

Taye couldn't help but smile as she bit into her slice of pizza. "Yeah, I'm sure he can be, Kennedy, but I know how to handle your father. We go back a long way, remember?"

Kennedy nodded, grinning.

"Maybe you ought to tell my mom about the man-hungry lady, Kennedy, so she can be prepared," Sebrina said before taking a huge swallow of iced tea.

Pretending ignorance, Taye asked, "What man-hungry lady?"

Kennedy rolled her eyes to the ceiling. "She's talking about our neighbor Mrs. Boykins. She has the hots for Dad. I tried to warn him, but he doesn't believe me. He thinks I'm too young to understand such things. But it's obvious that she wants him in a bad way and would love to get me out of the picture."

Taye frowned. "Why would she want you out of the picture?"

"Because she doesn't like kids. She gave hers away to her ex-husband."

Taye nodded. "You think your dad likes her?" After she asked, she wished she hadn't.

Kennedy wrinkled her nose at such a notion. "No. I know for certain that he prefers not being bothered, but he's too nice of a man to tell her." Her eyes suddenly took on a mischievous glint. "Maybe you can help him out by pretending to be his girlfriend tomorrow, Aunt Taye."

Taye laughed. "Oh, Kennedy, I couldn't do something like that. Besides, I probably won't even see the lady."

"Oh, you'll see her all right. She'll probably break her neck coming across the street to check you out. Like I said, she has designs on Daddy real bad."

Taye couldn't help wondering if Michael had designs on the woman as well. But she found it hard to believe, especially if Mrs. Boykins didn't like children. She couldn't imagine him getting serious about anyone who would not accept his daughter. He loved Kennedy very much.

"And you really think I'll see her tomorrow?" Taye asked before biting into her pizza.

"It's a sure bet that you will, Aunt Taye."

Taye nodded. In that case, she couldn't wait to meet the man-hungry Mrs. Boykins.

CHAPTER 26

Just as Rae'jean poured the last of the coffee from the pot into the sink, the doorbell rang. Wondering who it could be, she placed the coffeepot on the counter and headed for the front of her apartment. When she opened the door she found Grady standing there.

"Grady? What are you doing here? Is something wrong?" Before he could respond, she asked in an alarmed voice, "Lynn?"

He gave her a reassuring smile. "No, nothing's wrong and Lynn's fine. May I come in?"

"Sure." She stepped back. After he entered, she motioned him to the sofa. "I would offer you some coffee, but I just poured out what was left from this morning. But I could make more if you——"

"No," he interrupted. "I'm fine. I don't plan on staying long. I left Candace at the hospital with Lynn."

Rae'jean nodded as she sat in the chair opposite him. Although she hadn't seen Grady's sister, she'd heard from Shawna that she'd arrived. "And how is Lynn doing?"

Grady leaned back against the sofa. "She's improved greatly. In fact, they plan on releasing her to go home tomorrow."

Rae'jean smiled. "Oh, Grady, that's wonderful. I know you must be happy about that." After a few moments of silence, she asked, "Why are you here, Grady?" His visit was unexpected, and she decided not to beat around the bush with small talk.

"I wanted to talk to you privately. To thank you."

Rae'jean shrugged. "You don't have anything to thank me for, Grady."

"Yes, I do. Because of you I was able to be honest with myself regarding my true feelings. They were deep-buried feelings I thought I had gotten over, but in essence I really hadn't." He released a long weary sigh. "I feel bad about us, Rae'jean, and wanted you to know it. I couldn't stand it if you thought I intentionally used you in any way."

His words were a painful reminder of the gossip floating around the hospital. Rumor had it that he had dropped her like a hot potato when he realized he was still in love with the woman he'd been engaged to marry three years ago. Rae'jean had only shaken her head when she heard it. Anyone who knew Grady, who really knew him, would realize that he wasn't capable of doing that sort of thing. He was too compassionate a person to intentionally use anyone.

"I don't think that, Grady, and if you're referring to the hospital gossip, don't waste your time worrying about it. People will say whatever they want to say. We can't stop them. But you and I know the truth. Things just didn't work out for us and we decided to end our engagement. It's as simple as that."

"I still care for you, Rae'jean," he said softly.

"And I still care for you, but not the way it's supposed to be, and we both know it. I can handle the gossip, so don't worry about me. I'm fine. What we shared was too precious to get tarnished by people who don't know what they're talking about."

Grady smiled faintly. "They don't know, do they?"

"No, they don't. I don't regret letting you be a part of my life, Grady. Nor will I ever. You are a very compassionate and giving person."

"And so are you." He hesitated briefly before adding, "And I know there is someone out there who will give you the kind of love you deserve, Rae'jean. I wish you all the happiness one person could possibly endure."

A lump tightened in her throat. "Thanks, Grady."

"I also hope things work out with your finding your father. I know I had misgivings about your need to locate him, but now, after discovering how delicate and fragile life can be, I think maybe you should look for him." Grady released a long deep breath. "I think you should do whatever makes you happy."

Rae'jean couldn't help wondering if finding her father would make her happy.

Grady rose from his seat. "I better go. I promised Candace I'd be back in an hour or so. Since Lynn is being released from the hospital tomorrow, Candace wants to get her apartment in order."

Rae'jean nodded as she stood. "Thanks for coming by, Grady. I think the best way to ward off any more gossip is for us to continue to be friends. In time the gossip will die down as long as we don't give anyone fuel to keep it going."

"I agree."

"And I think it would help if I were to drop by to see Lynn before she leaves the hospital. What do you think about that?"

He smiled. "I think that's a wonderful idea. I know she would love seeing you. I've told her everything. She knows you're the one who forced me to face my true feelings."

Rae'jean nodded. "Then it's settled. I'll make it a point to drop by and see her."

After Grady left, Rae'jean walked over to the window and looked out. She couldn't help wondering if perhaps he was right and she should try to locate her father. Like he said, life was too delicate and fragile. Besides, there was a part of her that needed to know more about the man who had fathered her other than the fact that he'd been a door-to-door insurance salesman at one time. What had he done over the past thirty years? Was he married? Did he have any other children? More important, was he even still alive?

Turning, she walked over to the table and picked up the phone book. She decided to make an appointment to see a private investigator, one who specialized in finding missing persons.

CHAPTER 27

"You're right on time, Taye. I'm glad to see you're dressed appropriately for what you'll be doing," Michael said, grinning, as he stepped aside to let her enter his home.

"Flattery won't get you anywhere, Michael Bennett. I should have my head examined for letting you talk me into this. Even Kennedy is questioning my sanity. However, I assured her that I could handle you, so don't think you'll be working me to death today," Taye said, smiling. She glanced around Michael's living room. When she'd driven up, the first thing she'd thought was that the place was huge. You could easily fit two of her homes into this large one. It sat on a hill and had a big, beautiful landscaped yard.

"Nice place you have here, Michael." It was evident he had hired an interior decorator. Everything looked chic, elegant, and expensive.

"Thanks. Come on; I'll give you a personal tour."

The tour started in the living room, and when they ended back there Taye was still in awe. Michael's house was large and spacious. It was definitely a dream home. She was happy about his success and told him so. He thanked her for it. While in his bedroom she couldn't help noticing a picture of a woman on his dresser. Since the same picture had been on Kennedy's dresser as well, Taye could only assume the woman in the picture was his late wife. She had refrained from asking him about it, but from what she saw, Lynda had been a very beautiful woman.

"Come on; let's go out back to the toolshed, where all my gardening supplies and equipment are located," Michael said, leading her through his kitchen and onto his back porch.

The backyard, Taye noted, was just as beautifully landscaped as the front. His enclosed pool looked inviting, and she knew that by the time she finished helping him with the yard she would be eager to find out just how inviting it was. After giving her a quick lesson on how to operate the riding mower, Michael placed a pair of work gloves in her hands with strict orders for her to use them. He also handed her a can of mosquito repellent and a big straw hat with orders that she use them as well.

First they started working in the backyard. Michael trimmed the hedges, raked up the leaves, and placed mulch around the flower beds while she mowed the grass. They worked together amicably for an hour or so, then went into the house to drink some iced tea before tackling the front yard.

"How are you holding up, kid?" Michael asked her as he stood across from her drinking iced tea.

"So far, so good, but then I had the easy job."

"Want to swap?"

She looked up at him over the rim of her glass and smiled. "Not on your life. You've spoiled me. I may never want to operate a push mower again. I'm going to look into purchasing a riding mower for myself. It even seems safe for the girls to handle."

Michael returned Taye's smile. "It is. I let Kennedy drive it sometimes. Like you, she's soft."

Taye tried to put a frown on her face but failed when she couldn't keep from grinning. "Who's soft? I'd like you to know, Michael Bennett, that I'm made of some pretty sturdy stuff. All Bennetts are."

Michael shook his head, smiling. "True. Are you ready to tackle the front yard now?"

"Ready when you are. I just need to use the bathroom first."

After Taye disappeared around the corner where one of his bathrooms was located, Michael leaned against the counter and released a deep sigh. Boy, did she look good. She had shown up wearing a T-shirt, cutoff jeans, and tennis shoes and socks on her feet. Today she looked younger than her thirty years, but her looks weren't what had held his attention while they worked in the backyard. Taye Bennett was built. She had enough curves

to make the Indy Speedway jealous. The cutoffs she wore hugged her behind in a way that made one think the shorts had been designed especially
for her backside. When she had gotten off the mower to lean over to move
an object out of her way, he'd almost swallowed his tongue when he got
a pretty nice view of her curvy bottom. He closed his eyes, forcing his
mind not to go there. He had to remind himself what his and Taye's relationship was. She had a way of making him forget they were family. But
then, another part of his brain forced him to accept that they weren't actually family, at least not blood relatives.

He shook his head. It was hard to believe her daughter's claim that Taye
did not have a boyfriend. Single women who looked like she did had men
pursuing them in droves. So whoever the lucky guy was, for some reason
she had him tucked away from her daughters if they really thought she
wasn't involved with anyone.

"I'm ready, Michael."

He glanced up to see her reenter his kitchen. "All right, let's go. The
front yard awaits us."

After Taye and Michael had spent a couple of hours working in the front
yard, Kennedy's prediction came true. Taye sat on the riding mower and
watched as a woman hurriedly crossed the street. Michael, she noted, saw
her approach the same time she did, and a grim and annoyed expression
appeared on his face. So this was the man-hungry Mrs. Boykins.

"You're about to have company, Michael," Taye said, trying to keep a
straight face and hide the grin in her voice.

Michael picked up on it anyway. His face spread into a thin-lipped smile.
"That's my neighbor, Marcella Boykins. Sometimes I think she's on a man-
hunt for husband number four." He chuckled. "Maybe if we ignore her
she'll go away."

Taye doubted it. The woman appeared to have a determined look on
her face and walked with a purpose, boppin' her way toward them. As she
came closer, Taye noticed that she appeared to be in her late thirties or
possibly her early forties. As much as she might try, there were some things
a woman just couldn't hide. Wrinkles were one of them. But then, Taye
had to concede, the woman had very few and actually looked good for her

age, in both her body and her face. And it was obvious she didn't mind flaunting that fact. The makeup made her features appear almost flawless, and she was wearing a halter top and a pair of shorts that would make Daisy Duke look tame.

Taye got off the mower and walked over to Michael's side where he had stopped trimming the hedges. "If the two of you plan on having a private conversation, Michael, I can always go inside the house until she leaves," Taye whispered, easing a grin up at him.

"Don't you dare. Keep your butt right here. Just follow my lead. I thought of a way to finally get rid of her once and for all."

Taye looked up at him. "What way is that?"

"I'm going to pretend you're my lover. If she thinks I'm involved with someone maybe she'll back off and go hunting elsewhere."

Taye nodded, deciding not to tell Michael that Kennedy had come up with the same plan. He might not appreciate the fact that Kennedy had discussed his man-hungry neighbor with her. "Don't be surprised if it doesn't work. Some women thrive on competition."

Before Michael could respond, Marcella Boykins walked up to them. "Hi, Michael. I couldn't help but see you over here working," the woman said cheerfully to him but cutting her eyes at Taye, giving her a thorough once-over.

"Yes, I am," Michael said, smiling. Taye could tell it was a supreme effort for him to do so. Any prior thoughts she'd had that he may be interested in the woman got blown out of the water with his forced smile.

Not waiting to be introduced, the woman offered Taye her hand and said, "I'm Marcella Boykins, Michael's neighbor."

Taye took the hand obligingly. "I'm Taye Bennett."

The woman lifted a brow. "Bennett?" She looked from Taye to Michael. "You're related?"

Michael chuckled, apparently enjoying the woman's confusion at his and Taye's same last name. "No, we're not," he lied easily.

"But the two of you have the same last names."

"Purely coincidental," Michael said quickly, bringing Taye closer to his side and wrapping his arms firmly around her waist. "Taye and I are friends." He leaned over and began placing kisses on Taye's throat before adding, "We're very *close* friends."

"Oh, I see," the woman said in a cutting voice.

Taye lifted a brow and wondered if the woman really did see, and if she did, she hoped Marcella Boykins would go back across the street as soon as possible. Taye was having a hard time standing on both her legs. The feel of Michael's lips on her throat had her weak in the knees and made the muscles in her thighs vibrate. And if that wasn't bad enough, the feel of his arms around her waist was sending ripples of pleasure up her spine. "Marcella," she eased out slowly as she tried to breathe properly. "It's nice meeting you."

"Will you be visiting Michael often?" Marcella Boykins asked boldly when Michael leaned over and nuzzled the side of Taye's neck.

Taye somehow gathered her scattered wits and answered as she tried to ignore the warmth that was working its way through her body. "Mmm, yes. This will probably become my second home, so you can expect me to pop over anytime."

"How nice," Marcella replied with a slight chill in her voice.

Taye was tempted to tell the woman she didn't know the half of it. With the feel of Michael's hand around her waist, slightly stroking her on the side, she thought that if things got any nicer she would be tempted to stretch out on the grass and pull Michael down with her. She was getting just that turned on from his touch.

"Taye and I need to get back to what we were doing," Michael said, ignoring Marcella's frown. "We want to finish up out here so we can enjoy the rest of the afternoon. We've made plans for later."

Marcella nodded. "Where's Kennedy?"

"She's visiting friends for the weekend," Michael answered casually. He smiled. "Why did you ask? Do you need her for something?" He knew that wasn't the case since the woman wasn't overly fond of children. Not even her own.

"No, I was just wondering. Well, good-bye, and it was nice meeting you, Taye."

Michael and Taye watched as Marcella Boykins hurried back across the street.

"Well, hopefully that took care of that," Michael said as a broad grin split his face. He slowly removed his arms from around Taye's waist. "Come on; let's wrap things up so we can take that swim. I think I need it."

Taye nodded and walked back over to the mower thinking that at the moment she needed a cool dip a lot more than he did.

Taye sipped her ice-cold Pepsi and tried to act nonchalant as Michael removed his shirt and dropped his pants. But the moment he stood before the pool's edge wearing the sexiest pair of swimming trunks she had ever seen on a man, her breath caught and she thought it would be best to avert her gaze and concentrate on something else. So she studied the patio furniture around the pool and the pretty tile on the floor. It was only after hearing him dive into the water that she returned her attention to him.

"It feels good in here, Taye. When are you coming in?" Michael called out to her.

"In a minute," she replied, taking another sip of her cold drink. She tried being nonchalant again, but when Michael began doing breaststrokes across the pool, showing strong, muscular shoulders, Taye felt her body heat up just from watching him expertly maneuver through the water. The shimmering coolness of the pool looked extremely inviting. Thinking she should stop being a coward and join him, she stood and removed her top and quickly took off her shorts.

"Nice bathing suit, Taye."

She glanced up and saw Michael had stopped swimming and was studying her two-piece bathing suit. "Thanks." After removing her sandals she walked over the pool and said, "Ready or not, here I come. Catch me if you can." She then dived into the pool with him.

Michael caught her in his arms, laughing. "Nice catch," he said, slowly releasing her. "Come on; let's do a couple of breaststrokes. I want to see if you remember what I taught you."

Taye grinned. "That's right. You're the one who taught me, Alexia, and Rae'jean how to swim, aren't you?"

"Yeah, so let's see if those lessons paid off."

Together they swam several lazy laps before deciding to test their skill in the water by racing from one side of the pool to the other. Of course Michael won the races, since he was an expert swimmer and she barely found time to get in a pool these days.

"So, how did I do with the breaststrokes?" she asked him later, after they had moved to stand in the shallow end.

"Not bad, but you need to relax more. Your shoulders were kind of tense."

Taye was tempted to tell him that wasn't all about her that was tense. Before she realized what he had planned to do, Michael had turned her around and had moved behind her. He placed his hands on her shoulders, gently rubbing them. The sensation of his touch almost shot her out of the water.

"Relax, Taye," he leaned over and whispered close to her ear as he continued to rub her shoulders. He pressed himself closer to her back as he tried stroking away the tightness in her shoulders.

Taye forced herself to relax, but it wasn't easy. He was standing so close she could feel the front of his legs touch the back of hers. So close she could feel the hardness of his body touch hers. The feel of his hands on her shoulders was incredibly soft and gentle, she thought. As well as mind-blowingly erotic.

"Are your shoulders feeling better?" he asked softly near her ear.

"Mmmm," she said, unable to say anything else.

He took that for a yes. "Good. Tonight, before you go to bed, you may want to rub your body down with some type of liniment. It endured a lot of physical exertion today."

Not as much as I wished it could have, Taye thought and then was surprised she had thought such a thing. In the last ten years she had seldom given thought to making out with a man. But Michael's touch was making it hard for her not to think about it.

"Come on," Michael said, lifting her into his arms and sitting her on the side of the pool. "I think we've played in the water enough for now. It's time to feed you. You must be starving."

Taye nodded. She was tempted to tell him that she was starving all right, but food wasn't what she needed to appease the gnawing hunger embedded deep within her body.

Taye pushed back her plate. "That sandwich was good, Michael. It was so good it makes you want to reach out and slap somebody."

Michael laughed. "Sounds like you've been hanging around your teen-age daughter too long."

Taye smiled, shaking her head. "Yes, I guess I have. Where these kids come up with this stuff I'll never know."

"Probably the same place we came up with it. We had some pretty crazy sayings ourselves."

Taye nodded in agreement. "Yeah, we did, didn't we?" She took a sip of her iced tea as she watched Michael over the rim of her glass. They were sitting on the patio near the pool. He had fixed sandwiches, cooked French fries, and made more iced tea. "You're an efficient father, Michael. At least I don't have to worry about Kennedy starving."

He chuckled. "I make do." The amusement suddenly left his face. "After Lynda died I had to. Kennedy was mine and Lynda had left her in my care. She was the only thing of her mother I had left. That's probably why I'm so protective with her."

Taye reached out and touched his arm. "That's understandable, Michael." She had heard so much love in his voice when he spoke of his wife. She'd also heard his pain. "Tell me about her," she said, removing her hand from his arm and sitting back in her chair.

Michael lifted his gaze to hers. "About Lynda?"

"Yes. I never got the chance to meet her. None of us did. I know Alexia and Rae'jean went to the funeral, but I couldn't make it at the time. Both Monica and Sebrina had come down with the chicken pox."

Michael nodded. "I understand you couldn't make it. That's OK. To tell you the truth, I don't recall who was there that day and who wasn't. I was just that torn up. The only thing that kept me sane was Kennedy. Without her I would have lost it. I loved Lynda just that much."

Taye leaned her head back and gazed into his eyes. "How did you meet her?"

Slowly Michael submerged himself into pleasant memories. "In Japan. She was a navy nurse working in one of the hospitals there. It was love at first sight. She was such a good person. An honest person. You would have liked her. The entire family would have. Now I regret not bringing her home to meet everyone, but at the time I was having a rough time dealing with the fact that I'd been adopted."

Taye took a sip of her drink before asking, "When did you find out?"

"When it was time for me to report for duty. One of the things Uncle Sam needed was my birth certificate. Since the fire that killed my parents destroyed all their important papers as well, I ordered a duplicate. It came a few days before I was due to leave. That's when I found out, and I had a hard time handling it. Instead of being grateful that I was raised by two loving people and had grown up as part of a wonderful loving family, I felt resentment that I hadn't been told the truth. Then, to make matters worse, I felt I wasn't worthy to be called a Bennett."

His words surprised Taye. "Why would you feel that way?"

He met her gaze intently. "Because I realized I wasn't a Bennett by blood and to me that was the one thing I had to deal with, to come to terms with."

"And have you?"

"Yes. The Bennetts are a very special group of people. When they love, they love deeply and nothing can change that, and when they accept you as one of their own, it's final, complete." He leaned back in his chair. "They've accepted me, always have and always will. I can't ask for more than that. I'm a Bennett. Maybe not by blood but in all the ways that count. Family loyalty. Family love. Family honor. Family unity. If I ever had any doubt of that, things were brought back home for me at the family reunion. Once a Bennett, always a Bennett."

"True." Taye took another sip of her tea before saying, "But we're not perfect people, Michael, although there are some Bennetts who actually think they are. We've all made mistakes. Heaven knows I've made my share."

"The girls?"

Taye looked at him and smiled. "I don't think of them as mistakes anymore, Michael. I think of them as blessings."

"And you should."

"Yeah, but the mistakes were made in putting my trust in men who I thought cared for me. I should have known better after being exposed to Uncle Victor's and Victor Junior's womanizing ways." She tilted her head to the side. "I should have been smart enough to know a man can say, 'I love you,' and mean nothing by it."

Michael nodded, hearing the hurt and pain in her voice. After a few silent moments, he said, "Tell me about them, Taye. Tell me about the girls' fathers."

Taye glanced up at him. His request was really no different from the one she'd made of him to tell her about Lynda. "Sebrina's father is a guy I met my first semester in college. I was unprepared for the likes of him. I was barely seventeen and a freshman and he was a twenty-one-year-old senior looking for a conquest and I was game. We used protection, but somehow I got pregnant anyway. Go figure that we would be in that slight percentage of failure. I returned home that first semester from school feeling I had let the whole family down. I was supposed to be the smart one, but what I did was truly dumb. The family had high aspirations for me to make it to the top, and I felt I had failed them. That was a big burden for me to deal with. If it wasn't for Gramma Idella, Alexia, Rae'jean, and Sharon, I probably would have gone off the deep end. Momma placed a guilt trip on me like you wouldn't believe. And when Cousin Priscilla's daughter got pregnant in her junior year of high school, Momma actually accused me of being responsible because I hadn't set a good example for my younger cousins to follow. Can you believe that?"

Michael chuckled. "Knowing Aunt Otha Mae, I can believe anything. She gets carried away at times."

Taye shook her head. "That's an understatement."

Michael took a sip of his drink. "What about Sebrina's father? Do the two of you stay in touch?"

"Yes. Gary plays an important part in Sebrina's life, although he lives in New Jersey. He did own up to being her father and even wanted to give her his last name, but I wouldn't let him. If my last name was going to be Bennett, so was hers. At first he didn't like it, but he eventually came around, since he had no intentions of marrying me and changing my name just to make his daughter legit. I have to admit he does well by her. His parents are pretty well off, and they simply adore Sebrina. She's their only grandchild. She goes to visit her father and grandparents every summer. According to her, Gary is getting married next month."

"How do you feel about that?"

"I'm happy for him. I realized long ago, even before Sebrina was born, that I never loved Gary. I was infatuated with him. I'm happy he's found someone."

Michael nodded. "What about Monica's father?"

Taye's hand stilled in reaching to pick up her glass of iced tea. The subject of Monica's father was one she'd always avoided with anyone, including her best friend, Sharon. The family had gotten upset with her because she'd refused to reveal his identity. And because of that, they'd had their suspicions that he was a married man. Which he was. But what they didn't know was that she hadn't known he had a wife. For a long time she'd felt degraded and used.

She sighed, not wanting to discuss the subject of Monica's father but then feeling that with Michael she needed to. There had once been a time she had shared a lot with him, and now that he was back in her life she could use another ear to listen, someone to understand. When it came to the subject of Monica's father, Sharon was not the least bit objective.

"Monica's father is a married man, Michael. But I didn't know it at the time. He was living a double life. It was only after I'd gotten pregnant and told him that he told me the truth and that there was no way he could marry me because he was already married. He even went so far as to say his wife had told him that morning that *she* was pregnant. You can't know how I felt, knowing that not only had he betrayed me, but he had betrayed his wife as well, not to mention that he'd been sleeping with the both of us. That was ten years ago. Although he lives here in Atlanta, I've only run into him a few times."

"He hasn't ever done anything for Monica?"

"No. I didn't ask and he didn't volunteer. I guess you could say that I gave him the easy way out, but that's coming to an end soon, not that I want anything from him financially. Monica has begun asking questions about her father. I have a feeling that in time she'll want to know who he is, and I plan on telling her the truth. I'm going to meet with him sometime in the near future and let him know that my days of protecting him are over. I don't want Monica to go through what Rae'jean is going through now, agonizing over the identity of her father. She has a right to know."

"I think you'll be doing the right thing."

"Thanks, Michael. I don't know how he's going to handle it. My telling

Monica about him will force him to tell his wife he has an outside child. He's not going to like that too much, since he's kept things well hidden for ten years."

"Do you think he'll deny being her father?"

"He might, but it will be a losing battle, since blood tests can prove otherwise. Besides, I got pictures taken of us together during that time and letters he wrote me, supposedly when he was out of town on business, but he was actually right here in town sleeping with his wife. I hope he'll think twice before denying he's her father, because that will only hurt Monica."

Michael nodded. "Any man who fathers a child should own up to his responsibility." His head bowed for a few seconds before he met her gaze again. "What about now, Taye? Are you involved with anyone now?" he asked smoothly, with no expression on his face.

Taye met his eyes, deciding that she didn't want him to know that she hadn't dated anyone in over ten years. "No, I'm not currently seeing anyone. What about you?"

His dark eyes never left hers for an instant when he said, "No, I'm not seeing anyone, either. To be honest with you, I don't know how Kennedy would handle it if I were to began dating."

A probing query came into Taye's eyes with his words. "Are you saying you haven't dated at all since Lynda died six years ago?"

"Not openly. I was seeing someone for over four years, but our relationship was based on friendship and mutual need. We were close friends as well as lovers. She'd been abused by her ex-husband and didn't want a serious relationship, and I was trying to get over Lynda and didn't want anything serious, either. So, our relationship was built on that understanding and it worked out for us."

"Why didn't you see each other openly?"

"We preferred it that way. She's a flight attendant and we would only see each other and be together whenever we happened to fly together. That's the way we wanted things. Both of us liked our space."

"Your moving here ended things between you?"

"In a way, but things would have ended between us anyway. She met someone and fell in love."

Taye nodded. She tried not to feel resentment toward the woman who had been intimate with Michael for the last four years. "Do the two of you still keep in touch?"

"No, I'm officially out of her life. But I recently heard from a mutual friend that she's engaged to be married. I'm happy for her. She deserves all the happiness any one person can possibly receive. She's a very special person." Michael saw Taye's glass was empty. "Want some more iced tea?"

Taye shook her head. "No. In fact, it's about time for me to pick up the girls. We're going shopping and then later we're going to Fayrene's house for a cookout. Do you want to come along?"

"No. I'll give Kennedy her weekend without me underfoot. I'm going to relax and watch the ball game on television tonight. The Braves are playing."

Taye nodded as she stood. "Well, I'd better go. Thanks for having me over today, Michael."

He stood as well. "You're welcome to come over anytime. And thanks for your help with the yard, Taye. I enjoyed your company. It felt good to talk to someone."

She smiled up at him. "Same here, Michael. Same here."

CHAPTER 28

Alexia Bennett knew how to seduce a man. From the outfit she wore, a short black sexy, thin wisp of a dress, to the mouthwatering home-cooked meal she had prepared, she was ready to put her carefully orchestrated plan into motion. And to top things off, according to the chart she'd kept over the past few weeks that had recorded daily her body's temperature, tonight it would be at its hottest peak, which was the best time to conceive. All she needed was a virile, potent male partner, and Quinn Masters was her man.

The kiss they had shared two days ago had totally snapped her of control and still had her rocking and reeling and fighting to maintain her balance. A deep ache was radiating through her body just thinking about it.

Her experience with sensual desire was too extensive for her to have responded the way she'd done with a simple kiss. But the woman in her had to concede that there hadn't been anything simple about Quinn's sensuous onslaught on her mouth. For once she had lost control, and it wasn't supposed to be that way. There was never a time when she'd been kissed that she hadn't called the shots and set the pace, no matter how wondrous the pleasure. In Quinn's arms she had found herself letting go and wondering if she had truly ever been kissed before. His kiss had made every nerve ending in her body come alive. It had made her greedy for more and hungry for the taste of him.

Frustration and remembered desire had put her in a testy mood since then. At one point she had been tempted to call Quinn, make an excuse, and cancel her dinner invitation. But she had come too far to abandon her plans now due to a moment of weakness on her part.

Picking up the tray of deviled eggs, Alexia walked across the kitchen to the refrigerator and placed it inside. As she shut the refrigerator door the sound of the doorbell drew her attention. She hesitated for a second and took a deep breath. Her pulse began racing and a strange heat coursed through her body and settled dead center between her legs.

Those temperature charts were right. Her body was at its hottest.

Quinn stood back after ringing the doorbell of the spacious two-story home and waited with one hand shoved in the back pocket of his jeans while the other held an expensive bottle of wine. The house, he thought, like the woman living there, had style. Located in an upscale area of LA, where a number of other entertainers, including Babyface Edmonds and Mariah Carey, made their homes, the yard was meticulously well kept, with an assortment of flowers in bloom.

He took several deep breaths when the door finally opened. The first thing he noticed about Alexia was that she was wearing her hair differently. Instead of the thick mass flowing freely around her face and down her shoulders, she had confined it by tying it back with some sort of band.

Then his gaze settled briefly on her face—beautiful as ever—before moving to concentrate on her outfit. He immediately felt his body respond. The dress, he thought, was sexy as hell. He blinked twice, making sure it was indeed a dress and not a slip. It was just that sheer. It hugged her curves, molded her breasts, and the thin T-straps teased her shoulders.

Quinn took another deep breath, wondering if this was how Alexia Bennett operated—draw a man in, make him want her to distraction, sink her claws deep into his skin before yanking them out and leaving her mark. Unconsciously he rubbed the skin of his unprotected arms before saying, "I like your outfit, Alexia."

Smiling, Alexia stepped aside to let him in. "I'm glad you do. It's one of my favorites. It's easy to get into and easy to get out of."

The heat in Quinn's veins turned his body to molten liquid with her words. His hold tightened on the bottle of wine in his hand as his gaze roamed over her. She had just created a disturbingly intimate scene in his mind.

"Won't you come in, Quinn?"

Crossing over the doorstep, Quinn entered, then turned and stared at Alexia for an endless moment. Their eyes locked. He thought there was something different about her tonight, other than the way she wore her hair. Not able to figure out what that difference was at the moment, he handed her the bottle of wine. "Good wine to go along with what I know will be a very good dinner."

Alexia accepted the bottle of wine from him. "Thanks, and I hope you're hungry. I've prepared a feast."

"Trust me. I'm ravenous. Nothing will go to waste."

Something in the way Quinn said those words and the look in his eyes when he said them made Alexia's stomach clench with the feeling that he was talking about tackling more than just food. At least she hoped so. It would make her job easier later, when she made her move. "Make yourself at home while I go into the kitchen and put the finishing touches on dinner."

"Need my help?"

"No, I can manage, but thanks for the offer." She turned and started walking toward the kitchen, feeling the intense heat of his gaze on the back of her legs and the thin material of her dress. She felt her insides get hotter and wondered how such a thing was possible. She was at a burning point already.

Quinn stood there, assessing Alexia's attire with lingering appreciation until she was no longer in sight. He'd felt himself getting hard just from looking at her long, shapely legs. And from the way the slinky thin material clung to her body he seriously doubted that she was wearing anything underneath. How on earth was he supposed to sit across from her at the dinner table knowing she was completely naked under that dress?

He shook his head, wondering what the deal was with her, then quickly decided that whatever it was, he was game, especially if it would allow him to delve into the recesses of her mind to see just what made her tick. He didn't want to depend on what he'd read in *Essence, People,* or *Ebony* magazine. He intended to explore every facet of her psyche for himself and get to know the real Alexia Bennett. He was determined to do whatever he could to get close to the woman he had fallen in love with. And from the look of that easy-in, easy-out dress she was wearing, she had her own set of plans for tonight. There was no doubt in his mind that she intended to seduce him. No sweat. He could handle anything she threw down, but if she thought he would let her treat him like a hit-and-run or a one-night stand, she was wrong.

Tonight she would discover that with him, she had finally met her match.

Purely in the interest of common sense had Alexia made the suggestion that Quinn make himself at home in the living room while she escaped to the kitchen. There was just so much temptation any woman could handle, and Quinn Masters was temptation with a capital *T*.

Reaching the kitchen, she glanced at her watch. If dinner progressed at a leisurely pace, followed by certain events she planned on initiating, she and Quinn could be in bed by 8:00 P.M. and she could be pregnant by 9:00. She figured a second round of hot and heavy lovemaking by 10:00 would assure an accurate hit.

Alexia released a deep sigh. She wondered how Quinn would feel if he knew that his body would be used tonight as a baby-making machine. She tried not to think about the fact that she would be using him. After all, she planned to make it worth his while by making sure he got a good lay out of it. And if he ever discovered he was her baby's daddy, at least it wouldn't put a dent in his lifestyle, since she wouldn't be asking him to contribute anything for child support.

She took a deep breath and conceded that if committing herself, body and soul, to any man weren't so terribly wrong for her, Quinn Masters would be perfect in every way. It was too bad she wasn't interested in an affair. All she wanted from him was a baby. There was more chemistry flowing between them than there was in the science department at UCLA. Feeling hot thinking about all that snap, crackle, and pop, she tried recovering by turning to the sink and getting a glass of cool tap water. The intense heat between her legs that had intensified the moment she opened the door for Quinn would be better served later in bed.

Seeing him dressed in a polo shirt and a pair of tight jeans had caused goose bumps to form on her arms and legs. She took another swallow of cool water to get a grip. From the way hot passion was simmering inside of her, getting pregnant would be quick and easy.

She sighed. Dinner was ready, and unknown to Quinn, he would be the main course.

Quinn strolled around Alexia's living room trying to concentrate on all the things he saw, nice furniture, including a large oak bookcase, and a collection of every Diana Ross CD, album, and cassette you could imagine. He smiled. Like him, Alexia was a die-hard Diana Ross fan. Imagine that.

He then walked over to the bookcase. The tall shelves were lined with a wide array of books. Most of the volumes were works by African-American authors. Like him she also liked to read. Another coincidence.

He turned and noticed the huge photo album sitting on a table. Curiosity made him pick it up, and he began browsing through it.

"Those pictures are from my family reunion."

He looked up. Alexia had reentered the room. Because she had removed her sandals, the plush carpeting had silenced her entrance. "There are a lot of pictures in here," he said as he sat down on the sofa with the album in his hand. "Come sit beside me and tell me what I'm looking at."

Alexia wasn't sure sitting next to Quinn on the sofa was a good idea, especially before dinner. According to a book she'd recently read, *Pregnancy Made Easy,* a man's sperm count and sex drive automatically increased after he ate certain foods. Although she didn't have any fresh raw oysters to feed him, she had made a tray of deviled eggs, since the book claimed boiled eggs served the same purpose. Pleased that she was back in command of the situation, she walked over and sat down next to him on the sofa.

Quinn nearly forgot to breathe when Alexia came and sat next to him. He watched as she slipped her fingers beneath the cover to open the album. He immediately thought that she had nice hands. He could just imagine them on him, touching, rubbing, stroking . . .

"This is a family picture of everyone," she said, claiming his attention by pointing to the first picture she came to in the album. "This is my grandfather, Poppa Ethan. These are my parents, and these are my cousins Taye, Rae'jean, and Michael."

Quinn nodded as he concentrated on the face of the man she'd said was her grandfather. "How old is he?"

"Poppa Ethan will be turning ninety years old in a few months, but he still has a strong mind and gets around OK. My grandmother Idella died ten years ago."

"Were they still together when she died?"

Alexia lifted her head as if she found his question strange. "Of course. Gramma Idella and Poppa Ethan had been married nearly sixty years when she passed. They got married when she was only sixteen and he was twenty. They shared a good life together raising their six kids."

She sat back as she looked back down at her grandfather's picture. Her expression reflected a mixture of treasured memories, both happy and sad ones. "They were so close that we didn't think he would live long after her. I've heard of that happening when two people have been married for a long time and one of them dies. Often the other one gives up all hope for living."

"Long marriages run in your family?" he asked after they had looked at a few more pictures and she had mentioned that all her relatives, except for a womanizing uncle and his chip-off-the-old-block son, were married to their original partners.

She shrugged, thinking of her own short-lived marriage. "There probably aren't any more in our families than in others."

"I happen to disagree. My maternal grandparents are deceased, but my paternal grandparents are still alive. My grandmother is on her third husband, and my grandfather is on his fourth wife. And I don't know but one or two of my uncles who are still married to their original partner. The others are working on their second or third marriage. That's why my generation of Masterses have vowed not to marry until they're sure they've found the perfect mate."

Alexia's eyebrow shot up. "There's no way anyone can ever be sure of that."

"True, but we intend to try. That's why we're committed to finding our chosen one and not rushing into marriage until we do. So far it's worked. There hasn't been a divorce in the Masters family in over fifteen years."

She lifted her eyes to his. Since she knew for a fact she wasn't any man's "chosen one," she felt pretty safe. But still . . . "You're not interested in a serious relationship with anyone right now, are you?" she asked to be absolutely sure.

Quinn met her gaze. He knew why she was asking. If for one minute she thought he wanted a serious relationship with her, she'd probably not see him again. Therefore, his answer could not reflect the complete truth. There was no way he could tell her that she was the woman he intended to marry. He was more than willing to patiently wait for her to come around to his way of thinking. "No, not right now I'm not. However, although I'm not interested in a serious relationship, I do prefer dealing with committed relationships. They're safer. It's suicide for any single person to do it any other way. I wouldn't want the woman I'm sleeping with to also be sleeping with other men. Having multiple bed partners these days is dangerous."

Alexia nodded in agreement. She'd always had a policy of not being involved with more than one man at a time. It had also been a policy of hers to spell out their relationship up front. It ended whenever she decided to end it with no questions asked. The only reason she hadn't felt the need to give Quinn her spiel was because with him she was on a mission. She had an ultimate goal she intended to complete.

She closed the album. "We'll finish looking at this after dinner," she said, placing it back on the table. "Will you help me set the table?"

Quinn smiled. "I'd love to."

Over dinner they talked about anything that came to mind. His work. Hers. Their families. He told her about his sister's wedding, and she told him more about the family reunion.

Alexia shared with him information about Taye, Rae'jean, and Michael and how close they'd been growing up.

"You're very dedicated to your family, aren't you?" Quinn asked after devouring another deviled egg.

Alexia smiled, pleased. He had eaten half a dozen of the deviled eggs already. He should be good and potent by now. "I am now that I've taught some of them not to ask me for anything that has to do with money. When I began making the charts I had some family members—not even the real close ones—call me whenever they got behind in their bills, like I was the family bank or something."

He chuckled. "There are those kinds in every family. But weren't you always close to your family?"

Alexia leaned back in her chair. If she told him what he wanted to know, it would be the very first time she had shared such deep inner thoughts with anyone other than Taye, Rae'jean, and Michael. But for some reason she felt comfortable in sharing them with Quinn. He had that persona about him. He was an easy person to talk to. "No, not really. I was a big disappointment to my family."

Quinn frowned. "In what way?"

Alexia's throat tightened. Her chest burned at the childhood memories. She swallowed, willing her throat muscles to relax, and took a deep calming breath to ease the burning sensation away from her chest. "Rae'jean was always the pretty one, and if you ever saw her you'd see why. She's totally gorgeous. Those pictures I showed you of her don't do justice. While we were growing up everyone doted on her, understandably so."

Quinn nodded but said nothing.

"Taye," Alexia continued, "was always the smart one. She was so smart the school officials skipped her a grade. She graduated from high school at sixteen. Taye's a born mathematician and can add, subtract, multiply, and divide in her head like nobody's business. She has a memory out of this world and could ace any test the teacher gave her."

Quinn considered everything she had told him so far before saying, "You still haven't explained why you think you were a disappointment to your family."

With a voice a bit unsteady, Alexia said, "I was the darkest Bennett ever to be born. Besides that, I was overweight, had unruly hair, crooked teeth, and at times I was rather clumsy. I was considered the ugly duckling in the family."

Quinn shot her a disbelieving look as he concentrated on her beautiful dark skin, gorgeous figure, a nice set of straight white teeth covered by full, sensuous lips, and the mass of flowing hair on her head that made her look downright sexy. She was definitely a good-looking woman. He looked at her and saw the seriousness of her expression. "You're joking about being considered ugly, aren't you?"

She met his gaze. "No. As a child I constantly heard I wasn't attractive enough to ever amount to much."

"People would actually tell you that?"

"Not to my face. The conversations were always meant to go over my head or were supposed to be spoken when I wasn't around." She exhaled a long breath. "They didn't mean to be cruel, but constantly hearing those things kept me pretty sensitive, and hearing them didn't do a whole lot for my self-esteem. If it wasn't for my grandparents, my parents, Taye, Rae'jean, and Michael, I probably would have grown up with some sort of complex about the way I looked. Thank God for Weight Watchers, braces, and for a hairstylist who worked wonders with hair. And as far as being dark, black is beautiful, isn't it?"

Quinn pushed his chair back and stood. He walked slowly over to her and gently pulled her from her chair and into his arms. He was thankful there had been others around to make her believe in herself. He couldn't imagine anyone being cruel enough to say such things around a child. And these were people who'd been members of her family. "Yes, black is beautiful, and you are the most beautiful woman I've ever seen, Alexia."

She tried to laugh against his shoulder. She didn't want his pity. She didn't want anything from him. But still, being held in his arms felt good. She blinked the tears from her eyes, wondering why she had told Quinn about that part of her childhood. It wasn't that they were close friends, lovers, or anything. Why did she feel he was someone she could bare her inner soul to? Why was it so hard to stay on her toes around him, to stay in control?

Although she liked the feel of him holding her, she knew she could never let herself get close to any man. She pulled back out of his arms. "How about if you go on into the living room and resume looking at the photo album. I'll rejoin you as soon as I clear the table."

"I'll be glad to help—"

"No. I prefer doing it myself."

He studied her face. "Are you OK?"

She forced a smile up at him. She didn't think she could ever really be

OK around him. He had a way of messing with her mind, big-time. "Yeah, I'm OK."

He nodded before turning to walk out of the kitchen.

As soon as he was gone Alexia began clearing off the table. Her movements were slow, thoughtful. When the dishes began to shake in her hands, she immediately set them back down on the table. Sighing, she wrapped her arms around her waist, trembling. When she had come up with the plan to get pregnant, things were supposed to be simple, easy, uncomplicated. But Quinn was making things pretty damn difficult. She was letting him get too close. Way too close.

She was doing something she swore that she would never do, and that was let a man get the upper hand with her again.

CHAPTER 29

When Alexia joined Quinn in the living room, she squared her shoulders, mustered a bright smile, and walked over and sat next to him on the sofa. For the next ten minutes or so he turned the pages while she told him about the rest of the pictures that had been taken at her family reunion. After they had looked at the last photo he placed the album back on the table, then sank lower on the sofa and stretched his legs out before him. He began talking, telling her about a particular case he was working on, one involving a client who wanted her prenuptial agreement declared invalid.

"I thought a prenuptial was ironclad."

He shook his head, smiling. "A number of people think that. However, as with anything else, exceptions can be made, especially if the behavior of one of the individuals comes into play. In certain situations, a prenuptial agreement can be overturned."

Alexia tried not to analyze Quinn's features while he spoke but couldn't help doing so. Not only did she enjoy looking at him; she enjoyed listening to him as well. His voice was deep, rough, sexy. The sound of it made her insides tingle. She could just imagine how it would be to wake up to the sensuous sound of it each and every morning. While he continued talking, her eyes skimmed over his chest. She wondered if he had a hairy chest and if so, how her naked breasts would feel rubbing against it. Her gaze then moved to his lap. The thighs she saw covered in denim seemed strong, firm with sinewed strength. She thought about straddling those thighs while they were completely naked with his hands guiding her movements over him as she rode him in sure strokes, moving up and down, forcing him to climax inside of her as she ground herself more tightly against him, taking his seed into her womb.

"Alexia?"

The deep, sexy sound of Quinn's voice reclaimed her attention as it drifted over her. She raised her gaze and saw the eyes watching her were compelling, magnetic. She sucked in a deep breath when she also saw they were smoldering with fiery desire.

Their gazes held. Neither could look away. The room was quiet except for the shallow sound of their breathing. Then, as if he had been privy to her earlier thoughts, he reached over and lifted her onto his lap to straddle him. As he framed her face in his hands, his mouth hungrily covered hers. Greedily devouring her, more so than it had the other day.

She was not prepared for the magnitude of his kiss as his lips took complete possession, nibbling and sucking while arousing her to a feverish peak and sending new spirals of ecstasy through her. It made her body ache even more. He continued kissing her as his hands moved downward to lift her dress up to her waist.

Quinn moved his legs, stretching them apart and, in doing so, spreading hers wide open and getting easy access to the very heat of her. His mouth remained locked to hers as his hand slid under her dress, not surprised to discover she wasn't wearing any underwear. His fingers immediately went to work to explore, to touch, and to claim the heart of her sex.

When her body jerked from the sensation of his fingers' intimate touch, his mouth gentled her by his constant assault on hers, savoring every moment doing so, hungrily devouring her tongue, swallowing her sighs and moans of pleasure.

When Alexia felt herself succumbing to the domination and skill of his mouth, she pulled away, braced her hands on his shoulders while her head fell forward, limp with desire, on his chest. Currents raced through her body the likes of which she had never felt before. He was relentless in what he was doing to her. The pad of his thumb continued to stroke her, demanding her readiness. Her fingers dug into his shoulders, holding on as she abandoned herself to the sensations he was making her feel, sweetly draining all of her fears, doubts, and resistance and making her forget about her well-orchestrated plan. Even that couldn't compete against this uncontrollable passion and this intoxicating need.

No man had ever touched her so boldly, to the core, branding her sex his, making it crave his touch. And no man had ever made her moan aloud in sexual pleasure. His fingers were tearing away any self-control she may have had. They were tearing away any walls of resistance she may have erected. She felt some sort of rebirth, purely physical, emotionally uplifting. She felt her body getting hotter and wondered if he could feel her heat.

Quinn did feel her heat and gloried in it. He was staking his own claim to her body and, by slow degree, setting in place the groundwork for a future he intended to have with her. He loved her totally, completely, not just physically. But if physical loving was what he needed to start with, then he would. He was willing to do whatever it took. And in time, with love and patience, he intended to give her everything she deserved. She was definitely a woman worth loving and cherishing. And he wanted all of her.

When he felt her nick his shoulder with her teeth he decided it was time to give her what they both wanted. He removed his hand from beneath her dress, and in one fluid motion he lifted her dress over her head and tossed it to the floor.

Easy on. Easy off. That was no lie. With her completely naked before him, his mouth immediately set upon her breasts. It latched onto a nipple and began teasing it with his tongue, nibbling sensuously with his teeth, then sucking gently with his lips.

Alexia nipped Quinn's shoulder again when his torment to her breasts became unbearable, making the burning hotness at her center blaze out of control. When he moved to the other nipple and began the same torment, she closed her eyes as pleasure, too rich, too potent, too arousing to deny, flooded her.

"Quinn . . . oh . . . oh . . . Quinn."

Upon hearing his name moaned so sweetly from her lips, Quinn felt his heart thump loudly in his chest. He removed his mouth from her breasts and went back to her mouth to kiss her deeply, hungrily, intimately. Moments later he broke off the kiss to whip his shirt over his head.

Before his shirt hit the floor Alexia had reached out to explore the mass of hair on his chest, the swell of his muscles, the force of his broad shoulders, and the sheer beauty of his upper body in the naked flesh. She leaned forward, inhaling his scent before lowering her mouth to his chest, latching onto a budding tip, and encircling it with her tongue. When he expelled a long, shuddering breath, her insides grew hotter at the sound. She then attacked the other budding tip and performed the same torment at the same time that her hands went to work at the snap and zipper of his jeans. She wanted to be skin-to-skin with him.

Quinn grabbed hold of Alexia's hips, lifting her, hauling her closer to his chest, and placing her legs high on his shoulders to hang over the top of the sofa. Her hot, moist feminine mound rubbed against the upper portion of his bare chest, branding him, while he lifted his own hips to tug down his jeans. Her female scent surrounded him, becoming entrenched in his skin. It was the scent of a woman in heat. It was the scent of a woman who was ready to mate. It was intoxicating, invigorating, stimulating.

"You smell good," he whispered as he brushed kisses around her navel, then moved lower, teasing and tasting before his hands gently pulled her back down his body to straddle him again. His erection was hard, poised, ready, between her thighs. Passion tore through the veins of his turgid hard shaft and its tip began to throb, eager to get inside of her and be released from the pulsing torment.

But first he knew what he had to do before he could think about easing into her heated moisture. He had to protect her against an unplanned pregnancy. "Alexia, I need to protect you, baby."

"No," she whispered, splashing kisses across his mouth and cheeks. She had gotten so caught up in the way he had made her feel that she had completely forgotten about her plans to get pregnant. She had gotten caught up in fulfilling another kind of need.

"Alexia?" His mouth stilled against her skin. Horizontal lines formed on Quinn's forehead as he met her gaze. "You're on some type of birth control?"

Instead of giving him an answer, she leaned down and captured his mouth with hers. She wanted him to forget about protecting her and just concentrate on pleasing her and letting her please him. No man had ever made her body this hot, this needy, this greedy. She thought she would die if he denied her the feel of the fluid heat from his groin shooting deep inside of her, thick, heavy, and mixing with her own juices in an unbridled force that she knew would give her the ultimate in sexual ecstasy.

She wanted all of him and she wanted him now.

She tried lowering herself down on his lap, closer to his aroused erection, but he caught her hips in his hand and held her immobile. She broke off their kiss and met his gaze. His face was damp with perspiration; his breathing was ragged, his eyes glazed with desire.

But still he held back.

Her breath caught in her throat as she wondered if he would deny her the very thing she wanted because she had not answered him regarding birth control. "Quinn?" His name was a choked whisper from her lips.

She felt him touch her intimately. His fingers moved inside her, arousing even more the satiny flesh within and driving her beyond delirium. He stilled his fingers. His eyes locked with hers. "This is mine. Say it." His voice was deep and husky as he staked his claim to that part of her body.

Alexia, frantic for the pleasure he could give her, chewed on her bottom lip as she held his gaze, knowing there was no way she would say those words. No man dared to make such a claim to any part of her—heart, body, or soul. "No, I can't," she whispered. "I won't."

A part of her couldn't believe he would suggest such a thing of her. No man had the right to expect anything from her other than what she wanted to give him. The thought that Quinn believed that he was somehow above any of the others angered her. She didn't need this. She didn't need any man *that* bad.

She lifted her hips to remove herself from his lap, then stopped. He *was* above any others. Hadn't she placed him there when she decided that he would be the father of her child? Hadn't she seen something in him that she hadn't seen in a lot of other men? Had felt it? Had sensed it?

She sighed deeply. She couldn't fight the deep longing, the fiery need he aroused within her. Nor could she deny it. What he was making her feel was beyond reason. He had her body burning for him. She closed her eyes to the fierce need escalating in her lower limbs, aching for the hardness of him to be inside of her. But she fought giving in to him and to his demand.

When she reopened her eyes there was a calculated look in them as she held his gaze. She was determined not to let him get the upper hand in this and decided to do something about it, even if it meant not playing fair. Slowly she eased downward, silencing his protests with her lips. When her moist heat grazed the tip of his erection, teasing, enticing, taunting, she held it there, waiting, feeling heat ripple through her as her wet mound hovered over him, hot, ready. She held that position, beckoning him to finish the task and sheath his burning shaft deep into the core of her. She felt the tip of his erection stir, get harder and hotter against the mouth of her womanly core.

But still he held back.

Quinn broke off their kiss. He was testing his will, his strength to endure. He was determined to be just as stubborn as she. "This is mine, Alexia," he whispered again, with a little more force while guiding himself a little more within her. "Say it!"

She closed her eyes and fought for control as she felt the fierce hardness of him fill her a little more than before. She reopened her eyes. "No!" But even as she said the words, she eased down just a fraction more, and her fingernails sank into his bare shoulders. She fought back the moan that threatened to pour forth from her throat. He was inside her now. Just barely. Not even halfway. All she had to do was inch down just a tad, flex her hips, and make their union complete. She inhaled deeply when she felt her wetness bathe the head of his erection. The air encompassing them began filling with the mounting, hot scent of sex.

The breath Quinn expelled was a shuddering one. He closed his eyes and threw his head back when he felt her slick wetness surrounding him, and felt her fingernails digging deep into his flesh. He fought to retain control of his mind and pride. He didn't want to take the little of herself she was offering him, which was all she had ever offered any man. She believed she had a divine right to do things her way or no way. Damn it, he wouldn't let her play around with his heart. He loved her too much, and she could destroy him if he were to let her. He refused to go through all that pain just to be her flavor of the month. Giving in to his pride . . . and his love, he opened his eyes and saw her watching him. Slowly he placed his hand under her hips to lift her off of him, to bring an end to his torture. To keep his pride he had to walk away, even if doing so killed him.

Seeing his intent and realizing what she was about to lose out on shocked Alexia into awareness, admission, and an acceptance. She did belong to Quinn. She belonged to him in a way she had never belonged to another man. No man had ever made her body feel the way he'd made it feel tonight. There was something about him. Something strong, elemental, that had drawn her to him from the beginning. Deep down she'd known it hadn't been all lust. And now, at this very moment, she was willing to let him lay claim to that part of her that he possessed already.

Before he could lift her up off of him, Alexia took matters into her own hands and pushed downward and took the full length of him inside of her, making their union complete, joining their bodies to the hilt as one. She tightened her hand on his shoulder to hold her body in place. The shock of what she had done made passion rip through the both of them. Her eyes flew to his, dark, guarded, tormented. Even now he still wanted to fight her. He still wanted to resist. There was nothing calculated in his actions, she suddenly realized. He was a man who possessed a deep sense of pride. Pride that she had tried stripping away from him. Pride he was fighting to hold onto.

"Quinn." She breathed his name and reached out and framed his face into her hands. She tightened her pelvic muscles to hold him with her body and whispered softly, "This *is* yours."

Like a tidal wave, the force of her words, her surrender, engulfed him. He suddenly surged up, and without disengaging their bodies, he flipped her on her back, stretched out on the sofa, and began moving in and out of her body, with long, deep strokes. The dam inside of him had broken and his floodwaters were filling her to satisfaction.

Alexia lifted her legs and wrapped them around his waist. She lifted her body to meet him stroke for stroke, getting caught up in the rhythm of his thrusts as he went deeper, making her feel she was a part of him and reinforcing the fact that this part of her did belong to him.

She closed her eyes and appreciated the fact that her sofa had good springs and a comfortable cushion, because Quinn wasn't letting up any. He was making love to her hard, fast, complete, pulling all the way out, then thrusting all the way in again. Every part of her body felt the impact as he claimed her with demanding mastery while relentlessly exploring the depths of her mouth, making love to it as well.

Moments later she broke her mouth free when she felt a tremor move through his body to hers, igniting every nerve within her. "Quinn!"

He lifted her hips to receive more of him, going deeper, feeling stronger, hotter. He met her gaze and before he could demand that she say the words again, she tightened her legs around him, demanding the same of him that he'd demanded of her. "This is mine! Say it!"

He gave her the words without hesitation as he pushed deeper inside of her. "This is yours."

Alexia wrapped her arms around him as her body accepted his words to be true. An idealistic calm settled over her.

But not for long. Every thrust he made into her body ensnared a piece of her soul.

The pace of Quinn's lovemaking increased, bursting an inner flame within her. She became swept away into the maelstrom he had created as he continued claiming her, consuming her until there was no way she could take any more. A deep guttural sound erupted from his throat at the same time a powerful climax slammed into the both of them. She felt the hot fiery release from his groin shoot deep into her womb, pouring into all depths of her body.

"Alexia!"

The explosion was powerful. It was earth-shattering. It rocketed them to heights they'd never imagined possible.

He pushed himself farther and farther inside of her, flooding her insides with the very essence of him. Her womb milked him for all it could get as the force of their orgasm propelled them into a world of incoherent passion.

When he had given her all that he could, he whispered her name one last time and wrapped her in his arms. Exhausted. Satisified. Complete.

"Tell me about him."

Eyes closed, Alexia lay under Quinn in contentment. Her body satiated, still panting and shuddering from what they had just shared. She rubbed her nose against his chest, inhaling his scent and the robust aroma of sex. It took all the strength she could muster to open her eyes and meet his gaze and ask, "Tell you about who?"

"The man who made you so distrustful of others," Quinn responded

230   BRENDA JACKSON

softly. "The man who's to blame for your always being on your guard and not wanting to share a long-term relationship with another man."

Alexia thought about Quinn's question for a moment, although the feel of his body still connected to hers made thinking about anything other than making love to him again a challenge. "Richmond Fulton wasn't anything spectacular," she tried to say lightly.

Quinn cupped her chin with his fingers when she tried looking away from him. "But you loved him."

She took a deep breath as she remembered just how much she had loved Richmond and how he had effectively destroyed that love. "Yes, I loved him."

"Then I want to know about him."

Alexia studied Quinn's features and was once again amazed at the extent of just how far he assumed he could go with her. The man was a tad bit arrogant, to say the least. But then she had to inwardly concede that she sort of liked his arrogance. No man had ever really stood up to her before. In the past after making love with a man she would immediately put distance between them, dismissing him from her thoughts as well as her bed and sending him on his way, real quick-like and in a hurry. None had ever given her any flack about it, not that it would have mattered if they had. Quinn, it seemed, came from a different breed of men. With him it was all or nothing. The man was artful when it came to getting what he wanted, but not in a manipulative kind of way. She supposed in his profession as an attorney he had to be sharp, shrewd, and clever. There was no doubt in her mind that she had definitely met her match with him.

Her thoughts drifted back to what he'd said. He wanted to know about Richmond. She had never discussed her marriage with any of her past lovers. But Quinn was asking her to do that very thing. He wanted her to open up to him.

"Why?" she finally asked. "Why do you want to know about my ex-husband?"

"So I can fully understand what I'm up against."

Alexia shifted and turned her head so she was no longer looking directly into Quinn's eyes. "You're not up against anything or anyone."

"I believe that I am."

Alexia snatched her gaze back to Quinn's, more than slightly irritated.

How could he think such a thing after what they had just shared? He practically had carte blanche to her body. "I don't understand why you'd feel that way. He means nothing to me anymore. He—"

"—hurt you, damn it."

Quinn's words ripped into her and she buried her face against his chest. She heard the anger in his voice and was overwhelmed at the thought that it was there for her. "Yes, he did hurt me," she admitted, whispering the words softly against his throat.

Moments passed before either of them spoke again.

"Alexia?"

She kept her face buried. "Yes?"

"I can't take away the pain he caused, but I can promise not to ever hurt you. Will you trust me on that?"

She raised her head and met his gaze. He was pushing too far, asking too much. "You're always demanding something of me," she snapped.

Her words drew a soft chuckle from Quinn's throat. "Yes, but only because I want what's best for you."

"And just what do you think is best for me?"

Quinn's gaze intensified as he looked at her. "I am," he whispered hoarsely before leaning down and capturing her mouth, branding it the way he had branded her body, making it his.

His kiss was everything she'd come to expect. It was intoxicating, exhilarating, and by the time he ended it, it had her body quivering in need, in desire.

Quinn pulled himself up and sat back on his haunches, looking down at Alexia. Reaching out, he let his hand drift over each and every part of her naked body that he had touched, had tasted. His eyes were locked on her face, watching her reaction to his touch. "Will you, Alexia? Will you trust me or at least try?"

Alexia was trembling, not only from the feel of his hands on her, but also from the way he was looking at her. There was an intensity in his gaze that almost took her breath away. "Why should I?" she asked, barely breathing out the words.

Quinn inhaled deeply. He could easily explain in just a few words that the reason she should trust him was because he loved her. Deeply, completely. But he knew she wasn't ready for something as heavy as that just yet. So instead he said words that he knew she could handle and would accept. "I want you to trust me because I want you. There's a lot of chemistry between us, too much to let go to waste. For the time we're together I don't want any misunderstandings between us. I have to know that you believe I won't deliberately hurt you and that you're safe with me. I won't let you put up your guard around me, and you can only let your guard down if you trust me. Will you trust me, Alexia?"

It was a long moment before she answered, "Yes."

Smiling, he reached out and stroked her cheek with his thumb before leaning down and sealing her mouth with his. Unknowingly she had also sealed their lives together. There was no way he would ever let her go. Like he'd said, he would prove that he would not hurt her, and in the process he would heal her heart of the pain her ex-husband had caused her. In time, she would discover she could love again, and he intended to be the man she loved. He was a patient man, but then he was also a persistent man. Already he had jumped two hurdles tonight in building a relationship with her. She had let him lay claim to her body, and now she'd agreed to let her guard down and trust him.

He broke off the kiss and gathered her into his arms, hugging her close. "I think it's time for us to go into the bedroom, don't you think?"

Alexia took a deep breath, then smiled up at him. "Definitely."

CHAPTER 30

Rae'jean chided herself for being nervous as she entered the Heritage Building. She had a one o'clock appointment with a private investigator who she hoped could locate her father.

Now that she'd made the decision to act, she should have been feeling calm, relaxed, less stressed. But the unknown had her tense. Was the man who had fathered her still alive? Would he want to see her? If he had known about her, then why hadn't he taken the initiative to find her? Locating her would not have been difficult, since he knew where her grandparents lived. She sighed deeply. And knowing that had been the hardest thing for her to swallow. He had not sought her out, which put niggling doubt in her mind that she was doing the right thing spending her money to find him.

She immediately crushed that thought. From the time she'd been old enough to understand that other kids had fathers and she didn't, she had wondered about him. Who was he? What did he look like? Why couldn't he be there with her and her mother?

Since her mother, nor any other family member for that matter, hadn't been willing to provide answers to her childhood inquiries, she'd grown up speculating, curious. Now she hoped, with Ryan Garrison's help, her speculation and curiosity would come to an end soon.

She had gotten Mr. Garrison's name out of the phone book. When she checked with Consumer Services it appeared he had an astounding record of success when it came to locating people. He'd been highly recommended. His former clients had only good things to say about his professionalism and his manner of getting the job done. From what she'd heard, he was a man of action. She only hoped he wasn't backed up with assignments and would be willing to take on her case.

Since today was her day off from the hospital, she was dressed more comfortably than usual, having chosen a slim calf-length printed skirt and a rib-fitting blouse. The sandals she wore she had purchased during her shopping spree while attending the family reunion. Alexia had seen them first, and the both of them had ended up buying a pair. They were cute as well as comfortable. Deciding she hadn't wanted to be bothered with her hair, she had swept the long strands up on her head in an elegant French twist.

Entering the main lobby of the building, she immediately went to the elevator. When the elevator door opened, she stepped inside. By the time she had reached her destination the nervousness returned. She shrugged, determined to go through with this.

It wasn't hard finding Mr. Garrison's office. His nameplate was big as day on his office door: RYAN J. GARRISON, PRIVATE INVESTIGATOR. Inhaling a deep breath, she opened the door and went inside. An older lady, who she assumed to be Mr. Garrison's secretary, was seated in the spacious and elaborately decorated outer office. The woman looked up upon hearing her approach. "Yes, may I help you?"

"Yes. I'm here to see Mr. Garrison. I have a one o'clock appointment. I'm Rae'jean Bennett."

The woman smiled. "Yes, Ms. Bennett. You're early. Mr. Garrison hasn't returned from lunch. Do you mind waiting?"

"No, not at all." Sitting in one of the chairs, she picked up the latest issue of *Black Enterprise* from off the table in front of her. She had read several of the articles by the time the secretary called her name to get her attention.

"Mr. Garrison just returned and I've told him you're here. He'll be out in a minute."

Rae'jean nodded. Since she was certain no one had come through the room where she'd been sitting for the last half hour, she could only assume there was a back door to Mr. Garrison's office. She returned her attention to the article she'd been reading.

Moments later when she heard the door to Mr. Garrison's office open, she lifted her head. As soon as she looked into the man's face, she was stunned. She blinked twice, then a third time, not believing who she saw. Walking toward her was the man who'd been her neighbor. The man she'd lusted after on many occasions.

She took a deep breath, forcing air into her lungs. From the look of it, Ryan Garrison was just as shocked to see her as she was to see him. He stopped his approach and stared at her.

Rae'jean took another deep breath, not knowing what to do. She noticed the secretary had stopped typing and was eyeing them with curiosity. Mr. Garrison noticed his employee's interest as well and cleared his throat. He then took the final steps over to her. He cleared his throat again. "Ms. Bennett?"

She could only nod as she got to her feet.

He offered her his hand. "I'm Ryan Garrison."

Rae'jean wasn't aware she had given him her hand until she felt it encompassed in the firm, warm strength of his. After he had released her hand it still tingled from his touch. She somehow found her voice and said shakily, "I'm Rae'jean Bennett and I have an appointment with you." For some reason she felt the need to explain why she was there.

A quick smile tugged at the corners of his mouth. "Would you come into my office?"

Rae'jean thought that as long as he continued talking to her in such a deep, sexy voice she would go just about anywhere with him. And his smile wasn't half-bad, either. She took another deep breath, forcing herself to get a grip. She didn't want to be any form of entertainment for Mr. Garrison's secretary, who was still watching them.

Adjusting the straps of her purse on her shoulder, Rae'jean allowed Ryan Garrison to escort her into his office. He closed the door behind them, shutting them off from the secretary's prying eyes.

"Please have a seat, Ms. Bennett."

She immediately took the seat he offered, not sure how much longer her legs would be able to support her. She had begun to feel them buckling under her the moment she saw just who Ryan Garrison was.

"Well then," he said, sitting at his desk in a chair directly across from her. "What can I do for you?"

Rae'jean met his gaze and thought his question was a loaded one, with numerous possibilities. Her heart began thumping wildly against her rib cage. She was reminded of the first time she had seen him when she'd stood at the window, watching him move into her apartment complex. There had been something about him that had drawn her to him even from two floors up and across the span of the parking lot. It had been something immediate, tangible, forceful.

Pretty much like right now.

She watched his eyes probe deep into hers and knew that, like her, he was remembering that day and was probably also remembering another time their paths had crossed. It had been the day she'd been rushing to work and had accidentally bumped into him. He had touched her to keep her from falling. That touch had seared her insides. It was a contact she could not forget.

And from the looks of it, neither could he.

"You're no longer wearing an engagement ring," Ryan Garrison said, lifting his brow questioningly.

His words, soft yet husky, filtered through the room. She was not surprised he had decided to clear the air by confronting the strong sexual attraction that neither of them could deny.

"I'm no longer engaged," she said as she continued to meet his gaze. "We decided to be just friends."

He nodded slowly as he continued to watch her through dark, intense eyes. "I liked him, your former fiancé."

Rae'jean raised a brow. "You know Grady?"

He shrugged. "Not on a personal level. I know that, like you, he's a doctor. We ran into each other on the elevator a few times when he was visiting you. He's a friendly person."

Rae'jean couldn't help smiling. That was Grady all right. "How did you know I was a doctor?"

He hesitated before answering, "I saw you leave the apartments a few times dressed the part."

Rae'jean nodded. She wondered if he'd often done what she'd done, stand at the window and watch him come and go. "You moved," she suddenly blurted out, unintentionally making it sound like an accusation, a personal affront. She didn't know if he took it that way, since his expression didn't change. It was still intense.

"Yes. My house was finished."

"Your house?"

"Yes. I was having a new one built. My wife got the old one."

Rae'jean continued to stare at him, but that one word *wife* made a lump form in her throat. "Your wife?"

He nodded slowly. "My ex-wife, actually. I'm divorced."

"For how long?" Rae'jean didn't think for a minute asking him that was none of her business. For some reason she felt she had a right to know. Evidently he thought so, too, because he answered.

"Six months."

Which would have been about the time he had moved into the apartments, she thought. "Any kids?"

"No, and I take it you don't have any children, either."

"No, I don't have any." She waited for him to ask the next question, and when he didn't say anything but continued to look at her she chuckled softly.

"What's so amusing, Ms. Bennett?"

"This entire situation. I think the both of us can agree that it won't work?"

"What won't work?"

"My using your company to find my father."

"And why wouldn't it work?"

Rae'jean shook her head, wondering if she really had to spell it out to him. "Because . . ." She hesitated, looking for the right words to use.

"Because we're so attracted to each other that neither of us can think straight."

His straight-to-the-point, no-beating-around-the-bush attitude caught her off guard. She shifted in her seat and nervously crossed her legs. "Are you always inclined to say whatever's on your mind, Mr. Garrison?"

"It depends on timing. I was very much attracted to you when we were neighbors, but the engagement ring you wore made doing anything about it impossible. I don't believe in invading another man's territory."

"And now since you know I'm no longer engaged?"

He sighed deeply as he continued to look at her. "Bad timing again, since I have a policy of not getting personally involved with my clients."

Strange, Rae'jean thought, she should have been elated that things would be strictly business between them, since she wasn't ready to get involved with anyone again just yet. But still, his saying things would be strictly business between them was easy. The challenge would be in making sure things stayed that way. "And you're sure things will remain strictly business between us, Mr. Garrison?"

"I'm positive, Ms. Bennett." He sat up straighter in his chair. "Now that that's out of the way, let's discuss the real business at hand," he said, pulling out a writing pad. "You indicated that you want me to find your father."

Satisfied that things would be kept on a business level between them, Rae'jean began talking. For the next thirty minutes or so, she told him about her history and the information Uncle Victor had shared with her regarding her father. She watched as he periodically wrote down notes, thinking that he had a really nice set of hands. She mentally shook herself. She shouldn't be thinking of his hands, or any other parts of him for that matter, although she had to admit he looked just as good sitting across from her dressed in a suit and tie as he did the other times she'd seen him wearing T-shirts and jeans. She quickly decided she liked him better in jeans. He looked awfully good in them, she reflected.

"Ms. Bennett?"

Rae'jean blinked as she met his intense gaze. While he'd been talking to her, her mind had drifted elsewhere. She wondered what he'd think if he knew she'd been thinking about him. "Yes?"

"Like I was saying, finding your father shouldn't be much of a problem, since you have a name and a place where he was working thirty years ago. I'll keep you updated each week." Fees were then discussed and agreed on.

"How long do you think it will take?" Rae'jean asked and stood after he did.

"It depends. I'll have a preliminary report to you in a week. Do you want my courier to deliver the report or do you want to come by here and pick it up?" He came to stand in front of her.

Rae'jean weighed his question with serious consideration. If he had it delivered to her then she wouldn't have to come in contact with him. "You can have it delivered."

He nodded.

She reached her hand out to him. "Thanks. I appreciate all your help."

He took her hand in nothing more than a businesslike handshake. "And I appreciate your giving us the business."

With nothing further to say, Rae'jean turned and walked out of Ryan Garrison's office.

Ryan Garrison walked over to the window and looked out. His breath got caught in his throat the moment he saw Rae'jean exit the building and begin walking along the sidewalk. His senses heightened as he watched her retreating back as she crossed the street to her car. How many times had he stood at his apartment window and watched her walk across the parking lot? More times than he cared to count and then some. He'd gotten to pretty much know her schedule and would have his coffee in his hand as he stood at the window and watched her while sipping his coffee and admiring every damn thing about her. Especially her walk. It was pure sensuality in motion. He'd had no idea that a woman's walk could be a total turn-on. Even when she had turned to walk out of his office he'd gotten a rise out of it. Big-time. He was glad nothing had compelled her to glance back at him. There was no way she would have missed seeing the huge bulge straining against the zipper of his pants.

It was a considerable time later before Ryan could summon the energy or the inclination to go sit at his desk. He wished there was some way his mind could do an instant replay of what he'd just seen. Back at his desk he picked up the writing pad and glanced down at the notes he'd taken. Swearing creatively, he tossed it aside and rested his head back against his chair. If this just didn't beat all. In his line of business coincidences never ceased to amaze him.

When he had moved out of his apartment, he'd thought he would never see his sexy and gorgeous neighbor again, although he'd known he would continue to think about her and that images of her would sneak into his dreams at night. He'd hated the idea of lusting after another man's woman, especially a man who seemed to be such an OK guy.

He wondered why she and her fiancé had decided not to marry. Irreconcilable differences perhaps? That was a good one to use. At least that's the reason Cherise had come up with when she had divorced him. He guessed it wouldn't have been kosher to use the truth—that she had gotten pregnant from another man—as the real reason she'd wanted him out of her life, so she could be free to marry her baby's father.

His breath hissed through clenched teeth. The pain of her betrayal still hurt, although he told himself a million times a day that it didn't. And because of her, he now had an ironclad rule of not getting involved with any of his clients. Cherise had shown him the hard way the pitfalls of that.

So no matter how much Rae'jean Bennett interested him and regardless of the fact that she was no longer an engaged woman, he would make sure things stayed strictly business between them. He wasn't ready to get seriously involved with anyone, and from the looks of it, neither was she.

CHAPTER 31

"If I hear another verse of 'Zip-a-Dee-Dooh-Dah' I'm going to go nuts," Michael leaned over and whispered in Taye's ear as they watched the girls race off to yet another ride. They'd been at the Magic Kingdom theme park in Disney World since nine that morning, and it was now almost four o'clock. Sebrina, Victoria, and Kennedy still seemed to have an abundance of energy left. Monica hadn't made the trip, since she was still in Texas with Taye's brother Darryl and his kids.

Taye shook her head, grinning. "It was your idea to buy a four-day pass," she reminded him.

"Yeah, well, the next time I do something stupid like that, I give you permission to slap me silly." He glanced down at his watch. "How much longer do you think they'll want to hang?"

Taye smiled, hearing the weariness in his voice. They had arrived in Orlando early yesterday, and the girls had been eager to get her and Michael to commit to four days of fun at Disney's theme parks. She had held back from agreeing, but Michael had readily agreed, saying that he wanted the girls to enjoy themselves this week. "Do you want to know the truth?" she asked.

"Yes."

"I heard them say they wanted to stay until closing time."

"Closing time! Are they nuts? Have they forgotten we're supposed to get up early and do Epcot tomorrow?"

"Oh, they haven't forgotten. They just plan to make sure they get your money's worth, Michael."

He reached out and playfully grabbed Taye around the neck, bringing her closer to him. "Cute, Taye. That's real cute. You like rubbing salt into a wound, don't you?"

"As long as it's not my wound." The two of them laughed as they made their way over to where the three girls stood in line for Splash Mountain. The sign indicated a thirty-minute wait.

"Uncle Michael, do you and Aunt Taye want to ride with us?" Victoria yelled out.

"No thanks, I'll pass, but Taye may want to," he said, slanting a teasing grin down at her.

Taye shot him a 'don't even try it' look before answering Victoria. "I'll pass, too. My head's still spinning from that last ride."

"Come on then," Michael said, taking hold of her hand. "Let's go and find a place to sit and chill awhile." He turned his full attention to the three girls and made sure that, likewise, he had theirs. "When this ride is over, we expect the three of you to stay put here until we return. Understand?"

"Oh, Daddy," Kennedy said, frowning as she squinted up at him. "You're treating us like we're kids."

Michael smiled. "If I am, it's because the last time I looked, the three of you still were. And if you're not, you're doing a pretty good imitation by the way you're running around this park with a kid's look of excitement in your eyes. You almost knocked a couple down racing for Space Mountain."

Kennedy rolled her eyes skyward but said nothing.

Michael chuckled as he walked away holding Taye's hand.

"You seem to handle Kennedy quite well, Michael," Taye said, smiling up at him. She noticed he had not released her hand. To passersby, they would appear to be a couple.

"It comes with practice. She's been a cross to bear at times, trust me. But it's been a lot easier these past three to four weeks. I have your girls to thank for that."

"How so?"

"They're so well mannered and appreciative. Kennedy notices and it's rubbing off on her. She actually thanked me last week for the money I gave her to get her hair done. Boy, was I shocked."

Taye nodded. "Don't think Sebrina and Monica have always been Goody Little Two-shoes. I had some rough times with Sebrina a few years back. Whenever she returned from spending the summer with her father and grandparents she would drive me off the deep end. They would spoil her rotten while she was with them, and when she came home she would expect the same treatment. I had to nip that in the bud big-time." She sighed deeply before continuing. "And Monica was hell-bent on throwing temper tantrums at one time."

"How did you handle it?"

Taye smiled sheepishly. "I showed her that I could throw a few tantrums myself. For a week or two following a couple of my demonstrations, the girls tiptoed around me like I was a looney tune. After that we pretty much understood each other."

Michael couldn't stop from laughing. "Yeah, I could see how that might work. Last year Kennedy went through a lot of changes, and she tried explaining to me what peer pressure was, like that was a good-enough excuse for some of the stupid stuff she'd been doing."

"And what did you do?"

"I told her I understood peer pressure. But in my day peer pressure was nothing compared to a good behind whipping from Zoe Lee Bennett. If I had to make a choice between getting into trouble, with the possibility of facing one of Zoe Lee's heavy hands on my backside, and peer pressure I'd choose peer pressure in a heartbeat. You know for a fact that my mama didn't play, but then neither did yours."

Taye nodded, remembering those times. Otha Mae Bennett had been a force to reckon with. She still was. "If you ask me, the kids today got it made in the shade. They don't know the meaning of having it rough."

"I agree. The worst part of Kennedy's week is breaking a fingernail." They stopped and sat down on one of the park benches. Michael was satisfied that he still had a pretty good view of the girls. "OK, that's enough about the girls. Let's talk about us," he said, finally releasing her hand.

Taye's eyes were full of questions. "Us?"

Michael smiled. "Yes, us. We need to plan some fun time for ourselves."

"What do you have in mind?"

Michael turned to face her. His dark eyes were gleaming with the thrill of adventure. They were identical to how Kennedy's had looked that morning. "One thing I'd like to do is check out City Walk at Universal Studios. I heard that Motown Café is a must-do. How about if we go there tomorrow night?"

"That's fine with me, but do you think you'll have enough energy left after doing Epcot?"

Michael's smile widened. "Yes. We'll put our foot down and tell the girls we plan to leave Epcot at five o'clock. What do you say?"

Taye smiled at him. "I say that sounds like a plan that'll work."

Taye frowned, immediately wishing she could have gone straight to bed after her shower like the girls had done. But she had promised them she would talk to Michael.

She glanced around. The condo at Westgate Lakes Resorts was a vacationer paradise, a real dream come true, and she appreciated Michael for including her, Sebrina, and Victoria in his plans this week. She smiled when she thought of how well the girls were getting along and how much fun they'd had today.

But now, they were upstairs sleeping off exhaustion and here she was downstairs fighting off her attraction to Michael. Today hadn't been easy. She had forgotten what a touchy-feely person he was. It was nothing for him to hold her hand or wrap his arm around her shoulders while they strolled around the park. Even this morning at breakfast and tonight at dinner, he had sat close to her.

She reflected how things had been over the past three weeks, since that Saturday she had spent working with him in his yard. He and Kennedy had been over for dinner more than a few times. He'd even spent the night once, crashing on her sofa after he had arrived back in town late after a flight and she'd suggested that instead of waking Kennedy to take her home he just stay over for the night.

Each time that Taye had thought she'd begun to feel more comfortable around him, something would happen to make her painfully aware of how attracted she was to him. Like the time he had returned the favor and helped her work in her yard and he had taken off his shirt because of the heat. Seeing him shirtless in a pair of tight-fitting faded Levi's while trimming her hedges had nearly been too much for her to handle. But even with her constantly feeling overheated around him, she liked having him around, and the girls did, too. He was fun to be with and could turn some mundane situation into a pleasurable escapade.

Taking a deep breath, she slid the glass door open and stepped outside on the screened patio. Michael was standing with his back to her, gazing out at the lake. She immediately caught herself staring at the clothes he had changed into after his shower, a pair of running shorts and a T-shirt. For some reason, his striking, elementally male features were sharper tonight, probably because the moonlight reflecting off the lake was hitting him at an angle that was compelling. It was bathing his muscular limbs in a way that made him look too gorgeous and too distracting.

Scrambling to get her thoughts together, she took a deep breath and took her gaze off Michael and put it on another picturesque view—the lake. Michael had gotten a condo with a fantastic view of the lake. The three bedrooms had been built so each room could have a breathtaking view. The girls were occupying the master bedroom upstairs, since it was the largest of the three, with a king-size bed. She and Michael had taken the two guest bedrooms downstairs. It had been nice to wake up and look out the window and see how the sun blended with the waters in the lake, making various shades of blue.

Shoving back a bothersome wisp of hair from her forehead, Taye walked over to Michael. "The girls are out like a rock," she said, coming to stand next to him.

He chuckled as he turned to her. "Hell, they should be. Either they got too much energy or I don't have enough."

Taye shook her head, smiling. "Are you taking any vitamins?"

He lifted a brow. "No."

"Then maybe you should, since you're determined to keep up with them."

She saw his shoulders stiffen. "Are you saying we should let a bunch of young girls run wild in the park, Taye?"

Knowing this topic of conversation was one she and Michael would not agree on, she chose her words carefully. She had promised the girls she would talk to him and she intended to do just that. He had been the ferocious watchdog today, the overprotective father. "No, but I think they're mature enough in their thinking to stay together as a group and meet us at a certain location and time that's spelled out beforehand. I don't think we have to stay on their heels every minute."

Silence stretched so long between them that for a moment Taye began to wonder if he'd heard her. "What about that group of boys who were trying to hang around them today?" he finally asked.

Taye smiled and shrugged. "Show them pretty girls and boys will be boys."

"Yeah, and that's what worries me."

Taye chuckled and shouldered past Michael to sit in a patio chair. "You can't go around wanting to do bodily harm to every boy who looks twice at Kennedy."

Michael crossed his hands over his chest and looked at her. "Was I that bad?"

"I'm sure Kennedy thought you were. You scared those little boys to death."

"Little boys? They were fifteen. Too old to be sniffing behind thirteen-year-old girls. Besides, for all we know they could have been little criminals-in-the-making, future hoodlums of America."

Taye rolled her eyes upward. "Or they could have been geniuses in the making, future presidents of America, Michael. They only wanted the girls to sit next to them on some rides, not to elope."

Michael sucked in a deep breath. He admitted he probably had put the fear of God in those three boys and would even go so far as to admit he had enjoyed doing so. "You didn't have a problem with them hanging around?"

"No, I trust the girls."

"It's not the girls that I don't trust. It's those boys," Michael grumbled in such a way that made the smile tilting Taye's lips widen.

"Then, you'll have to trust the girls to make the right decisions."

Michael came over and sat in the chair next to her. "They're only thirteen, Taye. They shouldn't even be thinking about boys yet."

Who says? Taye thought. *I sure thought about you at thirteen.* "Michael, it's not as serious as you're trying to make it."

"It doesn't bother you that Sebrina likes boys?"

"No, and it shouldn't bother you that Kennedy likes them, either. It's natural. And how we handle the situation as parents is very important. I think the main reason I got pregnant once I went off to college was because for the first time I felt free. Momma was too strict on me; you know that. You had to follow me, Rae'jean, and Alexia around everywhere we went to make sure we didn't get into any trouble, but most important, to keep the boys away. And it worked. News got around fast that the three of us were your cousins and if any of the guys tried to talk to us that meant trouble."

"I was just following orders."

"I know, and they were well-intended orders, but I wished Momma would have loosened her rope just a little. If she had then I wouldn't have been so eager to get a taste of forbidden fruit after leaving home for school."

Taye let her thoughts reflect back to that time when she'd gone to college and had tried making up for all those things she'd missed out on during her teen years because of her parents' strictness. "I'm not saying you're not supposed to keep an eye on Kennedy and not be cautious of the guys who come around. All I'm saying is that you should trust her to make the right decisions about some things. If you don't, she'll resent you for it and do things for the hell of it just to aggravate you."

He gave a derisive snort. "She does that anyway at times."

"Well, then maybe she won't do it as often. Tomorrow at Epcot I suggest we let them explore the park without us following them around and have them check in with us every four hours at a designated place."

"Every four hours?" Michael squawked.

Taye laughed. "OK, how about every three hours?"

"How about every two?"

Recognizing his indisputably stubborn nature, Taye conceded. "OK, every two hours if it makes you happy." She'd known asking for any time beyond two hours would be pushing it but had tried her luck anyway. "Is it a deal?"

Michael shrugged, frowning. "I guess so."

Taye reached over and hugged him. "Cheer up, Michael; it's not going to be that bad. You'll survive."

The hug was meant to be innocent. Neither of them was prepared for the sudden surges of desire that swept through them or the disturbing amount of sensual heat that immediately engulfed them.

"Taye," Michael whispered softly as she slowly released him. But he replaced her arms with his own and wrapped them around her, pulling her to her feet as he stood on his.

"Michael?"

Her voice was shaking; he could hear it. Her body was trembling; he could feel it. He noticed the way she was looking up at him. It was the look of a woman who wanted the man she was with. That knowledge kicked low and seeped through his insides like a slow-burning flame. He wanted to fight his body's response to her and couldn't. He hadn't been able to fight it since he'd seen her again at the family reunion, although God knows he had tried. He'd felt that flicker of guilt that what he was feeling for her was wrong. Although they were not blood relations, they were in the same family. It hadn't been easy not wanting her. It still wasn't.

He'd tried fighting the response he felt whenever he was around her. Some days he'd succeeded; some days he had not. And now at this moment, with her standing before him, close, with his arms around her waist, with her eyes searching his for answers, the only thing he could think about was tasting her. Tasting those sweet lips that looked petal soft and pliant, moist and ready.

He looked deep into her eyes and wished he hadn't. They revealed so much. They showed signs she was going through the same torment that he was. Once again she was being faced with forbidden fruit. He wished that somehow he could find the strength to turn and walk away, to tell her good night and that he would see her in the morning, bright and early, well rested, ready to face another day, and all that good stuff.

But he couldn't.

In fact, he didn't want to.

He was losing a battle he'd never wanted to take on. For family's sake, for sanity's sake, he had tried resisting temptation. It hadn't been easy and now, standing before him with dazed eyes, labored and shallow breathing, she wasn't making it any easier.

"Damn, Taye," he said huskily, in a tone intended to quell what was happening between them, then and there, here and now. He knew if he kissed her, things would change. Things would be different and it would mean they would be more than kissing cousins, because he didn't think he would be able to stop at just kissing. The ache went too deep; the longing was too strong. If he kissed her, sooner or later, they would sleep together. He knew it and wanted to make sure she knew it as well. Understood it. Wanted it.

She spoke before he did. "We've got to stop what's happening here, Michael," she whispered softly, unconvincingly.

"I can't, Taye. I've tried, but I can't." He slowly lowered his head, and with a groan of defeat and a moan of pleasure he covered her mouth with his own. The immediate response of his mouth on hers sent his pulse racing, sent his hormones into overdrive. Blood, thick, hot, passionate, ignited into a flame through his veins. He took her breath away with his tongue; he fed desire into his loins with hers. The taste of her was heady. The feel of her in his arms was mind-blowing. This woman was literally rocking his world.

His hands on her waist sought to hold her to him, sought to bring her closer. He groaned while grinding the lower part of his body against her, acting out a heated emulation of lovemaking while they were yet clothed. But the material of their clothing wasn't a strong-enough shield against the fervor of what was taking place between them.

Both knew they should stop. But neither wanted to.

So they didn't. They continued kissing. They continued to grind their bodies in heated erotic movements. It was obvious from the rock-hardness of Michael's lower body that he wanted her, and likewise from the sound of her whimpering in his mouth that she wanted him.

They finally broke off the kiss to come up for air. Much-needed air.

"This is crazy, Taye," Michael whispered as he feathered kisses along her neck.

"I know." Those were the only two coherent words she could speak. They were the only two she could think of saying at the moment.

He kissed her cheekbone. "If the family knew we were carrying on like this they'd go bananas."

"I know."

He continued to scatter random kisses over her face, not able to get enough of the taste of her. "They won't like it one hell of a bit."

"I know."

He licked the lining of her lips. "They'll think we're insane."

"I know."

Blood pulsed full force into his loins. He became filled with the want of her. He stopped kissing her and held her gaze in the moonlight off the lake. He wanted her to know something else, too. "But at this moment, I don't give a damn what they might think or how they might feel. My mind is too concentrated on what *I* think and how *I* feel."

She pressed her hands to the center of his chest as their gazes continued to hold. "At this moment, I feel the same way, Michael."

Her admission to him was breathtaking. It was the thing that drove him over the edge when he pulled her back to him and took her mouth again as his heart pounded rapidly with his need for her, his want of her.

They immediately broke apart when they heard the phone ring.

Michael's heart clamored against his chest when Taye pushed herself out of his arms and raced off to answer it. Eyes closed, he took a deep breath. When he reopened them he didn't have any regrets for what he and Taye had shared. Something feeling that right couldn't be wrong. And he was determined for her not to have any regrets, either. They would take things slow if they had to, but they wouldn't have any regrets, and they wouldn't go back to status quo.

Never had he been driven to such need. If that phone hadn't rung, he probably would have taken her right there on the chaise lounge. He had wanted her just that much. Every time he was around her, new currents of awareness would sizzle within him. Even Stephanie hadn't been able to do that to him. She hadn't come close and deep down he knew why.

Even with his and Stephanie's close friendship, there had always been something that held him back from ever wanting more. He'd been complacent, knowing things between them would never go anywhere. They had been good friends, and their lovemaking had been an extension of that. With Taye it was different. Tonight, she had touched a part of him that no woman had touched since Lynda. Kissing her had affected him in a way he didn't think was possible—again. And even though he'd been without a woman for close to six months now, he knew it wasn't about lust. It was something deeper, but he shouldn't have found that thought surprising. Taye Bennett had always been able to get next to him. There had always been this special bond between them from the time they were kids. But now the question of the hour was just what he planned to do about it.

He lifted his head when he heard her return. "That was Momma," she said softly from where she stood across the patio. "She hadn't heard from us and was calling to see if we made it here OK."

Michael shook his head and snorted. "Figures."

Taye lifted a brow. "What figures?"

He slowly walked over to her. "That some member of the family would call right when we were on the path to doing something they would see as total damnation."

Taye lifted her gaze upward. "Maybe someone up there is trying to tell us something." She then lowered troubled eyes to him.

He decided to squash that look and that thought. "No. I doubt that very seriously. We weren't doing anything wrong, Taye."

"Weren't we?"

Michael frowned. "No."

Taye was silent for a moment. Then she said, "We're family, Michael."

"Yes, but we aren't blood-related. There's a difference."

She shook her head. "Everyone won't think so. Especially the family."

"They'll eventually accept it."

She walked across the patio to stare out at the lake for a moment before turning around. She had already disappointed the family twice; she couldn't risk doing it a third time. "What about the girls?" she asked softly. She swallowed hard and her eyes were glued to his.

"I don't think they'll have a problem with the idea of you and me together."

"It will be too confusing for them," she murmured. "Normally two people who consider themselves cousins don't suddenly become boyfriend and girlfriend." Taye paused. She studied him, realizing that she might be getting ahead of herself, since she had no idea what Michael wanted or where this attraction between them could be headed. "Maybe I'm reading more into this than what's really there. What do you want from me, Michael? A one-night stand? A week fling? A secret affair?"

Michael quickly covered the distance between them. "The first thing I want is for you to have no regrets. Then the next thing is for you to believe that I wouldn't use you that way, Taye."

She shrugged. "But you said . . . you told me that you'd had a lover, a secret lover, for four years and that Kennedy hadn't known about her."

"That's the way Stephanie and I wanted it for our own personal reasons. But with you I'd want things to be different. And I see no reason why they can't be."

Taye chuckled. "Oh, they'll be different all right. I can just see the family hauling us before Reverend Overstreet to talk some sense into us, if they don't try knocking it into us first themselves."

"Do you think we're crazy, Taye?"

She held his gaze. "Do you?"

"No. I think we're two people who're attracted to each other, who have been attracted to each other for a while, and who finally decided to take the first step tonight."

Taye lowered her head in thought. She could just see her mother pointing an accusing finger at her and saying, "Once again you've shamed this family, Octavia." She took a deep breath. "I don't know what to do. I need time to think."

"Take your time. I don't plan to go anywhere. And while you're thinking, think about the fact that tonight, for the first time in nearly six years, I felt something, Taye. I felt something with you in my arms, and I want to explore just what that something is. It shocked the hell out of me and it made me think. It seems we aren't thinking along the same wavelength, but that's OK. You continue to do your thinking and I'll continue to do mine. But sooner or later we're going to have to admit there is something between us, something deep. And it's going to take more than the family's disapproval to destroy it. Think about that."

With those final words, he turned and left her alone on the patio.

Even after she heard Michael's bedroom door closing behind him, Taye continued to stand on the patio. Her heart was pounding in her chest and she felt breathless. Kissing Michael the way she had, had rocked her world. It had been over ten years since she had been kissed. Ten years since she had been held in a man's arms and made to feel soft and womanly, desired.

She took a deep breath. She then searched her mind for an answer as to what she should do. Michael wasn't just any man she was attracted to; he was someone she had known all her life, and he'd always been a hero figure to her—*her hero*. And most important, he was her cousin. There was no way the two of them could ever let anything develop between them. It wouldn't work. She would have to act responsibly and make sure nothing did develop. It would be better for everyone in the long run.

Taye felt a heavy weight settle in her stomach with that decision. How was she supposed to be around him for the rest of the week and act like nothing had happened between them tonight? Now that she had gotten a taste of him, how was she supposed to put that taste out of her mind and forget about it? And how could she forget that for the first time in over ten years, she wanted a man? A man who was definitely forbidden fruit of the most delicious kind.

It wouldn't be easy. But the fact was—she had to do it. She turned to look at the lake and suddenly realized just how lonely she felt.

A little after 2:00 A.M., Michael found himself still awake, unable to sleep. He'd heard Taye go to her room and close the door hours ago and wondered if she was doing a better job of getting some rest than he was.

With a sigh he pulled his body up in bed and levered himself on his elbows. He was still not believing what had happened between him and Taye on the patio. Talk about spontaneous combustion. Once she had reached out to him, to hug him, that had been the straw that broke the camel's back. Her touch had made immediate heat race through his solar plexus. His reaching for her had been automatic, elemental. And their kiss had been everything he'd known it could be and more.

Tonight he had fulfilled part of his fantasy. It was a fantasy he'd tucked away in the back of his mind and had only allowed to surface at night while he slept. The fantasy had extended to his kissing Taye in every way a man could kiss a woman, his touching her breasts and seeing them become responsive to his touch and then having those long, gorgeous legs of hers wrapped around him in the heat of passion while he made love to her.

Then there had been another fantasy that had recently taken shape in his mind, one he couldn't get rid of. And that was the one of Taye's body rounded and ripe with a baby. His baby.

Michael ran his hand across his face, trying to remember just when that particular fantasy had begun. Maybe it had been that day the two of them had taken the girls out for pizza and the couple sitting at the booth across from them had their three-month-old baby with them. Taye, being the ever friendly person that she was, had struck up a conversation with the couple and had asked if she could hold their little boy, whose name, coincidentally, was Taye. The baby's mother was a big Taye Diggs fan and had named the child after the popular actor. Michael had watched while Taye had cuddled the baby to her, smiling and cooing down at him. The happiness on her face had been priceless. It had touched Michael deeply, resurfacing longings he'd always had for another child.

He released a deep sigh. All those feelings he'd been experiencing for Taye over the past two months no longer perplexed him. He suddenly remembered the promise he had made to Stephanie and the words she had spoken: *I believe there is a special woman out there for you. And although she won't ever take Lynda's place, I think she'll be able to carve her own special place in your heart if you let her. Promise me that when you do meet her you'll give her a chance and that you won't let anything come between you. You will need her and Kennedy will, too.*

Michael's gut twisted and he swallowed hard as emotions suddenly came over him, swamped him, and consumed him. When he made Stephanie that promise he had no idea that six months later he would find such a person.

But he had.

And to take it a step further, he would admit to himself now, tonight, that he had fallen in love with her. What he felt for Taye didn't tarnish Lynda's memory or the love they had shared. They'd had a good life to-gether; they'd made a beautiful child. Lynda would always hold a special place in his heart. But he knew she would have wanted him to get on with his life and remarry. But he'd never given that any thought, because for the past six years he'd felt that he would never get lucky enough to find love that strong, that pure, a second time.

But he had.

And the woman he loved was trying to put roadblocks in the way of their ever sharing a life together. He couldn't let her do that. He wouldn't let her do that.

Michael gave himself a long, determined smile. He'd promised Stephanie that once he found that special person he wouldn't let anything come between them. Now it seemed the thing that could keep them apart was something he held dear to his heart.

His family. Their family.

Michael lay there in the dark, his face illuminated by the moon's glow reflecting off the lake that shone through his window. As much as he loved his family, he would not let them come between him and Taye. But first things first. He couldn't tackle the family by himself. He would need Taye by his side. He would have to convince her that he loved her and that together they could handle anything. Including their family.

CHAPTER 32

How long are you going to try and ignore me, Taye?"
Taye glanced up sharply from studying her wineglass. Her gaze held Michael's. They were sitting together at a table at Motown Café. The small flickering flame of a candle that sat on their table illuminated his features while a song by Boyz II Men played in the background. "I'm not trying to ignore you, Michael," she said finally.

He reached across the table and took her hand, "I think that you are."

Taye felt a trembling deep inside her from his touch. She tried tugging her hand away, but his grip tightened its hold. "You don't have to hold my hand, Michael."

"And what if I said I wanted to?"

"I'd prefer that you didn't." She gave one more tug and this time he released her hand.

Michael leaned back in his chair. "How about cutting me some slack here, Taye? If you want to go on a guilt trip, that's fine, but don't try taking me there with you."

"I am not on a guilt trip."

"Aren't you? You seem to have been on one all day. You got up this morning barely saying anything to anyone. Even the girls noticed. I heard Sebrina whisper to Kennedy that you were probably PMSing."

Taye's shoulders slumped. "I was hoping that they wouldn't notice."

"Notice what? That you really are PMSing?" he asked, smiling at her.

Taye couldn't help but return his smile. Michael had always managed to get her out of whatever funk she was in, and it seemed that he still could. Even if he was the reason for her funk. "I'll be all right."

"Not as long as you deny what's between us you won't."

She frowned. "There's nothing between us, Michael."

"Only because you won't let there be anything between us."

She stared at him for a moment and then she wished she hadn't when she felt a deep stirring in the pit of her stomach. "Last night was just overactive hormones out of control," she said before taking another sip of wine.

"I don't have a hormone problem, Taye."

Her frown deepened. "Then maybe *I* do. It just so happens that I haven't been as sexually active over the last few years as you have." She hadn't meant to tell him that, but then maybe it would be best if he thought her attraction to him was only physical. It was a lie, of course, but she was desperate right now.

Michael looked at her with much speculation. "I know you mentioned that you hadn't dated anyone in a while. Just how long has it been since you've been intimate with a man?" he asked, arching his eyebrows back so far they almost became part of his forehead.

Taye shifted in her chair under his direct, intense gaze. "A long time."

"How long?"

"Long enough."

He inclined his head. His gaze intensified. "How long is long enough, Taye?"

She hesitated before answering. Then she looked elsewhere and not at him. "Over ten years."

He gaped at her before exclaiming, "Over ten years!"

"You don't have to shout, Michael," she said flatly, noticing others in the café had turned their attention to them.

"Sorry." After a moment he said, "Don't you think that's a rather long time?"

"For some people it might be, but not for me. After two pregnancies I decided to bail out of the lovemaking scene, since it appeared I was a walking baby maker. I was on the pill when I got pregnant with Monica.

For some reason birth control doesn't work for me, so I decided not to take another chance. A third pregnancy would get me kicked out of the family for sure."

Michael's fantasy returned. It was the one of her pregnant with his child. In his mind he could see her and could see himself as well, gently stroking her stomach knowing his baby rested inside.

"And since I'm not married," Taye went on, "celibacy is a surefire way not to have another baby out of wedlock." She took a sip of her wine before saying, "I responded to you the way I did last night because of overactive hormones."

Michael looked at her thoughtfully. If she hadn't had sex for over ten years, then he could probably believe that. Jeez, it's a wonder she wasn't climbing the walls. He had found out firsthand just how strong sexual needs could get. After Lynda had died he couldn't bear the thought of ever making love to another woman. But then within two years he'd had to rethink that idea. It was either that or become an alcoholic when those strong sexual needs began to take effect. He had stayed celibate for two years and seriously doubted he could have made it to ten. Not too many people could. Leave it to Taye to be one of the few. But still he refused to believe what they'd shared last night had been only physical on her part. A part of him believed she had been touched emotionally as well, just like he'd been.

"Don't look at me that way, Michael."

"What way am I looking at you?" he asked, matching her light tone.

"The same way Alexia looked when she found out."

"And what way was that?"

"Like I needed to have my head examined."

A smile touched his lips. "I don't think you need to have your head examined, Taye, but I am concerned that you're refusing to have a healthy, normal relationship with a man because of your fear of getting pregnant. There are other methods of birth control than condoms and pills."

"Thanks, but I'll pass on anything that's not one hundred percent foolproof. Besides, the fear of getting pregnant isn't the only thing keeping me celibate."

"What's the other thing?"

"Men who are liars and cheaters."

He thought about her past experience with men. "All men aren't that way, Taye."

"But enough of them are."

He studied her before carefully asking, "Do you think I'm that way?" His voice was relaxed, quiet.

She lowered her head, suddenly interested in the pattern of the tablecloth. "No."

"Look at me, Taye," he commanded gently, softly. "I want to see the truth in your eyes when you answer."

She slowly lifted her eyes to his. Their gazes locked. The air surrounding them nearly crackled with charged intensity. "No, Michael. I don't think you're a liar or a cheater."

He gave her a smile that she thought was utterly charming. "Good. Then you won't have anything to worry about in regards to me, will you?"

Taye swallowed hard, wishing she could somehow keep up with Michael's conversation. Somewhere along the way he had lost her. "What do you mean, I don't have anything to worry about with regards to you?"

"You just admitted you don't think I'm a liar and a cheater, right?"

"Right."

"And with me you don't have to concern yourself with getting pregnant. If you got pregnant from making love with me, it would be OK. I'd like another child anyway."

Taye frowned as she wondered what that had to do with the cost of tea in China. "This conversation with you is confusing. Why are you telling me that? You and I won't ever get together that way."

"Won't we?"

She tilted her head up. Her eyes were determined. "No, because I won't let it happen."

He took a sip of his wine before asking, "Because of the family?"

"Yes."

Michael nodded, deciding to let the subject rest for now. He then checked his watch. "It's getting late and I'd like to get at least one dance in before we leave if you don't mind."

Taye swallowed hard. She did mind. She didn't know how she could manage being in his arms. Frantically she tried thinking of an excuse she could give, but nothing would come to mind. "Do we have to dance?"

"I'd think you would want to. You used to enjoy dancing. Besides, tonight is our night for fun, remember?"

Taye sighed and decided not to waste her breath trying to get out of dancing with him since he seemed hell-bent on getting her on the dance floor. When he stood and reached out his hand to her, she took it. In the background she could hear the sound of Marvin Gaye's "Let's Get It On" starting to play.

Moments later when Michael took her into his arms on the dance floor the turmoil she'd felt all day returned tenfold. She took a deep breath and tried relaxing in his arms as she forced herself to concentrate on the music and not on him. And definitely not the feel of the palm of his hand stroking the center of her back. His caress was soft and gentle and was stirring her senses.

"Say what you want to say, Taye, but there is more between us than overactive hormones. You know it as well as I do. Admit it," he murmured softly in her ear.

"Michael . . . I . . . I can't. We can't."

He reached up and lifted a hand to her neck and slid it down the slender column of her spine with a feather-light stroke. "You can. We will." He leaned closer and kissed an area under her ear. "Trust me when I say that things will turn out all right," he added in a soothing voice.

Taye became dazed with the want of him, with the need of him, but still a part of her held back. "It's not about trust, Michael. It's about reality and what makes sense."

She felt the essence of his smile against her cheek. "That's good to know, sweetheart, because right now you're my reality and us being together makes perfect sense. But I'll give you time to digest what I'm saying, Taye. I don't want you all uptight for the rest of the week because of me. But I won't give up on you, Octavia Louise Bennett. So don't think that I will."

He slowed their movements on the floor to almost a standstill. She shivered as his fingers reached up and touched her cheek. His gaze held hers. It was dark, compelling, intense. Then he slowly bent his head and brushed his lips lightly, affectionately, over hers.

Taye held on to him as she felt her senses spinning out of control. The mere taste of him was hot, sensuous, and male.

He lifted his lips from hers and pulled her closer into his arms as they continued dancing while he trailed small kisses along her neck. "I need you, Taye," he whispered in her ear. "Kennedy needs you, too. We need both you and the girls."

Before Marvin Gaye finished his last note, Michael whispered softly in her ear, "And I love you, Taye."

Taye went still in his arms. She pulled back and looked up at him with disbelief in her eyes. She didn't want to believe it. She couldn't believe it.

"Yes, it's true," he said, smiling down at her, thinking her shocked expression was priceless, precious. "I came to terms with it last night after I went to bed. Now you have to come to terms with it, too. And when you do, we'll come up with a plan to deal with our family together."

Taking her hands, he walked her back over to their table as the Four Tops' classic "I Can't Help Myself" began playing.

CHAPTER 33

S he can't get away with this, Quinn. She can't!"

Quinn slid the papers into his briefcase before turning to Alexia. He watched as she paced the floor. To say she was mad as hell would be an understatement. As usual, Raisa Forbes was causing problems, but this time she had gone too far.

Court papers had been delivered to Alexia that morning that stated Raisa had filed a lawsuit against her. She was alleging that Alexia's first solo album, which was due to be released in a few months, contained two songs that Raisa had written. Upon being served the documents, Alexia had called Quinn immediately and asked him to represent her.

Quinn closed his briefcase with a snap. "As your attorney, I'll take whatever action is needed to get this matter resolved even if I have to file a countersuit for libel and slander."

He then walked across the room and took Alexia's hand in his and gently pulled her closer to him. "And as the man in your life, I'll give you all the support you need in dealing with this. I don't want you to worry about it, baby. I got your back." A teasing smile tilted the corners of his lips. "But then I have your front as well, don't I?" he whispered huskily.

Alexia frowned up at him. "I'm too mad for that right now, Quinn."

He chuckled softly. "Are you? Let's see." He leaned down and captured her mouth with his and immediately ignited a ripple of desire within her.

She tried to hold back and then conceded it would be a losing battle. No one kissed like Quinn Masters. And no one could make her become supple and yielding in his arms like Quinn could. Like now. In no time at all she could hear the sounds of her own whimpering and moans as his kiss drove her near the edge of insanity. He reluctantly released her mouth.

"Well, maybe I'm not that mad," she said breathlessly, her eyes dazed.

Quinn smiled down at her. "Don't waste your anger on Raisa Forbes. She isn't worth it."

"But what about the article that appeared in this morning's paper? The things she said?"

"You know they aren't true. What Raisa Forbes is trying to do is make any record company wary of doing business with you in the future. She figures if you can't get work as a solo artist then you'll be forced to return to Body and Soul with your tail between your legs." He pulled her closer to him and whispered, "Little does she know that there's something a lot more solid and sturdy that's going between those legs."

"Quinn!"

He laughed at her shocked expression. "What?"

"Behave."

He lifted a brow. "Do you really want me to?"

She looked at his sensuous, provocative mouth before moving her gaze lower, to the fly of his pants, thinking of his body part tucked away behind it. Taking a deep breath, she lifted her eyes to meet his gaze as memories of how his mouth and that certain solid and sturdy part of him—the part she did enjoy having between her legs—had nearly driven her insane with passion a number of times over the past four weeks. She felt comfortable in being scandalous with him. Brazen. Naughty. She would even go so far as to say he encouraged that behavior when they were alone. "It wouldn't do any good to ask you to behave. You wouldn't do it anyway," she finally said.

He pulled her to him and kissed her lips again quickly. "I would have surprised you today. Unfortunately, I have a number of appointments scheduled. How about dinner tonight at my place?"

"Your place?"

"Yes. Don't you think it's about time?"

Alexia only hesitated briefly before saying, "Yes, I suppose."

Quinn smiled, perfectly satisfied with her answer. It had been a month since they had first become intimate and she had yet to come over to his place, although he had invited her there a number of times. He was still taking things slow with her. Once in a while she would try putting distance between them. It was during those times that he let her know, in no uncertain terms, that he was not like the other men she'd dated. He had no intentions of putting up with her fickle ways.

He was being patient with her because he understood she didn't trust easily and that although she had agreed to trust him, it would take time. Having a man in her life who didn't let her call all the shots was new to her, so he gave her space every once in a while. But he'd made sure she understood that he considered her his woman, just like he considered himself her man.

"Do you want me to come pick you up?"

She shook her head. "No, I'll drive."

"All right." He knew why she wanted to drive herself over to his place and he didn't like it, although he decided not to push the issue. She had once explained to him that she preferred having her own wheels whenever she went out with someone just in case she felt the need to cut out unexpectedly.

He leaned down and kissed her lips once more before walking back across the room for his briefcase.

"Will you be meeting with Raisa's attorney sometime today?" she asked him.

"Yes. I'll call you later and let you know how it goes." He paused a moment before asking, "Will you walk me to the door?"

She shook her head as she met his gaze. "No. I don't want you to leave just yet."

Quinn lifted a brow as Alexia began unbuttoning her skirt. He watched it slide to the floor, leaving her completely bare underneath. His pulse escalated. He knew exactly what she was doing and why. Calling him to come over had made her feel vulnerable, dependent. Those were emotions she detested, since she was used to being in control.

"Alexia," he warned in a deep, husky voice. "I'm on my way to an appointment and have less than an hour to get there."

She tossed aside her blouse, then walked completely naked to where he was standing. She reached out and began toying with the zipper on his pants. "Then I guess we'd better make this quick, huh?"

Sucking in a deep breath, Quinn decided to let her have her way with him, giving in to her need for control. Eventually she would see that in a solid relationship no one was in total control.

His mind suddenly lost all thought when he felt her hands, soft and warm, on him. He breathed in deeply when she began stroking him. "Alexia." He released a tortured sigh as she continued to caress him.

"I want you, Quinn," she whispered. Her voice, he noted, was deeper and sexier than he'd ever known it to be. He looked at her; their gazes locked. His heart stopped when he saw the look of uncertainty in her eyes. "What's wrong, baby?"

She shook her head as she continued to look at him, stroke him. "Nothing's wrong. It's just that each and every time we do this, I get a little thunderstruck when I'm reminded of what a beautiful man you are, both inside and out, and how unselfish you are in your giving to me. Maybe that's why I . . ." She stopped herself from saying whatever she had intended to say.

"Maybe that's why you what?" Quinn asked quietly as his heart resumed beating double-time. "What was it you were about to say, Alexia?"

She lowered her gaze from his. "Nothing."

Quinn decided to let it go. He hadn't yet told her how he felt about her, that he loved her. He wanted to give her time to adjust to his being a part of her life before hitting her with something that deep.

He lost all sense of thought again when she rubbed her body against his.

"I want you, Quinn," she repeated before lifting her hips and sitting on the table behind her and unashamedly spreading her legs wide. "I want you now." She pulled him between her legs and guided the hardness of him into her moist core.

"Ah, Lex," Quinn groaned as he penetrated her deep, finding her wet and ready for him. He sucked in another breath when she wriggled her body several times to get comfortable on the edge of the table. He leaned down and pressed a kiss against her lips when she wrapped her legs around him. "You feel so damn good, Lex." He drew her closer and began to move inside of her. "So damn good."

At that moment he forgot everything except the woman he was making love to on the table in her breakfast room. Everything about her was an aphrodisiac. Her voice, her body, her scent. Everything. He forced his eyes open to look at her and saw her looking at him with eyes glazed in passion of the richest kind.

"This is crazy, you know," he said, pulling her closer, going deeper, faster.

She wrapped her arms around his neck. "No, this isn't crazy," she whispered raggedly. "This is everything making love should be." She moved with him, giving him all of herself and putting into her actions what Quinn knew she was not ready to say in words. But eventually the words would come. And when they did, he and Alexia would have a lifetime of loving, of mating, of being one.

"Quinn!"

It was only when he heard her harsh cry and felt her body shudder that he gave in to the hunger that was ravaging his body. He plunged one last time into her with an urgency that shook him. He felt his groin explode, shooting the essence of him into the depths of her. He hollered out his pleasure. He yelled out his satisfaction. He shouted out his release in a way that left him feeling drained and depleted. This woman whom he loved endlessly and intended to marry meant everything to him. She was his world, his heart, his soul, and a part of his body. And right now she held him at the pinnacle of mindless desire and fulfillment. She joined him there, pulling every single thing from out of him.

When he had completely emptied himself inside of her, with what little strength he had left he reached out and gently stroked her cheek. "You did that deliberately, didn't you?" he asked her, feeling weak, dazed. His gaze traveled the full length of her naked body.

He hadn't undressed. He hadn't unfastened a single button on his shirt. He hadn't even bothered to remove his pants. She hadn't given him time. The only thing out of place was his zipper, which was down to accommodate the part extended from his body to hers. They were still connected.

She fell back on the table with her eyes closed, her breathing shallow. Moments later her eyes opened slowly and she looked at him and smiled. "Yes. I did that deliberately," she said, her voice deep, even. "I wanted you to know how I feel whenever you take me spontaneously, unplanned and

unconstrained. I wanted to give you a taste of your own medicine. Did
I?"

He continued to stroke her cheek, loving her even more and wondering
how that was possible. "Yes, you did."

"And did I please you?"

"Most definitely." He watch the satisfied look in her eyes and was
touched to know that pleasing him meant so much to her. "You may have
spoiled me."

Her smile widened. "The way you've spoiled me?"

His hand moved from her cheek and down to her neck, stroking the
column there. "Have I done that, Sexy Lexy?" he asked huskily, still holding
his gaze to hers and using the pet name he'd given her.

She closed her eyes briefly and shivered. When she reopened them they
were filled with both wonder and awe. "Yes, I think you have. You treat
me special, Quinn. It's as if you . . ."

He watched her. He saw the look of uncertainty in her eyes again. "It's
as if I what?"

She shook her head and answered softly, "Nothing."

He continued to watch her. "You sure it's nothing?"

Instead of answering him, she nodded her head.

He pulled her up to him and leaned down and kissed her. She would
eventually tell him what had been in her thoughts and on her mind. Time
and love would continue to heal her hurt and pain. She was still fighting
him even now without fully realizing it. The hurt and pain her ex-husband
had caused had gone deep, and the shield around her heart was thick. She
saw no other recourse than to fight him to protect herself against ever
getting hurt again.

But one day he knew she wouldn't be able to fight him any longer.
And when that time came, when she was ready to commit herself to him
and she was ready to accept the love that he had for her and the belief in
her heart that he would never hurt her, he would ask her to be his wife.

Alexia slowly opened her eyes. She was naked in bed alone. She glanced
over at the clock on her nightstand that indicated the time was a little past
two in the afternoon.

Shifting in bed, she remembered Quinn picking her up off the table and carrying her to the bedroom, placing her under the covers. He had kissed her one last time before he'd left, telling her that he would see her at his place tonight for dinner.

She lay still for a moment, willing her body to stop tingling when she thought of the way she had made love to Quinn. On a table, for heaven's sake! But then, nothing she did with him surprised her anymore. Whenever they were together, he demanded the real Alexia Bennett and would not settle for anyone else.

She inhaled a deep breath. His parting kiss had been deep, sweet. The taste of him still lingered on her tongue. Her body missed his touch. What was there about Quinn that made her want him? Made her want to be a part of him? Made her want to love him?

She resolutely pushed that thought from her mind. Richmond had shown her the hard way what could happen if you left your heart open. But then a part of her knew Quinn was nothing like Richmond. Her ex-husband had used her for his benefit and would still be using her if she hadn't had the sense to leave. The night she had left him she had decided she had been manipulated and used for the very last time.

Alexia levered herself up on her elbows and stared at the wall. She had been doing a pretty good job of protecting herself until Quinn came along. Quinn Masters, who had the strength of steel, the stubbornness of a bull, and more kindness than any man had a right to show, had slowly eased his way into her heart. And just to think she had thought he was arrogant. Quinn wasn't arrogant, just confident. He had been confident in his ability to win her over by being a totally different type of man than she'd ever had to deal with before. He had also won her respect. There was something about him that demanded it. He had somehow found a way to conquer the heart of a woman who was afraid to let go of the past and love again.

But then, she conceded, he was making it easy for her to want to let go and love again by making her feel wanted, cherished, and loved.

Alexia shifted her gaze from the wall upward to the ceiling. There were different degrees of love. She believed that Quinn loved being with her and that he loved making love to her. But could she believe that he loved her? The way a man was supposed to love a woman, in the true essence of the word? Especially now that she knew she had fallen in love with him?

Her eyes went soft and moist. "I love him," she whispered quietly to herself. "It's not about good sex like I want to believe; it's about more. I truly do love him." And with that ardent confession her fear returned. But this fear went deeper than any she'd ever felt before. She feared the possibility of losing Quinn when he found out that she had set out to use him in the beginning to get a child, a child she was fairly certain she now carried in her womb. She was a week late and was too frightened to take a home pregnancy test to confirm what she suspected was true.

That she was carrying Quinn's child.

CHAPTER 34

E ven from a distance, Rae'jean could see that Ryan Garrison's stance was a casual one as he leaned against her car and watched her walking toward him. For long moments she wondered how he'd known what time she got off work and why he was in the hospital's parking lot waiting for her when it had been decided that any report she was due to receive would be delivered by someone other than him. She had counted on not seeing him again for a while.

She didn't want to worry about the strong sexual attraction between them or the fact that even now, when she was still over fifty feet away from where he stood, she could actually feel the air surrounding them hum with sensuous stimulation. She glanced down at her arms and saw goose bumps forming on them and noticed her breathing had deepened.

Seeing the only way to get out of her dilemma was to place her mind on something else, she thought about the hectic ten-hour shift she had just pulled and that the most important thing on her mind was getting home and going to bed. But moments later she found even thinking about that was impossible. Her mind was determined to remain on Ryan Garrison. Even from across the parking lot his gaze was burning into her.

With all the dignity she could muster, on unsteady legs she continued walking, determined not to let him know how much seeing him again was affecting her.

• • •

Ryan forced himself to break eye contact with Rae'jean and looked down and took a deep, shuddering breath. He needed to have his head examined. He had made a big mistake by coming here to deliver the report to her himself instead of sticking to the plan they had agreed upon. But he had wanted to see her again and this was the only excuse he could come up with to do so. Besides, for some reason he wanted to be there when she read the report about her father.

Without wanting to, Ryan lifted his head and let his gaze wander over Rae'jean once again. She was less than ten feet away now and was wearing her doctor's scrubs. She looked tired, he mused silently. Evidently it had been a very busy night for her. But then he felt tired himself. He wasn't getting much rest, either. Ever since he'd seen her that day in his office, she had dominated his dreams even more than before, making him wake up drenched in sweat during the wee hours of the night.

"Mr. Garrison? What brings you here?" Rae'jean asked when she finally stood in front of him, only a breath away, eyeing him with quiet defiance. She decided that had been a stupid question when she saw the big envelope he was holding in his hand.

"I thought I would drop this off with you myself, Ms. Bennett, since I was in the neighborhood," Ryan responded, loving the way her mouth had tightened into a disapproving frown. Seeing him again bothered her as much as seeing her again bothered him. He watched as she lowered her eyes and fixed them on the package he held in his hand.

"You've found something out about my father?" she asked in a voice that sounded anxious but fearful of what information the package contained.

"Yes."

"Good or bad news?"

"That's for you to decide after you read the report," he murmured softly.

Rae'jean inhaled a slow, deep breath, then released it. She didn't want to read the report. She wanted him to tell her what was in it. "Tell me, please."

"You should read it for yourself, Ms. Bennett."

A lump formed in her throat. "Yes, I'm sure I should," she said, just a little shakily. "But I'm afraid to. I—I've waited so long for this moment and now I'm . . ."

"Scared," he finished for her when the word couldn't come out. "I understand." After a few moments he said, "If you really want me to, I could brief you on what I found out, but you still need to read the report in its entirety yourself."

Rae'jean expelled a sigh that sounded like relief before saying, "And I will, but I'm too tense to read it now. Thanks for your willingness to go over it with me."

Ryan's heart began to hammer hard in his chest with the look of gratitude that shone on Rae'jean's face. There was something about that look that was indefinable and held him enthralled. "All right," he finally said. He glanced around the parking lot where various people were coming and going. "But not here. Is there somewhere we can go and talk privately?"

Rae'jean lifted her shoulder and let it drop, knowing the one place where they would find absolute privacy. "Yes, my apartment."

Ryan wasn't surprised by how the inside of Rae'jean's apartment looked. The decor offered a telling glimpse into her character more than it should have. She had exquisite taste. Evidently she liked soft colors, and the leather furniture in her living room, that was covered with numerous large throw pillows, looked comfortable as well as stylish. There was a huge fireplace of marble on one side of the room, but what really set off the spacious room was the huge floor-to-ceiling window that took up an entire wall. The very first time he had laid eyes on her, she had been standing at that window looking at him. The immediate attraction between them had been overpowering. It still was, but they were both fighting like hell to control it.

"You didn't say how you liked your coffee, Mr. Garrison."

The sound of her voice floated in from the kitchen, where the aromas of freshly brewed coffee and frying bacon seeped out as well. At this very moment she was in her kitchen making them breakfast. He had followed her in his car from the hospital, and once they got to her apartment complex they had ridden the elevator up together in silence. As soon as she had opened the door to her apartment, she had surprised him by inviting him to join her for breakfast, although for most people it was actually time for lunch.

Instead of turning down her invitation like he should have done, he had consented to join her. "Black!" he called back out to her.

"And how do you like your eggs?" she called back.

His brows rose, as he tried to remember the last time someone had cooked an egg for him or he had cooked one for himself. His day began with a visit to McDonald's to get an Egg McMuffin. "Scrambled would be fine."

"Well done, medium, or light?"

Ryan couldn't help but smile. He didn't know cooking an egg could be so much trouble. "Well done will be fine!" he called back out.

"OK." Then a few moments later she said, "You can set the table for us. Use the dishes from the china cabinet. Place mats and silverware are in the drawer."

He shook his head, thinking that using fancy, expensive china for breakfast didn't make much sense, but who was he to argue? He would do as he'd been told. Besides, he was thankful for anything to do other than idly wander around her living room. He walked over to her dining room and took down the dishes and mugs from the cabinet. He pulled open a drawer and found the place mats and eating utensils.

He had just completed the task of setting the table when she breezed into the room with two platters in her hand. One was filled with crisp bacon and the other with the fluffiest-looking eggs he'd ever seen.

"I'll be back in a minute with toast and coffee. What flavor jelly do you prefer?" she asked.

He frowned. "I'm not sure. What flavor do you have?"

"Umm, just about all flavors I could imagine. For the holidays, some of my relatives who know how much I enjoyed eating jelly as a child always send me those gift packs of miniature jars. They're always good to have on hand."

He nodded. "Grape will do."

She smiled. "OK, I'll be right back. You can go ahead and start filling your plate if you like." Before he could say anything else, she had breezed back out of the room.

Ryan's brow lifted as he tried to wonder just what to make of Rae'jean Bennett. He glanced down at the platters she had set on the table. One thing was certain: the woman could throw down when it came to a meal, and he had to admit he was definitely hungry. Following her orders, he immediately sat down at the table. He was just about to reach for the platter of eggs when she returned with a percolator in one hand and a platter of toast and jelly in the other.

"Now, we're all set," she said, placing the items on the table and then sitting down across from him. "First we say grace."

Following her lead, he bowed his head while she said a few words of thanks.

"Amen."

"Amen."

She smiled over at him. "Don't be shy; just dig in."

"Thanks," he said as he began filling his plate, and not with meager rations, either. He couldn't remember the last time a woman had cooked for him. In fact, he doubted one ever had. His father had raised him after his mother had died before his first birthday of breast cancer, and his ex-wife, Cherise, had not been the domestic kind. The only thing she did in the kitchen was pass through it. With her hectic schedule as an attorney she normally would eat on the run, leaving him to his own devices.

Rae'jean poured the both of them coffee. "I hope I didn't make it too strong for you."

"I'm sure it's fine." Then after taking a sip he said, "It's delicious." And he meant every word of it. As impossible as it seemed, the woman even knew how to make good coffee. "Who taught you how to cook?" he asked after trying the eggs and bacon. Like the coffee, they were absolutely delicious.

"My grandmother. I spent a lot of time with her while growing up, which meant I spent a lot of time in her kitchen. I enjoy cooking. In fact, I don't do enough of it since it's only me. Grady, being from the North, never appreciated a home-cooked meal." She smiled. "His idea of a good breakfast was a bowl of Cream of Wheat, and dinner was a steak off the grill with a tossed salad. He was definitely not a meat-and-potatoes man." After taking a sip of coffee, she asked, "Where are you originally from, Mr. Garrison?"

Ryan's coffee cup stopped midway to his lips and he met her eyes. "South Carolina."

She nodded. "I've visited there before. In college a group of friends and I rented a condo in Hilton Head during spring break one year. We had lots of fun. Do you still have family there?"

"No. My mother was an only child. She died before I turned one, and I didn't know any relatives on her side of the family. My father died while I was in college. He had a brother who passed away a few years back."

Rae'jean nodded slowly. "So you don't have any family?"

"No."

She chuckled. "Well, I have a bunch, more than I can count, and I'm definitely into sharing."

Ryan nodded. He liked her voice, all soft and mellow. The sound of it was doing crazy things to his heart rate. He knew he needed to take his mind off her voice and get their conversation on course. There was information he needed to share with her about her father.

He took a deep breath, wishing he didn't have to tell her anything, especially not during breakfast. So he decided to delay it awhile. "Where did you go to school?" he asked her as he refilled his plate with more eggs.

"I got my bachelor's from the University of Georgia and got my medical degree from Meharry," she replied.

He nodded. "I got both my bachelor and master's degrees from the University of South Carolina before going to work for the FBI."

She found that interesting. "How did you like being an agent?"

"It was OK, but I wanted to be my own boss. That's why I started my investigative business." He took another sip of coffee before asking, "Have you lived here in Boston long?"

She shook her head as she chewed the last of her bacon. "I've been here for two years now. I was working at a hospital in Maryland before transferring here."

Rae'jean pushed her plate aside and studied Ryan. It was obvious he was trying to avoid discussing the report that was sitting on the table in her living room. That made her even more nervous about what it said. She took a deep breath and gave him a nervous glance. "Mr. Garrison, I'd like to know what the report says."

He held her gaze. "You don't want to wait until after you finish breakfast to talk about it?"

She shook her head as the anxiety within her began to rebuild. "No."

He smiled faintly and nodded. "All right then." He leaned back in his
chair. "Finding your father was not hard at all. In fact, it was as easy as I
thought it would be. He's been living and working in Texas for the past
twenty-eight years. The insurance company his family owned went bank-
rupt around ten years ago. He's been employed with another major
insurance company as one of their top executives."

Rae'jean's heart fluttered with the news. "What part of Texas?"

"San Antonio."

She took a minute to concentrate on what he had said. Now that she
knew where her father lived there was nothing that would stop her from
going to see him and introducing herself to him. She would have to be
strong enough to handle whatever his reaction would be to her. Even rejection. "I have some time coming that I can take off. Other than my
cousin's wedding next month, I don't have anything planned. I think I'll
fly to San Antonio to meet him."

Ryan took another bite of his food, chewed, and swallowed before
saying, "Ms. Bennett, there's more."

She glanced up at Ryan. "What else is there?"

Taking a deep breath and holding her gaze, he said softly, "You can't
go see him."

Her expression turned puzzled. "Why can't I?" She felt a lump form
in her throat when she felt the effort he was putting into making sure he
said the next words carefully. He leaned forward. "I'm sorry to be the one
to have to tell you this," he said tightly. "But your father passed away in
January of this year."

Rae'jean's breath caught. She met his gaze, not wanting to believe what
he'd just said. It couldn't be true. The man who had fathered her couldn't
be dead, not when she had finally found him and had planned on getting
to know him.

She took a deep calming breath. "How did he die?"

Ryan looked at her, hating the thought that the news he was giving her
was causing her pain. "He was killed in a car accident less than ten miles
from his home while on his way from work."

Rae'jean took another deep calming breath, knowing she had to pull herself together. She reached over and began filling her plate with more eggs and bacon, enough for two people. "It doesn't really matter, you know," she said quickly, as if to convince herself and not him. "I didn't even know him, so news of his death really doesn't bother me."

Ryan watched as she absentmindedly sprinkled sugar on her eggs instead of salt. "I don't understand what reason I have to feel bad about him dying," she continued. "He knew I existed and never came to see me anyway. I can't believe I'm letting myself get worked up over this for—"

Ryan immediately stood and closed the distance between them. He was long past caring about the promise he'd made to her to keep things strictly business between them. He reached out and gently pulled her from her seat and into his arms, letting his chest absorb her tears. "It's OK to cry. It's OK. Whether you ever met him or not, he was still your father and you cared. You cared enough to want to find him. I'm just so sorry it was too late," he said in a husky voice.

She nodded her head as she smothered her face in his chest, appreciating the comfort she found there. "It's so unfair. So unfair."

On that he had to agree with her. "There is something else I have to tell you that may be good news, though."

She lifted her tear-stained gaze to his. His expression was one of deep concern and compassion. "What?"

"You have a sister."

Her eyes widened in surprise. "A sister?"

"Yes," he answered with hesitancy. "Your father got married shortly after leaving Macon, and he and his wife had a daughter. She's only two years younger than you, and the two of you look so much alike it's uncanny."

Rae'jean's heart pounded. "You saw her?"

"No, but the guy who works for me out of Texas did. In fact, he took pictures and they are included in his report. Do you want to see them?"

"Yes."

Taking her hand in his, he led her over to the sofa, and they sat down. He opened the package and pulled out several pictures and handed them to her. He watched as she studied each one of them.

"We do favor each other a lot, don't we?" she asked quietly with utter amazement. No one could deny they were sisters.

"Yes, probably because her mother was Hispanic, which accounts for the both of you having the same coloring. The two of you must have favored your father."

Rae'jean nodded. "Do you have any information on her? What's her name? What does she do?"

Ryan smiled. He was glad to hear the excitement return to her voice. "Her name is Danica, but she goes by 'Dani.' She's twenty-eight and finished school at the University of Texas with a master's degree in accounting. She works as an accountant for a large firm in San Antonio. She's single; however, she's been dating the same guy for over a year. He's an attorney who works for the same firm that she does."

Rae'jean stared at Ryan, amazed. "You were able to get all that information?"

"Yes."

Rae'jean smiled. "Is there any more?"

"Yes. Her mother died when she was ten, and your father raised her. They were very close."

She nodded. "Does she know about me?"

"My man was advised not to make contact of any kind, so I don't know if your father ever told her about you. Under the circumstances, I doubt that he did, but who knows?"

Rae'jean stood and began pacing the floor. "I'd like to go to Texas and meet her."

He nodded, not surprised. "All the information you need is inside that packet, including her address." He stood and looked at her steadily. "Do you have any more questions about anything?"

She shook her head. "No."

He nodded. "Then that concludes your business with my company. A bill will be sent to you within a week."

Rae'jean waited to see what else he would say, since it appeared he was getting things back on a business level with them. When he didn't say anything, she stood, reached out, and presented him her hand. "Thanks for everything, Mr. Garrison. I appreciate everything that you did."

He looked down at her hand for almost a second before taking it in his. He didn't try fighting the warm feeling that settled in his chest from the feel of it encompassed in his. "Don't mention it, Ms. Bennett, and thanks for breakfast." He released her hand.

She looked up at him and smiled wryly. "Anytime."

He smiled, hoping she actually meant that, as relief washed through him. Now that their business was concluded he had wondered what excuse he could come up with to see her again. "How about tomorrow?" he asked huskily.

Rae'jean blinked. "Excuse me?"

Ryan hesitated, wondering for the second time that day if he needed to have his head examined. He was totally forgetting his ironclad rule of not getting involved with a client. But then, he reasoned, she was no longer a client. "You said we could do breakfast again anytime, so I was wondering about tomorrow."

"All right," she said, almost at a loss for words. "Tomorrow would be fine. Do you like pancakes?"

He decided not to tell her that he always enjoyed the ones he got from McDonald's, but he knew any she made would probably taste a lot better. "Yes, I like pancakes."

She smiled up at him. "Good. We'll have pancakes, eggs, and sausage tomorrow."

That sounded mighty good to him. He glanced down at his watch. "I'd better go."

"OK."

"Is there anything I need to bring tomorrow?"

She shook her head and grinned. "No, just a healthy appetite."

He glanced over at the table. "Do you need help cleaning up? I can call the office and—"

"No, I can handle things here. Then I plan on going to bed and getting some sleep. I have to report back to work at ten tonight."

He nodded slowly. "But you'll be getting off in the morning at ten just like today, right?"

"Right." She tipped her head to the side as she gazed up at him. "Just out of curiosity, how do you know the hours I work?"

He smiled mischievously. "I'll tell you tomorrow." Turning, he headed for the door. He pulled it open and started through it, then turned back around. He smiled again, but this time his smile as well as the gaze was focused and intense. "Good-bye, Rae'jean."

Hearing him say her first name for the first time sent her pulse racing and the lower part of her stomach simmering. She returned his smile, inhaling deeply, then releasing it slowly. "Good-bye, Ryan."

Rae'jean watched as he walked out of the apartment, closing the door behind him. She shook her head. She had no idea how they had gone from uninvolved to involved in less than two hours.

CHAPTER 35

R yan leaned back in his chair. "Mmm, breakfast was fantastic again. Do you ever rent out your cooking services?"

Rae'jean had risen and was already clearing off the table. She smiled when she looked at Ryan. "No, but like I told you yesterday, you're welcome to breakfast anytime. Every once in a while I find time to cook dinner, but because of my hours at the hospital that usually doesn't happen." She lifted a brow. "And speaking of my hours at the hospital, you never did say how you knew what shift I worked."

Ryan stood and began helping Rae'jean remove the items from the table. He smiled at her. "Didn't I?"

"No, you didn't." Conversation during breakfast had really been nice. They had talked about Samuel Jackson's latest movie, delved into a discussion of politics, and talked about the house Ryan had recently moved into. But neither had discussed their respective jobs.

"It must have slipped my mind," he said easily, following her into the kitchen, where he deposited their used dishes on the counter. He leaned against the counter and watched as she put the syrup, milk, and orange juice into the refrigerator.

"Yes, it must have." She walked over to the sink and began making dishwater. "So how did you know what time I got off work yesterday?"

The room got quiet and Rae'jean glanced back over her shoulder at him. He was looking at her intently. "When I lived here I used to watch you leave every night. I would stand by my window and watch you get into your car. Although the parking lot was well lit, I had to know you were safe," he finally said.

Rae'jean was suddenly unsure as to what she should say. Knowing he had watched her leave each night because he cared for her safety touched her. She cleared her throat. "Thanks. I didn't know."

His impressive shoulders lifted slightly. "There was no need for you to know. To be totally honest with you, I didn't have a right to stand there and watch out for you the way I did. You belonged to another man," he said, raising his eyes to Rae'jean. "But I also happened to notice your fiancé was never here at night when you left, nor did he spend the nights over here on your days off. Why?"

His question took her by surprise. She started not to answer him, thinking her past relationship with Grady was none of his business. But if she wanted to satisfy her curiosity about him, then she had to satisfy his curiosity about her as well. "Once I agreed to marry Grady I made him promise that we wouldn't sleep together anymore until our wedding night. We had just gotten engaged the day before you moved in."

Ryan nodded. "Making a promise like that didn't bother him?"

Rae'jean grinned as she reached for the dishes off the counter to place in the sudsy water. "I wouldn't say that, but he was a good sport about it."

Ryan crossed the room to get the dish towel off the rack. He went to her side and began drying the dishes she had washed. He tilted his head and looked at her and asked, "And did it bother you?"

She glanced up at him, vitally aware of him and how much space his masculine physique took up in her kitchen. "What?"

"The abstinence."

"Oh, heavens no," she said, blushing somewhat at their topic of conversation. "I'm not a passionate person anyway, so it didn't bother me at all."

Ryan almost dropped the plate he was drying. He stared at her, stunned, astonished at such a notion. "Excuse me?"

Her blush deepened. "I said I'm not a passionate person, so the abstinence didn't bother me," she said flatly.

Ryan continued to stare at her. That was what he thought she said. He put the plate he was holding down. "What gave you that idea about you not being a passionate person?"

Rae'jean shrugged, wondering how on earth they had gotten on this topic of conversation and just what she could do to get them off of it. She gazed levelly and said, "Because I know I'm not. In my profession as a doctor there's as much excitement, tempestuousness, and intensity as I can handle. I don't want nor do I need those things to spill over into my personal life as well. I much prefer the calm, sedate, tranquil. I don't like the turbulence that full-fledged passion can bring. Somehow my body has built an immunity to it. Grady understood that and I appreciated him for it."

Ryan shook his head as he dried another plate. The corners of his lips tilted into a faint smile. Unbelievable, he thought. If this woman thought she much preferred calm in a relationship rather than passion she was really fooling herself. He wondered what she thought the two of them were feeling whenever they came within two feet of each other. Why did she think they were working so hard even now to keep it in check? She probably had more passion in her little finger than most women had in their entire bodies. But evidently it was bottled passion, and as far as he was concerned, around him the cap wasn't on the bottle too tight.

He had definitely felt passion emitting from her that day he had seen her standing at the window looking at him. And then that other time, when they had collided in the hallway, he had felt it. It had been so thick he could have cut it with a knife. And then, even more recently, the time in his office and yesterday and even today. Did she know what real passion was? Whether she admitted it or not, she was full of it. And if she was bottling it inside of her, he could just imagine how it would be once it got unleashed. That would be one hell of an explosion.

"I know it's different for some men," she then remarked as casually as if they were discussing the weather and not such an intimate subject as passion. "Passion is important to some men, isn't it?"

Even her voice sounded passionate and desirable, he thought. "Depends on who it's coming from and how deep you feel about that person."

She nodded. She wouldn't be surprised if Grady felt a lot stronger passion for Lynn than he had for her now that he'd accepted the fact that he was in love with Lynn. She wondered if the reason the two of them never shared earth-shattering passion was because they hadn't been in love with each other.

Rae'jean and Ryan continued doing the dishes in silence. Rae'jean thought that since she had shared something about herself with him, she wanted to satisfy her curiosity about him. "You mentioned you're divorced. Are you and your ex-wife still on friendly terms?"

He was reaching up and putting the juice glasses back in the cabinet. He slanted her a look that was minus his usual smile. "No. It's hard to stay on friendly terms with a woman who got pregnant from another man while married to you," he said coldly, his jaw tensing.

Rae'jean stopped what she was doing and turned to him apologetically. "I'm sorry."

"Why? You didn't do anything."

"I brought up a subject that must be painful to you."

He shook his head dismissively and turned his focus back to drying the dishes. "I've gotten over it. You learn from your mistakes. She was mine."

Rae'jean nodded. "How did the two of you meet?"

Without turning to look at her, he said, "She came to me as a client. She's a defense attorney and needed my help solving a murder her client had been charged with. She won the case and we went out and celebrated one night and lost our heads. She got pregnant. I did the honorable thing and asked her to marry me, and she accepted since it wouldn't have looked good for her to be a single mom in the prestigious law firm where she worked."

"How long were you married?"

"A little over two years."

Rae'jean pressed her lips together when she remembered something. "I thought you said you don't have any children."

"I don't. She lost the baby in her fourth month, but we decided to remain married and make it work." He replaced the dish towel on the rack. "At least that's what I thought we had decided to do. I didn't know she had resumed an affair with another attorney in her office who was married. They decided they wanted to be together, especially after she got pregnant with his child. He divorced his wife of ten years and she divorced me."

"Did they get married?"

He turned to face her. "Yes. They got married the same day our divorce became final. They have since left the firm they were working for and have now formed their own law office."

She nodded. No wonder he'd been adamant about not mixing business with pleasure. The last time he'd done so had turned out disastrous for him. Before she could say anything else the doorbell rang. She breathed in deeply, relieved by the interruption. "Excuse me while I answer that."

Leaving the kitchen, she walked into the living room to the door and opened it. "Grady?" She was surprised but happy to see him. Since Lynn had been released from the hospital and was going through rehabilitative therapy, Rae'jean didn't see Grady much anymore.

"Hi, Rae'jean. I got some good news to share with you," he said, entering her apartment when she stepped aside.

She could feel his excitement. "What is it?"

Before Grady could respond he glanced over her shoulder and a surprised expression appeared on his face. Rae'jean turned to see what had caught his attention and saw Ryan standing in the doorway that led to the kitchen. She looked from Ryan back to Grady. "Ryan mentioned the two of you ran into each other in the elevators a few times but haven't actually met," she said diplomatically.

Grady shook his head as he kept his eyes on the man standing across the room. "No, we haven't."

Ryan crossed the room to stand next to Rae'jean, and she was suddenly aware how the two men were staring at each other. "Grady, this is Ryan Garrison. He was my neighbor for a while some months ago, and he's the investigator I hired to find my father."

Grady nodded. Although Rae'jean had painted a picture that indicated her relationship with Ryan was business, Grady could tell by the way Ryan was looking at him that the man wanted more. Grady wanted Rae'jean to be happy, and for some reason he felt the man standing beside her could make that happen. "Good seeing you again, Ryan." He smiled, offering him his hand.

Ryan felt the sincerity in Grady's smile as well as in his handshake. He relaxed his guard and began feeling less awkward. "Same here, Grady."

"So what's your good news, Grady?" Rae'jean asked, relieved that there was now a more relaxed atmosphere surrounding the two men.

Grady's smile widened. "I got a call from Dr. Morris Donovan. He wants me to come to San Diego General and work closely with him in the cardiology department there."

Rae'jean let out a squeal as she threw her arms around him. "Grady, that's wonderful! I know how much you wanted that position. How soon will you be leaving?"

"Not for another month or so. I told him about Lynn, and he understands." Grady then looked at Rae'jean thoughtfully. He felt better telling her what he was about to tell her with Ryan standing by her side, since it was obvious to him the man was interested in her. "There's something else I have to tell you, Rae."

She lifted her brow at the serious tone in his voice. She looked up at him. "What is it, Grady?"

"Lynn and I have decided to get married this weekend. I wanted you to know."

Grady watched as Ryan instinctively stepped closer to Rae'jean's side. "Oh, Grady, that's wonderful. I'm so happy for the both of you," she said, smiling.

He nodded, knowing that she truly was. If it hadn't been for her, he would not have realized his true feelings for Lynn until it was too late. "Thanks, Rae'jean. Now what about your father? Were you able to find him?"

Rae'jean told him about Ryan's report. "Oh, Rae'jean, I'm sorry. I know how much finding him meant to you."

"I'm OK. Now I'm looking forward to meeting my sister."

After Grady left, Rae'jean was quiet. Ryan was just as quiet. Then he spoke. "It doesn't bother you that he's marrying another woman a little more than a month after the two of you ended your engagement?"

Rae'jean looked up at Ryan and shook her head. "No. I'm glad I was able to get him to see just how much he loved Lynn before he made a mistake and married me."

When Ryan cast her a confused look she told him the entire story, including her part in bringing Lynn and Grady together. "So you realized the two of you were not in love?" he asked.

"Yes. We love each other as friends but not the way two people who plan on getting married and sharing a life together should love each other."

Ryan nodded. No wonder they had been quick to settle for a passionless relationship. He knew if he and Rae'jean ever became involved, it would definitely not be that way with them. "I'm leaving later today for Miami. I'll be gone for a couple of days. When I return will you have dinner with me?"

"You don't have to do that, Ryan. I—"

"I want to, Rae'jean. I enjoy your company. Will you be free Friday night?"

"Yes, I'm not working that night."

"Can I come pick you up around seven then?"

Rae'jean lowered her head and studied the floor. Where would all this lead, the breakfasts and now dinner? Did she want to know? Did she dare find out? Maybe it was best if she didn't. She raised her eyes to him and shook her head. "I'm not ready for a serious involvement with anyone right now, Ryan."

He nodded. "Neither am I. But having breakfast together twice hasn't killed us and I doubt sharing dinner will, either. I'm not asking you to move in with me, Rae'jean. All I'm asking is for you to have dinner with me. Will you?"

The odd note of pleading in his voice helped Rae'jean make the decision. "Yes, I'll go out to dinner with you."

A smile curved his lips. "Thanks." He glanced back down at his watch. "I'd better go," he said in a voice that was thick and taut.

"All right. I hope you have a safe trip to Florida, and I'll see you when you return on Friday."

He nodded, reached for the door, then paused. He stared at her, as if going through the motions of making up his mind about something. Then he reached for her and lowered his head. Rae'jean met his lips without hesitation.

He kissed her possessively, thoroughly, and she kissed him back, putting everything she had into it. It was a greedy kiss, as he continued to taste her as if he were sampling the sweetest wine. His tongue mated with hers, sucking hers deeply and sparking a demand from her. When he heard the moan from deep within her throat, his kiss became hotter, more electrifying.

Just when Rae'jean was certain she wouldn't be able to endure his kiss a minute longer before her body began going up in smoke, with excruciating slowness he pulled his mouth away.

She heard him utter a soft chuckle as he continued to hold her in his arms. "If that wasn't passion, Rae'jean, I'd like to know what it was."

She swallowed as she looked up at him. The burning inside of her was too intense to say anything at the moment.

"Take care, Rae'jean," he whispered into her ear before releasing her.

Before she could gather her wits he had opened the door, walked out, and closed it behind him. Taking a deep breath, she licked her tongue to her lips, savoring the taste he'd left behind. Her insides quivered at the memory of how it felt to be held in his arms. Sensations raced along her nerve endings. She had felt simmering heat. She had felt tingling in her toes. She had felt turbulence of the most jolting kind, a fierce throbbing need in the very center of her body.

She placed her arms around her waist as heated blood rushed through her veins and she acknowledged what all of that meant.

In Ryan's arms she had felt passion. Unmistakable earth-shaking passion. And she had liked it.

CHAPTER 36

"Thanks for a lovely evening, Ryan."

"I'm glad you enjoyed it."

Rae'jean covertly studied Ryan as they stood in front of her apartment door. The restaurant he had chosen had had good food as well as good entertainment, a live jazz band. And as much as she hated admitting it, she'd been glad to see him when he had shown up at her place at exactly seven o'clock to take her to dinner.

As if they had a mind of their own, her eyes lingered on the sensual fullness of his lips, and she remembered their kiss of three days ago. She had actually melted in his arms. As she continued watching his lips, she suddenly noticed they were moving and realized belatedly—with deep embarrassment—that he'd said something to her.

"I'm sorry; what did you say?"

His smile and the amusement lurking in the depths of his eyes made her think he knew where her mind had been. "I asked when you were leaving for Texas?"

"Tuesday morning."

He nodded. "And you still plan to surprise your sister?"

Rae'jean heard the censure in his voice. "You don't think that's the best approach?"

He conceded that with a nod. "Not all people like surprises. Why don't you give her a call first?"

Rae'jean blew out a breath, not wanting to tell him that she had dismissed that idea for fear Danica Turner would refuse to see her. At least if she showed up unannounced they would be forced to meet face-to-face.

"It will be a blessing for her to want to meet you, Rae'jean. If for some reason she doesn't want to meet you or get to know you, it will be her loss."

Rae'jean met Ryan's gaze. He had read her thoughts explicitly. He knew her doubts and fears. "I want things to turn out right for us. We're sisters."

"But you're also different people who may not have the same values and the same feelings about things. You were raised differently. You've always been surrounded by family. After reading the report I'm sure you know that your father was all the family she had. It may be hard for her to accept he had another daughter, especially if he didn't mention it to her."

Rae'jean nodded. "But we look so much alike. Surely she won't deny that we're related."

"No, but acknowledging that the two of you share the same blood doesn't necessarily mean she'll want to strike up a relationship of any kind with you. You may want to be prepared for that."

Rae'jean saw the point he was trying to make. "You're right and I appreciate the advice." After a few moments of silence she asked, "Would you like to come in . . . for coffee or a drink?"

With his gaze never leaving hers, he said, "Yes, I'd like to come in just for a minute."

Ignoring the faint trembling of her fingers, Rae'jean opened her apartment door, and the two of them stepped inside. Ryan closed the door behind them. Breath became suspended in Rae'jean's throat when he placed his hand on her wrist to stop her from going anywhere.

"This will only take a minute," he said huskily before leaning down and joining his mouth to hers.

There was a huge explosion or the loud popping of fireworks. Rae'jean wasn't sure exactly which sound she heard the moment Ryan's lips touched hers. A tiny moan broke past her lips and was captured by his as his mouth moved over hers with hungry abandonment. She pressed her body against him and felt the proof of his maleness as well as his want and his desire.

His ravaging of her mouth was too delicious, too wonderful, and too passionate.

She had thought all this time that she didn't need or want passion. But the onslaught of his mouth on hers was proving otherwise. She was melting in his arms again.

He pulled away briefly. His voice was thick against her mouth when he said, "Do you still want to downplay passion, Rae'jean? Can you still honestly say you don't want or need this—the passion, the turbulence, the fire? Can you still settle for calm?"

Her response was breathy when she spoke. "I—I don't think so."

"I don't think so, either." He curved a hand to her neck and brought her closer as he dipped his head again and captured her mouth. The intensity of his kiss conveyed a deep emotional yearning; it bestowed an even greater emotional need. He gave them both the purest of pleasure in this mouth-to-mouth contact as their tongues mated.

Slowly he pulled away, his breathing deep. "I'd better go," he whispered against her lips. "While I still have the mind to do so."

She nodded. Yes, he had better go, while she still had the mind to let him. With a sigh she took a step back. A small warning pricked at the back of her neck reminding her that she did not want to get seriously involved with someone else this soon. She looked away from him as her insides began tightening in tangled knots. She wasn't sure what she wanted anymore.

"Think about it, Rae'jean."

His words invaded her thoughts. She didn't have to ask him to elaborate on what she needed to think about. He had read her thoughts again. Somehow he knew she was having doubts about their getting together. "And will you do the same, Ryan?" she asked, looking up at him. She knew that because of his fairly recent divorce, he had issues to deal with as well before thinking about getting involved in a serious relationship.

"Yes, I'll think about it," he replied huskily. After a few brief moments he asked, "How long will you be gone?"

"I plan to be in Texas for a couple of days; then after a pit stop in Macon I'm flying to Jamaica to attend my cousin's wedding."

He nodded. "So you'll be gone for a week?"

"Actually, it will be ten days."

Ryan hung his head as if in deep thought. When he lifted his head and looked into her eyes, the gaze that held hers was intense. "We should know by then what, if anything, we want from each other. A serious relationship or just friendship."

She nodded. "I agree. I can't become sexually involved with anyone I don't care deeply about, Ryan. I'm not into casual affairs."

"Neither am I. I lost my head to passion one night and it ended up costing me two years of heartache and pain. I don't ever want to go through that again. I want to take my next relationship with a woman slow. I won't risk there being any misunderstandings between us by rushing things. I would want for us to get to know each other better, spend time together, and see what happens from there."

If Rae'jean was thankful for one thing, it was for the way Ryan saw things. He didn't want to rush anything between them. He wanted to take things slow and was willing for them to sort through things and determine just where, if anyplace, they wanted to go.

"I hope things turn out the way you want them to in Texas. Will you at least call me and let me know something?"

"Yes, I'll call you."

He leaned down and brushed his lips against hers. "Good-bye, Rae'jean."

"Good-bye, Ryan."

She then watched as he opened the door and walked out of it.

FIVE DAYS LATER IN SAN ANTONIO, TEXAS
Rae'jean looked around the plush restaurant, feeling grateful that Danica Turner had agreed to see her.

At first the young woman had staunchly denied that her father could have fathered another child without her knowing about it. There was no way he would not have told her that she had a sibling somewhere, she had said over the phone. He wasn't the type of man to keep something like that a secret. She had taken Rae'jean's number at the hotel anyway and said she would talk to someone who would know the truth, a man who'd been her father's best friend for over fifty years.

It had been another full day before Danica returned Rae'jean's call. Her father's best friend had confirmed that David Turner had gotten a young woman pregnant nearly thirty-one years ago while working in Macon, Georgia. However, after he moved to Texas his grandfather told him the young woman had miscarried the child. Blaming himself for the heartache and pain he'd caused the young woman and her family, he had made a decision not to contact the young woman again.

Rae'jean glanced up when she heard someone's approach and saw the young woman walking toward her table. She studied the features of the young woman and thought once again that it was simply amazing how much the two of them favored each other. The other woman evidently thought the same thing. She stopped dead in her tracks and stared at Rae'jean, then somehow collected herself and continued walking toward her.

Placing a cheerful smile on her face, Rae'jean stood and nervously extended her hand out to Danica. Staring into a face that looked so much like hers was almost a bit much. "Hi, I'm Rae'jean."

"This is amazing," the young woman said softly, clearly astonished. "I wish Dad could have lived for this moment. He would have been speechless and deeply shocked to know he'd been lied to all those years, Ms. Bennett."

Rae'jean nodded as the two of them sat down. "There's so much I want to know about him. Mom never talked about my father. She died eight years ago, and only recently was I given his name."

Danica smiled, shaking her head. "I'll tell you anything you want to know. And I should apologize for doubting what you said over the phone."

"An apology isn't necessary. Your reaction to my phone call was understandable." She looked deep into Danica's eyes and said, "It's hard to believe that we're actually sisters. I've never had a sister before."

Danica chuckled. "Neither have I, and I would love to get to know you better."

Rae'jean smiled. "Same here."

They had both taken the first step.

Later that night Rae'jean placed a phone call to Ryan and told him everything that had happened that day.

"I'm glad things worked out the way you wanted them to, Rae'jean."

She held the phone tight in her hand; a part of her wished he were there with her. "Thanks, Ryan. She plans to visit me in Boston for Christmas."

"What about her fiancé? Did you get a chance to meet him?"

"Yes, and he's a very nice person. I think they're getting married sometime next year."

They both became quiet; then after a few moments Ryan said, "I miss you, Rae'jean."

Rae'jean inhaled deeply. She hadn't realized that such a deep male voice could sound so soft and raspy. "I miss you, too, Ryan." As she said the words, she wondered how it was possible. They had only shared breakfast together twice and had shared dinner together once, but for some reason Ryan Garrison was becoming a very intricate part of her life.

"Rae'jean?"

"Yes?"

"I hope to see you when you get back."

You will, she wanted to say but knew she couldn't. She still had a lot more thinking to do. She had to be sure she was ready for more than just friendship with him. "Good night, Ryan."

"Good night, Rae'jean. Pleasant dreams."

When Rae'jean went to sleep that night she did have pleasant dreams, and just like the nights before, they were about Ryan.

CHAPTER 37

Taye forced open sleepy eyes when she heard the doorbell chime downstairs. It had to be past midnight, so who would be dropping by this late?

Shoving the bedcovers aside, she tucked her feet into the Tigger from *Winnie the Pooh* slippers the girls had bought for her while in Orlando. Walking over to the window, she peeped down at the street below and saw Michael's car parked in her driveway. She'd known his flight to Connecticut would not return until fairly late, but why had he come by her place? Had he forgotten the girls were staying overnight at Fayrene's house?

Picking her robe up off the bed, she thrust her arms through the sleeves, thinking that a good night's sleep had been too much to hope for. The AKAs were holding their national sorority convention in Atlanta this weekend, and Taye had prepared more sistahs' heads for the event than she cared to remember. She had arrived at the salon at seven that morning, and it had been nonstop from then on. She had done more weaves today than she'd done in a long time. Everyone wanted the Alexia Bennett look. As far as Taye was concerned, that particular hairstyle—which should have retired right along with Diana Ross—was being brought back by Alexia and in a big way, which wasn't surprising, since Diana was Alexia's idol. Everyone wanted the long, full-looking, wild hairstyle and was willing to pay good money to get it. She shook her head thinking of the number of sistahs who didn't seem to mind that the amount of hair on their heads was out of proportion with their faces.

The doorbell chimed again before Taye could make it down the stairs. She saw the silhouette of Michael's body through the door's beveled glass. After freeing the chain and the dead bolts, she quickly opened the door. "Michael? What are you doing here? Did you forget the girls are spending the night with Victoria at Fayrene's house?"

Michael leaned against the doorway, produced a charming smile; then very softly he said, "No, Taye, I didn't forget."

She glanced at him warily. "Then why are you here?"

"I just got in and didn't think I could make the drive the rest of the way home."

Taye narrowed her eyes. *The rest of the way home was only a whopping two miles.* "Are you saying you couldn't drive those two extra miles to your own house?"

He leaned in closer. "I probably could have had I really pushed myself," he said smoothly, slipping her another charming smile. "But I like your place better. With Kennedy gone my house will be lonely."

Taye shook her head, returning his smile although she didn't want to. "Haven't you gotten with the program yet, Michael? Parents aren't sup- posed to miss their kids when they're away for the night. You're supposed to rejoice, count your blessings, and relish the peace."

He chuckled. "Then, no, I guess I haven't gotten with the program yet. I'm used to coming home from a flight knowing Kennedy's home with the sitter or that she's over here with you and the girls."

Taye nodded and her voice turned serious. "You do know that she's OK over at Fayrene's, don't you?"

"Yes, I know that. Old habits are just hard for some fathers to break." He released an aggrieved sigh. "Are you going to make me stand out here all night or are you going to invite me in and let me use your sofa?"

Taye's sigh was as deep as his. "What kind of person would I be if I were to force you to go on home to an empty house?" she said, stepping aside so he could enter. "Besides, I'm too tired to argue with you at this hour."

"You had a busy day?" Michael asked as he stepped into her living room.

"You can definitely say that. A sorority convention is in town this week.

I earned enough money today to cover a lot of my bills for the month and still have some chump change left." She yawned. "I'll be back in a minute with some blankets for you."

"You sure you don't mind if I crash here tonight?"

"Nope," she said as she headed for a hall closet that was off the living room. "Why should I mind that you prefer my lumpy couch to a nice, comfortable bed at your house?" She tossed him a sheet and a blanket. "I'm going back to bed. If there's anything else you need, just help yourself finding it. Sleep tight."

Michael sighed with resignation as he watched Taye go back up the stairs. He growled under his breath as he mentally took a long, slow count to ten. The woman looked utterly tempting wearing a plain white cotton bathrobe. Jeez. Octavia Bennett wasn't making things easy for him, and he was fast losing his patience.

Ever since their Orlando trip, whenever he tried taking two steps forward with her she would counter his efforts by taking two steps back. She was determined to keep things in a family way between them. He was beginning to get sick and tired of this family crap, since it was keeping them at arm's length. She was willing to sacrifice what he knew they felt for each other for the sake of the family.

He cursed softly. It had been nearly three weeks since they had returned from vacationing in Orlando, and the memories of that night on the patio were driving him crazy. He thought about her constantly, and whenever he was around her for long periods of time he nearly went out of his mind. Even the girls' presence didn't downplay his desire for her like it used to. He was too far gone. He would sit and watch how she would take time with her girls as well as with Kennedy, who had lacked a woman's presence in her life for the past six years. He'd longed for that same kind of loving attention that Taye was unrestrictedly giving her daughters and his.

Michael sucked in a deep breath. He had missed his daughter true enough, but he'd known that she was OK with Fayrene. What had really driven him to this house in such a mad dash had been this desperate need to see Taye.

The thought of making love to her was constantly on his mind, and knowing that she was under the same roof, upstairs in her bed, only made the longing worse. He glanced down at the items she had handed to him.

There was no sense getting worked up over something he couldn't do a thing about until she saw for herself that the two of them were meant to be together.

Upstairs, Taye lay in bed unable to get back to sleep knowing Michael was downstairs and that they were the only two people in the house. Other times when he'd slept over, Kennedy and her girls had always been here with them. Now, that wasn't the case.

It was just the two of them and they were alone.

Taye rolled over on her back and looked up at the ceiling, thinking about how good Michael looked tonight dressed in his pilot's uniform. There was just something sexy about a man in a uniform.

She heard the front door downstairs open and then close a few minutes later. Michael had evidently gone out to his car to get his overnight bag. When she heard the sound of water running, she knew he was about to take a shower. The thought of his naked body standing beneath a spray of water made her feel all hot inside, and she couldn't help but think about that night in Orlando. That was the night they had crossed the bounds of acceptable family behavior. Since then she had been plagued constantly with memories of that night when he had held her in his arms, against his hard body, and kissed her in a way that had left her body hot, bothered, and hungry for more.

She inhaled deeply, trying to fight off the hungry longing that had been tormenting her for three solid weeks. She couldn't be in the same room with him for long periods of time without wanting to jump his bones, which meant her bond of restraints was beginning to rage out-of-bounds. Even now, when she should have been too tired to think about anything, thoughts of him were consuming her mind. She couldn't help but imagine how it would feel for his naked body to be pressed against hers, inside of her, making love to her. Those thoughts made a fevered need burn deep within her. It was a need she was slowly losing control of as her body began protesting ten years of denial. She tightened her legs together and gripped the bedcovers, forcing her body to cool down, relax. She had never known such agony before and wasn't sure if she could endure what she was going through much longer.

• • •

Michael had settled in on the couch and was staring up at the ceiling for a long time. He couldn't sleep and there was no excuse for it. He had taken a shower and felt refreshed, cool. But his body was beginning a slow throb at the sound of Taye moving around upstairs. He wondered what she was doing. He'd thought she would be asleep by now, but from the sound of things above him, she was pacing the floor. Was she OK? Had she worked herself into a tired frenzy today and couldn't settle down and rest?

After a few moments when he still heard the sound of her pacing about, he pushed back the covers, slipped into his pants, and slowly began walking up the stairs.

In the privacy of her bedroom, Taye was going through pure hell.

She had gotten out of bed and had begun pacing the floor. Breathing deeply, she tried to fight the urges that had been tormenting her for weeks and were now raging out of control. She'd had a hefty amount of sensuous dreams over the past few years that had been so steamy she would wake up drenched in sweat. She would even admit to getting really turned on while watching one of those after-dark adult movies that she'd come across on the cable channel late one night when she couldn't sleep. But no matter what, she had always been in complete control of her mind and her body.

But not now.

She was losing it and losing it fast. In truth, she had already lost it. She had never known this sort of agony before. The very center of her body, the area between her legs, felt hot, electrified, intensified, sensitized. In need.

It took the last of her strength to make it over to her bed and sit down on the side of it. She tightened her thighs together as a throbbing sensation ripped through her loins. A deep, tortured moan escaped her lips, and she wrapped her arms around her stomach and bent her body to ease the ache, the pressure, and the desire that were pounding through her.

"Taye? Are you OK?"

The sound of Michael's voice penetrated her feverish mind, her tormented senses. She could barely raise her head to look at him standing in the open doorway, but when she did, the look on her face and the way she was holding her abdomen must have alerted him that she was in some kind of pain. He began moving quickly toward her.

"What's wrong, Taye? Are you having a bad stomachache? Side ache? Bad cramps? What is it, baby? What's wrong?" He sat next to her on the bed and gently gathered her into his arms.

"Michael," she said in a tormented voice, barely above a whisper. "I—I ache."

Total concern covered Michael's features. "You ache where? Should I call a doctor? Take you to the emergency room? What do you want me—"

"Michael," she said in a deep, ragged voice, interrupting the panic she heard in his voice. Way past the point of feeling shame, she said, "I ache *here*." Taking his hand, she pressed it against her gown to the area that ached between her legs.

Michael inhaled deeply as he broke eye contact with her and brought his head down until it nearly touched hers. He pulled her closer to him when he realized what her torment was all about and just what part of her was aching. He breathed in deeply again as he continued to hold his hand pressed against her while she began trembling in his arms. "It's OK, baby. It's OK," he said softly in her ear.

Taye tried twisting her head away from him. *No, it isn't OK,* she wanted to scream as she continued to lose touch with reality. Her body was beginning to feel hotter and hotter. His closeness and his touch, even through the material of her cotton gown, were pushing her over the edge and destroying her last hold on reality.

"Michael . . ." His name was again forced from her lips. The sound was tormented, desperate. "It's—it's not OK. I need . . ."

"It *is* OK, baby; I'll take care of you," he said soothingly as he eased her onto her back in the bed. "Trust me, Taye." He looked down at her as he tried fighting his way through her desire-hazed mind. "Will you trust me to take care of you and know I'd never do anything to hurt you?"

With the last shred of sanity she had left, she nodded. In her heart she knew that Michael would never hurt her, just like she knew in her heart that she loved him and had always loved him.

Michael fought back his own rampant need as he lifted Taye's gown up to her waist. He breathed in deeply and whispered her name as he eased his hand between her legs. At first she stiffened against his intimate touch and tried pushing his hand away. But he wouldn't let her.

"Trust me, Taye. Let me take away the ache, baby."

The sound of his voice soothed her mind but not her body. "Michael, I—I can't help this. I need . . ."

He leaned down over her. "I know, sweetheart. I know what you need. Just trust me, Taye," he murmured before stretching out beside her and kissing her.

He slowly began stroking her mouth with his, the same way his hand was stroking the sensitized flesh between her legs. She was wet, intensely so, and she was hot. He forced the thoughts from his mind of how it would feel with him inside of her as he felt himself get thick and hard. At the moment, her needs outweighed his. He was determined to release her body from the torment raging inside of her from having gone without for so long.

So he continued to stroke the sensitized flesh between her thighs, touching her in the most intimate way a man could touch a woman without making her completely his, but giving her deep gratification nonetheless. Over and over his fingers pleasured her, pushing her higher and higher as he eased the ache within her. He watched her close her eyes as her body accepted his caresses, his tantalizing treatment. Her moans of pleasure touched him and made him fall in love with her that much more. And when she began lifting her hips against his hands he could feel sweat pop out on his forehead.

"Michael," she breathed slowly when the touch of his hand became more profound, stroking the heat inside of her into the greatest pleasure she had ever known, as she trembled, succumbing to her primal craving to be satisfied. She reopened her eyes and looked at him.

"I want you inside of me, Michael." She slid her hand up to his face, wanting him to join her in the mind-blowing passion she knew lay just beyond her reach again. "The ache won't completely go away until you're inside of me, because you're the one my body is aching for," she whispered as hunger flamed desire all through her once more.

Michael closed his eyes to fight against her words, her plea. When he reopened them, he saw her looking at him with eyes heavily laden with desire. "Are you sure, Taye? What about your fear of getting pregnant?

What about your fear of the family finding out about us? I got condoms to protect you, but I can't have you for just tonight. If I make love to you, things can't ever go back to being the way they were between us. You do understand that, don't you?" he murmured hoarsely.

Taye slowly nodded her head. She had waged a fight not to love him and had lost. In the end love had won. She couldn't deny what she felt for him anymore. She couldn't deny what she wanted with him. "Yes, I understand," she whispered softly.

"Are you willing to love me and to be with me regardless of whether the family gives their blessings or not?"

He saw the look in her eyes and knew she wasn't sure they would give it, but then neither was he. But at this point, he was beyond caring. As long as their girls accepted things, and he truly believed in his heart that they would, he was determined that he would have a life, a truly rich and meaningful life, with her. "Are you willing, Taye?"

She stared deep into his dark eyes and softly said, "Yes."

Michael breathed in deeply before withdrawing his hand and easing off the bed. Before sliding down his pants, he pulled out his wallet and got two condom packets. He looked down at her. "I really think one will work, but to ease your fears I'll use two."

Taye's throat was tight. She was deeply touched by his thoughtfulness. And because of it, she was no longer fearful of anything. "One is OK."

Michael held her gaze. "Are you sure?"

"Yes, I'm sure."

He nodded. To be honest, he didn't want to use one at all but knew they had to act responsibly. He wanted a child with her, but he also wanted things to be done right. He didn't want her ever feeling guilty about getting pregnant with his child.

Taye watched Michael prepare himself for her as the heat in her body began getting hotter and the need within her began getting fiercer. Moments later, after completely removing her gown, he came to her and the weight of his naked body pinned her to the sheets. Automatically her legs opened for him as his mouth found hers.

The feel of Taye's wetness as well as her tightness was almost more than Michael could stand when he slowly entered her. By the time he had gone as deep into her body as he could go, his body was wet with sweat.

He sucked in a deep, agonizing breath when he felt Taye's tongue lick a portion of the sweat from above his lips. That gesture pushed him over the limit, and he ground his body against hers, going deeper and claiming her in the most elemental way. She lifted herself to him, moaning, demanding fulfillment.

And he gave it to her.

With overwhelming intensity and an obvious concern with her ten years of celibacy, he made love to her with compelling tenderness. At least he tried being tender, but she wouldn't let him. She didn't want him to suppress his desire to fulfill hers.

So she whispered in his ear and told him exactly, in blatant erotic terms, what she wanted him to do to her. The flagrant crudity of her words surprised him but elated him, pushing him over the edge. He immediately increased the rhythm and the tempo of their lovemaking. "I'm going to do just what you've asked, baby, so hang on."

And she did.

He tightened his arms around her, thinking that never before had making love been this good. Taye touched him in places he hadn't known existed, which attested to just how much he loved her. Her body was accepting all he was giving, as well as giving fully of herself as she arched upward to meet his every hard thrust, grateful her bed had good springs and grateful still they were the only two people in the house. Both her body and her bed were getting a workout like they'd never had before.

Taye and Michael continued straining toward each other, giving each other pleasure. He could barely breathe when she reached up and pulled his mouth down to hers, kissing him in a way that melted his insides.

She let go of his mouth to scream out his name when a fierce climax rammed through her. But it didn't stop there. He held himself back as once again he brought her body to a second climax, then a third, releasing ten years of sexual need stored within it.

Finally, when he could no longer not give in to his own body's demands, his head fell back as he pushed himself deep inside of her when a climax with more force than a freight train and tornado combined ripped through him, wringing groans from him. Passion, the likes of which he'd never experienced before, possessed him, took control of his body and his mind. His arms gripped her hips, bringing her closer to him as he felt her shudder again uncontrollably beneath him.

Moments later, when his strength had been totally consumed, he took her face in his hands and looked down at her, touching her cheek with trembling fingers. "I love you, Taye," he said in a voice made rough by what they had just shared as well as the deep emotion in his heart that he felt for her.

He saw her smile. He saw the tears wetting her eyelids when she said, "I love you, too, Michael."

"Oh, Taye," he said, slumping against her and pulling their sweat-dampened bodies together in a warm embrace. Closing his eyes, he held her in his arms, wanting to hold on to this moment for as long as he could. He slowly lifted up and looked down at her. "Because we love each other, we'll be able to handle anything. Believe that, Taye."

She looked at him, knowing that somehow he would give her the strength to handle anything as long as he loved her. "I do believe it, Michael." She then inhaled deeply. "That was truly amazing," she said softly. "It was one soul-shaking experience."

He smiled. "You think so?"

She looked up at him, smiling. "Yes."

He leaned in close and put his lips to her ears and whispered, "Want to soul-shake some more?"

Breathless, her heart fluttering, her pulse racing, she said, "Yes."

With a deep groan from the back of his throat, he joined their mouths together in a long, passionate kiss. He then slowly pulled away. Upon seeing the questioning look in her eyes, he said, "I got to make a change before we do this again, baby."

When she still looked at him, confused, he said, "I need to put on another condom."

"Oh. I'd forgotten about that," she said softly.

He leaned over and brushed a kiss across her lips. "Umm, that's OK. I meant it when I said that I would take care of you." His voice was a warm caress that stroked across her body. "You're going to be here when I get back?"

She smiled up at him. "You bet." She then watched him get up out of the bed, pick up the other condom packet off the nightstand, then turn to walk, naked as a jaybird, into the bathroom. She sighed as a satisfied smile curved her lips. She wondered what Rae'jean and Alexia would think of her now. She had gone from celibate to totally wanton in a single hour. And she loved it! Just as much as she loved Michael. She refused to think about how the family would react when they found out. She would think about that tomorrow. Then maybe she wouldn't think about it at all. Telling the girls first was the most important thing. Sebrina, Kennedy, and Monica had grown close over the past months. Taye wondered how they would handle the news that she and Michael were serious about each other. What if they were appalled at the idea, the very thought? She clutched the bedspread tightly in her hands. She refused to worry about anything tonight. The only thing she wanted to concentrate on was Michael. Loving Michael.

"Ready?"

The sound of his husky voice made her turn in the direction of the bathroom. He leaned against the door frame. She let her gaze rake over his entire body before returning to meet his eyes. "I see that *you* are."

He smiled as he slowly walked back over to the bed. "For you, always." He reached out and pulled her into his arms, holding her tight enough to imprint his body onto hers. "This time we'll take things slow."

"You think so?" she said brazenly, challengingly.

He chuckled. "Just what have I unveiled here?"

She shrugged her shoulders and grinned sheepishly. "A woman with a very hungry appetite, maybe?"

His smile deepened. "I guess after ten years I shouldn't really be surprised, should I?"

Taye pulled him back down into the bed with her. "No, you shouldn't."

Much later, after their bodies were satisfied once again, Michael gathered Taye closer into his arms and held her with his jaw resting against the top of her head while she peacefully slept. He made a silent promise that from this day forward her life would be filled with love and happiness.

Total love and complete happiness.

She belonged to him now, and their family may as well get used to the idea.

CHAPTER 38

Pretending to be asleep as she felt Michael's attempt to kiss, stroke, and taste her awake, Taye fought to keep her eyes clamped shut. With the bright sunshine peeking through the bedroom window announcing it was a new day, it seemed he had plans to continue what they'd done most of the night.

Boy, he's determined, she thought as he gently kissed her eyelids before moving down to the corners of her mouth. Playing possum wasn't easy, but she was curious to see just how far he would go to wake her up.

Then again, maybe pretending to be asleep wasn't such a good idea after all, she concluded when he rubbed his unshaven chin against the delicate skin of her breasts just moments before his tongue made a wet trail around the darkened nipple. It took everything she had not to moan out loud from the sensation.

"How long are you going to pretend to be asleep, Taye?" he whispered.

She opened her eyes and smiled up at him. "How did you know I wasn't really asleep?"

Amusement played around the corners of his mouth. "That little catch in your breath when I touched you here gave you away," he said, reaching down and again touching the very essence of her. "If you were really asleep, you wouldn't have been able to feel a thing."

She looked up at him, almost breathless again, when he continued to intimately caress her. "I seriously doubt that."

He chuckled. "Why were you pretending to be asleep? Am I boring you already?"

"Hmm, definitely not. I was curious to see just how far you would go to wake me."

Propping himself up on one elbow, he leaned over and kissed around the corners of her mouth again. "Do you really want to know?"

"Yes."

"Then I'll tell you." He leaned closer and whispered something scandalous in her ear. She actually blushed. "Michael! You wouldn't have!"

He chuckled again. "Oh, yes, I would have, and enjoyed every minute doing so. Wanna see?"

She tried backing away from him. "No, you can't."

He stopped her retreat and pulled her back toward him. "Wanna bet?"

Taye's breath caught in her throat as she watched him lick his tongue across his firm, full, and determined lips before moving closer and closer to . . .

The sound of the doorbell interrupted his intent. He pulled back. "Expecting someone, sweetheart?" he asked, refusing to remove his hand from between her legs just yet. He liked touching her that way.

She released a little moan from the back of her throat before answering, "It's probably the paper carrier collecting his weekly fee."

"Umm, you know that for sure?" he asked as his hands continued to stroke her.

"No," she replied in a throaty whisper. The only thing she was sure about at the moment was how he was making her feel. The man was a master at foreplay. Whenever he touched her this way it was immensely reactive, to every nerve cell in her body.

"Then I'd better check," he said, moving away for what Taye hoped would only be a moment. She was enjoying all the wonderful things he was doing to her body, she thought, watching him walk, totally unselfconscious of his nakedness, to the window. He eased the curtain aside.

"Does your paper carrier drive a late-model black Olds Ninety-eight?"

Taye closed her eyes and snuggled under the covers when the doorbell chimed again. "No." Seconds later she snatched her eyes back open when she suddenly realized just who did. She quickly sat up in bed. "What color is the interior?"

Michael turned around and looked at her curiously. "You expect me to be able to tell that from way up here? My vision is good, Taye, but not *that* good."

Already she was scrambling off the bed, grabbing her robe, and coming to the window to join him. She almost passed out when she saw the car. "That's Mama's car! Good grief! What's she doing here! She seldom comes to visit."

Michael heard the anxiety in her voice. He reached out and rubbed her shoulders. "Calm down, sweetheart. If we don't open the door she'll think no one is here."

"Fat chance. She's seen your car in my driveway. She doesn't know it's yours and probably assumes I'm up here in bed with my lover."

He laughed, bringing her closer into his arms. "You are."

Taye pulled away from Michael and quickly slipped into her robe. "You know what I mean." She stepped into her slippers. "I'll go see what she wants."

Michael watched Taye hurry out of the bedroom. Even if she told her mother that the car parked in the driveway was his, making things appear quite innocent, since he was family, he wondered how she was going to explain all those passion marks he'd placed over her body during the night, especially the ones that were quite visible on her neck.

Passion marks were the last thing on Taye's mind as she rushed down the stairs to open the door for her mother. Pulling her robe together, she glanced at the clock on the wall. It was nearly noon. Had she and Michael slept that late? But then, they'd had a rather busy night, so it was definitely possible.

Taking a deep breath, she opened the door, then nearly passed out. Her mother was not alone. "Mom? Cuzin Sophie? What are the two of you doing here?" Taye's heart almost stopped. Why did her mother have Cuzin Sophie, of all people, with her?

The two older women walked in when Taye moved aside. "What took you so long to open the door, Octavia?" her mother asked in a no-nonsense voice that was filled with disapproval as she stepped into the living room and glanced around. Otha Mae's gaze went immediately to the sofa that was still covered in a sheet and blanket. "You had an overnight guest, I see. At least you had the decency to let him sleep on the couch."

Taye·inhaled deeply, forcing herself to be calm. Quite naturally her mother would automatically assume that her overnight guest was a man. And what if it was? She was thirty years old, three months shy of turning thirty-one. This was her house and what she did or didn't do in it was really no concern of her mother's. "Yes, I had an overnight guest. Michael spent the night," she said honestly.

Since she and Michael were cousins, her mother and older cousin would see nothing wrong with that. They would never suspect that there was something going on between them. Taye watched as her mother's ramrod-straight spine loosened up some. "Oh, that's Michael's car," she said with relief in her voice. "I didn't recognize it."

Taye looked at both women but specifically at her mother. "Whose car did you think it was?"

Otha Mae shrugged. "You never know with you young people. Some of you lack morals these days, having all sorts of men coming and going out of your homes."

Taye was about to open her mouth to say something about that comment when she noticed the two women glancing behind her to the stairs.

"Michael," they both said at the same time, smiling.

"It's good to see you, sweetie," Cuzin Sophie added. "Come give us a hug."

Taye turned around and her breath caught in her throat. Michael was coming down the stairs wearing just his pants. His chest and his feet were completely bare, and he moved with the fluid grace of a panther. He looked sensuous, sated, and irresistible—like a man who'd spent most of the night making love to a woman and, if given the chance, would continue to make love to her again today.

Taye wondered if her mother and Cuzin Sophie noticed that look about him or if either of the two women thought it odd that she and Michael both looked like they had just gotten out of bed.

"Good morning, Aunt Otha Mae, Cuzin Sophie," Michael said to the two women and proceeded to do as they'd asked and give them hugs. "You two are out visiting early, aren't you?"

Cuzin Sophie laughed. "Early? Why, it's nearly noon."

He gave them a charming smile and said smoothly, "Is it? I overslept then. Since I knew Kennedy and the girls were spending the night over at Fayrene's, I decided to stay over here with Taye instead of going home to an empty house when my flight got in last night. I always enjoy Taye's company," he said, turning to smile at her.

Taye's heart rate increased with that smile. He was being totally honest with the two women, but he definitely wasn't telling them everything, thank goodness. "So, what's the reason for this visit?" Taye asked. She was surprised and couldn't pretend otherwise. Although her father usually visited her and the girls at least once a week, her mother rarely made the drive from Macon.

"Well, I knew you would be leaving in a few days to attend Brandy's wedding, and Sophie and I wanted to send our presents by you," her mother said, placing a JCPenney shopping bag on the table.

"Yeah, that's why we came by," Cuzin Sophie tagged in and said. "Besides," she continued, "I've never seen your house and thought this would be a good chance to do so."

So that you can go back and gossip about what you saw, Taye thought. "I'll make sure Brandy gets your presents," she said. She had no plans to give Cuzin Sophie a tour of her home. She could only imagine what the older woman would think if she were to take a peep into her bedroom. It would be quite apparent to anyone that her bed had been well used last night.

Taye frowned when she couldn't help but notice that for some reason Cuzin Sophie, who noticed everything, was paying a lot of attention to her neck. Taye's frown deepened. Had she broken out in a rash or something? If so, her mother and Michael hadn't seemed to notice.

"Cuzin Sophie? Is there something wrong?" Taye finally asked moments later after having gotten tired of the older woman's intense stare.

The older woman didn't even try to look contrite for having been caught staring. "I should be asking you that question, Taye, since you're the one with all those little marks on your neck."

That comment certainly got everyone's attention. Taye couldn't help noticing her mother suddenly zeroing in on her neck as well. Taye swallowed deeply. After last night she could only imagine what sort of marks Cuzin Sophie was referring to. She pulled her robe tighter around her. "They're just marks. No big deal," she tried to say lightly.

Unfortunately, making light of it didn't wash with her mother. Otha Mae Bennett crossed her arms over her chest and glared at Taye. "It's obvious what kind of marks they are, Octavia. I would like to know how you got them."

Taye returned her mother's glare. She noticed that Cuzin Sophie had taken a seat on the sofa, not to miss any of the proceedings. "Mama, I don't owe you an explanation about anything that goes on here in this house."

Her mother's spine went back to being ramrod straight. "Yes, you do if I think you're not setting a good example for my granddaughters. I expect them to have a good Christian upbringing."

"I raise the girls right and you know it. Besides, they're spending the weekend over at Fayrenc's."

Otha Mae huffed. "And you think their absence gives you the right to act indecently. What about Michael and his opinion of you now? I'm sure when he got here last night and saw all those marks on your neck the first thought that came to his mind was that you'd become a woman with loose morals."

Her mother's words hurt because Taye felt there was no reason for them. She hadn't dated a man since Monica had been born, but for some reason her mother failed to believe she hadn't been involved with anyone all these years.

Michael, his fists balled in anger, went immediately to Taye's side. "I think you've said enough, Aunt Otha Mae," he said in a voice that was clearly upset. "And you're wrong about what I think of Taye. I hold her in the highest regard, and as far as I'm concerned she is above reproach."

"Above reproach! How can you fix your mind to even think that?" her mother snapped. "She's had two babies out of wedlock and now it seems she may be working on a third. Look at those marks on her. I may be old, but I'm not stupid. I know what they are. She's let some man put—"

"No!" Michael said, loud enough to freeze Otha Mae's words in midsentence. "Taye didn't let *some* man do anything. *I'm* the one," he said, pointing at himself, "who put them there."

Michael's confession, Taye saw, shocked both her mother and Cuzin Sophie speechless. Their eyes bulged. Their mouths gaped open. And she was sure that if it weren't for the straw hats they were wearing, their hair would be standing straight up on their heads right now.

"What do you mean, you put them there?" Cuzin Sophie asked, clutching her heart like Michael's confession was enough to give her a heart attack.

Michael placed a hand around Taye's waist and gently brought her closer to him. "I meant just what I said. Taye and I are in love and what we do and how we spend our time is our business, no one else's."

Otha Mae recovered quickly. "In love! You can't be in love! You're cousins, for heaven sakes! What the two of you are doing is a sin!"

Michael rolled his eyes to the ceiling. "It's not a sin for two people who love each other to express their love in a physical and intimate way. And as far as us being cousins, everyone knows I was adopted into this family, so in actuality, Taye and I aren't related."

"But you're family. If you don't want to think about yourselves, then think about the girls. This will totally confuse not only the family but the girls as well."

"Then it's time for everyone to get unconfused. I'm not worried about how the girls will take it. I have good reason to believe they'll handle it just fine. And to be honest with you, I really don't care how the family is going to take it. Those who love me and Taye and want us to be happy will accept the fact that being happy for us will mean being together."

"No, Michael, you don't mean that. It's wrong," Otha Mae implored.

Michael shook his head and looked down at Taye. He smiled and reached out and cradled her face in his hands. "There's nothing wrong about me loving Taye or her loving me."

He then turned his attention back to the two women who stood staring at them. "Accept it and be happy for us."

Shock turned into anger and it ripped through Otha Mae Bennett's body. "I will never accept it! No one in the family will!" She turned angry eyes to Taye. "You have succeeded yet again in bringing shame to this family, Octavia. You have disgraced us all."

Otha Mae then turned and walked out of the house with an indignant Cuzin Sophie following behind her.

CHAPTER 39

M ichael pulled Taye closer into his arms and looked down as he studied her face. "You OK?"

Leaning back, she met his gaze. "As well as any woman could be whose mother thinks the worst of her," she said, trying to make light of things but failing miserably.

"You know your mom, Taye. She's always had this self-righteous air about her. Maybe it stems from her father being a Baptist minister and her expecting everyone to act a certain way. Don't let what she said bother you. She really does love you; you know that."

Taye sighed. "Yes, but sometimes she has a funny way of showing it, Michael. She has no reason to question my morals. I haven't been involved with anyone since Monica was born, but she doesn't want to believe that. She knows Monica's father was a married man, so of course that definitely lowers her opinion of me. She even questioned how I was able to get this house, and that really pissed me off. I didn't even tell her that I borrowed money from Sharon to make the down payment. She's convinced I have a sugar daddy."

Michael grinned at her. "You do. I can be quite sweet when I'm enticed enough."

Taye smiled, but her heart wasn't in it. "I can truly believe that." She walked out of his arms and went over to the sofa and began folding up the blanket and sheet. "You know we have to tell the girls soon, don't you? I prefer that they hear it from us rather than from the gossip Cuzin Sophie will be spreading around."

Michael nodded as he sat casually on the arm of a wingback chair and watched her. "I don't have a problem with that. Do you?"

Taye turned to him and shrugged her shoulders. "No, but I was hoping we would have more time before we had to tell them. I wanted for us to just enjoy our moments together without anyone knowing but the two of us."

Michael slowly nodded. He had wanted that, too, although he'd never intended to keep their newfound love a secret. In a way he was glad things had been forced out in the open. He wanted everyone to know he loved her. For a moment he watched what she was doing as she folded the items, then placed them aside. He could tell that Otha Mae's opinion of her had hurt her deeply. He slowly crossed the room and sat down on the sofa and pulled her down onto his lap. "Let me hold you, Taye."

She willingly went into his arms. "Kiss me, Michael. Please kiss the hurt away."

He couldn't have denied her request even if he had wanted to, which he didn't. The coiling need to ease her hurt was great. He leaned down and touched his mouth to hers, kissing her fiercely. He wanted to take her hurt away and replace it with love. The kind of love a man had for a woman. His woman. Reaching his hand down, he slowly opened her robe and began stroking her quivering belly in the same tempo that his mouth was stroking hers. Then, moving his hand lower, he felt her legs automatically part for him and his touch.

The kiss deepened as he brought her to throbbing need with his hand. He continued to touch her, stroke her, probe her until he felt her shudder in his arms as hot, intense sensations raced through her. He felt each and every tremor as her body exploded into tantalizing pleasure. When she moaned into his mouth, his tongue soothed her. It comforted her. It consoled her. It was taking her hurt away completely.

Moments later, he slowly lifted his head and looked down at her with darkened eyes. Her mouth was a mouth that had been thoroughly kissed, and her glazed eyes revealed a woman who'd just been sexually satisfied.

Taye returned his gaze. She had no idea that she'd been capable of such passion and such desire. But once she was in his arms Michael was able to make her feel things she had never felt before. "You have quite a knack for being able to do two things at once," she whispered softly, almost in a purr. "And you can do both of them extremely well, I might add. You're remarkable."

He was touched by her words. "No, Taye, you're the one who is remarkable. You've taken a man who thought he would never love again and proven him wrong. Lynda will always have a special place in my heart, but I love you now. I really do love you, Taye."

She acknowledged his words with a smile and reached up and placed her arms around his neck. "And I love you, too."

He softly caressed the area of her neck. "I didn't mean to put these here, Taye," he said of the passion marks that were clearly visible there.

"I know, but I don't mind wearing your brand. However, I'm going to change into something that will cover them before the girls get here."

He nodded. "When do you want me to go and get them?"

Taye sighed. "You may as well go get them now. Gossip spreads fast in this family."

Michael nodded. He knew Sophie's reputation for being a compulsive gossip. "All right. I'll leave now." He looked at her. "You're not alone in this, Taye. Promise me you'll try not to worry about anything."

She looked at him steadily. The force of the gaze made her shiver a little. "I promise."

He smiled and slowly slid her off his lap into the seat next to him. He then moved and got off the couch and went down on his knees in front of her. He looked up at her.

Taye caught her breath at the intense look in his eyes. "I want to make you a promise as well, Taye," he said, taking her hand. "Right here, in front of you and before God, I promise to love you, protect you, and keep you and the girls safe. Regardless of who their fathers are, I want them to become my girls, too. I want me, you, Monica, Sebrina, and Kennedy to be a family, and the only way that can happen is if you marry me. Will you marry me, Taye?"

Tears suddenly sprang into Taye's eyes. A number of people, including her mother, had convinced her that no man in his right mind, unless he was old as dirt and wasn't worth having anyway, would want to commit himself to a woman with a ready-made family, especially one with two children. But Michael was proving them wrong. Here he was before her, on his knees, offering to love and protect not only her but her girls as well.

"Will you marry me, Taye?" he repeated when she did not respond.

"Yes, Michael, I'll marry you."

Taye found herself pulled off the couch as he got to his feet. He wrapped his arms around her and kissed her, sealing their commitment to each other.

Taye stood at the living room window and watched Michael's car pull into her driveway. Seconds later she watched as the girls got out. It was obvious all three were disappointed that their fun time at Fayrene's had been cut short, although Taye's two daughters were trying hard not to show it. Kennedy, however, didn't mind letting her father know she was not a happy camper. The pout on her face spoke volumes.

Not waiting for them to knock, Taye immediately padded barefoot across the carpeted floor and opened the door. She had taken a shower and had changed into a pair of shorts and a short-sleeve turtleneck blouse. Although she felt refreshed, she also felt nervous as heck. "Hi, girls."

"Hi, Aunt Taye," Kennedy greeted her casually and automatically gave her a hug. "Why did Dad bring us home? We were having so much fun and were about to go to the mall."

Taye then hugged her own two daughters. "Would you believe it if we said that we missed you?"

"You just saw us yesterday, Mom," Monica said, grinning.

Taye smiled. "Yeah, that may be true, but we missed the three of you anyway."

Kennedy looked back over her shoulder as her dad came through the door and closed it behind him. "Am I in trouble or something?"

Michael lifted a brow. "Should you be in trouble about anything, Kennedy?"

Kennedy gazed at her father with uncertain eyes. "Not unless the school contacted you," she said softly.

Michael leaned back against the door. "No one at the school has contacted me."

Kennedy shrugged. "Well then," she said calmly, as if dismissing the discussion.

"Why would the school be calling me, Kennedy?" Michael asked. He had no intention of dismissing it.

Sebrina suddenly appeared at Kennedy's side. "It wasn't her fault, Uncle Michael. Cherry Burgess started it all."

Michael looked at Taye, who hunched her shoulders to let him know she had no idea what the two girls were talking about. "And just what did Cherry Burgess start?"

"She said a lot of bad things about Kennedy," Monica said.

Taye lifted her brow as she looked at her younger daughter. "Monica, how do you know about any of this? You don't attend their school."

"But they told me all about it and said it was supposed to be a secret and not to tell."

Taye tried not to smile, wondering if Monica realized that she *was* indeed telling. "Thanks for your contribution, Monica, but we prefer hearing the entire story from Sebrina and Kennedy." Taye then turned her attention to the two older girls. "OK, ladies, let's hear it."

Kennedy met Taye's gaze. "Cherry Burgess said something mean about me in class, so I sort of pinched her."

Michael lifted a brow. "You sort of pinched her?"

Kennedy nodded. "Yeah, sort of."

Michael ran his hand over his face. "Kennedy," he said slowly, trying to maintain his cool. "How can you *sort of* pinch someone?"

"Do you want me to show you, Daddy?"

Michael glared at her, wondering if she was serious or was just being a smart-mouth. "No. What happened after you *sort of* pinched Cherry Burgess?"

Kennedy shrugged. "She sort of hollered."

Michael shook his head and inhaled a deep breath. "What happened next?"

Kennedy swallowed as she looked up at her father, trying to decipher his mood. "I sort of got sent to the office."

Michael took another inhaling breath. "And?"

Kennedy clasped her hands tightly together as she studied her father through apprehensive eyes. "And you have to take me to school on Monday to talk to Mrs. Jones, the dean of girls."

Michael stared at his daughter for a second. He then glanced down at her nails, freshly polished, nicely manicured, and long. Her could just imagine the abuse Kennedy had given this Cherry Burgess. "Kennedy, why on earth would you pinch that girl?"

"Monica already told you why, Daddy. Cherry said some bad things about me. She's been mean to me ever since I started that school. She doesn't like me because I wear nice clothes and my hair looks good every day. And she said that I was a—"

"Kennedy, it doesn't matter what she said," Michael said, interrupting his daughter. "Is whatever she said true?"

"No, sir."

"Then why should it matter to you?"

"It didn't."

"It must have for you to have pinched her. Sort of."

"But—"

"But nothing, young lady. I've told you time and time again not to care about what people say. You know what you are and who you are and that's all that matters. Understand?"

"Yes, sir."

"I would put you under punishment if I wasn't feeling so happy right now."

Kennedy looked at her father under lowered lashes. "What are you happy about? Did you win the lotto?"

Michael stepped farther into the room. "I wish. No, that's not it. Will the three of you have a seat on the sofa?"

The three girls studied him and Taye thoughtfully for a moment before walking over to the sofa and taking a seat. They continued to look at the adults expectantly.

Michael began talking. "Kennedy, do you remember when I told you about being adopted into the Bennett family?"

Kennedy nodded. "Yes. You said you didn't find out until you were eighteen."

Michael nodded. "Yes, that's true. And I also told you that adoption or no adoption, the Bennett family is the only family I know and as far as I'm concerned I am a Bennett."

Kennedy nodded, understanding that. "Yes, sir."

"But my not being a blood Bennett also means something else."

Kennedy frowned. "What?"

"It means that in all actuality, Taye and I aren't really related."

"Yes, you are," Monica piped in. "Momma is your cousin."

"Yes, she's my cousin, but she's not my *blood* cousin. Do the three of you see what I'm getting at?"

Three heads shook no at the same time.

Taye walked over and stood next to Michael. "Michael and I have discovered something that's simply wonderful," she said, smiling as she tried to put on a brave front.

"What?" Sebrina asked cautiously but curiously.

Taye looked at Michael. Michael looked at Taye. They then looked at the girls. "We love each other," Taye finally said softly.

Monica chuckled. "Momma, you're supposed to love each other. You're cousins."

Taye smiled back at her younger daughter, but her gaze was steadfast on Kennedy and Sebrina. As they were three years older and somewhat wiser, they caught on to what she was getting at.

"You mean that mushy man-love-woman sort of stuff?" Kennedy asked in utter amazement, looking from her father to Taye. "The kind that sort of leads to marriage and babies?"

"Yes, that's the kind we mean," Michael answered.

Sebrina smiled. "Hey, that's off the chain!" she exclaimed loudly. "That means you might get to live here or that we might get to live with you. And that Kennedy, Monica, and I won't have to hang out together just on the weekends?"

Michael laughed, shaking his head. "Yeah, I guess it would mean all of that." He looked at his daughter. "What do you think of it, Kennedy?"

He saw the huge smile on his daughter's face. He hadn't really been concerned about her reaction. She had mentioned to him a number of times how much she liked Taye and wished that Taye were her mother instead of her aunt. "I think it's great. But I didn't know people in the same family could get married."

"Normally they can't, Kennedy," Michael explained. "But Taye and I have a rather unique situation since we aren't actually blood-related."

"Oh." Kennedy looked at Taye. "I would love having you for a mother. You're so cool. And you're so pretty. And you're so smart. I can see why Daddy wants you for that mushy man-love-woman sort of stuff."

Taye shook her head, grinning. "Thank you." She then opened her arms and Sebrina and Kennedy automatically went into them, giving her joyous hugs. It was only a second later that Taye noticed Monica had not moved from her spot on the sofa and had tears in her eyes.

"Monica? What do you think about it?" Taye asked concernedly, although it was apparent Monica had been bothered by the news.

Monica stood, looked at Michael and then at her mother. "I think it sucks; that's what I think. I'm worse off now than before," she said, her body shaking with suppressed sobs. "Sebrina has a daddy and Kennedy has a daddy, but I still won't have one." She then whirled and made a dash for the kitchen and was out the back door before anyone had time to react.

Michael took in Taye's stricken face before she moved to go after her daughter. "I have to go talk to her, Michael."

He placed his hand on her wrist to stop her. "No. Let me handle it. You stay here with the girls and explain the rest of it to them. The family matter."

Taye started to protest. The mother in her wanted to go after her child and comfort her.

"She has to have a father's assurance, Taye, and I'm the only one who can do that," Michael said softly. "Trust me."

Taye slowly nodded and stepped back. She then watched as Michael walked out of the living room and went into the kitchen, to go after Monica.

When Michael stepped out on the back porch he saw Monica sitting on the grass under a huge oak tree with her head bowed. He knew she was still crying. Taking a deep breath, he slowly walked over to where she sat.

He gently lowered his body on the grass next to hers and reached out and gently brought her into his embrace. "Don't you like me, Monica?" he asked softly.

She slowly lifted her head and met his gaze. Her eyes, Michael saw, were still filled with tears. "Yes, I like you," she said, still shaking from the onslaught of her emotions. "But that doesn't mean anything. I still won't have a father and it's not fair."

The heartbreaking pain he heard in her voice touched him deeply. He inwardly cursed the man who had fathered her but had never come to see his child, to be a part of her life. "When your mother and I get married, I will become your father, Monica. That is, if you want me."

Monica looked up at him. She swiped at the tears in her eyes. "Why would you do that? You already have a daughter."

Michael breathed deeply, wondering how he could say the words to let this precious child know how he felt. His voice was rough and unsteady when he said, "Yes, but after marrying your mom, I'll have three daughters. They will be three daughters that I will love and cherish equally."

Several tense moments passed and then Monica spoke. "But why?"

"Because I love your mother, so there's no way I couldn't love you or Sebrina and think of you as my daughters, too. And I hope the two of you will think of me as your father."

Monica frowned. "Sebrina already has a father and he sends for her every summer and he sends her stuff every Christmas. Lots of stuff."

Michael nodded, hearing the hurt in her voice. This beautiful little girl whose features reminded him so much of Taye's when she was Monica's age.

"I didn't have anyone," Monica added, roping Michael's thoughts back in.

He tightened his arms around her. "Well, you got me. In fact, how would you like to be my best girl at the wedding?"

Monica's eyes widened. "You gonna have a wedding?"

Michael smiled. He hadn't talked to Taye about having one, but he wanted a wedding. When he had married Lynda, they had gotten married in a small chapel on the military base with only the two of them, the minister, and two witnesses from the administration office. He wanted the chance to watch Taye walk down the aisle to him, surrounded by friends and family. He sighed when the thought occurred to him that they might have more friends than family present. "Yes, we'll have a wedding and you'll be my best girl. I will have a best man and a best girl."

Monica smiled at the very thought of that.

"So does that mean you will accept me as your father once I marry your mother?" he asked her.

"Yes," Monica said softly.

"And does that also mean you've agreed to be my best girl in the wedding?"

Her smile widened. "Yes."

Michael chuckled. "Good."

Monica then gazed at him apprehensively. "Does—does that mean I can start calling you Daddy after the wedding? I never called anyone Daddy before."

Michael didn't think he could love this child any more than he did right now. She was asking the question like it would be an honor for her to call him Daddy. "Yes, just as long as I can introduce you to everyone as my daughter."

"OK."

Michael slowly got to his feet. "It's all settled then. You're my best girl until the wedding. Then you'll become my daughter. How does that sound?"

Monica gazed up at him as he towered over her. "That sounds good."

Michael reached out his hand to her. "Come on. Let's go tell your mother our plans."

CHAPTER 40

They lay facing each other. Naked. Satiated. Contented.

Quinn gazed at Alexia as he forced his breathing back to normal. The long, luxurious mass. of hair on her head totally surrounded her face, and he thought she was the most beautiful woman he had ever seen. No woman should look this breathtaking just minutes after making love. He didn't think he would ever be able to erase from his mind the picture of her above him, taking control, setting the pace and gliding them higher and higher until they soared together.

He felt his throat constrict when he thought about just how much he loved her and how much he wanted her in his life permanently. They had been seeing each other exclusively for the past three months. Three glorious months. Things had gotten off to a rocky start, but then they had grown comfortable with each other. She had begun trusting him, confiding in him, and making him a part of her life. They did things together and, more often than not, they shared the same bed each night, whether it was at his place or hers. Things were good between them, but he wanted them better.

He wanted forever.

He thought about what was inside his pants pocket. It was a box he had picked up from the jeweler that morning. An engagement ring. He had intended to pop the question as soon as he arrived, but when she had greeted him at the door wearing nothing but her panties and bra, his mind had immediately gone blank. They had barely made it into the bedroom. He'd barely had time to tell her the good news that Raisa Forbes had dropped her frivolous lawsuit before Alexia had begun removing his clothes.

"Do you want to take a shower with me, Quinn?" Alexia asked softly.

He heard her question, but for the moment he could only stare at her and soak up her beauty. Finally he spoke. "I don't think I have the strength to move," he said huskily. "Were you trying to kill me just now?"

She smiled that smile that always made his heart do flips. "No. I wasn't trying to kill you." Then after a few moments she added in a still softer voice, "I don't want anything to happen to you. You mean too much to me, Quinn."

Quinn took a sharp intake of breath. This was the first time she had admitted that to him. More than anything he wanted to believe her. "Tell me," he said. His eyes and mouth issued a challenge to her. "Tell me what I mean to you."

Alexia blinked, clearly understanding what he was asking her to do. Was she ready to tell him how she felt about him? That she loved him? Was now a good time to tell him about the baby, since she'd gotten the official word after visiting her gynecologist earlier that day?

Yes, she thought. She couldn't put off telling him both things any longer. But first she had to take a shower. When she told him, she wanted to feel refreshed, and she hoped to God that he loved her as much as she loved him, and that he would be OK with the news about the baby. Their baby.

So instead of answering him she avoided the question by saying, "I'm going to take a shower. You're welcome to join me if you like." Without waiting for his response, she quickly slid out of bed and went into the bathroom, closing the door behind her.

Quinn remained where he was and sighed deeply. There was something different about Alexia today. Something he couldn't quite put his finger on. For some reason her mood seemed a little subdued, although she'd almost killed him while making love. She was a passionate person, a real hellion in the bedroom, but he wouldn't want her any other way.

At that moment her phone rang. He decided that he was too tired to reach over and pick it up and would let her answering machine get it. It was probably Abbott Bodie calling about the tour being set up for her that would start in a couple of months.

"Alexia, this is Rae'jean," an urgent voice said. *"Evidently you aren't in, but I hope you play back this message before you leave for Jamaica tomorrow."*

Quinn raised a brow as he remembered that Rae'jean was one of Alexia's ace-boon-coon cousins, the one who was the heart doctor. She'd told him that the other cousin she was close to was Taye and that she lived in Atlanta. Alexia would be flying out in the morning for Jamaica to attend one of her cousins' wedding.

"Girl, all hell has broken loose in the Bennett family," Rae'jean continued. *"Aunt Otha Mae and nosy Cuzin Sophie found out that Taye and Michael are having an affair. Now the family is split down the middle. Half want to give them their blessings and the other half want Reverend Overstreet to exorcise the demons from their bodies. They're convinced Taye and Michael are possessed by the devil."*

Quinn covered his mouth with his hand to keep from laughing out loud.

"Trust me, Alexia. This is no laughing matter."

He stopped laughing immediately, felt contrite for doing so, and was grateful she hadn't heard him.

"Taye and Michael need our support, so be prepared when you see them this weekend. And I'll tell you all about that business with my father when I see you. Bye. Wait! I forgot to ask how things are moving on your end. Have you gotten pregnant from that attorney yet?"

Quinn raised a dark brow.

"Alexia, you know I love you and I'll support you in whatever you do, but please be careful. No man likes being used. I know how much you want a child, but there are other ways you can go about it without deliberately deceiving someone. Well . . . that's my two cents. Think about it. I'll see you in Jamaica."

Quinn sucked in a deep gulp of air, refusing to let his heart shatter into a million pieces. Evidently he'd heard wrong. He'd misunderstood what the caller had said. With the sound of Alexia's shower going in the background he pulled himself up to sit on the side of the bed and pressed the replay button on the telephone.

He listened to the message all over again.

Quinn didn't think he could get a full breath of air past the excruciating tightness in his throat. Moments later he slowly stood as he tried to get a grip on his emotions. The past three months had been nothing but an act on Alexia's part to get pregnant? She'd been that desperate for a baby that she had set a plan into motion to use him for stud services? Nothing more than a breeding machine? She had actually led him to believe that she'd been on some sort of birth control.

He shut his eyes against the pain and heartache that suddenly racked his body. He'd been a fool to believe she had cared for him. He'd even convinced himself that she had begun falling in love with him and that eventually she would love him as much as he loved her. The media had been right. Alexia Bennett didn't love any man. She used them until she had her fill, then tossed them aside.

He opened his eyes when he heard the shower stop. Crossing the room, he picked up his pants and shirt and began putting them on. His heart began aching even more when his hand brushed against his pants pocket and felt the box inside. It was the box that contained the engagement ring he had planned to give her tonight. How could he have been so stupid? The tigress had definitely done a job on him. She had used her long, sharp claws and completely ripped his heart in two.

Quinn didn't turn around when he heard the sound of the bathroom door opening.

"Quinn? Why are you getting dressed? I thought you'd be staying tonight," Alexia said behind him.

He turned around slowly to face her.

The smile on Alexia's face vanished when she saw the dark, cold look in Quinn's eyes and the tight way he was holding his chin. It was obvious that he was upset about something. "Quinn, what is it? What's wrong?"

"You got a call while you were in the shower," he said quietly.

Alexia wondered what call she could have gotten that had upset him so much. "What did they want?"

His dark eyes blazed in anger, but his voice was rather calm when he spoke. "It was your cousin Rae'jean. I didn't pick it up. She left a message for you on your answering machine. I suggest that you replay it."

Alexia heard the quiet anger in his voice and was confused by it. "All right." She walked across the room and pushed the replay button.

And she listened.

At the end of the recording she took a deep breath, knowing she had a lot of explaining to do. She slowly turned around to Quinn. The anger she felt radiating from him was so thick that even from across the room she could cut it with a knife. "I can explain things, Quinn," she said softly, meeting his gaze.

"Can you?"

She heard the pain in his voice and her heart began to ache. "Yes."

He continued to stare at her before saying, "Just answer this for me. Did you set me up, Alexia? Was the only reason you invited me over that first night to get pregnant from me?"

The room got completely quiet. The only sounds were their breathing. It seemed like an eternity before Alexia finally answered. "Yes," she said miserably. "That was my initial plan, but—"

"No!" Quinn said, the sound so loud that it thundered off the walls. "If that's true, then there's really nothing else you can say, is there? You lied to me. You deliberately used me." He then began walking to the door.

"Quinn! Wait! Please let me explain."

Quinn stopped walking. "There's nothing to explain." He then thought about the number of times they had made love without protection because he'd assumed she was on some sort of birth control. "Did you succeed in getting what you wanted, Alexia? Are you pregnant?"

Alexia inhaled a deep breath. She started to lie but then changed her mind. Lying would only make things worse between them. She met his dark gaze. "Yes. I found out today that I'm pregnant."

Quinn's insides twisted into knots. The woman he loved was carrying his child, but she had lied and deceived him to get it. "There's something you should know," he said in a voice laced with steel as his eyes held hers. "I will take you to court to gain full custody of my child. By the time I finish with you, you won't have anything left, not even a decent name or a singing career, and you sure won't have my child. I'll make damn sure of that, Alexia. You've used a man for the very last time."

Tears shimmered in Alexia's eyes. "You don't understand, Quinn. I fell in love with you. No matter what my intentions were in the beginning, I love you now. Please believe me."

"I don't believe anything you say," he said coldly. He turned around to leave.

"You lied to me, Quinn."

Quinn stopped walking and turned around slowly. "What the hell are you talking about? Don't try shifting guilt here, Alexia. You aren't the one who got used, so don't pretend otherwise."

· She swiped at her tears. "You did lie to me. You promised you wouldn't hurt me and that I could trust you."

Quinn just stared at her, taken aback by her words. Before he could give her a flaming retort, she continued.

"But you are hurting me, Quinn. You're hurting me by not believing in me and by not trusting me. You asked me to believe in you and to trust you, but you never intended to believe in me and to trust me. And knowing that hurts."

Quinn inhaled deeply. His feelings and emotions were too raw to deal with this right now. What she was saying wasn't making a whole lot of sense. As far as he was concerned, she was deliberately trying to confuse the issue and place the blame on him when all he'd ever wanted to do was love her. Totally. Completely. He inhaled another deep breath, and without saying anything, he turned and walked out of the bedroom.

It was only when Alexia heard the sound of the front door closing behind him that she hugged her stomach and gave in to her tears.

CHAPTER 41

MONTEGO BAY, JAMAICA

"So, you two," Victor Junior murmured as he joined Taye and Michael on the hotel's patio as they enjoyed tropical drinks. "When you want to stir up things, y'all go all the way. There hasn't been this much excitement in the Bennett family since everyone found out Cuzin Louis was gay."

"Umm, you're probably right," Taye murmured, looking up at him. "I hear the family is split down the middle. What're your feelings?"

Victor Junior sat back in his chair. "Hey, I don't have a problem with it. Like you said, it's not like the two of you are blood relations, so if you get pregnant we don't have to worry about your having a water-head baby or anything like that."

He then leaned in closer. "You might as well know that Daddy didn't have a problem with it, either, until he started listening to Valerie. So watch out for her. The witch has her broom and is riding pretty high on it."

Michael met his cousin's gaze. "Taye and I aren't worried about Valerie or anyone else, for that matter."

Victor Junior took a sip of his drink before saying, "What about the grandfathers? You should be worried about them. Word's out that Poppa

Ethan and Cuzin Henry are calling an emergency family meeting at Poppa Ethan's house as soon as you two return home."

Michael nodded as he looked down into his drink. In the past, he had always gotten his grandfather's support on anything he'd ever done. He wondered if his Grampa Henry would support him on this. "If there's a meeting, Taye and I will be there. We don't like the rift it's caused between the family and want it resolved." He reached out and captured Taye's hand in his and lovingly met her gaze. "But there's no way, whether we get their blessings or not, we will sacrifice what we feel for each other."

Victor Junior shook his head, chuckling. "Damn, man, you two got it bad."

Michael returned the chuckle. "Has anyone seen Rae'jean lately?"

Victor Junior shrugged his shoulders. "Not lately. I understand she's around here somewhere babying Alexia. Word's out that Alexia's boyfriend dumped her. She hasn't taken those shades off her eyes since she's gotten here. Can you imagine Alexia actually crying over anything? Especially over a man? I thought she was a lot tougher than that. I heard Valerie tell Dad she hopes Alexia's puffy eyes clear up before she has to sing at the wedding."

Taye shook her head. "Valerie is all heart, isn't she?"

"Yeah," Victor Junior said, smiling. "If you like the frozen kind." His smile widened. "And of course she had something to say about the white man dumping Rae'jean."

Taye started to say something about Victor Junior's comment but happened to see Brandy rush across the patio. She appeared to be upset about something. "Excuse me for a minute," Taye said to Michael and Victor Junior. "I need to see Brandy about something."

Getting up from the table, Taye followed the same route Brandy had taken a few minutes earlier, which led her to a storage room. She started to knock on the door, but when she heard Brandy crying inside she opened the door and went in.

Brandy was sitting across the room on a huge plastic can with her back to Taye, weeping miserably. Taye quietly closed the door behind her and wondered if Brandy was going through what most people referred to as bridal jitters.

"Brandy, are you all right?"

Brandy turned on her fuming. "What are you doing here? I came in here to be alone, Taye. May I have some privacy please?"

Taye immediately went on the defensive. "Hey, that's fine with me. I thought you were upset about something and decided to come check on you. Forgive me for caring."

Taye had turned to leave when she heard Brandy say in a heart-wrenching, sobbing voice. "I'm sorry, Taye."

Taye turned back around. Surprised. Shocked. She'd never heard Brandy apologize for anything, especially for having been rude.

"I'm just feeling so confused about everything right now," Brandy continued.

Taye lifted a brow. "Are you starting to have doubts about whether or not you really love Lorenzo?"

Brandy shook her head. "No, I love him, but . . ."

"But what?"

Brandy lifted her head to meet Taye's gaze. Her eyes were filled with tears. She hesitated a few moments before saying, "He—he's having an affair."

"What!"

Brandy nodded as fresh tears flooded her eyes. "Yes. I just found out."

This news was a little bit much. Taye leaned against the closed door. "What do you mean you just found out?"

Brandy swiped at her eyes a few times before answering. "You know that at the wedding reception we planned to show videotapes taken during our courtship of places we visited together?"

Taye nodded. "Yes, I heard something about it."

"Well, before leaving the States to come here I went by Lorenzo's apartment and collected them all. Most of them were easy to find, but some I had to really look hard for, since his apartment is so cluttered. Well, I found one that didn't have a label on it on the top shelf in his closet. I assumed it was one he forgot to mark, so I put it in the bag with the rest and brought it along."

Taye shook her head. "Go on."

"Well, a few minutes ago, while alone in my hotel room, I took the time to watch them, thinking the unmarked one was the tape he made when we went hiking in the North Carolina mountains earlier this year."

Brandy swiped at her eyes again when more tears appeared. "But that wasn't it. It was a videotape of Lorenzo and another woman making love."

Taye's eyes widened. "You actually saw Lorenzo having sex with another woman on a video?"

"Yes. And the tape was dated last month."

Taye shook her head. What a blow for a woman the day before her wedding. "Did you recognize the woman with him in the video, Brandy?" she asked quietly, curiously.

Brandy nodded again. The tears in her eyes got fuller. "Yes. That's what hurts so bad, Taye. The other woman was Jolene."

"Jolene! Your best friend, Jolene?"

"Yes!" she wailed. "Can you believe that!"

That news angered Taye beyond logical thinking, and she went off on a tangent. "Oh, that's real deep. That's really cheap. The low-life sneak." Taye couldn't help but remember all the attention the woman had given Michael at the family reunion. "Jolene is supposed to be your best friend and she is caught on video making out with your fiancé? I can't believe it!"

"Neither can I," Brandy said, as she started to sob all over again. "How could she do this to me? How could he have done this to me? There's no way I can marry him now. All of you came here for nothing."

Taye quickly walked over to Brandy when she began sobbing and wailing unmercifully, letting it all out. To say Brandy was in complete agony was putting it mildly. Taye leaned down and placed her arms around Brandy's shoulders. "It's OK, Brandy. At least you found out what a dog he is before the wedding," she said, handing her some paper towels from out of a case stored nearby.

Brandy nodded as she continued sobbing. "Momma's gonna have a cow. If I call off the wedding she'll be totally embarrassed. She invited a lot of her friends to come here."

Taye nodded. Knowing Valerie, she definitely would be embarrassed. She'd been walking around with her chest poked out gloating that her daughter was marrying into money. "Don't worry about your momma having a cow. She'll be in good company. My momma has had two cows already, and just a few days ago she gave birth to a third."

Brandy chuckled through her tears. "Oh, Taye, what am I going to do?"

Taye took a deep breath. She wasn't good at handing out advice, but there was one thing she knew for certain that she could tell Brandy. "The first thing you're going to do is stop crying. Lorenzo isn't worth your tears. Then we'll decide what's the best way to go about calling off the wedding. But for right now you should come to my room until you can pull yourself together."

Brandy nodded and swiped at her eyes some more. "OK. I don't want anyone to see me like this."

"Come on then. We'll take the back elevator up to my floor."

"Shhh, Rae'jean, please try and keep your voice down. Brandy is in the other room trying to rest. Poor thing cried herself to sleep."

Rae'jean glared. "I'm too mad to keep my voice down," she said, lowering it anyway. "I can't believe the nerve of some men."

"Or of some women," Alexia added as she leisurely took a sip of coffee. "Let's not forget Jolene's part in all of this." Alexia had finally taken off her shades, but her eyes were still slightly swollen. She'd told herself not to cry any longer. She had gotten herself in this mess with Quinn and she was determined to get herself out of it somehow by doing whatever it took to convince him that she really did love him. She had sent something to him earlier that day and wondered if he had gotten it yet.

"The two-bit hussy," Rae'jean said, her tone sharp. "I can't believe Jolene would do this to someone who is supposed to be her best friend."

Alexia stood and walked over to the coffee maker to refill her cup. "Well, if you ask me, Brandy got just what she deserved."

Taye and Rae'jean glared at Alexia. "That's a cruel thing to say, Alexia. No woman deserves finding out her man is cheating on her," Rae'jean said.

Alexia glared back. "If the two of you want sympathy from me for Brandy, forget it. And why are you trippin' over this for her benefit? She's never been nice to us."

Rae'jean was fuming. "No matter how nasty Brandy has acted in the past, Alexia, you've forgotten one very important thing."

"What?" Alexia snapped.

"She's family."

Taye nodded. "I agree, and the first thing we need to do is help Brandy come up with a way to call off the wedding."

Alexia came and sat back down. As much as she hated admitting it, Taye and Rae'jean were right. No matter what, Brandy was family. "Why call off the wedding?" she asked smartly.

Rae'jean raised her eyes to the ceiling. "Lex, be for real. What woman in her right mind would go ahead and marry a man whom she caught on videotape screwing her best friend?"

A mischievous smile tilted Alexia's lips. "A pretty smart one if she plays her cards right."

Taye lifted a brow. "What are you talking about?"

Alexia leaned back in her chair. "Look around you. Lorenzo and his family are loaded. If I were Brandy, I'd get him right where it would hurt—in his bank account. I'd go ahead with the wedding, and before the ink dried on the marriage license I'd be filing for a divorce and demanding that I got half of everything he owns."

Rae'jean laughed. "Hey, that's rich, no pun intended."

Taye shook her head. "It won't work in this case."

Alexia's smile vanished. "Why not?"

"Because Brandy mentioned that she signed a prenuptial agreement yesterday."

Alexia's smile returned. "It still might work. I remember Quinn sharing something with me regarding the legality of a prenuptial agreement. He said that in certain situations they could be overturned. I would think that this would be one of those situations." She sat up straighter in her chair, smiling. "But to cover our bases, I have another great idea."

"Oh, no," Taye said miserably. "The last time you got that look on your face, we were fourteen and got into big trouble for sneaking onto the Parkers' place and stealing one of his prized watermelons because you'd developed a craving for fresh fruit."

Alexia frowned. "It wasn't stealing, Taye. It was feeding the hungry. Now hush; let me think this through." After a few minutes she said, "I assume Brandy signed the prenuptial agreement with the Ballentines' family attorney, Mr. Gleason."

Taye nodded. "Yes. He's the same man who tried talking you up to his hotel room last night. Can you believe he's married? I understand his wife won't be flying in until the day of the wedding."

Alexia nodded. "If he hasn't left the hotel since those papers were signed, chances are he still has them somewhere in his room."

"Probably," Rae'jean said. She raised a brow at her cousin. "I hope you're not suggesting we break into the man's hotel room and steal those papers."

"No. I plan to let you into his room."

Taye crossed her arms over her chest. "And how will you manage to do that?"

"Tonight I'll let Mr. Gleason think he's talked me into going up to his room for a drink." Alexia's smile curved her lips. "Well, actually, I'm going to let him think I'm going up to his room for something else. I'll leave his hotel room unlocked, and at a specified time, while I have him somewhat occupied, the two of you will sneak into his room and find the papers."

"We won't have time to find any papers because we won't know where to look," Taye said, not liking Alexia's plan. "Besides, there's bound to be other copies out there. I'm sure Lorenzo has his own copy."

"More than likely Gleason's copy is still in his briefcase. And as far as Lorenzo's copy is concerned, it should be easy enough for Brandy to secretly confiscate that one. Once we get all the copies we can destroy them."

"It will never work," Taye said, shaking her head.

"Yes, it will," Alexia countered.

"No, it won't. We'll get caught and go to jail. Besides, Michael won't let me do it."

"Then don't tell him. For Pete's sake, Taye, you don't have to tell him everything. Just make up a reason for wanting to spend time with Rae'jean and me tonight."

Rae'jean studied Alexia. "Thanks to me, you're already in hot water with Quinn. Don't make matters worse. Just how far do you plan to go to keep Mr. Gleason occupied?"

"Relax, Rae'jean. I'm not going *that* far. My body belongs to Quinn, no one else." Alexia sighed. She hadn't thought she would ever openly admit that any part of her belonged to a man. "It will probably be easy for me to get Gleason tipsy, since he seems to enjoy hitting the bottle anyway," she said. "So what do you ladies think?"

"I'm still not sure about this," Taye said.

"I think it might be fun," Rae'jean added. "We haven't gotten into some big-time trouble in a long time."

Alexia looked at her two cousins for a few minutes. She knew that although Taye had misgivings, she would go along with the final decision. "We need to wake up Brandy and run things by her to make sure she's cool with them."

"And if she is?"

"Then we'll put our plan into action." Alexia studied her manicured fingernails. "I have another idea which will definitely seal Lorenzo and Jolene's fate, just in case our plan with the prenuptial backfires."

"Heaven help us," Taye groaned, afraid to ask what else Alexia could think of.

Rae'jean didn't share Taye's fear and asked, "What's your idea?"

"Show the tape at the wedding."

Taye's eyes widened a hundred degrees. "Are you nuts!"

"No, but I sure as hell want to get even, and showing that videotape at the wedding will be the clincher. Even if Lorenzo's attorney finds a way to make the prenuptial legal, showing that video will generate such a scandal that the Ballentine family will pay any amount of money to avoid the negative publicity. Something like that could ruin them financially. When Brandy gets a divorce, she'll get enough of the Ballentines' millions to live happily for the rest of her life."

Taye nodded, finally buying into the plan for Brandy's sake. "After all the stress she'd been through today, she'll deserve every penny."

Quinn looked up when he heard a soft knock on his office door. "Yes?"

The door opened and his secretary walked in carrying a vase filled with calla lilies. "These just arrived," she said, sitting the large vase of flowers on his desk. She was out of the office before a speechless Quinn could say a word. He pulled off the card and read it.

> *Quinn, no matter what my initial plan may have been, I'm the one who got caught in the trap by falling in love with you. I really do love you.*
>
> *Alexia*

Quinn tightened the card in his hand and closed his eyes. He hadn't gotten much sleep last night and was forcing himself to work today. He stood and walked over to the window and looked out. Instead of seeing downtown LA, he was remembering Alexia and how she'd looked last night right before he had walked out of her house. The words she had spoken were still very clear in his mind.

You lied to me, Quinn. . . . You promised you wouldn't hurt me and that I could trust you. But you are hurting me, Quinn. You're hurting me by not believing in me and by not trusting me. You asked me to believe in you and to trust you, but you never intended to believe in me and to trust me. And knowing that hurts.

Quinn balled his hands into fists at his sides. Didn't Alexia know he was hurting as well? No man liked being used, and she had deliberately set out to use him.

He was jolted out of his reverie when the phone rang. Walking quickly back to his desk, he picked it up. "Yes?"

"Your sister Mrs. Norris is on the line, Mr. Masters."

"Thanks, Rita. Please put her through." A few moments later his twin sister came on the line. "Quinn?"

He smiled. "Quinece. What's happening, Sis?"

There was a pause. "I should be asking you that. Are you OK? There's something bothering you. I can feel it."

Quinn sat down in his chair. He and Quinece had discovered a long time ago that at certain times they could feel each other's pain. "And what do you feel, Quinece?"

There was another pause. "Like my heart is breaking."

Quinn nodded. "You almost got it right. You just forgot to use the past tense. My heart has been broken."

"Oh, Quinn, I'm sorry. Is there anything I can do?"

He smiled gently. As always, he appreciated the closeness he and his sister shared. In fact, he appreciated the closeness that he shared with all his siblings. They were a close-knit family. "Just continue to love me, Que-Two."

"You know I'll do that anyway, Que-One." After a pause, she asked, "Do you want to tell me about it?"

Quinn ran a hand over his face. What man wanted to tell anyone about being made a fool of? But then, he could tell Quinece anything. So he began talking. A few minutes later, after he was finished, he said, "So as you can see, I have good reason to feel the way I do."

"Do you still love her, Quinn?"

"Of course I do. You don't stop loving someone overnight."

He could hear the smile in Quinece's voice when she said, "No, you don't." There was another pause. "I've never told you how Kendall and I met, have I?"

Quinn lifted a brow. "I know the two of you actually met at a health spa."

"Yes, but I never told you that I had watched him a good month or so before I approached him and asked him to take me out."

Quinn chuckled. He wasn't surprised that she had been that forward with a guy. His sister was definitely a women's libber. She always had been.

"The main reason I wanted him to take me out was because, of all the men that I had been checking out, there was something about him that made me know he would be the one."

Quinn nodded. "The one you would marry?"

"No. The one I would sleep with. I knew he would be the one I would give my virginity to."

Quinn almost dropped the phone. "Say that again?"

Quinece chuckled. "You heard me right, Que-One. I had put a plan into motion to rid myself of my virginity. Here I was approaching my thirtieth birthday and was still a virgin and decided to do something about it. And Ken was the one I chose."

"You actually intended to use him that way?"

"Yes. I came on to him like I was a very experienced woman and he found out differently the first time we slept together. To say he was mad as hell would be an understatement. He dropped me after that like a hot potato."

Quinn nodded. "But he ended up coming back and falling in love with you anyway."

"Yes, he forgave me after realizing something that even I hadn't realized at the time."

"What?"

"That subconsciously, he was the one I had chosen. I had seen something good, something worthwhile in him that I hadn't seen in all those other men I'd checked out, that made me want him to be the one. My mind knew he was special even if at the time my heart did not." There was a slight pause. "I'm saying all that to say that there's a reason Alexia selected you to be the father of her child. Her mind knew you were special even though her heart didn't at the time. Now her heart has caught up with her mind. Don't punish her for it. Like you, Kendall felt used initially. But then, after going off for a couple of weeks and thinking about it, he realized just what a lucky man he was to be my first. Just think of what a lucky man you are to have a classy woman like Alexia Bennett admit to loving you and being pregnant with your child."

Quinn leaned back in his chair as he remembered the look on Alexia's face moments before he'd walked out. His words to her had been cruel, threatening.

"Well, I've said my piece. It's time for me to go, but I did call you for another reason, too," Quinece said.

"What reason is that?"

"To tell you that Kendall and I are expecting."

Quinn smiled. "Quinece, that's wonderful. I'm really happy for you."

"Thanks. And from the sound of it, me and Alexia will be delivering about the same time."

He nodded. "Yes, it seems that way, doesn't it?"

"Momma will be tickled pink to get two grandbabies all at once."

He nodded. "Yeah, but she'll be able to handle things."

"Of course she will. That woman is made of some pretty sturdy stuff. Well, I'd better let you go. I'm sure you have a lot of work to do and a lot to think about."

"Give Ken my best."

"I will. Love you, Que-One."

"Love you, too, Que-Two." After hanging up the phone, Quinn looked at the flowers Alexia had sent and picked up the card and reread it. Moments later he stood and walked back over to the window to think.

CHAPTER 42

Later that day the four cousins sat around Alexia's suite and viewed the videotape. After watching a good thirty minutes of it, Brandy commented that she hadn't known Jolene was so acrobatic. Alexia mentioned that she hadn't known there were so many positions to make love in and filed a few in the back of her mind to use later when she got Quinn back. Rae'jean, who'd always taken a nonpassionate approach to making love, got to see what she'd been missing and couldn't wait to see Ryan again. Taye had gotten hot and bothered and wanted to immediately go find Michael and jump his bones.

"Maybe we ought to sell copies. Some people would find it very entertaining," Rae'jean said, smiling, after the viewing was over.

"Some would even find it educational," Alexia said.

"And stimulating," Taye threw in.

"Or disgusting," Brandy said angrily as she ate a chocolate bar, at the moment not carrying that she'd probably have a zit somewhere on her face tomorrow as a result of it.

Alexia, Rae'jean, and Taye looked at Brandy and immediately felt bad. For a while they had forgotten how she must have felt seeing the man she had loved and planned to marry having sex with another woman, a woman who was supposed to be her best friend.

"Brandy, are you sure you want to go through with showing this at the

wedding tomorrow?" Alexia asked with concern in her voice. "You're being very brave about all of this, and I can't help but admire that. If it were
me, I'd be tempted to murder somebody—namely, Lorenzo and Jolene."

Brandy nodded with a wry smile. "Yes, I'm positive that I want to do
it. My vows tomorrow will be a farce anyway, so I may as well make the
most of it. I'm going to play the innocent, wounded bride. I even plan to
faint when the videotape starts playing." She giggled. "Once I'm brought
back around, I will become the drama queen, asking for a divorce and
demanding to be compensated heavily for my humiliation."

Rae'jean smiled. She could just imagine Brandy being dramatic. "All
the plans are final for tonight?"

Alexia giggled. "Yes, Mr. Gleason doesn't know what he's in for. He's
going to find out the hard way, right along with Lorenzo and Jolene, that
you don't mess with a Bennett."

"Really, Mr. Gleason, I don't think it's necessary for us to get undressed to
enjoy this glass of wine," Alexia purred to the old man sitting across from
her on the love seat in his suite.

"I watched you on that HBO special five months ago," the old man
crooned. "And I wondered what a man had to do to get a woman like
you. You have such a beautiful voice, and I bet you have a beautiful body
to go along with it."

Alexia forced a smile. The man had been trying to get her out of her
clothes ever since she had come up to his room. She, however, was trying
to get him intoxicated. Unfortunately, he seemed to be able to hold more
alcohol than she had counted on. She crossed her legs, deliberately baring
her shapely thighs and hoping that would be enough for him, because that
was as much as he would get. The thought of his hands on her was beginning to make her ill. She reached over and refilled his glass with more wine.

"You're not drinking any," he observed.

She smiled sweetly at him. There was no way she would tell the old
coot that she wasn't drinking because she was pregnant. "Wine doesn't
agree with me. It usually makes me sick." She sweetened her smile. "And
you don't want me to get sick, do you, Mr. Gleason?" she asked, batting
her lashes at him.

"No, of course not. However, if you do feel ill you can always stretch out on my bed to rest."

Alexia forced another smile. "I'll keep that in mind." At that moment they heard a sound coming from the other room.

"Did you hear anything?" Mr. Gleason asked, getting to his feet . . . but just barely. The alcohol was beginning to work on him, and he couldn't stand straight.

"No. I didn't hear anything," Alexia said quickly, knowing Rae'jean and Taye were now inside the man's hotel room. To take his mind off what was probably going on beyond the door, in the sitting area, she stood and crossed the room to the window, knowing his eyes had nearly popped out of their sockets at just how short her dress was. She had borrowed the outfit from Brandy, who was the same size as her but shorter. If she were to bend over he'd be able to see next Christmas and well into the New Year. "The ocean is beautiful at night," she said, looking out the window.

She heard him come up behind her on wobbly legs. The man was about gone. It shouldn't be long now before he was out like a light. She tried not to stiffen when she felt his hand on her shoulder and felt him come stand directly behind her. She almost got sick when with his drunken breath he whispered in her ear, "Can I take off your dress, Al?"

Alexia inwardly cringed. She hated it when people shortened her name to Al. "Yes, if you really want to," she whispered silkily, knowing he wouldn't be able to get the zipper down. Even if he didn't have drunken fingers, the zipper wouldn't work. She'd had Taye stitch the zipper in place to make absolutely sure of that.

She inwardly smiled when she felt him trying, without much success, to get the zipper of her dress down.

"It's stuck," he finally said.

"It can't be," Alexia said smoothly. She heard him release a frustrated breath before trying again without any success. She turned to face him. "I tell you what; why don't you just go on and get in the bed, under the covers, and wait for me? I'm going into the bathroom and take it off. I'll be back in a little while."

"But I want to watch you get naked," he pouted drunkenly.

Not in this lifetime, old man, Alexia thought. "I'm much too shy to get undressed in front of you," she said innocently.

"Sure, honey, I understand," he said, patting her thigh. "You go on and get undressed in the bathroom. I'll be in bed waiting for you."

Alexia deliberately remained in the bathroom for a good twenty minutes. When she opened the door to come out—still fully clothed—she couldn't help but smile. Mr. Gleason had removed his shirt but hadn't taken off his pants before passing out on the bed. And he was snoring loudly.

Grabbing her purse, she quickly left the hotel room.

Mission accomplished.

It was nearly two in the morning and Alexia, Brandy, Rae'jean, and Taye were all sitting around Rae'jean's room recounting what they had done that night. Alexia had had them in stitches while telling them about her episode with Mr. Gleason.

After a while Rae'jean asked Brandy, "Were you able to get your copy of the prenuptial from out of Lorenzo's room?"

Brandy nodded after taking another sip of wine. "Yes, all copies should be accounted for. I suggest we tear them in tiny bits and flush them down the toilet."

Alexia laughed. "Sounds like a good plan to me."

Brandy sighed deeply. Today was the longest period she had spent with her cousins in a long time, and she had enjoyed their company. She smiled. She was touched by the way they had rallied around her and had given her their support. She now regretted that she had missed out on their friendship while growing up. "I want to say something to the three of you."

When the room got completely silent and all eyes were on her, Brandy continued, "I know I haven't been the nicest person to each of you over the years, and for that I am truly sorry. I let my mother's resentment at how things didn't turn out for her and my father influence my relationship with the Bennett family. I see now what I missed out on and what I could have been sharing with you. It will forever be my loss, because the three of you have proven tonight, beyond a shadow of a doubt, that family does matter, and that blood is thicker than water and that when you need them, your family will come through for you."

Tears misted Brandy's eyes. "I love Lorenzo. Even now, with everything he's done, I still love him. But I will get over him and I will make him pay dearly for hurting me this way. But I believe that somewhere there's a man who will love me as I should be loved."

She turned to Taye. "He will be like your Michael, Taye, and will be willing to fight heaven and hell, even family if he has to, to be with me." Her gaze moved next to Alexia. "Or he might be like your Quinn, Alexia, who even now, when you think you may have lost him forever, still brings a sparkle of love and passion to your eyes." She then turned to Rae'jean. "Or he may be like the new man in your life, Rae'jean, the one you want but are so afraid to have. The one who makes your blood race with just a look. I will have all of that one day, and when I do," she said, her smile widening, "the three of you won't just be invited to the wedding; you'll all be in it."

Cheers went up in the room and the four women stood and, for the first time ever, they embraced with love in their hearts for one another. Crying all the while and knowing they had accomplished something that was a long time coming.

"Hey, you guys," Alexia said, wiping tears from her eyes. "I got just the right song to top this off. My agent sent it with me because he wants me to think about doing a remake of it. At first I rebuffed the thought, but now it may not be such a bad idea after all."

She went over to the CD player and began playing the song, "We Are Family," by Sister Sledge. Everyone in the room joined in, dancing and singing at the top of their lungs, with Alexia doing the lead. They replaced the word *sisters* in the song with the word *cousins*. After singing it a few times, Taye, Rae'jean, and Brandy concluded that if Alexia ever did a remake of the song, she would need the three of them as her backup.

CHAPTER 43

Even with overcast skies, it was a beautiful day for a wedding. At least four people in particular thought so.

Taye nodded to Rae'jean. Rae'jean nodded to Alexia. Alexia nodded to Brandy just minutes before everyone took their places. This would be a wedding everyone would remember for a long time to come. The four Bennett cousins had gone out of their way to see to that.

The Ballentines had paid a lot of money for their son's wedding to the American woman with a Ph.D. who was as educated as she was beautiful. She would give them beautiful and brilliant grandchildren, they thought as they watched her walk down the aisle on the arm of the huge bulk of a man who was her father. She was glowing with all the radiance of a beautiful bride.

"Do you want to tell me what you, Rae'jean, and Alexia were up to last night?" Michael asked as he leaned over and whispered the question in Taye's ear. They were sitting halfway in the middle of the church. After the wedding, everyone would be returning to the hotel, where a huge and costly reception had been planned in the ballroom.

Taye smiled at Michael. She wasn't ready to tell him anything yet. Like everyone else, he would find out soon enough. "What makes you think we were up to something?"

He cocked a brow at her pretense of innocence. "I wasn't born yester-

day. Besides, last night you actually giggled in your sleep a few times."
Taye almost laughed out loud at that one. Instead, she said, "Oh."

On the other side of Michael, Rae'jean sat listening as Brandy and
Lorenzo exchanged vows. It was a beautiful wedding. It was just too bad
the groom was a dog and the maid of honor was a slut. Rae'jean shook
her head at the indecency of it all. She then thought about Ryan and what
he'd shared with her regarding his own wife and how she had gotten pregnant from another man. He, too, had had his share of pain from an unfaithful mate.

Rae'jean sighed deeply. She really missed him and had thought of him
constantly since she'd been gone. In such a short while he had made a huge
impact on her. She had decided that she did want a deeper, more meaningful relationship with Ryan. She only hoped that he felt the same way.
She couldn't wait to get back to Boston to find out.

Alexia sat on the end of the seat next to Taye. She was slated to get up
and sing in a few minutes, right after the last of the vows were spoken and
right before the minister announced that Brandy and Lorenzo were man and
wife. The song that had been selected for her to sing was about everlasting
love, something she intended to have with Quinn. Now more than ever, she
intended to make him see just how much she loved him and that her baby,
their baby, needed them to be together and not apart. When the time came
for her to sing her song, Alexia stood and walked toward the front of the
church.

As he sat at the back of the church, in the last pew, Quinn's gaze captured
Alexia within its scope the moment she stood and walked toward the front
of the church. He had arrived on the island with just enough time to drop
his luggage off at the hotel and come straight to the church. Abbott Bodie
had given him all the information he had needed to find her.

His gaze studied Alexia as she closed her eyes and began singing. The
entire church got quiet as her sultry voice flooded the audience. The impact
of the sound on him was devastating . . . just as devastating as her beauty.
And he knew at that very moment that he loved her and wanted her back
in his life.

It had taken almost a full day for his sister's words to sink in, really sink in. Once he had gotten over his bruised ego, he had seen reason. No matter what plan Alexia had originally initiated, the bottom line was that she loved him now. She loved him and she was having his baby. That meant everything to him.

After she had sung the last lyric, Alexia smiled at Brandy and moved to go back to her seat. As she walked back toward the middle of the church, her gaze absentmindedly swept over the rows of guests. Her heart nearly stopped beating when her eyes met the penetrating stare of the same dark eyes she had looked into countless times over the past three months while making love. She blinked, thinking she'd been thinking of Quinn so much that her mind had somehow conjured him up. But after blinking a second time she came to realize that he was here. He was really here, and he was looking at her not with anger but with love radiating from his strong, handsome features and his dark, compelling eyes. The man was drop-dead gorgeous. Today even more so.

She took a deep breath, wanting to go to him immediately and throw herself in his arms and beg his forgiveness. But she held back from making a scene. Today belonged to Brandy. At the moment, knowing Quinn had come was enough. Later, they would straighten out things between them.

After the final vows had been said and the bride and groom and their bridal procession had flowed out of the church, everyone in attendance rushed to follow them. Telling her cousins that she would be joining them at the reception as soon as possible, Alexia waited until the church had gotten completely empty, except for one person.

Quinn.

They began slowly walking toward each other and didn't stop until they were standing directly in front of each other. He was the first to speak.

"You're beautiful, Alexia," he said huskily. "No matter what our problems are, we'll work things out, because I have no intention of letting you go. I love you, you love me, and you're having my baby. I don't know what else a man could ask for to be truly happy."

"Oh, Quinn." Alexia threw herself in his arms, wanting and needing to feel him hold her. And he did. He tightened his arms around her, and she closed her eyes in silent prayer to God for bringing this man into her life. And then, moments later, he was kissing her. He was kissing her in a way that bound her to him forever. It was in a way that made her heart soar with everlasting love and made her insides tremor with the knowledge that this man was her baby's daddy. And he was the man who would love and cherish her and in return she would love and cherish him.

He was her soulmate.

Beneath a ten-tiered chandelier in the ballroom, Lorenzo and Brandy shared the first dance. To anyone looking on, it seemed the man truly loved the woman he held so tenderly in his arms. But at least three persons looking on knew better. Make that four if you wanted to count Jolene, who stood on the sidelines clinging to the man holding his arm around her waist. That must be her boyfriend, Rae'jean thought, frowning. The duplicity of some people amazed her. She wondered what Jolene's boyfriend would think of her when he saw firsthand how she spent her free time.

Rae'jean looked across the room at Alexia, who was standing next to the man who had shown up at the wedding to claim her. She was happy for her cousin and thought it was a long time coming. For years, Alexia had been a tough cookie to crack. Now, not only had she softened up, but she had a man she loved and who truly adored her. And to top things off, she was pregnant. She was getting both the man and the baby she wanted.

Rae'jean then glanced around to find Taye and Michael. They were standing away from everyone else, holding hands. She could feel the love that was radiating between them and knew what they felt for each other was special. She hoped the grandfathers gave the pair their blessings.

Everyone's applause after the couple had completed their dance vibrated through the room. Then other couples began moving onto the dance floor.

A half hour or so later, after everyone had taken their seats to be served the wedding dinner, two huge movie screens that had been erected in the front on both sides of the ballroom glowed as the images of Lorenzo and Brandy came into view. The screens showed footage of them walking to-gether on a Hawaiian beach, holding hands like two people very much in love. The next frame showed them getting into a horse-driven carriage in the Virgin Islands for a romantic ride.

Rae'jean braced herself for the next one.

The frame flickered before it moved to the next one. The next one, with the theme from *The Bad News Bears* blaring in the background, showed a bedroom scene . . . and two people making out. The crowd of onlookers gasped at what they saw. It was evident that the man in the video was the groom—his dreadlocks couldn't be denied—but the woman who was all on top of him, then under him, then on top of him again as they mated wildly wasn't the bride.

It was the bride's maid of honor!

Everyone, including the groom and the maid of honor, was too shocked to do anything but stand there and watch the scene being played on the two big screens.

Then, as planned, Brandy became hysterical, screaming loudly before fainting in her father-in-law's arms. The groom rushed over to his bride, but her father, who looked like he was ready to hit somebody, barred his way. Victor Senior actually did take a swing at the groom but missed when Lorenzo ducked. The bride's mother, who earlier had come across to everyone as such a very sophisticated lady, began calling the groom all sorts of obscenities. Mothers of small children were covering their little ones' ears from all the profanity being slung around, as well as shielding their eyes from what was being shown on the screens as they quickly ushered them out of the ballroom.

The video kept right on rolling, and now the theme to *Rocky* was playing. Amid the mad chaos, no one thought about turning it off, and both screens were aglow with images of Lorenzo's and Jolene's naked body parts as they made out like there was no tomorrow.

Rae'jean glanced over to where Jolene had been standing with her boyfriend earlier. The man was gone and she'd been left standing alone in total embarrassment and shame. All eyes, those not glued to the screen, were on either Lorenzo or Jolene.

"Hey, this is good," Victor Junior whispered to Rae'jean. His eyes were glued to the screen. "Boy, look how Jolene moves. If I had known she was giving her stuff away like this, I would have worked harder getting some of it."

Rae'jean rolled her eyes to the ceiling. It really didn't surprise her that he was thinking that way.

"I wish I had a copy of this," he added wistfully.

At some point, someone decided the best way to end the fiasco was to stop the video from rolling. But there were some present who were actually enjoying what they were seeing on the big screens and boldly blocked the path of anyone who tried to end it.

The place became a madhouse. The setting of Jamaica's wedding of the year had turned into a porno theater.

Brandy, it seems, had been brought back around. It was then wished by some, especially the Ballentines and their attorney, that she'd remained passed out. Playing the part of the humiliated, dishonored, and defrauded bride, she began screaming demands of her husband. She wanted compensation for this humiliation as well as a divorce that would give her half of everything he owned.

Michael shook his head as he looked down at Taye. "You wouldn't know anything about what's going on here, would you?"

Taye smiled up at him sweetly. "What would give you that idea?"

"Because this entire production has the three Bennett cousins' names written in the credits."

Taye grinned. "Make it four."

Michael cocked a brow and looked at her thoughtfully. "Brandy was in on this?"

Instead of saying anything, Taye widened her smile.

Alexia was rolling in laughter. Quinn looked at her like he thought she had lost her mind. "You think it's funny that your cousin just got married to a man who made love to her best friend?"

Alexia wiped the tears of laughter from her eyes. "Yeah." Seeing his confused look, she said, "I'll explain everything to you later. Right now I need to go support Brandy."

On cue, the three cousins assembled at Brandy's side as the Ballentines and their attorney hurriedly tried to bring calm and order to the madness by ushering the bride and groom from the ballroom and into a private room. Lorenzo, talking a mile a minute, was apologizing under one breath and denying everything under another.

Brandy, playing the part of the dishonored bride to the hilt, was sobbing uncontrollably. "I can't believe you would humiliate me this way, Lorenzo, and with Jolene. She was my best friend. She was to be the godmother of our first child. How could you?"

"Yes, how could you?" his own mother and father asked simultaneously. They had really liked Brandy.

"It was a mistake, sweetheart," Lorenzo was saying to his wife. "I'll make it up to you; I promise."

"No, you won't," Brandy snapped as she stopped sobbing almost immediately. "I have nothing I want to say to you. I'll see you in court. You'll pay for all the humiliation you've caused me today."

"Yes, you will certainly pay for this!" Victor Senior bellowed loudly, glaring at the man who was his short-term son-in-law. "And where in the hell did that tape come from anyway?" he thundered through the room, looking around accusingly at everyone except his daughter and three nieces. "I want to know who would embarrass my daughter this way."

Brandy patted her father's arm to calm him down. She knew he could be hell to deal with when he really got mad about something. And one thing he loved, besides women, was his children—all twenty or so of them. But she knew, as she'd always known, that to him she was special. She was his first daughter and had come from the body of the only woman he had really, truly loved and probably still loved. Whether he admitted it or not, he and her mother were in a constant love-hate relationship. Brandy knew for a fact that her parents had slept together quite a few times over the years and that they had even slept together a couple times here at the hotel. He hadn't deliberately left his wife home for nothing.

"It doesn't matter, Daddy. Whoever did it wanted me to find out the truth, and I'm grateful. I just want to go home," she said as she began sobbing again. She looked at Lorenzo before turning to leave the room. "You have truly hurt me this day," she said with genuine pain in her voice. "I don't ever want to see you again, and you will be hearing from my attorneys."

She then left the room with the train of her bridal gown flowing behind her and her three cousins following in her wake and her father bringing up the rear.

• • •

Later that night, the Bennetts threw a party in the penthouse of the hotel that contained what should have been Brandy and Lorenzo's honeymoon suite. Also, as part of her honeymoon package, Brandy had tickets for two weeks to Rome, Italy, which she still intended to use later. For the moment she just wanted to chill and enjoy her family. Her mother had somewhat recovered from the ordeal and was somewhere in one of the hotel rooms being comforted by Victor Senior.

The tale of how today's activities had unfolded was shared, and everyone was sworn to secrecy.

Quinn shook his head upon hearing that the showing of the videotape had been Alexia's idea. Michael was surprised at mild-mannered Taye's involvement, and Victor Junior was in hog heaven because Brandy had given him his personal copy of the videotape.

"Now you see what you're in for, Quinn," Michael said to the man jokingly. "Are you sure you want to become a member of the Bennett family?"

Quinn looked down into the face of the woman he loved. "Yeah, I'm sure. We're getting married as soon as things can be arranged."

Later Rae'jean exclaimed to everyone, "The next stop, you guys, is Macon for the family meeting! We need to be there to give Taye and Michael our support. We know they deserve to be together."

All the Bennetts in the room applauded in agreement. "We would appreciate that," Michael said, holding Taye in his arms. "We'll need all the support we can get. But no matter the outcome, this December Taye and I are going to get married and live happily ever after."

And everyone in the room truly believed that.

CHAPTER 44

E than Allen Bennett glanced around his front porch. The place looked
like a circus. There were more Bennetts than he could count. Assem-
bling together like this twice in one year was a miracle, he thought. First
it had been for the Bennett family reunion. Now it was for the Bennett
family civil war. It was evident that the lines had been drawn. The older
Bennetts, those who opposed a match between Michael and Taye, were all
sitting or standing on one side, and the younger, more free-thinking Bennetts were grouped on the other side.

He took a deep breath. He knew the final decision would be his and
Henry's and no matter what decision was made, everyone would abide by
it. Although he also knew that some, like Cuzin Sophie, would have a lot
to say about it for years to come, even after he finally went to join Idella
in the great beyond.

Both he and Henry had prayed over their decision and knew that in
the long run it would be the best thing for the entire family.

"Michael! Taye!" he called out to them. "Henry and I want to see you
two inside." When he saw the whole mass of cousins who were grouped
with them getting ready to follow, he added, "Alone."

He then turned to the other side and sought out his son and daughter-
in-law. "Joe and Otha Mae. You come, too."

When everyone he had summoned was inside, he closed the door behind him and pulled down the shades to the front windows. What they couldn't hear, he knew, the Bennetts outside were counting on seeing, and he wanted to make sure they didn't see or hear anything. He loved the lot of them, but Lord knows they were a nosy bunch.

"Everyone, be seated," he said in his authoritative voice. Henry was already sitting in a rocking chair. His arthritis was acting up today.

Ethan watched as Michael and Taye sat on the sofa holding hands. He could remember them as little ones, doing practically the same thing at one time or another. The two of them had always been close. Maybe if he had paid more attention he would have seen it coming, but in truth he hadn't. The fact that they were courtin' had come as a complete surprise to him. But it hadn't to Henry. He claimed that he'd known all the time and had been concerned about it when they were teenagers and Taye used to follow Michael around like a puppy with love in her eyes. But he'd figured she would grow out of it.

Evidently she hadn't.

"Now then," Ethan finally said when everyone looked at him expectantly. "We all know why we're here." He then turned his full attention to Michael and Taye. "I understand the two of you have stirred up a hornets' nest with this talk of being in love."

Michael's hold tightened on Taye's hand, something both grandfathers noticed. "Yes, sir, and if being in love with Taye has stirred up a hornets' nest, then so be it."

Poppa Ethan frowned. "So you're willing to cause problems in the family?"

"Yes, sir, if it means loving Taye."

"And you think you love her, son?"

Michael nodded. He wondered if everyone had failed to notice that he was not some sixteen-year-old boy. He was a man of thirty-three, three months shy of turning thirty-four. He'd been married before and had a thirteen-year-old daughter. He knew about love and didn't need anyone questioning him about it. However, the man who was asking was someone he respected and held in high esteem and someone that he and Taye loved dearly. "I *know* I love her, Poppa Ethan."

"And you're willing to do what's best for her?"

"Yes, sir."

"Even giving her up if you have to?"

Michael paused. That particular question had been asked by his own grandfather. He shifted his gaze from Poppa Ethan to his Grampa Henry. "Yes, Grampa, if I had to. But I don't have to. There's no reason for me to have to do that."

"What about to end the feud in the family?"

Michael inhaled deeply. He then looked at Taye before gazing back at his grandfather once again. "I love the family, but I love Taye more. She means everything to me. The girls have accepted what we have, and we want all of you to do the same. But if you don't, then we'll do what we have to do to be together. We are Bennetts, that can't ever be taken away from us, but if the family wants to disown us then that's their choice."

"See there, Poppa?" Otha Mae wailed. "What did I tell you? Taye has bewitched him. Michael has always had good common sense, but being around Taye these past few months has made him lose some of it. No soul in their right mind wants to marry their cousin, blood or otherwise."

"I did," Poppa Ethan said, feeling completely exhausted. It didn't take much for Otha Mae's hysterics to nearly drain the very life out of him. "I married my Idella."

Otha Mae frowned. "But the two of you weren't related."

"If you ask me, all black folks are related some way or another. Who can be rightly sure they ain't, the way our families were split up and separated during slavery times?" He sighed deeply. "Idella's ma and pa took me in and raised me as one of their own when I was barely sixteen and my own folks died. So in a way it was like being part of her family. In fact, I considered myself as such. And when I went to them at the age of twenty and told them that I wanted to marry Idella, they didn't have a problem with it." He sat back in his chair and stared at his son and daughter-in-law. "Just like I don't have a problem with Michael and Taye marrying. Neither does Henry." He shook his head before gazing intently at his son. "You need to learn how to put a lid on Otha Mae every once in a while, Joe. She gets too carried away with things."

Otha Mae stood fuming. "I can't believe you, Poppa. In your eye Taye can do no wrong. You were just as accepting of those two pregnancies of hers as you were of this. And it's wrong. What type of example is she setting for the family?"

Michael stood to say something in Taye's behalf, refusing to let anyone, even her mother, say anything against her. But Grampa Ethan touched his hand. "Sit down, son, and let me handle this."

Michael hesitated, but after looking into the old man's eyes, he relented and returned to his seat.

Grampa Ethan just sat there and gazed up at Otha Mae for the longest time before finally saying, "Ever since that child was born, I've watched you trying to make her into something perfect. Then the first time she made a mistake, you couldn't handle it; you all but disowned her. But you of all people should have understood. Therefore, I can say this and I can say this without batting an eye. You, Otha Mae Robbins Bennett, are a hypocrite. How can you fault Taye for having a baby out of wedlock when you had one out of wedlock yourself?"

Poppa Ethan didn't know which of the two women, Otha Mae or Taye, gasped in shock the loudest.

Otha Mae dropped back down in her seat. "I don't know what you're talking about. I've never had a child out of wedlock. You must be——"

"Yes, you did, so stop lying," Poppa said in a firm tone. "Your father told me, and he had no reason to lie on his own daughter."

Otha Mae hung her head down, and for the longest time she didn't speak. When she did, she raised eyes full of shame to Poppa Ethan and asked in a quiet voice, "How long have you known?"

Poppa Ethan sighed deeply. He loved his daughter-in-law, even with all her faults. But someone had to get her straight once and for all, and since Joe wasn't trying to do it, then for the family's sake the task fell on him. "I've known since before you and Joe got married. Your father, being the honest and religious man that he was, felt I had a right to know that the woman my son had chosen to bring into our family had had a child out of wedlock at the age of fifteen. It was a child that he and your mama gave to a childless couple who once belonged to his congregation before he was called to a church here in Macon."

Otha Mae nodded. She then forced herself to meet her husband's gaze. "Did you know?"

Joe gazed at the woman he'd been married to for going on forty years. He'd known he should have put his foot down countless times, but it was easier just to let her have her way. "Yeah, I knew. Daddy told me about it before I married you."

"And you married me anyway?" she asked incredulously in a soft voice.

"Yeah, because I knew you were a good woman and I wanted you for the mother of my children. Any mistakes you made before we got together didn't matter to me."

"Just like any mistakes Taye has made don't matter to Michael, either," Poppa Ethan said, leaning forward in his chair. "Knowing about your past, Otha Mae, how could you be so unforgiving to your own daughter? A sin is a sin, big or small, one or two. Taye made a mistake, but then so did you."

Taye sat beside Michael speechless. She had had no idea that her upright, Bible-toting mother had given birth to a child before she married Taye's father. To find out that she had done so was a shocker.

"I didn't want Taye to make the same mistakes I did. I didn't want to think that the reason she had made those mistakes was somehow connected to me and my past. I didn't want to think of myself as a bad seed," Otha Mae said, beginning to cry softly.

Taye immediately got up and went over to her mother and knelt down. "Oh, Mom. You aren't a bad seed. You are an inspiration to my girls and me. I made two bad decisions in life, for which I've learned lessons and for which I plan to set good examples for my girls, and I've done that. I hadn't been involved with a man in over ten years, because I was too afraid of making another bad decision which could cost me your love."

Taye took a deep sigh as she wiped tears from her mother's eyes from the handkerchief her father had handed to her. "But what I feel for Michael is right. It's good. I love him. He loves me. I know you love Sebrina and Monica and want the best for them. Then please want the best for me, too. And Michael is the best."

Otha Mae nodded slowly, accepting her daughter's words, then reached out and hugged her youngest child to her. Then they both cried together, washing away years of hurt and misunderstandings.

"I think," Poppa Ethan said moments later, "that what's been discussed here among us should stay here among us. There's no one beyond these walls who needs to know what's been said. What's important is that we continue to love each other as a family, to support each other, and to always be there for one another."

He leaned back in his chair. "Some days I feel so tired I think this may be the night when I'll lie down for the last time before going to join my Idella. But so far, the good Lord hasn't seen fit to take me on home. But when he does, I want to know that my family ain't back here cuttin' the fool. I want to believe I left them with at least a grain of good sense. Although nobody's perfect."

He slowly stood to his feet. "Now me and Henry are gonna go out there and tell everyone our decision. Some gonna like it. Some ain't. But those that ain't just have to get over it. The ones that will like our decision are the ones that are gonna continue to keep this family strong. They're the ones like Taye, Michael, Rae'jean, Brandy, and Alexia." He then shook his head, ashamed. "And the one who's hell-bent on keeping the family populated is Victor Junior. But then there's no hope for the boy. He got it honest."

Michael walked over to Taye and gently pulled her from her mother's arms into his. "Later today, we're going shopping for an engagement ring," he said, hugging her tight.

The younger Bennetts decided to have a fish fry to celebrate the grandfathers' decision to give their blessings to Michael and Taye. The older Bennetts, those who weren't happy with the decision, decided to stop their grumbling for the time being—at least until after they could get a good-tasting fried fish sandwich into their stomachs.

Michael, Victor Junior, and Quinn—who'd been adopted into the family already—had gone to Chucky's Seafood and purchased at least twenty dozen blue crabs. A fire was lit under a huge pot in the backyard, and now the spicy aroma of boiling crabs floated through the air. Everyone was having a good time, and after a while they forgot there was supposed to be a division in the family.

Rae'jean was in the kitchen with Aunt Otha Mae and Cousin Agnes to help with the pies they had decided to bake when one of Cousin Fred's kids came running inside and told her there was a man in the front yard who wanted to see her.

Wondering who it could be, she wiped the flour off her hands and left the kitchen. Walking through the living room, she smiled when she glanced up at what once had been her grandmother's prized "wall of frame" with the Kennedys' and Martin Luther King, Jr.'s pictures hanging proudly. She saw that her grandfather had recently added John F. Kennedy Jr.'s picture on the wall beside that of his father, John F. Kennedy, Sr. Rae'jean's smile widened, as she knew her grandmother would have liked that.

Opening the front door, Rae'jean stepped outside on the porch, then stopped short when her breath got caught in her throat. Ryan was standing by the huge oak tree in her grandfather's front yard.

"Ryan? What are you doing here?" she asked him as she came down the steps and walked over to him. "How did you know where I was?" To say she was glad to see him was an understatement. It had been ten days since she had seen him, and she had missed him every one of those days.

He smiled. "I'm an investigator. Finding people is my specialty." He reached out and covered her hand with his own. "I had to return to Miami for that case I'm working on. When I called back to the office, my secretary gave me your message that your return back to Boston would be delayed a few days because of a family matter. I couldn't wait to see you, so I decided to come here."

He took a deep breath as he continued to look at her. "I want to know what you've decided. Do you want for us to have a serious relationship or be just friends?"

"What do you want?"

"I asked you first."

Rae'jean smiled as she looked up at him. "I want us to have a serious relationship."

Ryan grinned happily. "So do I."

Her smile widened, tilting the corners of her lips. "So it's official we'll be doing the dating thing now?"

"Yes, it's official, and we'll be doing the dating thing now."

"So can I consider myself your girl?" she teased.

He shook his head, grinning, wanting so much to kiss her. "Oh, yeah, you're my girl all right."

She wanted to kiss him, too, but out of the corner of her eye she saw nosy Cuzin Sophie watching them. Rae'jean decided that she would make time for them to go someplace private and kiss—and maybe do some other things—later. "Come on; let me introduce you to my family," she said, taking his hand and leading him to the backyard. "I may as well warn you that they can be a rowdy group." She thought she should at least warn him, since she wasn't sure if he knew what antics went down in a large family, and hers could take the icing off the cake.

"Really? How rowdy are they?"

"Oh, you're about to find out."

Rae'jean cast her eyes to the man sitting in the car beside her. "Thanks for bringing me back to the hotel, Ryan."

"Don't mention it," he said, holding her gaze. The hotel's neon sign reflected off the shine in his eyes.

Then were was silence. Simmering heat. Swelling tension. It had been like that between them all day. Even with her family around she had felt his eyes on her every movement, and whenever she had looked up to meet his glance she had felt the desire and the hunger within him. It had been there all through her family's friendly game of volleyball, all through the seafood they'd consumed, and all through her family's nosy questions and pointless inquisition.

And it was there now and it was affecting her big-time.

She had never felt this way before, this hot, this keyed up, this intense, this filled with desire and wanting. She was very much aware of him. She urged her gaze away to look at the beautiful landscape of the building. "Do you want to come up to my room for a drink?" she finally asked to break the silence.

"I'd love to."

She then waited for him to get out of the car and come around to open the car door for her. "I forgot to ask what hotel you're staying at," she said as they began walking up the sidewalk to the entrance of the Marriott Hotel.

He smiled and it increased the hunger growing inside of her. "This one."

Her eyebrows drew together. "Oh? What a coincidence."

"Not really. I knew you were staying here."

She nodded, tilting her chin toward the ground. "Due to your investigative skill, right?"

"That's right."

She smiled and glanced back at him. "You're good at it. Was it hard to find me?" The thought that he had gone through all that trouble to see her had touched her.

"No, mainly because I was determined to find you. I wanted to see you, although I wasn't sure how you would feel about seeing me. For all I knew, you could have made the decision that you didn't want any type of relationship with me. I took a chance in coming."

They walked in silence until they reached the entrance to the hotel. Then they stopped walking. They stood facing each other, their gazes locked, each hearing the unsteady beat of their own hearts. They knew their relationship would change once they crossed over the hotel's threshold and needed to make sure this was what they wanted. They had already decided earlier that day that they wanted to have a relationship, one that meant more than an assuaging of overworked hormones.

"Ryan, I—"

"Shh, it's OK," he said softly, reaching up and gently stroking her lips with his thumb, holding her silent. "It's a big step for me, too. We don't have to if you aren't ready for it."

"Are you ready for it?"

He hooked a finger under her chin and lifted her gaze to meet his. "I think I've been ready for it since the first time I saw you, standing that day at your window. But I knew you were off-limits. But that didn't keep me from wanting you, thinking of you often."

He skimmed his palm against her throat. "And then when you showed up at my office that day, I was thrown for a loop. After finding out you were no longer engaged, it seemed like fate had intervened, but I didn't want to believe it. The pain of my ex-wife's betrayal had gone deep, and another serious involvement was what I didn't want. But I couldn't stay away from you, Rae'jean. I had to accept the fact that even without my knowing you intimately, you're in my blood. There's this thing between us that won't go away. It's been there since the first time we set eyes on each other. Making love won't get rid of it; it will only intensify it, strengthen it. I think you should know that up front. This has to be your call."

He continued to watch her watch him. He wanted her more than he had ever wanted a woman. He wanted to possess her mind, body, and soul. He wanted to brand her his with his passion; he wanted to show her how special he thought she was. He had felt honored that she had shared her family with him today, a family he'd never really had. Even with the questions her grandfather had asked outright, regarding Ryan's intentions toward his granddaughter, he hadn't felt pressured or been made to feel like an outcast. After just meeting him, the Bennetts had included him within their close-knit fold.

"So, it's my call?" Rae'jean finally said, breaking the heated silence. "Then I suggest we call it a night. There's no need to pay for two separate rooms when I think one will suffice; what do you think?"

He thought he wanted to kiss her right then and there, under the moonlit sky. "I think you're right. I'll move my stuff to your room in the morning."

Reaching out, Rae'jean took his hand in hers as they walked through the entrance of the hotel. They stepped into the elevator and stood on opposite sides. Rae'jean tried to take her mind off just how much she wanted him.

"Rae'jean?"

She looked up when Ryan called her name. Her gaze met his. "Yes?"

"I think you have a super family. You should feel blessed."

Her smile widened as she thought about her family; even nosy Cuzin Sophie had some good in her at times. She knew every family had someone like Sophie; that couldn't be helped. "I do. I feel extremely blessed."

The elevator came to a stop on her floor. "What floor are you on?" she asked Ryan as they stepped out.

"This one."

For some reason, Rae'jean wasn't surprised. Moments later she blew out a trembling breath when she couldn't get her key to work in her room door.

"May I try it?" Ryan asked.

"Yes."

He expertly opened the door with no hassles, then stood back to let her enter. As soon as she heard the door closing and locking behind him, she turned back around to face him. He stood leaning against the door, watching her.

"I'm safe," she said, releasing a deep breath. "I had a physical a few months ago. And I'm still on the pill."

He nodded. "I had my annual physical last month and I checked out fine, too."

Rae'jean nodded; then an involuntary shiver touched her body. "I'm not used to this, Ryan. I've never wanted the passion before, but now I want it so much I can't think straight."

He eased from the door and walked over to her. "I don't want you to think at all. I just want you to feel. After tonight you will know my body as well as I'll know yours," he said, his voice hoarse, barely above a breath. "After tonight there will never be any doubt in either of our minds that this is what we want and that being together is our fate."

He pulled her against him. "Feel, baby. Just feel."

And she did.

When he brought his mouth down on hers, she almost felt her knees buckling. Without breaking the kiss Ryan picked her up into his arms and carried her over to the bed. His hands then went everywhere, all at once, as he removed her shorts, top, and underthings.

Ryan broke off the kiss long enough to undress himself, but Rae'jean refused to just watch. She had a vested interest in this and intended to participate. She rose up on her knees and began fumbling with the button and zipper of his jeans. He accommodated her by pulling them down over his hips, and her breath caught in her throat when he stood before her wearing nothing but a pair of the sexiest briefs she had ever seen on a man. Her gaze scanned the hardness of him, the length of his erection clearly outlined.

Then something happened to her that had never happened before. She felt needy. She felt greedy. She felt totally, unequivocally aroused. She felt driven with a voracious hunger she had never felt before.

And all for this man. She felt undiluted passion. Reaching out, she began stroking him, wondering how she had gotten so bold, so wanton, and so filled with desire.

Ryan drew in a deep shuddering breath with her touch. "Rae'jean, let me take my briefs off."

She relented and watched, fascinated, as he removed the last barrier of his clothing. Then she felt herself heating up all over again.

Coming to the bed, he lifted her into his arms and sat on the side of the bed with her in his lap and kissed her into sweet oblivion. Then when she couldn't stand it any longer he placed her back in bed and covered her body with his. "I want you," he whispered as he continued to touch her everywhere, her breasts, her stomach, her thighs, and the very center of her being, as he prepared her for him.

Rae'jean's entire body felt over the rim brimming with excitement, wanting, passion.

Passion. The kind she had thought she didn't need or want. Ryan was proving otherwise in a way that ignited every nerve in her body. And when she felt the length and thickness of him ready, waiting, poised at the entrance of her womanly core, she shimmied her hips upward, against him, anticipating being a part of him.

Wanting it. Needing it.

And within seconds, Ryan gave her what she wanted as he slowly and gently eased inside of her, letting her feel his hard, male thickness, claiming her, branding her, and even now growing harder just for her.

When she tried lifting her hips to meet his some more, he grasped her hips and held her in place. "No," he said in a raspy voice. "Don't move. At least not yet. I want as much of you as I can get. I want to go deeper. I want to stay in longer," he whispered in a husky voice. "I want you burning for me like I'm burning for you."

"I am burning, Ryan," she was able to say, barely. The feel of him inside of her was too much. It felt too good. So right.

Unknown to Rae'jean, her long, shuddering breath aroused Ryan even more, and he continued pushing inside, determined to go to the hilt. And determined to share with her something he had wanted to share with her from the first.

Passion.

And he took her hot, tight, and enticing womanly core there. Almost pulling out, then pushing way back in. Deeper, timelessly, rhythmically, he made love to her, giving her all of himself, from the top of his head to the bottom of his feet. Every cell in his body was primed for her total satisfaction. For her passion. And he was demanding it from her in the most elemental way. The most primitive way.

He heard her keening cry of pleasure. He felt her fingernails brand his back and felt the tiny bites she was taking off his shoulder. But he didn't stop. He couldn't stop. He was home. Inside of her was where he belonged, giving her what she needed, what he wanted, maintaining a steady rhythm as he moved against her in sharp, hard, pumping thrusts as the scent of their heavy lovemaking saturated the sultry air.

"Ryan!"

"Not yet, baby," he whispered in her ear. "Hold on; don't go there yet."

Ryan tried to stay in control as he continued to take her over and over the edge of mindless passion. Over and over until neither of them could hold out any longer, finally giving in like there would be no tomorrow.

"Now," he murmured against her lips as he surged into her one final time, holding himself in deep, hard. "Now!"

Her body exploded when the long length of him found the center of her most erotic point, making her shatter into a million pieces of glowing, fulfilling passion. At first she made a little sound at the back of her throat before letting out an earth-shattering scream, which Ryan's kiss immediately absorbed. Her body erupted and continued to explode when she felt his body jerk and felt the hot molten liquid of his release shoot deep inside of her, joining with her feminine juices at the most exquisite point. The feeling was unexpected, consuming, breathtaking, powerful.

She tightened her legs around him, wanting, needing, to feel every hard, throbbing inch of him that was still exploding inside of her, deep within her body. Their connection complete, and somehow she knew it was permanent. "Ryan . . ." Her voice was barely above a whisper, strangled.

He must have read her thoughts, because he continued to hold her hips to him, determined to give her every last drop of him. She was shaken to the core by what they had shared and how he had made her feel. And to think that for a long time she'd thought she'd needed the quiet, peaceful, and serene type of lovemaking. Ryan had just proven her wrong, and a part of her knew there was more between them than good sex. In her heart she knew it. In her soul she felt it.

Ryan lifted his head to look down at her. At that moment, words between them weren't needed. As he continued to look at her he felt his body renew itself with desire.

With him still inside of her, Rae'jean felt it, too. Without any hesitation, she reached up. "Again," she whispered before bringing his mouth down to hers.

EPILOGUE

I, Ryan Jamaal Garrison, take this woman, Rae'jean Elizabeth Bennett, to be my lawfully wedded wife."

Ethan Allen Bennett, who was sitting in the front pew of the Mount Calvary Baptist Church in Macon, Georgia, couldn't help but smile. He hoped that his deceased daughter, Colleen, was just as happy as he was today. Her only child was committing her life, before God, family, and friends, to the man she loved and who loved her.

It had taken nearly every bit of physical strength Ethan had had to walk his granddaughter down the aisle, but he had done so. He was glad Rae'jean had understood his need to walk at a slow pace and had graciously slowed her walk for him. The walk had probably taken longer than usual, but she hadn't seemed to mind. In fact, no one in the church had.

He didn't have to glance around the church at the guests to know who was there. Alexia and her husband, Quinn, along with their five-month-old twin boys—Bennett and Blake—had arrived at the beginning of the week. Taye and Michael had driven into town last night to partake in the wedding rehearsals and dinner party. Taye was expecting a little one but was barely showing. She claimed that according to the doctors she was having a boy, whom she intended to name Ethan Henry Bennett. Ethan had been tickled pink that she would want to do that. She and Michael had built another house in Atlanta, a larger one, for the three girls and new baby. Taye had finished college and had landed a job working for a huge accounting firm.

Brandy had arrived last night and had brought along a man whom she introduced as her fiancé. Like the last one, the man wore those long braids on his head. Ethan shook his head. His granddaughter evidently had a thing for men who didn't believe in getting haircuts.

Rumor had it that Victor Junior and Evelyn were on the verge of getting a divorce, which wasn't a surprise to anyone. In fact, Ethan knew that a lot of the family members were walking around chanting, "Good riddance." Rose had finally left Victor Senior, and as far as Ethan was concerned, it was about time she wised up. Everybody knew he'd been whoring around with Valerie for years.

Ethan had been surprised to see Rae'jean's ex-fiancé, Grady, show up for the wedding. He had even brought his wife and their new baby. Even Rae'jean's sister, the one she'd found somewhere in Texas, had come to the wedding. Twice he had approached her thinking she was Rae'jean. They looked that much alike.

The preacher's words recaptured Ethan's attention.

"By the powers vested in me, I now pronounce you man and wife."

Ethan smiled broadly as he watched the couple kiss. He figured it wouldn't be long before they began increasing the Bennett–Garrison line.

After the couple had kissed and began strolling out of the church with their wedding procession following behind, Ethan, like everyone else, stood.

Today was a good day and he knew his Idella was up there rejoicing.

SIX MONTHS LATER

Poppa Ethan walked through his house and turned off all the lights. Feeling somewhat tired tonight, he moved slower than usual.

Taye and Michael had visited him that day, bringing their new little one for him to see. Ethan Henry Bennett was such a little thing, but the boy had a strong grip and a good appetite.

Rae'jean had called earlier in the day to say that she and Ryan were having a baby, which didn't surprise him, and he'd seen Alexia on TV last night getting an award for having the best song of the year. It had almost brought tears to his eyes when she had stepped onstage to receive the reward and, after giving respect to God, thanked her grandfather, Ethan Bennett, and her grandmother, Idella Bennett, for encouraging her to pursue singing when she was just a little one. He knew Idella was up there as proud as could be.

Brandy had called a few minutes ago to say that she had accepted a job somewhere out of the country, but he'd forgotten just what country she'd said. He shook his head. He was forgetting a lot these days.

Ethan made it to the bed and sat down on the side of it as he glanced around the room. A lot of things were still as Idella had left them, and he preferred it that way. He knew that whenever he came into this room, which for so many years had been their bedroom, where all of their children except for one had been conceived, her presence would always be in here with him.

For some reason he felt her presence even stronger tonight. He supposed she was just beside herself in happiness—just like he was—that their family was doing fine and the majority of the grands were married and successful. Cousin Agnes was already hard at work planning a family reunion for next year, which everyone was looking forward to. A decision had been made to have a family reunion every two years, and he was glad for that.

A moment later, after removing his house shoes, Ethan lay down on the bed and rested his head against the pillow and closed his eyes. In the morning Joe and Otha Mae were coming by to pick him up for church.

As sleep overtook him he saw, as he'd been doing a lot lately, a vision of his Idella. But this vision was different. She was wearing a different kind of smile on her face, and the robe she had on was whiter than ever before. It was so white it almost glowed. And her skin appeared soft, with a smooth translucent color of honey brown.

And for the first time, she was holding her hand out to him. He felt his heart rate increase when she spoke. *It's time, Ethan. It's time to come join me on this side. You are leaving behind a legacy we can both be proud of, and now the two of us can be together again.*

Ethan Allen Bennett took Idella's hand and smiled happily the same exact moment he felt himself slipping away.

He was going home to be with his beloved Idella. The next family reunion would be without him in body but not in spirit. He knew in his heart that the Bennetts would forever carry on.

Idella was right. He was leaving behind a legacy he was proud of.

AUTHOR'S NOTE

Family reunions are special. A reunion is a time when the entire family gets together to celebrate their existence with an abundance of good food, recreational activities, and, above all else, talk and getting acquained and reacquainted. It's a time to recognize past generations, descendants, and living elders for their contribution to the family structure. And most important, it is a special occasion for reaffirming family ties.

I hope my book takes you down memory lane, because the Bennett family can represent any African-American family. No matter what, in the end, "blood is thicker than water," and your family will always be there for you.

I would like to thank my friends who shared memories of their family reunions with me. It was a delightful experience. I want to especially thank my good friend Denise Coleman. When I shared the idea for this book with her, she became as excited about it as I was.

I want to thank my family, the Randolph family, for holding the first Randolph Family Reunion during the summer of 1999. It was everything a family reunion should be. I look forward to our next reunion.

If your family has not held a reunion, please do so. All it takes is one person taking the initiative to get the reunion organized.

The results will be rewarding and worthwhile.

If you enjoyed this story, please check out my Web site for information about other books written by me at www.brendajackson.net.

Please write me at:
Brenda Jackson
P.O. Box 28267
Jacksonville, FL 32226

READING GROUP GUIDE
A Family Reunion

1. Do you think that Taye should have initiated conversations with Monica about her father before she heard about her daughter's curiosity?

2. Should Michael have told Kennedy about Stephanie and at some point introduced the two of them?

3. Once Rae'jean realized she was attracted to another man, should she have broken off her engagement with Grady? Why or why not?

4. Should Rae'jean have questioned the family about her father when she knew it was a closely guarded family secret? Why or why not?

5. Do you feel Rae'jean was right to give up Grady to another woman? What would you have done?

6. Was Quinn justified in feeling used once he learned of Alexia's plot to get pregnant?

7. Was it wrong for Taye and Michael to become involved, even though Michael was only an adopted Bennett? Explain your answer.

8. Do you think Brandy was justified in exposing Lorenzo and Jolene the way she did at the wedding reception?

9. Do you look at Grampa Ethan's death as too sad an ending or do you think it was a happy ending? Why do you feel this way?

For more reading group suggestions visit
www.stmartins.com.

Get a
Griffin St. Martin's Griffin

CPSIA information can be obtained at www.ICGtesting.com
Printed in the USA
LVOW081219190513

334469LV00001B/127/P